RIPPLES

Deborah Fowler

SPHERE BOOKS LIMITED

SPHERE BOOKS LTD

Published by the Penguin Group
27 Wrights Lane, London w8 5TZ, England
Viking Penguin Inc., 40 West 23rd Street, New York, New York 10010, USA
Penguin Books Australia Ltd, Ringwood, Victoria, Australia
Penguin Books Canada Ltd, 2801 John Street, Markham, Ontario, Canada L3R 1B4
Penguin Books (NZ) Ltd, 182–190 Wairau Road, Auckland 10, New Zealand

Penguin Books Ltd, Registered Offices: Harmondsworth, Middlesex, England

Published in Great Britain simultaneously by Michael Joseph Limited
and Sphere Books Limited, 1988

Printed and bound in Great Britain by
Richard Clay Ltd, Bungay, Suffolk

THE BEGINNING:
The Island of Rhodes, June 1968

CHAPTER ONE

Laura stood still for a moment, apparently contemplating the water below her. Then her slim, naked body tensed and she executed a perfect swallow dive, her hair streaming out behind her.

'You look like a mermaid,' Francis called, leaning over the rail of the yacht to watch her.

'Come on in, it's gorgeous.'

He shook his head. 'Not likely, far too energetic for me.'

'You're hopeless, Francis.'

He smiled down at her, not with warmth but with an arrogance which instantly rankled. 'We'll see if that's still how you feel a little later, shall we, darling?'

With a splash, Laura turned on to her front and began swimming strongly away from him. His words humiliated her for, while she no longer loved him, his attraction for her was as strong as ever, and he knew it. She swam until the frantic pace exhausted her. It had been a long, surprisingly hard, sail round from Rhodes and most of it she had tackled single-handed. Her tired muscles shouted in protest and at last she gave in to them, rolling on to her back, and cradled by the gentle motion of the sea, she gazed up at the mountains that dominated the coastline.

To Laura, the Greek islands had always felt like her spiritual home, and it was not such a fanciful notion for her mother, Katrine, was Greek. On the surface, Laura had inherited nothing from her mother but her thick, black hair, but she never felt so truly at peace as she did when in these waters. It was why she had brought Francis here, hoping somehow that the magic would wash off on them and their relationship and cure a marriage which, in just two years, seemed to be spiralling into an abyss of acrimony.

Laura shivered – the heat had left the sun and the cool

water, so deliciously welcoming minutes before, now seemed to be chilling her to the very bone. Still she hesitated, reluctant to return to the yacht which had become a prison for all their anger and resentment.

Francis was waiting for her when she clambered wearily aboard. Wearing only the briefest of swimming trunks, the beauty of his body was impossible to ignore – lean, golden brown with a light dusting of fair hairs bleached white by the sun.

'See, my darling, you're absolutely exhausted now. It's just as well one of us is, how shall we say, still feeling vigorous.' He leaned forward and placed a hand on the nape of her neck. His skin felt cool and dry in contrast to her own sticky wetness.

She tried to turn away. 'Stop it, Francis, leave me alone, I just want to shower and relax for a while.'

The pressure of his hand increased, he was hurting her. They eyed each other silently for a moment and, subtly, Laura's anger began to change direction – it was now aimed towards herself as she felt the all-too-familiar warmth begin creeping insidiously through her body.

His eyes did not leave her face as his hands moved to her breasts. Her nipples, rose pink, were already hard with desire as Francis placed his hands over them and began gently to roll them between finger and thumb.

Laura shut her eyes momentarily, to try and stem the tide of mounting sensation. In theory, it was not too late to pull away with a sharp rebuff, yet her body already told her the moment had passed. She heard a sound, a moan of longing. Her eyes snapped open to the realization that the sound had come from her own lips – it *was* too late.

With shaking hands she began trying to untie the string of his swimming trucks, but his hugely engorged penis, rearing against the flat of his stomach, was hampering her. Francis's smile was full of self-satisfaction as in seconds he deftly removed his trunks so that they stood quite naked before one another. Then the smile left his face as suddenly as it had come. He pulled her into his arms and almost threw her on to the deck, forcing his way into her, his fingers digging into her breasts, his body pounding hers again and again. There was no gentleness, no loving caress. This was rough, raw passion . . . and they loved it.

It was the hardness of the deck that finally roused her. Her body felt languid and heavy, and her muscles seemed uncoordinated. Francis lay beside her, one arm flung across her. He appeared to be sleeping. Carefully, so as not to disturb him, Laura moved his arm and sat up. He did not stir. For a moment she sat watching her husband thoughtfully. His looks so perfectly reflected his character. Peter Pan incarnate – the boy who had never grown up. His soft, straight fair hair was brushed back from his brow, his cheeks, pink and healthy, his features, even in manhood, reminiscent of a cherubic choirboy. He really was impossibly good-looking, but in sleep the weakness showed. What caused that, Laura wondered. Was it in the slight smile or simply the relaxation of his face muscles which revealed the flaw. It was hard to tell. She let out a sigh. Why was it that whenever she was most angry with him, their lovemaking was always at its best? After a raging row, filled with hurt and recrimination, he could take her to dizzy heights she would not have believed possible. It was certainly true of their relationship that love and hate walked hand-in-hand, and yet just now, somehow, it had been different. There had been another element, impossible to define, yet oddly poignant and certainly quite unlike their lovemaking of late, where lust playing the major role always left Laura feeling empty, bereft and somehow vaguely unclean . . . But not this time – this time she felt fulfilled, almost happy. She stood up, gingerly, still very aware of her aching muscles and went below to take a shower. Perhaps this feeling was a good omen – perhaps there was still hope for their marriage after all, she thought as she scrubbed the salt from her tired body.

Half an hour later, they were both on deck again, showered and changed. Francis poured Laura a tumbler of wine, and then returning to his favourite seat, took a hefty gulp from his glass and lit a cigarette.

Laura watched him in silence for a moment. 'You know you really ought to take more exercise.'

Francis grinned up at her through a haze of smoke. 'Why?

I'm not fat.' It was true, his body appeared as trim and muscular as any athlete's.

'That's because you're only twenty-seven,' Laura said, 'you wait until you're forty.'

'My darling girl, I know *you're* a fitness freak, but there's nothing to do on a boat except swim, and swimming really isn't my thing, as you well know – it's too much like hard work.'

'Well, if you won't swim, you might at least give me some help with the boat,' Laura said, exasperated. 'I know you don't think much of the *Empress* because she doesn't have the creature comforts of a five-star hotel, but she is quite a large yacht to handle single-handed.'

'Darling, this holiday was your idea – remember. You know I haven't a clue about anything connected with sailing and boats, and nor do I have any desire to redress the balance on this appalling lack of skill. I told you when you suggested the idea, I was quite happy to come, provided you expected me to do nothing more than sit in the sun with a bottle of wine. So, my darling, stop griping. What's for supper?'

'The shrimps we bought in the market.'

'Wonderful. I hope you have plenty of garlic?'

'Of course, and lemons and a crusty loaf and salad. No one can say I don't cater for your every whim.' Her voice was heavy with sarcasm.

Francis set down his wine glass and began refilling it. 'That's true,' he said, sagely, 'that's very true.' He hesitated. 'Actually, darling, I want to have a serious talk to you this evening, there are things we need to discuss. You go and cook and I'll set the table, just to prove I'm not completely useless . . .' His words surprised Laura. Francis loathed serious discussions on any subject, indeed he would go to any lengths to avoid them. The fact that he was anxious to instigate one was totally out of character, as was the offer to lay the table. Laura went below with a sense of mounting unease.

Soon they were tucking into their shrimps, sitting at a little table Francis had erected on the after-deck. It was almost dark now and their meal was lit by an old kerosene lamp which hung from the boom above their heads, casting a soft, warm glow around them. They were moored in St Paul's Bay, at least a mile from the shore in any direction, and as the night crept in, isolating them in their pool of light, they could have been the last two people left on earth.

By now they were well into their second bottle of wine. 'Right,' said Laura, 'what is it you want to discuss?'

'Let's wait until we've finished the meal,' Francis suggested.

'I'd rather not,' said Laura. 'If you have something you wish to say, I'd like you to say it now.'

Francis made a great play of refilling their wine glasses and then leant back in his chair. 'I want to talk to you about ... about money, my darling.'

Laura was instantly on the defensive. 'I'm not lending you any more, Francis. I told you that last time. We need all of my income to live on – to feed and clothe us and give us holidays like this. I've long ago given up any hope of your contributing financially to our marriage, but you have to paddle your own canoe when it comes to financing your ... how shall I put it, *business interests*.'

'Don't be so touchy, darling,' said Francis. His face was unusually serious and Laura detected a certain uncharacteristic tenseness about him. 'I appreciate that since our marriage my business ventures have not borne much fruit, but when considering the contribution I have to make to our life together, Laura, you need to take a long-term view. It's easy to be critical, but my kind of work is very different from yours. You have a regular job and are paid a regular salary. It may not be a very good one, but it is at least consistent. I am taking a little longer to produce an income, but when I do, we'll be able to live like kings, not scrape the barrel as we do now. That's where our differences lie.'

His patronizing attitude was just too much. 'How dare you criticize my job,' said Laura, bristling with indignation. 'Just where would we be without my salary – in fact where would we be without *me*? We're in a flat *my* father provided, living off *my* salary, we're currently having a holiday in a yacht owned by a friend of *my* family ... your contribution is nil and yet you have the gall to complain about what *I* earn.

Dammit, Francis, when I think how I slave away at that office all day and come home to find you lounging around the house, talking about the big deals you're always *about* to do and dropping cigarette ash all over the carpets, you make me sick, you really do.' The resentment and anger which had been welling up in Laura for months had chosen this moment to erupt. All her efforts in the past to try and be tactful and curb her irritation had taken their toll. Now she did not care what she said – the time for protecting egos was over.

'Darling, you're quite right,' Francis said, soothingly. 'I'm a rotten swine. You're a marvellously talented woman, and I so admire your energy and drive. Look at the way you sailed the boat today, then cooked this lovely meal, not to mention the little interlude in between. No man could be luckier than I – don't think I'm not aware of it.'

Laura stared at him in amazement. This really was something new. Normally when criticized, Francis leapt into a counter-attack, his anger flaring to match her own. Momentarily she was thrown – she eyed him warily across the table, their meal now long forgotten. 'What exactly is it that you want, Francis?'

'It's not so much a question of wanting something – really it's more a question of what I have to offer.'

'To whom?' Laura said.

'To your father, actually.'

'My father?' Alarm bells began ringing in Laura's head. 'Surely you're not bringing up that old chestnut again, Francis? I've told you repeatedly – and so incidentally has my father – that there is no way he's going to invest in any of your mad-cap business schemes. He's worked too hard over the years to throw away his money now.'

'Yes, yes,' said Francis impatiently, 'but this is different, this is an investment in property. It is not, as you so charitably put it, one of my mad-cap schemes. This involves the best collateral there is – good old solid bricks and mortar.'

'Go on,' said Laura, wearily.

'You remember I mentioned to you that I was setting up a business with Douglas Fairley selling homes abroad?'

Laura searched her tired brain. 'Yes, I think I vaguely

remember,' she said. Long ago she had ceased to listen properly to Francis when he talked of his schemes – they were fairy tales so far as Laura was concerned.

'You must do, darling, we've talked about it a lot. Anyway it's working terribly well – in fact there's a huge demand for the property. The trouble is, Douglas wants out and I need to find a partner to take over from him.'

Laura frowned. 'Francis, that doesn't make any sense – the business is a howling success so Douglas wants to pull out? Where is the property, anyway?'

'All over – South of France, Italy, Algarve, here in Greece too – in Crete, to be precise.'

'Let me get this straight. You and Douglas have bought land and want to develop it, or are you buying existing property?'

'A mixture of the two,' said Francis, warming to his theme. 'In the South of France, it's a plot ready for development, in the Algarve, we've found some existing old property which is truly beautiful, and just needs a few bob spending on it.'

'And then you'll advertise and resell the property as holiday homes?'

'That's right,' said Francis, 'and we're having absolutely no problem finding clients, absolutely none at all. People are falling over themselves. Look, I have this brochure to show you.' Delving in the briefcase beside his chair, Francis pulled out a fat, glossy brochure. *New Horizons Ltd*, Laura read. She flipped through the pages – they were full of photographs and details of apartments, houses and villas.

Laura looked up at Francis. 'Francis, there must be hundreds of thousands of pounds worth of property here. Don't tell me that you and Douglas own all this?'

'No, of course we don't – *yet*. As you rightly say, it's a big investment, and in any event, Douglas's other business interests have meant he cannot tie up any further capital.'

'How much money are you looking for?' Laura asked.

'Three-quarters of a million,' Francis replied. '£600,000 for the property and its development and the balance for promotion and expenses.'

'I'm sure, potentially, it's a very good idea,' said Laura,

carefully, 'but I know it's not the sort of thing that Pop would want to become involved in.'

'How can you say that?' said Francis. 'What safer investment in the world can there be than property? Let's face it, the Stock Market is a dead loss these days and besides which, even looking on the black side, your father can afford to lose that much and not even notice it.'

Laura stared at Francis. His nervousness, she realized, had increased – there was a thin line of perspiration across his brow. 'You really need this money, don't you, Francis?'

He nodded. 'Honestly, Laura, it *is* a good investment and I'm sure if you put in a word for me with your father, it will be enough to convince him. If he wishes, he or you could be involved, as a director of the company. Without Douglas, I'll need some help. You could write all the copy for the brochures and that would mean you could give up that bloody silly job . . .'

While Francis was talking, Laura was continuing to leaf through the brochure. The word 'Antibes' leapt out from the pages at her. It showed the front elevation of an apartment block and then two pages of interiors, listing a variety of apartment sizes. Three of the apartments were shown as already sold. Laura felt her heart begin to pound. 'Francis?' she interrupted.

'Yes?'

She glanced up at him. He had relaxed a little, obviously believing he was gaining some ground. 'I thought you said you had only acquired a *plot* in the South of France at the moment?'

'Yes, that's right.' Francis spoke with confidence.

'But in this brochure you're showing actual apartments.'

'True, but that's no problem. The architect who is designing the apartments we will be building also designed the ones shown in the brochure. They're going to be exactly the same in every detail.'

'You mean, you're offering apartments for sale which aren't even built yet?'

'That's right,' said Francis, 'but it's perfectly normal, it happens all the time. People realize that if they're in on the early stages of a project, they can command the best price. Once we start building, the prices of the properties will soar.'

'So are you saying you've actually sold some of these apartments?'

'Good Lord, yes,' said Francis.

'Even though they don't exist?'

'I told you it's normal practice.' Francis shifted uneasily in his seat.

'And even though you don't have the money to build them?'

'Look, Laura, you're a journalist – I'm the businessman of the family.'

'You're in trouble,' said Laura, flatly. It was a statement, not a question.

'No, of course I'm not.' Francis stood up abruptly and turning his back to her, he leant over the rail.

Laura's voice was icily calm. 'I think you've been selling apartments that don't exist and then pocketing the money. That explains why you haven't been asking me for money for the last few months. Douglas must have found out what you are doing and, very understandably, he wants to terminate your partnership fast – I'm right, aren't I, Francis?'

There was a long silence. 'Certainly, Douglas withdrawing his backing has put me in a difficult position,' Francis admitted, cautiously.

'It's fraud,' said Laura, 'it is fraud, isn't it?' Her words hung in the still night air.

'Of course not,' said Francis, 'but I'll admit there have been a few complaints. One stupid couple I did a deal with a few months ago went out to examine their property last month. There was a misunderstanding as to where it was located and as a result, they are causing quite a stink.'

'You mean, they've reported you to the police?' Laura asked.

'Well . . . yes, as a matter of fact, they have,' said Francis, 'but I can explain everything – there's no problem, really. It was all just a misunderstanding.'

'How much money has Douglas actually invested in this joint venture?' To Laura the conversation was becoming more terrifying by the moment, but she had to know the truth.

'He hasn't actually made an investment at all,' said Francis. 'He promised me backing initially, but now he has decided not to proceed. That's what has caused all the problems. The man's a fool – it's a marvellous opportunity but he just doesn't seem to see it.'

Laura's strongest instinct at that moment was to play the ostrich, but, bracing herself, she continued to strip away Francis's defences. 'How many of these apartments have you actually sold, Francis?'

'About a dozen.'

'And have you been paid for any of them?'

'Not in all the cases – but mostly, yes.'

'You bastard!' Laura could contain herself no longer. 'You're nothing but a thief. Who are your victims – retired people spending their life savings on the promise of a rosy future in the sun, I suppose?'

Francis swung round to face her. 'Oh, don't be so dramatic, Laura. This is just a temporary setback, and if your father would come up with the backing, the problem would be completely solved overnight.'

'You have to be joking, Francis! Pop would have no part in a venture like this.'

'And just how will Pop feel about having his precious little daughter being married to a jailbird. The press would have a field day. The Honourable Francis Melhuish, son of Lord Campling, ex-cabinet-minister: The Honourable Francis Melhuish, son-in-law to top industrialist, Sir Bernard Beecham – jailed for fraud. It would kill my old man, you know that, and yours wouldn't exactly be over the moon, now would he?' There was a menacing tone to Francis's voice which Laura had never heard before and it made her blood run cold.

'This is blackmail,' she said.

Francis regarded her in silence for a moment and then unexpectedly produced one of his dazzling smiles. 'Come on, old girl, don't be like this – I just don't want my problems rebounding on any of our parents. That's fair enough, isn't it?'

'Don't add insincerity to your crimes,' Laura said, savagely.

'You don't care a jot about the parents, you're just trying to use them to your best advantage. I may have helped you before, but this is one crisis you're going to have to get out of yourself. All your life people have been bailing you out of scrapes, because of your charm, your good-looks and your title, but not this time – this time you've gone too far, this time you've utterly destroyed the faith I once had in you.'

'So,' said Francis, 'you've given up on me, have you? Funny, it didn't seem that way earlier this evening.' He let his gaze rest on her breasts and then slowly, arrogantly, travel down the length of her body.

'You destroy and debase everything – even love,' Laura said, her voice barely above a whisper. 'I loved you once so much, I'd have done anything in the world to help you, despite being warned against you, repeatedly. I had faith in you then, Francis, and I'd have followed you to the ends of the earth. The trouble is, you've treated me no differently from anyone else. You saw my love and trust in you as weakness. It was something of which you could take advantage, not something precious to hold on to, to build a lifetime around.'

'Don't start that again,' said Francis, 'I've heard it all before and it's not really relevant any more. Rather than venting your spleen on me, Laura, basically you have just one decision to make. When we return to England next week, either Bernard has to come across with the money or I will be arrested by the Fraud Squad – it's as simple as that.'

Laura stared at him for a long moment. It was difficult to tell, these days, whether Francis was speaking the truth or not. Something though, in his eyes, told her that he was scared – very scared. She took time before she replied, aware of her answer's implications for them both, and by the time she spoke, there was no anger left, only sadness. 'I have to tell you, Francis, that I will not help you raise money from my father. You can go to him direct, of course, but he will make no move to help you without first consulting me. In the circumstances, if he asks me what I think, I shall tell him that in my view he should not lend you the money.' Francis visibly blanched. 'Knowing you and the way you can charm yourself out of most of the problems you create, I'm sure you'll find a way round this one, too . . . but I have to say, it won't be with the help of my family.'

'You bitch!' said Francis. 'You're enjoying this, aren't you? It must be like watching a rat in a trap. It's at moments like this, Laura, that your background really shows.'

'What's that supposed to mean?' Laura said.

'Self-made rich men and their progeny are all the same – money is king. It's all too obvious why the rich become rich – because they're too bloody mean to part with a brass farthing, unless they absolutely have to. Precious Pop bought you everything he could – a private education, a pony, a swimming pool, exotic holidays . . . his money even enabled you to enter the social scene, which in turn made it possible for you to acquire a peer's son for a husband. However, what your father can't buy you, Laura, is breeding. When the family name is in jeopardy, breeding should tell you that you must do everything in your power to salvage it from ruin.'

His words bit deep, but Laura was not going to show how much he had hurt her. 'That is preposterous! I agree, it will be terrible for your father and brother if your name is dragged through the courts, but ask yourself who has put the family name in jeopardy? *You*, with your precious breeding, got yourself into this – all I'm saying, Francis, is that you have to get yourself out of it too.'

'Is that your final word?' Francis's hair was flopping into his eyes – he looked both dishevelled and anxious – so out of character from his normal well-groomed, laid-back self.

For a split second Laura hesitated. 'Yes,' she said, 'that is my final word.'

Francis leant forward, picked up his wine glass and drained it. Then he refilled it. 'Well, I don't know what *you're* going to do,' he said, 'but I'm going to get drunk.'

A terrible weariness swept over Laura. 'I'm going to go to bed,' she said.

'That's fine by me,' said Francis, 'in fact, don't give me another thought.' As always, when something did not go his way, Francis was immediately enmeshed in self-pity.

Laura stumbled down the ladder into the cabin. Despite the fact that all the windows were open, it was stifling. She undressed quickly and slipped under the covers of the double bunk. Lying alone in the dark, she was conscious of a slight swell as the *Empress* rode her anchor. She felt vaguely sick and wondered whether she should get up again, but the thought of facing Francis kept her where she was. She was never seasick – it was a combination of shock and too much wine, she reasoned. She rolled on her side, desperate for sleep to come and obliterate her thoughts, but her mind churned with images of Francis in court, Francis in prison, Francis being taken away in handcuffs. How could this have happened? When they met, they had fallen so deeply, so irrevocably in love, it seemed impossible that anything or anyone could touch them – yet in two years, it was all over. Tears would have helped, but she could not cry. She simply lay silently, staring into the darkness, until at last, mercifully, sleep claimed her.

Bright sunlight streaming through the cabin window woke Laura the following morning. Her first conscious thought was of her thumping head – this made her think of the wine she had drunk, which in turn brought back the scene with Francis, with horrible clarity. She turned over in bed but Francis was not beside her and, clearly, had not come to bed all night. She was not surprised. His sleeping on the deck was inevitable – he had probably drunk too much to find his way below. She stretched and considered the day ahead. Given the circumstances, another whole week of being imprisoned together on the yacht seemed impossible. Her practical mind considered the alternatives. Probably it would be best if they put into Lindos that morning. It was a pleasant enough little resort, with plenty of bars and tavernas – the sort of place that would suit Francis. A week's mooring at Lindos would ensure that they did not crowd one another, and then they would just have to sail the boat back to Rhodes at the end of the holiday. A quiet week would give Francis the opportunity to think out a plan and enable both of them to take stock of the future. In the light of day, Laura felt more optimistic – she could not believe that Francis would not come up with some solution to his dilemma. He always did.

Laura climbed out of bed and slipped into her bikini – a swim would clear her head. There was no sound on the deck above – Francis, clearly, was still sleeping. She popped her head through the hatch and gasped aloud. It was a devastatingly beautiful morning. The sea was sparkling blue, fading to all possible shades of aqua nearer the coastline, and the mountain tops were pink and purple in the early morning light. For a moment, her troubles forgotten, Laura gazed around her, and then she clambered out on to the deck.

'Francis!' she called. He was nowhere to be seen. The debris from their supper of the night before remained on the table, as did the two empty wine bottles. Laura frowned and climbed up on to the roof of the cabin, for a view of the whole length of the yacht, confident of seeing Francis's prone body stretched out on some part of the deck. He was nowhere to be seen. She jumped down to the hatch opening again and shouted his name. 'Francis, are you in the loo?' No reply – she opened the door. There was no one inside.

For the first time, Laura had a feeling of disquiet, and thoughts began jangling to and fro in her mind. Perhaps he was taking a swim, and yet he hated swimming, but if he had a hangover . . . she was back on the deck in a moment, gazing wildly round her. She began calling his name. 'Francis, Francis, where are you?' Her voice echoed across the water, mocking her, the silence immediately closing in again as if she had not called out at all. 'Francis, Francis . . .' She told herself to calm down, and began methodically searching the sea, sweeping her gaze backwards and forwards, looking for a head bobbing in the water – there was nothing.

Her mind tried to grasp at alternative possibilities. The tender, of course, the tender – he was sulking with her, so he had probably rowed ahead of her into Lindos. The town was only just around the corner of the bay, he knew that. She ran to the stern. The tender was still there, nosing against the rudder, the oars in place.

The realization, at that moment, that Francis was truly missing struck her with such force that she almost screamed. Telling herself to stay calm, she tried to look for explanations. Had there been an accident – had he fallen overboard in a drunken stupor and drowned? Her mind recoiled from the thought. Had he, perhaps, swum ashore to deliberately frighten her, or simply to get away from her? She studied the nearest point of the shoreline – it was a long swim, even for her – for Francis, she judged, it was impossible. The only remaining possibility produced a stream of tears as Laura fought her rising sense of panic. Had he deliberately killed himself to avoid arrest? No, not Francis, not self-indulgent Francis, and yet . . . She stumbled, half falling down into the cabin again and made for the drawer under the chart table. She pulled it out so far it fell off its runners, spilling the contents on to the floor. She fell to her knees and slowly began putting item by item, back into the drawer. There were both passports – hers and Francis's – also their cheque books, a wallet of travellers' cheques and a purse of Greek currency. It was all there, nothing was missing. Laura sat very still on the floor, staring down at the items before her. One thing was clear – whatever had happened to Francis, he had not made a planned exit from her life.

Slowly, Laura rose and once more climbed back up on deck to search the sea around her. The solitude of their mooring, so pleasant until this moment, was suddenly sinister, and the mountains seemed now to be crowding in on her, menacingly. All about her the silence prevailed as though the whole world had momentarily held its breath.

Francis Melhuish, it seemed, had disappeared off the face of the earth.

CHAPTER TWO

Andre Koyokopis was not having a good week. His problems had begun the previous day – his wife, expecting their third child, was having a difficult pregnancy, and she was taking it out on him. It had been his day off and he had been looking forward to it. It was the first for three weeks. A quiet day at home with his family was what he had planned – well away from the tourists and their problems. By lunchtime, though, his wife's nagging had driven him out of the house and down to the harbour taverna. He had meant to have just one raki and then return home, but his old friend, Miki Theodoris, was there and soon they were in a heated, political debate which continued through the afternoon and late into the night. The result, this morning, was an agonizing headache, a raging thirst and, he had to admit, a quite justified dressing down from his wife . . . and now this girl – he stared across the counter at her.

'Since you're clearly not going to help me, I demand to see the Chief of Police.' She tossed her head angrily. She was a pretty little thing, with unusual colouring – big blue eyes and a tumble of thick black hair. She was so small and petite, she could have passed for fourteen, yet, clearly, she was older – a married woman – and her manner was self-assured, arrogant even. His eyes rested on her T-shirt for a moment, noting the firm outline of jutting young breasts. She was his sort of woman. Curse his job which required him to be a pillar of the establishment. He forced himself to concentrate. 'Madam,' he said, drawing himself up to his full height, 'I am the Chief of Police.'

She seemed satisfactorily deflated by his announcement – then she rallied. There were traces of colour high on her cheekbones, her eyes were too bright – she had been crying, he could tell. 'If that is the case, you ought to be ashamed of yourself. This is a very serious matter. Tell me, are you married?'

The question surprised him. 'Yes.'

'If your wife went missing, would you just assume she would return sometime – wouldn't you be worried?'

In her current mood, Andre was tempted to say that Matia going missing would be a blessing. 'I understand your worry, Madam, but I do not see what I can do. You tell me you woke up on your yacht this morning and that your husband had gone. You tell me that you had drunk much wine last night and had angry words.' He shrugged his shoulders. 'Either your husband fell overboard when he was drunk or else he has swum ashore to punish you.' He held up his hands in a gesture of surrender. 'If he fell overboard, then he is drowned. If he swam ashore, he will come back to you.'

'But you don't understand . . .' Tears began coursing down the girl's face. 'He's not a strong swimmer. He may be hurt or injured somewhere, perhaps swept on to rocks. Surely you have some people available to search the beaches.'

'No, Madam!' Andre slammed his fist on to the counter to emphasize his point. 'This time of year the sea is, how do you say, like a lake. There is no danger in it, no currents, no big waves, no wind. If your husband can swim, he is quite safe in the sea. If he cannot swim . . .' Andre shrugged his shoulders.

The girl was trying to control herself. 'In England,' she said, angrily, 'missing people are taken very seriously.'

'In Rhodes, too,' said Andre, resenting the criticism, 'but if I was to worry about every tourist who had a fight with his wife, I would do nothing else but look for missing people. You go back to your boat and wait for your man there. He will come back to you when he is ready.'

The girl gave a great sigh, wiping the tears from her face with the back of her hand, like a child. 'Can I at least leave you my name and a description and photograph of my husband, in case there has been an accident?'

Andre too, sighed. Without answering, he turned and left the room, returning moments later with a pad and pen. 'Write your name here, Madam, and the name of your yacht, also your husband's name and description.' Andre watched as the girl wrote, her face frowning in concentration. He felt a sudden wave of sympathy for her. She was so young and so very obviously distressed. There was something about her bone structure and dark hair that made him wonder whether, despite her accent, she had any Greek ancestry. 'OK, Madam, I will watch for your husband, but he will be back to you soon – don't worry.'

She must have sensed the softening in his attitude for she pressed home the advantage. 'But surely you have coastguards?' He looked puzzled and she struggled for words to explain. 'Police who search the sea for missing people.'

The girl was as bad as his wife. Why did women never know when to be quiet? 'No one goes missing in the sea at Lindos,' Andre said emphatically, 'not unless they want to.' He picked up the piece of paper she had given him and the photograph she had placed beside it. It showed the face of a fair, good-looking young man. He studied it briefly and then looked up at the girl, surprised to see her still standing there. 'You go now,' he said, firmly. Her eyes searched his face desperately, looking to him for comfort he could not give. Andre felt suddenly inadequate, but dismissed the uncomfortable thought hurriedly. Lovers' tiffs were not his business – he was a policeman.

Out in the hot street, Laura was blinded by tears again. Normally, she considered herself to be a fairly capable person, but at that moment, she felt hopelessly out of her depth. Slowly, like an old woman, she picked her way down the cobbled street, back towards the harbour. Perhaps the Chief of Police was right, perhaps she was over-reacting. Yet knowing Francis's lazy nature, there was no way she could see that he would have deliberately swum ashore, however much he wanted to punish her. It was too much like hard work for Francis Melhuish.

Laura reached the edge of the harbour. It was almost noon now and very hot – the sun dazzlingly bright. She caught sight of the *Empress* and felt a surge of optimism, Francis would be there waiting for her – suddenly she was sure of it. She broke into a run, dodging the sauntering holidaymakers, many of whom turned to watch her – this pretty girl, her dark hair streaming out behind her.

She reached the yacht and jumped over the rail, eyes desperately searching the deck. 'Francis?' The deck was deserted. With a shaking hand, Laura opened her bag, took out a bunch of keys and started unlocking the hatchway. They only had one key to the cabin and therefore Laura knew Francis could not be inside. None the less, trembling with heat and exhaustion, she found it necessary to climb down the ladder and peer into the gloom to satisfy herself that he really had not returned.

The question was, what to do now? After bringing the yacht single-handed into Lindos, followed by the exhausting interview with Andre Koyokopis, it was tempting simply to lie out on the deck, to wait and see what happened, as the policeman had suggested. However, it was not in Laura's nature to give herself up to inactivity. She stripped off her T-shirt and shorts, both ringing wet with sweat, and digging around in a locker found a clean pair of shorts and an old T-shirt belonging to Francis. Somehow, wearing a piece of his clothing helped to keep her grip on reality. It seemed so long since their quarrel, so long since she had seen him, it was almost as though she had imagined everything that had taken place since. Perhaps I'm going mad, she thought – at that moment it did seem a serious possibility. On deck, she found a pair of sailing shoes which would be better for walking in than sandals. Putting a few drachmas in her back pocket, she locked the hatch again and climbed up onto the harbour wall.

Leaving Lindos, on the coast road, Laura toiled along what was little more than a dusty track. No traffic passed her, except a man on a bicycle and an old woman urging on a pitifully thin donkey, laden down with baskets of olives. It took Laura over an hour to reach the headland that separated Lindos from St Paul's Bay, by which time she was almost faint from the blazing heat. Rounding the headland she had an excellent view of the bay. By gazing out to sea, she could pinpoint almost exactly the small cluster of rocks beside which she had been able to drop an anchor the previous night. It was a fair swim from there to the shore, but it was possible. Exhaustion temporarily forgotten, she clambered down the steep rock face on to the beach. It was a beautiful stretch of golden sand, thick and powdery. She walked a few steps and looked behind her. Her tracks were barely visible. Footprints in the sand were clearly going to be of little help. She walked on along the beach, watching the rocks to her left and the sea to her right. Almost a quarter of a mile later, she saw that the rocks parted and that there was a little path leading directly up the cliff face – it was almost exactly in the centre of the bay and on a direct line from where the yacht had been moored. A dry wind had got up and was blowing sand around the beach. Laura, already caked in dust from the road, was oblivious to this fresh assault as sand clung to her hair and damp body. She started up the path, which was clearly well used. It twisted and turned, climbing steeply. It must lead back to the road, she decided, but as she rounded a corner of rock, she saw the true purpose of the path. Its immediate destination was a house, little more than a shack – a stone, single-storey building outside which a few scrawny chickens scratched the dry earth. Smoke was coming from a crooked chimney, and a row of washing suspended across the yard indicated signs of life. Without pausing for thought, Laura walked up to the front door and knocked.

A dark-eyed child, of perhaps five or six, answered the door. She gaped at Laura in silence for a moment and then ran back into the house, speaking hurriedly and excitedly. Moments later, the child returned, half hidden this time behind her mother's voluminous skirt, and Laura found herself staring into the face of a young Greek woman. She is probably no older than me, Laura thought, yet already the woman looked dried out with fatigue and hard work. Bitter lines ran from nose to mouth and her face was sallow and grimy.

'I am English,' Laura began. 'I am looking for my husband . . . a tall man.' She turned and pointed down towards the bay. 'He would have come from the sea . . . swimming. Have you seen anyone?' Laura made breaststroke movements with her arms. The woman stared at her blankly, as though she had not spoken at all, and not for the first time that day, Laura wished she had submitted to her mother's pressure to learn her native tongue. She tried again. 'A man, tall,' she raised her hands above her head, 'this tall. He came from the sea.' Again, she made swimming motions. 'Have you seen him?' She put her hands to her eyes. By now her audience was swelling. Four pairs of eyes regarded her at different heights, from behind the woman's skirt, but nobody's expression changed – everyone seemed to be waiting to see what she would do next. Laura remembered the photograph she had left with the police. If only she had another. There was no justification for the thought, but somehow, instinctively, she felt that Francis had been to this place. She tried again. 'A man, my husband, he came from the sea, from St Paul's Bay, swimming. Have you seen him?'

For a moment it looked as though the woman was going to remain as blank as before – then suddenly, she began vigorously shaking her head. 'No one here,' she mouthed.

Laura stared at her incredulously. 'You speak English?'

The woman shook her head some more. 'No one here,' she repeated.

Laura looked deep into her eyes, seeking understanding. There was something odd going on but it was hard to define quite what. Why did this woman know only those three, but highly appropriate, words of English? 'Is your husband here?' Laura asked.

'No one here,' the woman repeated, once more.

It was hopeless. 'Well, thank you anyway. Goodbye.' Laura tried a smile then turned away and began trudging on up the path. As the path disappeared from view into the hillside, she looked back. The woman and her children had come out of the doorway, to get a better view of her departure. She raised an arm and waved at them, but none of them responded.

By the time Laura reached Lindos harbour again, she felt very sick and the pain in her head was almost unendurable. She was so deflated by her abortive excursion to St Paul's Bay that she did not even expect to find Francis on the *Empress* and was barely disappointed at there being no sign of him. She took two aspirin and surveyed herself in the mirror. She looked dreadful – dirty, dishevelled and utterly defeated. She knew the water tanks were almost empty and that certainly there was not enough left in them for a shower. Somewhere on the harbour she would be able to get fresh water, but it seemed too much of an effort. It occurred to her that part of her problem might be lack of food. She had eaten nothing since the abandoned meal with Francis the night before.

Not caring how she looked, Laura left the *Empress* and walked across the harbour, to the nearest taverna. She sat down at a table, festive with its red checked tablecloths, candles and flashing neon light proclaiming it to be the Taverna Knossos. The evening light was soft and golden but she saw none of it. She ordered spaghetti and half a carafe of wine and sat patiently waiting for her meal, her mind so exhausted now that it had quite ceased to function. The wine, when it arrived, was dry to the point of being arid, but it was cold and she drank back a tumbler quickly. The steaming bowl of spaghetti which followed smelt good, but when Laura tried to eat it, her throat seemed to close against the food. She wearily pushed away her plate, rested her head on her arms and once again gave way to tears.

Chris and Eleanor Berry lay exhausted amongst the twisted sheets. Eleanor rolled over and squinted down at her husband, 'You're a randy old sod, Chris.'

He smiled up at her. 'You've noticed.'

She nuzzled his ear. 'It had filtered through.'

'Well, these days one can't miss an opportunity of having you to myself for a moment. It is a miracle – this early in the evening.'

Eleanor's face was suddenly serious, a frown criss-crossing her smooth brow. She ran a hand through her soft brown curls. 'Do you regret bringing the babies on holiday?'

'No, of course not.' Chris smiled up at her worried face. 'Honestly, darling, if we'd come away without them, especially without Eddie, you'd have been a real misery and worried yourself sick. Besides which, they're having a ball, aren't they?'

Eleanor relaxed a little. 'Yes, they are. It's lovely being able to spend so much time with them, both of us together like this.'

'Are you finding being back at work more difficult than

you'd expected?' It was a question he had asked many times before, but he sensed the relaxed atmosphere of their holiday might elicit an honest answer.

'At times like this, when we're all together, I wonder what the hell I'm doing. Yet, let's face it, if I wasn't working, we wouldn't have been able to afford a holiday at all.'

'Marrying an impecunious publisher was a grave mistake on your part,' Chris suggested.

Eleanor bent and kissed him. 'Marrying an impecunious publisher was the most sensible thing I've ever done in my life.' They lay contently together in silence for a few moments. 'We're very lucky,' Eleanor said softly.

'*I* certainly am,' said Chris, 'and I'm also very hungry.'

Eleanor slapped him. 'The last of the great romantics strikes again.'

'Ouch,' said Chris, 'that's my sunburn.'

'Rubbish,' said Eleanor, climbing out of bed. 'You really are the most appalling hypochondriac.'

'Why else do you think I married a doctor?'

As soon as they were dressed, they crept into the children's room next door. Eddie, in his wicker carrycot, which was really too small for him, lay on his stomach, his cheeks flushed in sleep, his fair hair smooth and clean.

'Absolutely angelic,' Chris whispered.

'No comment,' said Eleanor.

Thomas, on the camp bed, beside his brother, lay on his side, clutching his much loved rabbit, Peter. His thick brown curls, the image of his mother's, framed his face, his long dark lashes fluttered on his cheeks.

'Why can't I have eyelashes like that?' Eleanor said, 'they're wasted on a boy.'

They kissed their children and then hurried down the stairs to the taverna below. 'I'm going to have at least three courses tonight, and a couple of litres of wine,' Chris insisted.

'The trouble with your appetites, darling, is that they're totally insatiable,' Eleanor said, somewhat smugly.

The patron greeted them at the bottom of the stairs. 'Ah, Mr and Mrs Berry, I was just coming to find you.' His face was solemn and concerned.

'What is it, Nikki, is something wrong?'

'There is a girl here, outside at one of the tables. She is English, I think. She does not seem well and she is crying very much.' He looked at Chris. 'You say your wife is a doctor? I think perhaps you can help, yes?'

'Of course,' said Eleanor. 'Where is she?'

'Come, I show you a view of her. You decide what to do then.'

The patron led them through the kitchen and out of the side entrance of the taverna, from where they could view the front of the bar unobserved. It was almost dark and the tables were now fully occupied. The girl sat alone. There was an empty wine carafe beside her and a meal apparently untouched. She seemed to be staring into space. Her face was blotchy with tears and streaked with dirt.

'How long has she been here?' Eleanor asked.

'An hour, perhaps more,' said Nikki.

'Has anyone asked if she's OK?'

'Yes, I have asked and she told me to go away. She has paid her bill,' he added as an afterthought.

'She's absolutely filthy,' said Chris. 'Perhaps she's a hippy. I wonder if she's on drugs. Did you smell anything on her?' Nikki shrugged his shoulders.

'I don't like the look of her,' said Eleanor. 'I'm going over to talk to her. Give me a few minutes on my own, Chris, and then bring over some wine and three glasses.'

'Yes, Ma'am,' said Chris.

'Excuse me,' said Eleanor, 'is anyone sitting here?'

Laura did not glance up. 'No,' she said. Her voice was barely audible.

'Would you mind if I joined you?'

Laura dragged her eyes away from where apparently she had been staring at nothing and glanced at Eleanor. 'No, of course not. Actually I'm just leaving.' She half-rose, swaying slightly as she did so.

Eleanor put a restraining hand on her arm. 'No, don't go, not for a moment. Actually I wanted to talk to you.'

'Talk to me, why?' The girl looked confused.

'I've been watching you. There's something wrong, isn't there? I'm a doctor, is there anything I can do to help you?'

For a moment it looked as though the girl was going to turn and leave. Eleanor increased the pressure on her arm and she sank back in her chair. 'No, there's nothing wrong with me,' she said, with a sad little smile, 'at least I'm not ill, if that's what you mean.'

'So, what's the trouble?' Eleanor asked. Laura met her eye properly for the first time. She's absolutely exhausted, Eleanor thought.

'This is going to sound ridiculous,' said Laura, after a pause, 'but I seem to have lost my husband . . .'

By the time Chris arrived with the wine, Eleanor had the full story and she quickly repeated it to Chris while Laura sat in helpless silence.

'That Police Chief ought to be shot,' said Chris. 'Shall I go and have a word with him? They're a funny lot the Greeks – to them women are definitely second-class citizens. Perhaps he'll take more notice of me.'

Laura smiled at him, gratefully. 'I don't think he will, he's just not interested in the antics of tourists. His view is that because Francis and I had a row, Francis has disappeared to teach me a lesson, and, of course, he may be right.'

'Tell me to mind my own business if you like,' said Eleanor, 'but has your husband ever done this sort of thing before – disappeared I mean, after a row?'

Laura shook her head. 'The whole thing is out of character.' Up to that moment she had not mentioned Francis's financial trouble, but there seemed no point in keeping anything back from this couple – they were kind and interested and three heads were better than one. 'The only thing that has made this row different from the others,' Laura began carefully, 'is I discovered last night that my husband is in some sort of financial mess. My – my father's very rich,' she glanced at them a little self-consciously. 'You know Beecham Stores?'

'Yes, of course,' said Chris.

'Bernard Beecham is my father, and last night we argued about whether Francis should ask for his help. Francis is involved in a rather dubious business scheme, you see, and things appear to have gone very wrong. He wants my father to bail him out, but I told him my father wouldn't help him. I don't know exactly how much trouble Francis is in, but he did mention the Fraud Squad.'

Chris stared hard at Laura. 'Are you suggesting you think he might have . . .' He couldn't go on.

'Committed suicide?' Laura said. Sharing the burden was making her stronger. 'It has crossed my mind, but I honestly can't believe he's the type. He's so, well, self-indulgent.' From nowhere, tears welled up and began running down her face. I'm sorry, it's just such a relief to tell someone – I'm just so worried about him.'

Chris glanced at Eleanor over Laura's bent head and made a face. 'Stay here a moment,' he said, to Laura. 'I have an idea.' With a jerk of the head he indicated that Eleanor should join him. They left Laura and hurried into the taverna.

'What is it – quickly, tell me,' said Eleanor, 'I don't like leaving her alone, Chris, she might do a bunk.'

'Do you believe her story, then?'

Eleanor stared up at her husband. 'Yes, of course. Why, don't you?'

'It seems so unlikely. The girl looks filthy and unkempt – it hardly fits the image of her well-connected relations.'

'She's explained all that,' Eleanor said impatiently. 'She's been tramping up and down St Paul's Bay all afternoon, trying to find her husband – small wonder she's in such a mess.'

'Are you sure she's not on drugs? She may believe what she's saying at the moment but it could all be fabrication.'

'She could be,' Eleanor admitted, 'but I somehow doubt it – certainly there's no obvious evidence to suggest she is, and she seems quite lucid – just exhausted and worried sick, poor girl.'

'And what about Sir Bernard Beecham being her father, do you believe that, too?'

'Well, why not?' Eleanor said. 'There's no reason for her to lie about that.'

'Not unless she's some sort of down and out, hoping to screw a few bob out of us with a hard luck story,' Chris said.

'Well, I for one believe her,' Eleanor said emphatically. 'I think we should try and put a telephone call through to her father and, in the meantime, offer her our bathroom, so the-poor girl can clean herself up. It must be awful for her, Chris. Imagine me in similar circumstances – you'd expect fellow countrymen to rally round and help.'

'I admit I'm a cynic, but the trouble with you is you're such a sucker you believe everything you're told.' Eleanor's expression remained determined. 'OK, you win, I know when I'm beaten. You two go upstairs and I'll have a word with Nikki and try and organize a call to England, though goodness knows if they have any telephone lines out of this place.'

'They must have, Chris, and at least a call to Bernard Beecham will put a stop to your unpleasant suspicions.'

'I'll do my best, but I tell you this – unless somebody, sometime, allows me to have some supper, there's no chance of your being the recipient of any more of my unbridled passion this night.'

'No stamina!' Eleanor called, over her shoulder.

Lying in a warm bath, with water up to her chin, Laura felt her energy begin to return. She had behaved ridiculously, she realized. She should have been firmer with the Chief of Police and should have thought about ringing England before. However, she was always reluctant to ask for help, particularly from her father, and this had hindered her decision, she knew. That was certainly one reason – the other was because of the argument with Francis. It had undermined her normal confidence, for, deep down, she knew that whatever had happened to him was a direct result of their last conversation. There was no escaping that fact, which in turn meant she alone was to blame for whatever fate had befallen her husband.

'Chris has booked the call to England,' Eleanor shouted through the bathroom door. 'We're just going to go down and have some supper. You take as long as you like in the bath.'

'Bless you,' Laura called, 'I'm feeling hugely better already. I am grateful.'

'No problem,' said Eleanor. 'Just relax – we'll call you if we manage to get through to England.'

The telephone at the Taverna Knossos was not ideally situated, being halfway down the narrow passageway which separated the kitchen from the outside tables. Although by now it was well after midnight, the taverna life of Lindos was still in full swing and Laura had to flatten herself against a greasy wall every time a waiter, laden with dishes, passed by her. 'Mummy, it's me, Laura. Laura, Mummy – it's Laura.'

'Laura! What is it, darling, are you ill, are you hurt? Tell your mother quickly what is wrong with you. You should not frighten me like this – what has happened, what can be the trouble?'

Despite the agitation of the moment, Laura felt a flicker of amusement – getting a word in edgeways where her mother was concerned was always difficult. 'No, I'm fine. Mummy, I'm in Rhodes . . .'

'Of course you are, I know you are. Have you had an accident – the boat, it is shipwrecked?'

'No, no, nothing like that.'

'Where are you calling from? You sound like you're in a railway station – or an airport. Are you on your way home?'

'Please let me explain.' A brimming plate of calamari whizzed past Laura's ear. The line crackled and became suddenly very faint – at any moment she expected to be cut off.

'Laura, darling – are you still there. Please tell your mother your trouble.'

'It's Francis,' Laura said, 'he's vanished.'

'Vanished, what is this vanished? Has he left you, he has gone off with another woman? I will kill him, your father will kill him – what are you saying, Laura?'

'Mummy, I think it might be easier if I spoke to Pop.'

'Laura, I don't understand, what is going on?'

'Please, Mummy, we could be cut off at any moment, and it's taken hours to get through to you. It is important – truly.'

There was a pause. 'Laura, love?' Her father's gruff voice, far away though it was, offered immediate comfort. 'What the hell's going on, sweetheart?' Quickly Laura explained the situation. '. . . and you say the local police won't help?'

'Not exactly *won't* help, but certainly they're not taking me very seriously. They believe Francis is simply sulking.'

'What do you think has happened to him, Laura?' The question was uncompromising.

'I honestly don't know, Pop, I can't make it out. It's so unlike him.' Her voice faltered. 'It's why I think there must have been an accident.'

'Right, love, this is what we'll do. I'll find the name of the Head of Police in Athens and get your mother to ring him. Meanwhile, we'll book a flight out to Rhodes and be with you as quickly as we can. Where are you?' Laura gave the address. 'OK, love, don't worry. We should be with you tomorrow or, if not, first thing the next day.'

'Pop . . .,' Laura hesitated.

'Yes?'

'I think you'd better tell Lord Campling what's happened, don't you?'

'I'm not speaking to that man . . .' Bernard began.

'Pop, you must – it is his son who has gone missing. Whatever you may think of him, whatever you think of his attitude, just imagine if the situation was reversed, and he didn't tell you if I was in trouble.'

There was a pause. 'You're right, I'll get your mother to ring him, but I won't speak to him – not after the way he's behaved.'

'I understand that, Pop,' said Laura patiently, 'but for heaven's sake make sure he's informed – he does have a right to know.'

Eleanor and Chris were waiting anxiously in the bar, when Laura joined them. 'What happened?' they asked in unison.

Laura gave them a ghost of a smile. 'Pop, efficient as ever, is taking care of everything. He's going to get hold of the police in Athens, presumably to apply some local pressure and then he'll fly out here tomorrow.'

'Wonderful, what a relief,' said Eleanor. 'Poor old Laura, I should think you could use a drink – and are you hungry now?'

Laura shook her head. 'Honestly, I think it's sleep I need. I'll go back to the *Empress* now and perhaps see you in the morning. I am grateful for all you've done.'

'You're not going anywhere,' said Chris, 'we've booked you a room here, at the taverna. Neither of us liked the idea of your sleeping on that yacht alone, in the circumstances.'

'I'm alright, honestly,' Laura began, but even as she spoke, she knew she was in no state to argue. A lonely yacht in the darkened harbour was the last place she wanted to be. She smiled at them gratefully. 'I can't believe it, you've been so very kind – you feel like old friends already and yet I hardly know you.'

Eleanor smiled back. 'Frankly, Laura, I think you could use a friend or two just at the moment.'

Laura was not about to argue.

CHAPTER THREE

Andre Koyokopis could not understand it. The phone call had been tantalizingly brief. Georgios Theodakis, Assistant Chief of Police in Athens, was on his way to Rhodes and Andre was to meet him at the airport. No, the young sergeant telephoning had assured Andre, he did not know what it was all about.

The police station at Lindos, never the most salubrious of places, was a lamentable mess. The previous night, he had been forced to lock up five drunks. It had upset Andre. They were young Greek boys, learning bad ways from the tourists. He had let them go in the morning because he could think of no charge upon which to hold them, but they had left the station in appalling disarray. Andre had just three hours' notice of the impending arrival of the great Georgios Theodakis, but he did not dare ask his wife for help. He called instead on his sister, Elese, and together, brother and sister cleaned up the vomit, swept the floor, polished the counter and washed the windows. As a final gesture to order out of chaos, Elese picked a bunch of flowers and placed them in a vase on the window sill. Pleased with the transformation, Andre checked his watch, then climbed into his battered old car and took the coast road to Rhodes.

Georgios Theodakis was first off the plane and instantly recognizable because he was almost completely square. His extraordinarily short stature and vast frame meant that he had to walk with a rolling gait, and Andre watched with growing trepidation as his chief propelled his way across the tarmac. Whilst not a centimetre over five foot, Georgios made a formidable sight which matched a formidable reputation. Andre held out a hand to him. 'Welcome to Rhodes,' he said, cautiously.

'Is there a room here at the airport, in which we can talk? I have to catch the next plane out in half an hour,' Georgios said. He kept walking as he talked.

Fleetingly, Andre thought of the now spotless station back at Lindos. Clearly all his and Elese's work had been for nothing. 'I – I'm not sure.' Andre's apprehension was mounting – the whole situation was odd. Fear stifled his ingenuity.

'Oh well, no doubt you have a car. A car will do, it's probably best, anyway.' The two men walked through the airport building in silence to where Andre's car was parked. Georgios squeezed himself into the passenger seat. 'Drive the car into the shade,' he demanded, mopping his brow with an enormous handkerchief. Andre did as he was told and, moments later, parked the car in the shade of an airport hangar. More agitated than ever, he fumbled with the gears and then cut the engine. 'The missing Englishman, there's no further news on him, I assume?' The question was barked out without preamble and, for a moment, Andre's mind reeled. Missing Englishman, what missing Englishman? He stared at Georgios blankly. 'An Englishman was reported missing off a yacht yesterday,' Georgio said with studied patience. 'His wife came into the station to see you.'

That missing Englishman – Andre nodded. 'Yes, yes, that's right.'

'Well?' said Georgios, clearly irritated, 'nothing of him yet?' Andre shook his head. 'I see. His name, as you no doubt know, is Francis Melhuish. In fact he is the Honourable Francis Melhuish, son of an English lord – Lord Campling, who also happens to have been in the last Government – a British cabinet minister – a very important man,' he added for Andre's benefit. Andre was sure this was supposed to mean something to him, but he could not think what. He nodded his head enthusiastically but he did not fool Georgios. 'English lords,' Georgios continued, speaking slowly, as if to a child, 'are a type of royalty in England. This man who is missing is not particularly important, but his father is. When his father heard his son was missing he was able to telephone straight through to the Colonels. He has that kind of influence, Andre.'

At the mention of the Colonels, Andre felt a tingle of fear run down his spine. 'We have organized a search party and are looking for him most earnestly,' he said, hurriedly.

'What do you think has happened to him?' Georgios asked.

Andre's brain struggled to remember the details. 'I think perhaps, he is punishing his wife by pretending to be missing,' Andre said. 'The couple, they had a quarrel on the yacht and then he disappeared during the night, I think he may have swum ashore and then gone off somewhere.'

'But he has not yet turned up?' Andre shook his head. 'If it was a quarrel, I think he would be back with his wife by now, don't you? I believe there may have been an accident, in which case, Andre, it is most important that no body is found.' Andre frowned and although Georgios had not intended to give the man an explanation, he realized something of the sort was necessary. 'Diplomatic relations between Greece and England are not good at the moment. The English have given King Constantine a home, which does not please the Colonels. Then there has been the problem of one or two English people, how shall we say, disappearing. Remember the case of the English girl tourist in Athens?' Andre nodded emphatically. 'I am assured by the Colonels that Francis Melhuish's disappearance is not political, and that if he is dead, it is purely an accident. However, the Colonels feel that any such accident might be misinterpreted, and since he is the son of an English lord, who was also in Government, they think a body could put an intolerable strain on an already difficult situation. I don't like the tourists, neither do you, but as a nation we need them. A break in diplomatic relations could very seriously damage the economy at this moment. Do you understand all that, Andre?'

Andre nodded. 'No body.'

'That's right, no body. Some of my men are being flown over to help you. There will be a helicopter search. All this will take place before Lord Campling and his party arrive in Rhodes. If there is a body you must find it, and if there is a body, you must then lose it.'

Andre looked at his chief questioningly. 'Lose it. How?'

'Well, don't just throw it back into the sea, you fool. Bury it, feed it to pigs, I don't know, but make sure it is never found.'

Andre nodded slowly. For a moment into his mind came a

picture of the distraught young wife. He frowned. 'Is something wrong?' Georgios demanded.

'No, no, nothing.'

'Good.' Georgios consulted his watch, 'Now drive me back to the airport building, I have only ten minutes in which to catch my plane.'

Georgios Theodakis stood watching as Andre pulled his car out into the stream of airport traffic, an arm extending from the window in a friendly wave. A nice man, but stupid, Georgios thought. Once the search was over, body or no body, Andre would have to be moved from Rhodes; it was too risky to leave him there. A few rakis too many one evening and the conversation they'd just had was bound to be repeated. It was unlikely, too, that such an important English family would give up the search easily. There was going to be press coverage, a great deal of it, and he was sure Andre was not up to that. He would offer him a place on his staff in Athens. If he was not co-operative – well, he was expendable. Georgios tried to remember whether Andre had a family. He was not sure, but either way the man would have to be silenced. Georgios watched, squinting against the sun as the car took the perimeter road. He hesitated and then raised an arm to return Andre's parting wave. In the circumstances it seemed churlish not to do so.

For Nikki Takis of the Taverna Knossos, trade could not have been better. He had prepared two more letting rooms for the very important English who were arriving today – lords and ladies he had been told – and now people were flocking to his taverna, to ask what was happening. There was a helicopter flying overhead and a police boat searching along the coast. Both had attracted a great deal of attention and Nikki had been able to tell people that the missing man's wife was actually staying here, in his taverna. Andre Koyokopis had told him that soon newspaper men would be arriving and would ask him questions. The Taverna Knossos was to be in the newspaper – not just in Athens but in England and perhaps America, too. 'This will make us famous and very rich,' Nikki told his wife, confidentially. 'At the end of the season, we must build on, make more rooms, buy a deep freeze, extend the bar. We must also have Greek dancing every night.'

'Oh you and your dreams,' she said, dismissively.

'No, no, Lea, this will happen,' Nikki insisted. 'At least it will if they do not find the Englishman's body too soon. While he is still missing, people are interested, people will come here and eat and drink . . . I will speak to my brother. If he can find the body first, he could perhaps hide it for a little while.' Nikki's brother was a fisherman.

'He could get into trouble, and anyway, the Englishman may still be alive,' Lea suggested.

'No.' Nikki was adamant. 'His wife is a lovely girl, he would not leave her alone for so long.'

Three taxis drew to a halt outside the Taverna Knossos late the following afternoon. In the first was Sir Bernard and Lady Beecham, in the second Lord Campling and in the third, four pressmen – three from England and one from America. Laura was totally unprepared for the arrival of the press and after an emotional welcome from her mother, she turned to Bernard for an explanation.

'I'm afraid *I* can explain the press's presence, here, my dear.' Lord Campling had entered the taverna bar behind them. Although Laura had never met him before, she would have recognized him anywhere – his lean, good-looks were very reminiscent of Francis, as was the same natural elegance. After a flight and a long, hot taxi ride, he looked completely unruffled, in light linen trousers and jacket. His shock of hair, white instead of the pale yellow of Francis's, was perfectly combed into place. However, as he walked forward towards her, Laura noticed that he stooped badly and suddenly seemed every inch of the seventy-four years she knew him to be. Instantly, her heart went out to him, despite the fact that he had rejected her as his daughter-in-law. 'There have been serious developments.' Lord Campling addressed the Beechams generally. 'We need to talk, to pool resources. I have some information for you and, no doubt, Laura has some for us. I assume, Laura, Francis has not been found?'

She shook her head. 'No,' she said quietly.

Bernard Beecham had said not a word but the aggression he

felt towards Lord Campling was evident in his face. Katrine took the initiative. 'I think that's a very good idea. Is there somewhere we can talk quietly, Laura, darling?'

In the end, they assembled in Lord Campling's bedroom. It was cramped but that was not such a bad thing as it gave them all an immediate sense of intimacy – false, but in the circumstances, useful. 'If you can bear it, Laura, could you tell us the whole story from the beginning?' Lord Campling asked. Laura repeated the now-familiar story. No one asked any questions, and when she had finished, Lord Campling thanked her with great courtesy and then addressed them all. 'What I have to tell you is not a pretty story. I do not know whether it throws any light on Francis's disappearance or not, but I suspect it does. Shortly before leaving for the airport today, I received a visit from the Fraud Squad. Apparently Francis is in very severe financial trouble. He has been dabbling in – how shall I put it – the overseas holiday market, and as far as I can understand it, has been selling non-existent holiday homes.'

Bernard let out a long whistle. 'Have you any idea how much money is involved?'

'About a quarter of a million pounds.'

'Jesus, and this is the same man you considered too good for our daughter?'

'I'm glad you've raised that point now,' said Lord Campling. 'I *was* very opposed to your daughter marrying my son, but it was no reflection on your daughter. It was just that my son has been a wastrel all his life and I thought marriage was the last thing he should have been contemplating at the time. As Laura knows, Francis and I haven't spoken to one another for over two years.' He looked at Laura. 'I know this is a hurtful thing to say, my dear – particularly in the current circumstances – but I have always feared that he married you for your money, or rather your father's money, and it was for that reason I would have no part of it. When Francis came to see me to tell me your wedding plans, I told him that in my view he should get himself a steady job so that he could support a wife, before he considered marriage to you or anyone. I also said that if he persisted in marrying you, I would not attend the wedding and would cut him off without a penny. I'm afraid he laughed in my face.' Lord Campling looked directly at Bernard Beecham. 'The inheritance I can offer my children does pale into insignificance, I suspect, compared with what you can offer yours. It was rather a hollow gesture, but I do want to assure you that whatever Francis may have told you, I was not opposed in any way to his marrying your daughter – in fact quite the contrary, I was simply concerned as to his motives.'

'My poor baby,' Katrine burst out. 'Is that what you too believe now – that this husband married you only for your money?'

Laura seemed to consider the question for a moment. 'I don't know, I don't really know any more, the last few days . . .' she broke off.

Bernard sat down beside her on the bed and placed an arm round her shoulders. 'So what's to be done?' he asked, bluntly.

'There's not much that can be done,' Lord Campling replied, 'except to try and minimize the story so far as the press is concerned. Unfortunately they know the Fraud Squad are involved – indeed, they've already asked me about it. For Laura's sake, I think it is vital that we ensure the story attracts the absolute minimum of exposure. As to Francis – if he turns up, he'll be arrested and I'm sorry, Laura dear, but I for one will do nothing to help him.'

'Nor I,' said Bernard.

Laura looked into the face of her father and then in turn at her father-in-law. They were so confident in their total condemnation of her husband. She felt a sudden wave of pity for Francis – so far as any of them knew, he could be already dead, his body perhaps being battered against rocks or submerged in some lonely cove. Yet here they were, these men, apparently content to hand him over to the police, if by any chance he should survive.

Lord Campling saw the expression on her face. 'You think we're being too hard on him, Laura, but I suspect this business with the Fraud Squad came as no surprise to you. Am I right?'

She nodded. 'It was what we were arguing about the night . . . the night he disappeared.'

'You're the boy's father, what do you think has happened to him?' Bernard demanded.

'Like Laura, I don't think he killed himself, not intentionally anyway. However, it is difficult to form a view particularly when there is no trace of his movements. I gather the search of the coastline has been fairly thorough.'

Laura nodded. 'Yes, it has, but it didn't start for twenty-four hours after Francis disappeared. That was my fault, I should have telephoned to England sooner. I was such a fool.' Tears slid down her face but she did not seem to notice them.

'If he has drowned,' Bernard said, more gently, 'I don't think when the search party was called would have made a lot of difference, love.'

Lord Campling nodded. 'I think the important thing now is to get Laura away from here and back to England.'

'I agree with that,' said Katrine, 'but I can stay here, if you like, as I am Greek and can make sure the police keep busy.'

'What about the yacht?' Lord Campling looked at Laura.

'It needs to be taken back to Rhodes,' she said, wearily.

'There's no need to worry about that,' said Bernard. 'I'll arrange for someone to sail it round to Rhodes.

The following morning, Laura went alone to the yacht, to collect her and Francis's belongings, and to tidy up. Both her mother and Eleanor had wanted to come and help but she had insisted on doing it alone. It was a private pilgrimage, breaking the last tangible link with her husband. It took her no more than a quarter of an hour to pack away their clothes and belongings and only a little longer to clean up. She worked quickly and efficiently, purposely closing her mind to all conscious thought.

When she had finished, she sat down quietly in the cabin and looked around her. What did she feel for Francis now? She tried to sort out her feelings. He was a criminal, who – as his father had suggested – may well have married her for her money. Yet, thinking back to the early days of their marriage, she could not believe it. They had been so in love – hadn't they – or was it all an illusion? The man she thought she had loved was, after all, only the image Francis projected, not his true self, which surely, she now realized, she must never have known.

The question she had been asked so often in the last few days surfaced again in her mind. What did she think had happened to him? She did not, could not, know. This fraudulent stranger who had vanished from her life bore no resemblance at all to the man she believed to have been her husband.

Wearily Laura stood up and began lugging their two suitcases on to the deck. In the hatchway she stopped and stared down the length of the after-deck. It was here she'd had her last sight of Francis – wine bottle in hand, lolling back in his chair, his eyes cold and insolent. If that was how it was to be, it was not a good last memory to have of the man she had once loved so much.

The strange affair of the disappearing Englishman, Francis Melhuish, affected many lives. For Nikki Takis, it was the best thing that had ever happened. As he had accurately predicted, trade poured into his taverna to see the place where the Englishman had vanished. He renamed it Taverna Melhuish and when, a year later, his wife presented him with his first son, he called the boy Francis, feeling it was the least he could do. Andre Koyokopis was not so lucky. Like the man he had been seeking, he too disappeared without trace, just six weeks later. His family made enquiries, another perfunctory search of the coastline was made, but Andre was neither seen nor heard of again.

For Eleanor and Chris Berry, the influence of Francis Melhuish was less tangible, but still keenly felt. For one thing, a lifetime of friendship lay ahead with Laura Melhuish. For another, it demonstrated to them the frailty of life, and of marriage, something with which they would become only too familiar in the years that lay ahead.

And as for Laura – for Laura the unexplained disappearance of her husband was like the dropping of a stone into a still pond. The ripples that fanned out from that moment were to shape the rest of her life.

CHAPTER FOUR

David Lawson gave a deep sigh and leant back in his chair. He was sitting in the little shed that served as his office. In front of him, spread out on the desk, was a selection of the day's newspapers. The headlines were all in the same vein – 'Missing Peer's Son Wanted by the Fraud Squad. Francis Melhuish, son of Lord Campling, involved in Big Holiday Home Swindle'. The pages were plastered with mug-shots of Francis, but David's eyes kept straying to the photograph of Laura and her father, arriving at Heathrow. Bernard Beecham looked grim and very angry – his expression suggested that at any moment he might punch the photographer. David smiled. Knowing Bernard's short temper as he did, he guessed the press did not realize that they had enjoyed a very lucky escape. It was Laura though, as always, who held his attention – Laura's lovely face, framed by her long, dark hair. Even at that moment, of what for her must have been extreme grief and anguish, she looked controlled. She was leaning heavily on her father's arm, he noticed – otherwise there was no outward show of what must have been enormous inner turmoil. She stared straight into the camera, meeting its eye with her calm, steady gaze. The black and white photograph, of course, could not do her justice. He looked into those big, round, sad eyes, knowing their colour to be that of cornflowers or of the sea on a sunny day.

Enough of this, David thought. With a swift and easy movement, he stood up, straightened the hinge of his leg caliper and limped out of the door. The sight he greeted always cheered him, winter and summer, whatever the weather. The Thames, flowing almost beneath his feet was pearly blue on this early July morning. Here, just upstream from Henley, the river was already gaining some of the power and width that would take it past the Houses of Parliament, the

Tower of London, and so to the sea. He leaned on the rail and looked down into the water. He never tired of it – it was like watching a rich pageant, and somehow the timeless quality of the great rolling river always eased his worries and calmed his fears. Matched against the river's size and history, the frailty of man was all too apparent. It helped David to keep a sense of perspective, he felt.

He shifted slightly to lean more comfortably on the rail. The sun shone on his dark-brown hair, which sprang away from his face in a riot of curls, which he loathed and women adored. He had an extraordinarily handsome and sensitive face – high cheekbones, a permanent tan from his outdoor living and deep, dark, kind brown eyes. His physique – to the waist – was magnificent – broad shoulders and a deep, muscular chest. It was the body of an athlete, yet in reality had been created by years of heaving himself around on crutches and in and out of wheelchairs. He turned and began walking up the landing-stage towards his workshop. His walk was light and agile. He swung his useless leg, straightened and strengthened by a caliper, easily from the hip. This was his legacy from the childhood accident which had left his mother dead and himself crippled for life. The years of fighting against his disability, fighting to lead the normal life which his father clearly believed was impossible for him, had not embittered him – it had strengthened him. He was a better person, he knew, with a paralyzed leg, than he would ever have been without it. All he wished was that he was taller. At only five foot six, his penchant for tall women was inappropriate. He had always been attracted to tall women, except for Laura. Laura barely reached his shoulder. Laura, who had wandered in and out of his dreams since he was seventeen years old. Laura, forcing his attention upon her yet again . . . For David, the moment could hardly have been less appropriate, yet unfortunate timing had always played extravagant tricks where his relationship with Laura was concerned.

'Lawson, Lawson, come and meet my sister.' Edward Chattaway, David's closest school friend, was sauntering across the lawn towards him, a girl on either arm.

Whilst the rest of Eton College were elegantly dressed for this, the Fourth of June, or else flexing their muscles at some appropriate sport in front of proud and admiring parents, David, by contrast, was hot and sweaty, and wearing a grubby T-shirt and jeans. He had just finished helping to launch the various crews for the Head-of-the-River race. He was an excellent oarsman and rowed a great deal in his spare time, but the caliper excluded him from competitive sport. Now he stood awkwardly, acutely aware of his inappropriate appearance, waiting for the party to reach him. Edward looked tall and elegant in his tailcoat. Sylvia Chattaway, in contrast to her brother, was short, plump and red-haired – David barely noticed her. It was her friend, whom Edward described as one of Sylvia's chums from school, who riveted David's attention. Her name was Laura Beecham, he was told. She was tiny, slim and small-boned, with thick, dark curly hair, forced into a severe pony tail. Her eyes were the brightest blue and her heart-shaped face was exquisite. Her expression however, was troubled and stormy. Sylvia, David noticed, was staring at his leg. It did not bother him, it was how strangers always reacted. Laura, by contrast, seemed not to have noticed. She affected boredom and stared out across the river.

'We're just off for strawberries and cream, Lawson. Are you coming?'

David laughed, uneasily. 'Not like this, I'm not. I'll have to go and change, I'll see you later.'

In his room, he stripped off and washed, selected a clean shirt and took his time over getting dressed. He had shaved that morning – it was still a new experience and he had cut himself. He ran a finger thoughtfully over his chin. There was no hint of stubble, nor would there be for at least another twenty-four hours. Shaving, as yet, was something of an affectation, he had to admit. When he was dressed, he made a vain attempt to plaster down his curls with water, but they sprang straight up again. He sighed, hating the restriction and formality of the clothes. He hated all formal occasions come to that. Perhaps if his father had been here it would be different, but he rarely attended any school functions. At prep school, it had bothered David, but not now, not any more.

David left his room and began walking down the corridor. Two figures ahead of him stood in a doorway embracing – a tall, fair boy was kissing an equally tall, willowy, dark-haired girl with great thoroughness. There was a lot of giggling and the boy's hands moved up and down the slim, young body. The sight of them aroused David and made him feel hot and uncomfortable until he realized the identity of the boy.

'Hop! What the bloody hell are you doing here?' The boy's voice was rough and angry. 'I suppose you're spying on us, just because you can't get it for yourself. Is that right, Hop?'

His tone angered David more than the use of his childhood nickname. He had been known as 'Hopalong' at prep school. It was an affectionate term which at the time had never upset him. Used now though, it irritated and humiliated him, particularly in front of the girl. 'I was just passing, Melhuish. I do apologize for interrupting you . . . both.' He hoped his exaggerated tone sounded suitably cynical. He hurried round the corner but not before he heard Francis Melhuish's ringing tones, saying, 'I bet he *was* spying on us, darling, I'm so sorry. Still, I suppose he has to get his kicks somehow. Cripples give me the creeps, don't they you?'

David joined Edward and his party because he had promised to do so. Mrs Chattaway made a great effort to be friendly to him. Mr Chattaway wrung him warmly by the hand and questioned him closely about his academic work, with as much interest as if he was his own son. Yet Francis Melhuish's words had put him out of sorts. He felt oddly detached from the group and longed to be somewhere else, though where, he was not sure. The cricket match was reaching an interesting stage. Carrying bowls of strawberries, the party moved off to watch. David, seated in the shade of the marquee, felt disinclined to go with them. He sat, staring at the grass, thinking of the evening's activities ahead with no great enthusiasm.

'Are you hating this as much as me?' A crystal clear voice, high, light and very feminine, broke into his consciousness. He looked up. The Laura girl was standing before him. She was wearing a silly pink dress which seemed far too young for her, but her face was as arresting as ever.

'Yes.' He stood up awkwardly, strawberries in one hand clicking the hinge of his caliper, with the other. 'Yes, I'm hating it. Why don't we escape – go for a walk or something?' His boldness surprised him. He set down the unfinished strawberries.

'Yes, let's – anything to get away.' The face that had been so sullen was now bright and alive with mischief.

'How did you get the day off school?' David asked, as they walked along behind the backs of the spectators.

'Chicken pox,' she said. 'There's an epidemic at Wycombe Abbey at the moment and so we've all been sent home.'

'Well, I hope you're not going to give it to me,' said David. 'I think it's about one of the few things I haven't had.'

'I haven't either,' Laura said, 'and I simply mustn't get it, or Mother says I'll end up pock-marked.'

David looked at her candidly. 'That would be a shame.'

The girl smiled. 'Do you like being at Eton?'

'It's alright,' said David, 'but I do find these occasions hard work.'

'Aren't your parents here?' Laura asked.

He shook his head. 'No, my father has business commitments. I have a step-sister at Benenden. He and my stepmother are visiting her at the weekend, and he cannot take off any more time.'

'They should have been here for the Fourth of June.' Laura frowned. She wanted to ask about David's mother but decided against it.

'If they had been, I wouldn't have been able to run away with you,' said David, pleased with this logic.

'That's true.' Laura laughed, a light tinkling noise that delighted his ear.

'I tell you what,' he said, 'why don't we go punting?'

'I'm not sure,' said Laura, doubtfully. 'Remember I'm with the Chattaways.'

'What time did they say they were leaving?'

'Oh not until after prize-giving. Edward's won tons of prizes, Sylvia says.'

'Yes, he has,' David confirmed. He looked at his watch.

'Prize-giving's not for over an hour and it goes on for hours. We'll never be missed – honestly.'

'Then I'd love to go punting,' Laura said decisively.

David was reasonably skilled with a punt pole, and though he had some difficulty keeping his balance, they made steady progress and were soon away from the rest of the milling boats and people. Laura lay back on the cushions, as she imagined one was supposed to do, and trailed her fingers languidly in the water. She felt positively sophisticated, which, at fourteen, was something of a novelty. David removed his jacket and struggled manfully on, determined on playing his part in creating the image.

It was the heron which caused the problem. Suddenly, Laura sat up in the punt. 'David, look, look over there, isn't he beautiful?' David looked behind him. Standing in the hollow of an old tree stump was a heron, vast and very still. At the sound of Laura's voice, it turned and stared at them and then slowly opened its enormous wings, flapped lazily a few times and was airborne. David and Laura watched spellbound, and so engrossed were they, that they did not see the branch of the willow tree. It struck David's shoulder, catching him off balance and sending him straight into the water. Laura burst out laughing. 'Idiot!' she called. 'What *are* you doing?' David's head appeared above the water, several feet from the punt, which was flowing swiftly downstream. Almost immediately he disappeared again. Laura continued to laugh. 'David, stop messing about. Are you saying it's good in there, shall I come in too?'

When he came up the next time, fleetingly, she knew immediately that something was very wrong. He was not above water long enough to catch the expression on his face, but all her instincts told her that he was in serious trouble. Desperately she looked around the bottom of the boat, and found a paddle. She had been brought up on the banks of the Thames, and expertly, with a few strokes, she swung the long length of the punt so that the end furthest from her was more or less where David had been before he sunk. It was probably seconds, but it seemed like minutes before his head broke the surface again. He must have caught sight of the punt inches from him for one arm shot out of the water and caught the edge. Laura dropped the paddle and ran down the length of the punt, clambering over the seats. She reached David in time to catch his other arm as he struggled to hold on to the punt. He was fighting for breath. 'C-can you take the punt inshore? I can't get aboard,' he managed.

'Can you hold on?' He nodded. She ran back to the paddle and soon had the front of the punt nosing into a little creek.

David's feet must have touched bottom for suddenly he was standing beside the punt, his body bent forward wracked with coughing and retching. Laura jumped off the punt, secured it to a willow branch, then she went back for David. Taking his hand, she helped him on to the bank. 'I'll be alright, in a minute,' he managed.

'Don't talk.'

He lay on his stomach, his whole frame still heaving. She sat beside him, uncertain what to do. Gradually his breathing eased and he turned over. His face was very pale now. 'I'm so sorry,' he said. 'I don't know what you must think of me.'

'What happened, I don't understand? Can't you swim?'

He smiled at her. 'Oh yes, I swim like a fish, but not when I'm wearing this bloody caliper. It weighs a ton.'

'But you must have known that when you suggested we went punting,' said Laura.

'Of course I know it, but it's never normally a problem. I was showing off, that's the trouble. I do punt, but usually with a group of pals who know they have to haul me out fast. It was silly of me not to have settled for paddling with you today. I'm sorry if I frightened you – but for your quick thinking, I'd have been fodder for fish.'

'Don't,' said Laura. Instinctively, she reached out and took one of his hands in both of hers. 'Don't, David.' He smiled at her, it felt good to have someone so concerned about him. 'We ought to go back,' she said. 'You'll catch your death of cold.'

'Rubbish.' He hesitated. 'Would you mind if I took off my shirt?'

She watched as he removed his shirt and hung it on the branch of a tree. His physique was more that of a man than a boy. His chest, deep brown and powerful, made her feel strange, nervous and slightly in awe of him. She lowered her eyes. She could not look at him without wanting to touch him, and she did not understand her feelings. There was an awkward silence between them. Then Laura said, 'Tell me about your leg, David, that is if you don't mind. I expect you get awfully fed up with people asking.'

He laughed, instantly easing the tension. 'As a matter of fact I don't, because no one, and I literally mean *no one*, ever asks me directly what the problem is – not even Edward. It's typical English reticence, I suppose. I was born in South Africa, my father was working out there – he's an engineer, very high-powered. When I was two, my parents took me on Safari. One afternoon, while my father was waiting for a telephone call, my mother took me in a jeep out into a game reserve – the idea being to show me some of the animals.

'It was considered quite a sensible, safe thing to do – no one worried until we had not returned by nightfall. A search party was quickly sent out and they found us shortly after dawn. Apparently our jeep had been rammed by a rhino. The animal turned over the vehicle and . . . and trampled my mother to death. I was trapped under the jeep – alive, just, but with crushed vertebrae and a damaged spinal cord.'

'Oh David.' Tears came into Laura's eyes. She turned her head away so that he should not see them. 'How dreadful – what on earth happened next?'

'Hospital in Cape Town, then Great Ormond Street and finally Stoke Mandeville. It was a fair old haul to get me back on my feet.' He grinned good-naturedly – there was no hint of self-pity.

'Do you remember the accident?' Laura asked.

'No, which is a good thing. What is sad, though, is I don't remember my mother either. I have photographs of course, but my memory is a clean slate before the accident. I regret that, very much.'

'Poor David,' said Laura.

'Not poor David at all. If you have to go through something like that, two is the perfect age. I can't remember walking normally. As far as I'm concerned, I've always been like this, so I have no comparisons to make and nothing to regret. At two, imagination does not hamper and one is infinitely more resilient. Learning to walk with a caliper was just another of the learning processes – like piling one brick on top of the other.'

Laura nodded. At fourteen, she considered herself quite adult for her age, yet, for the first time, she was dimly aware of how easy and privileged her life had been. This boy – no, in her eyes, this man – had been through so much, had to cope with so much. Instinctively, she knew he was light years ahead of her in understanding. 'Your father?' she said after a pause, 'it must have been awful for him.'

'Yes,' said David, 'it must.' He hesitated. 'Actually, we're not very close. My father would rather I had died in that accident than ended up like this.'

'David, that can't be right.' Laura was appalled.

'Don't misunderstand me, I'm not criticizing him.' Having embarked on such a painful subject, David was anxious to explain. 'He's very much an action man – polo, tennis, big game hunting – cricket, too. He puts great store by his fitness and he just cannot imagine being hampered as I am. In his view, life just wouldn't be worth living – literally. For years, I could tell, he could hardly bear to see me. Then he remarried, and his new wife has done a great deal to help bring us together. I have a step-sister now, too, as I mentioned – she must be a little younger than you. This is her first year at boarding school and she's hating it. Her name's Jessica.'

'Do you get on well, you and Jessica?' Laura asked.

'Quite well,' David replied, 'but I don't really know her. My father still works abroad most of the time, and I don't go home every holiday – I tend to stay with my godfather, or the Chattaways.'

'I can't imagine what it's like not to be close to your family,' Laura said, 'it must be horrid.'

David smiled at her. 'You get used to it. Hey, come on, I'd better take you back to the party. I hope your dress isn't too wet.'

'I don't care if it is, it's absolutely ghastly, anyway,' said Laura.

They paddled back together. David put on his wet shirt and

his dry jacket over the top. The effect was not too bizarre. They paddled in silence but there was no awkwardness between them now – in fact a strange contentment. What Laura could not have known was that it was the first time David had ever discussed his problem outside the immediate family. He wondered now what had prompted the conversation – perhaps it was the shock of his falling in the river. When they reached the boathouse they abandoned the punt and skirted round the back of the houses – anxious to avoid the main crowds and, above all, prize-giving, which the loudspeakers told them was now well under way.

'You go up and change,' Laura said, when they reached the front door of David's house. 'I'll wait for you here.'

'Are you sure?'

'Yes, I'll sit in the sun.'

This time he hurried over his changing and when he returned, David found Laura sitting waiting for him, her legs swinging in the sunshine. Impulsively, he reached out and took her hand. 'Come on, if we hurry round the back, we can join the crowds without anybody noticing.'

Laura ran and David hopped with surprising speed. The warmth of the day meant that the prize-giving was outside. They reached the back of the vast group of people and paused to catch their breath. 'Are you alright?' Laura asked anxiously.

David looked surprised. 'Yes, of course.'

'I mean, first of all, nearly drowning and then all this dashing around.'

'I'm as fit as you are,' said David. 'Fitter probably.'

'I didn't mean . . .' Laura began, blushing.

'I know, I know you didn't.' He squeezed the hand he was still holding. 'We're friends, Laura, aren't we?' he asked, gently. She looked up at him and nodded, her eyes bright with warmth and happiness. It was that moment which enslaved David . . . forever.

Over the next few years, David saw Laura occasionally, but not nearly as often as he would have liked. David's father, Timothy Lawson, had been transferred to Tehran and gradually, under his step-mother's influence, David was drawn more into the family circle. David was under no illusion – Eton had given him a certain polish, and his scholastic excellence gave his father something to brag about, which in turn made it easier to overlook his son's disability. Each holiday there were flattering invitations to spend as much time as possible with the family, and, with the exception of the short Easter break, David tended to accept, travelling both ways with Jessica, with whom he still found it difficult to communicate. When he did see Laura it was at the occasional school dance, or the odd weekend at the Chattaways. On each occasion, they reacted like homing pigeons, spending every available moment together. Yet when they parted, it was without plans to meet again.

Everything changed in the summer holidays of 1963. Laura, by this time, was seventeen. She had left school after O levels, much to her father's fury, and had just completed a year's secretarial course, which included tuition in journalism. David was in his first year at Oxford, reading mathematics and hating it. Edward Chattaway, as always the true friend, was aware of David's dissatisfaction with university, and also of his very special relationship with Laura. Whether it was because of his disability or his natural reticence where close relationships were concerned, Edward did not know, but David had formed no real attachment to any girl – the only one who seemed to interest him was Sylvia's little friend, Laura. So Edward, with a flash of insight, invited David to spend a fortnight of the summer vacation at the Chattaway's shooting lodge on the west coat of Scotland, and persuaded his sister to invite Laura.

Neither David nor Laura were prepared for the presence of the other, for Sylvia and Edward had intended it to be that way. After the initial surprise and pleasure, the two quickly became inseparable, alienating themselves from the rest of the party by using the excuse of David's leg as restricting their walking activities on the moors. In fact, they roamed for miles, exploring the strange and beautiful sea lochs of the west coast, sometimes picnicking among the rocks or taking shelter in a pub, against the inevitable vagaries of the weather. They compared notes on the future mapped out for each of them, largely at their parents' behest, and found their circumstances strangely similar.

'Pop assumes I'm going to follow him into the business,' Laura said, 'but I'm just not that interested in clothes. I make an effort to look nice, but only if I've got nothing more important to think about.'

'That makes you very unusual,' David suggested. They were sitting on a promontory of rock, looking over the Island of Luing. It was a cloudy evening, but warm, and they were in no hurry to get back to the Chattaways.

Laura looked surprised. 'Do you think so?'

David nodded. 'Most of the girls I know are *only* interested in how they look. They're forever disappearing off to powder their noses or change their clothes. You make a refreshing change.' He hesitated. 'OK, so you don't want to go into Beecham Stores. What do you want?'

'I want to be a journalist.'

'Yes,' said David, slowly, 'yes, I can see that. You're good at making people talk about themselves – at least you're good at getting me to talk about myself.' He smiled at Laura ruefully.

'I won't be interviewing anyone for ages,' Laura said. 'I'll just be covering weddings and funerals, that sort of stuff, when I'm not making the coffee and sweeping the floor.'

'You mean you've got a job already?'

'I've been offered one at the *Maidenhead Advertiser*, but I'm too frightened to take it.'

'Why?' David asked.

'My father will go mad. He thinks this business of me not wanting to join Beechams is just a whim. He doesn't understand, David. He made it on his own and I want to do the same thing.'

'Have you talked to him like you're talking to me?'

Laura nodded. 'Endlessly, but he's very old-fashioned about the whole thing. Literally, I think he'll throw me out without a penny if I don't do as I'm told.'

'Would that worry you?' David asked.

'Not in the least,' said Laura, 'but it would upset my mother and that in turn would upset me. She's very emotional – it's the Greek blood – and I'm her only child.'

'I think you must follow your own star, though heaven knows, I'm a fine one to give you advice. Look at me!'

'Why,' said Laura, 'what's wrong with your life? Surely you're enjoying Oxford?'

'In some respects, yes,' said David, 'but I loathe maths, I can't think why I got such a good A level – it certainly wasn't for the love of the subject.' He smiled. 'My father sees me as a potential merchant banker, carving my way in the City. It's not what I want.'

'So,' said Laura, 'what do you want to do?'

'Build boats.'

'Build what?' Laura started to laugh.

'You see, you're not better than my father,' said David. His words were spoken casually, but he looked hurt.

'I – I'm sorry, I didn't mean to upset you. It just seems so unlikely, even if Old Etonians do have a reputation for being a peculiar bunch.'

'I'm sorry too, I shouldn't be so touchy, it's just that . . .'

'Tell me what sort of boats,' Laura interrupted.

'Nothing dramatic,' said David. 'You must have noticed that more and more of the boats on the river are being built of fibreglass, rather than wood.'

'Yes and ghastly they look, too,' said Laura.

'I agree, but that's because they are badly designed. Most of them look more like floating caravans than boats. I've been tinkering around with designs for ages. My idea of bliss would be to have a boatyard on the Thames. With a few lessons in engineering, I think I could build a fibreglass boat of which even you would approve.'

'Then do it,' said Laura, recklessly.

'No money, no energy to fight my father – I'm hardly the ideal candidate for private enterprise.'

'If you can summon up the courage to be a boat-builder, I'll be a journalist. Do we have a deal?'

David held out his hand. 'Alright, a deal.' They shook hands solemnly and then David stood up, stiffly. 'Come on, we'd better be going back, or we'll get rheumatism in some embarrassing places.'

The pact between them did not take on any tangible form

in the remaining days of their holiday in Scotland, in that they made no firm plans about their future. However, the fact that they were linked by a common desire to do something other than that which had been planned for them, lent a greater depth to an already strong and developing friendship. The Chattaway family were very fond of them both and left them largely alone. Nobody teased them about their growing bond and so they were completely unselfconscious about their preoccupation with one another. It was, in fact, this very atmosphere of calm which made them feel there was no need to rush into any deeper intimacy, that they had all the time in the world. It appalled them, therefore, to suddenly find that it was the last day of the holiday.

The Chattaways had arranged a large family party to celebrate their last evening. Discovering this, David suggested to Laura that they should spend their last day together on the Island of Luing, having lunch at a little restaurant they had discovered on a previous visit. They both loved Luing and the journey to get there – first the bridge on to the Island of Seil and then taking the ferry to Luing itself. They arrived on the island in high spirits and went straight to the restaurant. They ordered a sumptuous meal and David chose a bottle of white wine to accompany it. The atmosphere was festive. There were no clouds on their horizon and after lunch, a little drunk, but pleasantly so, they wandered along the beach. It was Laura who changed the mood in a single sentence. 'I just can't imagine getting up each morning and your not being there.' The words were spoken spontaneously, lightly, without a great deal of thought, but the moment she had spoken, they both realized how true they were.

David stopped and turned to face Laura, the easy pleasure of a moment ago, quite gone. He did not stop to consider what he was doing, he simply placed his hands on her shoulders, his lips on her lips and drew her to him. It was a gesture that was to change their lives.

CHAPTER FIVE

On returning from Scotland, David went straight to his godfather's flat in London. Justin Goodfellow kept open house for his godson, in as much that he never raised any objection to David's sudden arrivals and departures. Justin was a delightful character. Small, round and terribly myopic, his entire life was devoted to the British Museum, for whom he worked long hours for a pittance. This did not matter, since Justin's enlightened father had recognized very early on in the child's life that his boy would always have difficulty fending for himself. He had therefore left Justin adequate capital and an endowment upon which he could live for the rest of his days. Justin had been a contemporary at Eton of Timothy Lawson. Theirs had not so much been a friendship – it was more a question of mutual need. Justin was a natural victim, subject to endless bullying and practical jokes. By contrast, Timothy Lawson was tough – six foot and a demon rugger player by fifteen, he was not often crossed. However, whilst his physical prowess stood him in good stead, he basically was not very bright. Just as Timothy stood between Justin and his persecutors, so Timothy benefited by having Justin supervise and correct his work, and, on occasions when the call of the rugger field was too strong, Justin would complete two sets of work. The friendship, such as it was, had never matured but they had stayed in touch and Justin had seemed a natural choice as godparent to Timothy's first and only son. It was a far more intelligent decision than Timothy could ever have known, for whilst Justin was certainly not worldly, he understood, only too well, what it was like to be different. Not to be able to readily hunt with the pack presents a very special set of difficulties of which he had personal experience, and it gave him a unique understanding of David's particular problems during his childhood and adolescence.

On his first night in London, Justin had insisted on taking

David out to dinner, and over dinner David poured out his feelings of frustration regarding his career up at Oxford. He imagined his godfather's reaction would be utterly predictable. Justin Goodfellow was an academic, through and through. To suggest throwing up a career at Oxford, for Justin, would be worse sacrilege than selling one's soul to the Devil.

David could not have been more wrong. Happily into his second bottle of claret, Justin's advice was terrifyingly simple. 'Follow your heart, boy, follow your heart.'

'You can't mean it,' David said, aghast. 'In any event, you know father – if he's dead against something, there's no way one can change his mind. He won't back me, and I've no money of my own.'

'He may not,' said Justin, 'but I will.'

David stared at him. 'Justin, it's very kind of you, but you can't get involved in something like this.'

Justin's pale blue eyes twinkled behind his pebble glasses. 'Why ever not? I have no children, no wife. My friends are all richer than me and don't need my help. You're the nearest thing I have to a family, boy, so why don't we form a partnership? I'll put up the money. I can run to, what . . . £5000, that should be a start, and you can do all the work. We'll split the proceeds, fifty–fifty, until you've paid me back. There'll be no interest charge, of course. What d'you say . . . eh, eh?'

Later, in Justin's little bachelor flat in Harrington Gardens, David was still stunned by the offer. 'But think of the risk – what if I lose it? I might make a complete nonsense, Justin. I've no experience, either of the boat-building trade or of any sort of commerce at all.'

'If you lose it, I'll only have myself to blame. Besides, it won't make any difference to me. I've enough income to live on and there's no mortgage on this flat. All the money does is sit in the bank.' By this time they were drinking vintage port and smoking two enormous Cuban cigars. They were also both extremely drunk. 'It is really as simple as this, boy,' said Justin, 'take it, or leave it.'

'I'll take it,' said David, and when in the morning he woke to a crucifying hangover, he did not, for a moment, regret the decision.

Justin's unexpected backing filled David with a restless kind of energy he had never experienced before. By lunchtime the following day, he had written a letter to his father, to his tutor and to his landlady, explaining his decision to leave Oxford. With these letters in the post, he was on the M4 in under an hour, heading for Henley. His choice of location was quite deliberate. Henley was a tourist centre. The annual Royal Regatta brought thousands of people to the town, and a boatyard in the area was bound to benefit from this. In addition, the all-year-round traffic on that part of the Thames was increasing. He had also identified a very strong urge to live in the country, which he could not have achieved on the Thames anywhere nearer London. Above all, though, he was only too aware that Meadows Reach, the home of Sir Bernard Beecham, was only seven miles from Henley.

It took David two days to find the right property and a further day to coax Justin down to inspect it. Justin did not approve of the country. A trip down the M4 seemed to him like a journey into the wilderness but he bore up bravely for David's sake. A week later, the lease was signed and David moved in. It was spartan to say the least – an old boathouse just downstream from Fawley, above which was what the estate agents had laughingly described as a flat. It was in reality one vast room, with no running water and one power point. From a secondhand-furniture dealer in Henley, David bought a table, a chair and a double bed. A plumber fixed the barest essentials for a bathroom, which he boxed in at the far end of the room. Rush mats provided the floor covering and an old pot-bellied stove provided heating and cooking facilities. He also acquired an electric kettle, half a dozen mugs, a few glasses, a tin opener, a bottle opener, and, somewhat out of context, a splendid solid silver dinner service, which Justin insisted on giving him as a house warming present. Only when all this was achieved, did he telephone Laura.

David sat on the edge of a little chintzy chair, which was pretty but uncomfortable, sipping a pink gin, which he loathed. The bay window in front of him afforded a glorious view across a sweep of lawn to the Thames. One one side of the lawn ran an exquisite herbaceous border, and willows framed the view of the river. It was a beautiful golden evening and David had rarely felt more nervous in his life. It seemed to him that Sir Bernard Beecham was actually reading his mind, and he understood with perfect clarity, why this man had made a fortune and built an empire in his own lifetime, where others had tried and failed. To say that he was formidable was a gross understatement.

'So, where did you say you were taking Laura this evening?' David hadn't said, as Bernard well knew.

'I thought we'd just go and have some supper somewhere, sir. I haven't quite thought where yet.' He could not meet Bernard's eye because he knew exactly where he was taking Laura – to his boathouse. A bottle of wine, French bread, cheese, paté and fruit were already laid out on the table. Candles had been dotted around the room. In his mind's eye, David pictured the scene and could swear that Bernard was plucking the thoughts right out of his head.

'Not very efficient, not to know where you're taking a girl on your first date.'

David was about to protest that it was not his first date with Laura. Then he wondered, suddenly, whether she had mentioned that he, too, had been in Scotland on holiday with the Chattaways. 'I expect we'll probably go to the Catherine Wheel in Henley, sir.'

'Adequate, but hardly exciting.'

Bernard's aggression was very close to the surface and it was an enormous relief to David to hear the sound of voices coming into the drawing room behind them. He stood up and stooped to fasten his caliper. When he straightened up he saw Bernard was watching him, an expression of distaste on his face.

Laura almost ran to greet him. Her dark, curly hair fell loose around her shoulders. She wore a simple, pale blue cotton dress, nipped in at the waist, with a wide skirt. Her eyes shone brilliantly, picking up the colour of the dress, and spots of colour highlighted her cheekbones. David was stunned. It seemed for a moment that she would run straight into his arms, but something of the strained atmosphere must have got through to her for she slowed her pace and simply pecked him on the cheek. 'Hello, David. How nice to see you. I see you've met Pop.'

David smiled, wanly. 'Yes.'

'And this is my mother.' Katrine Beecham was a most extraordinary contrast to her husband. A small, vivid, vivacious woman, she burst into a long stream of chat, so much at odds with the dourness of her husband. Bernard stood silently by while his wife talked, but David noticed a change in his attitude – he smiled indulgently at his wife. He clearly adored her.

It took David and Laura another ten minutes to extract themselves from the house and into David's rather battered, but newly acquired Mini Pickup. 'Did Pop give you a hard time?' Laura asked.

'A bit,' David admitted, 'but never mind, we've escaped. It's lovely to see you, Laura, I've missed you dreadfully.'

'Same here,' she said, 'And I began to think I'd done something wrong. I was sure I would hear from you much sooner than this.'

'Ah, there's been a reason for my silence. You just wait and see.'

'Tell me, tell me. What's happened?'

'Just be patient,' said David, laughing.

'No, I want to know now.'

'Well, you can't. Ten minutes and all will be revealed.'

Laura wandered round the boathouse in silence, while David explained about Justin. 'I had another bit of luck today,' David said. 'I was in Hobbs, buying some chandlery stuff, when I bumped into this guy, who was trying to buy a fibreglass boat with a small cabin. I told him what I was planning to do, and he said if I draw up some plans, he might commission me to do a one-off prototype. It would be wonderful – that way I would get paid for my research and development. I was absolutely straight with him and explained I'd never done anything like it before, but he seemed really keen to back me.' Laura looked surprisingly solemn and said nothing. Deflated, he hurriedly opened the wine and gave her a glass, feeling increasingly disappointed. 'You don't approve, do you? You think this is just some mad-cap scheme.' He gestured around the room. 'Look, I know it's not much, but it's a beginning.'

Laura set down her wine untouched. 'Oh, David, it's not what I think at all. I think it's wonderful. I think you're so brave, I admire you enormously and I know you'll make a success of it, I just know it.' Her eyes were full of tears. 'I just wish I had your courage.'

David, too, set down his glass and slipped his arms around her. 'You can do it, you can be anything you want. You're clever, bright, funny, beautiful. The world's at your feet, Laura, it's yours for the choosing.'

She drew away from him a little and looked deep into his eyes. 'I'm supposed to be going up to Manchester next week for three months. Can you believe it? Pop says I have to start at the bottom and learn how the garments are made. That's fine, it's all very worthy, but it's not starting at the bottom that worries me – it's starting at all.'

'What does your mother think about it all?' David asked, curiously.

'She just doesn't look on it as a big problem. No woman of my mother's class in Greece ever works. She feels that since Beecham Stores is entirely responsible for the very comfortable standard of living we enjoy, the least I can do is to pander to my father's whim for a few months, until, as she sees it, inevitably I marry some highly eligible man.'

'Perhaps she's right,' David said, dully.

'I hope you don't mean that.' A tear escaped from the corner of Laura's eye and rolled down her cheek.

David bent and kissed it away, then taking her hand, he led her to the bed.

He was determined not to make love to her – it was too soon for both of them. None the less as they lay together in each other's arms, David could not control his violent trembling. He gently kissed away the tears, murmuring to her softly. He had imagined this scene so often lying alone, it was almost familiar. He kissed her lips – they were warm, soft, yielding to his. He felt that if he were to die at that moment, he would have no quarrel with his maker – there could be nothing on earth better than this. Their kissing intensified, their breathing became increasingly uneven. Laura's cotton dress was sufficiently flimsy that David could feel her breasts in every detail beneath the stretched and straining fabric. He was on fire, he wanted her so badly, the pain seemed to permeate throughout his whole body. It was almost too late and yet not quite. With a sudden desperate effort, he drew away, swung his feet on to the floor and stood up shakily.

Laura lay where he had left her – with eyes questioning, full of hurt. 'Why did you stop, David?'

He shrugged his shoulders helplessly, backing away from the bed. If he touched her again at this moment, he knew he would be lost. 'It's not right, too soon, we must wait.'

'For what?' Her eyes were full of tears. 'Don't you want me?'

'Of course I want you.' He felt a little calmer but dare not take her in his arms yet. He sat down cautiously on the edge of the bed. 'Darling, I've dreamt of this, of us being together, so often it feels more like reality than most of the things that happen to me in an average day. The fact is, though, at present we have no future. I am committed now to staying here – at least until I can repay Justin. You are about to go to Manchester for several months. To embark on, well – an affair – only to part in a few days – it would be intolerable for us both.'

'You're so jolly logical.' Laura rolled over in the bed, turning her back towards him.

'I love you, I respect you and you are my best friend. I also happen to think you are the most beautiful girl I've ever met. But it's because of how I feel, Laura, I don't want to mess things up.' Explaining his reticence was proving difficult – he did not truly understand it himself, yet the instinct to control the development of their relationship was very strong. 'Please don't be angry, it is right, honestly.'

She turned to him suddenly – her face tear-stained. 'Hold me, please.'

He joined her on the bed again, this time prepared to keep himself in check. Lying in one another's arms calmed them both. 'I love you, too,' Laura whispered after a while, 'more than anyone, ever.' Her childish words thrilled him.

'I know,' he whispered, and somehow their words made everything alright again.

It was after eleven by the time they finally left the bed. They sat around the table in the candlelight and attempted to eat the bread and cheese. The evening had grown chilly. David stoked the stove until the coals glowed brightly. They became acutely aware of the silence outside the boathouse – broken only by the occasional splash of water as moorhen, water rat, duck and their like played nocturnal games. The isolation suited them.

'It is lovely,' said Laura. 'I feel more at peace here with you than I have ever felt anywhere in my life.'

'So . . . what *are* you going to do?' David persisted, picking up on their earlier conversation.

'If I refuse to be involved with any aspect of Beecham Stores and insist on journalism, I think living at home is going to prove intolerable. Once or twice, when I've tried to go against my father's wishes, I've retired defeated in the end because he just keeps on and on until he gets his own way.' Laura hesitated. 'None of the things we have argued about before have ever been as big an issue as this. Beecham Stores has been Pop's life and I know it's true to say he built it to pass on to his children and grandchildren. I know I'm selfish, I know it's my duty, in some respects, to realize his dream, but I just know I'll never be any good at anything which doesn't interest me.'

'So, if you take this job with the *Maidenhead Advertiser*, you're saying you'll have to leave home.' Laura nodded. David hesitated. 'I don't want to put any additional pressure on you at this moment, Laura, but you can always stay here.' Laura started to protest. 'No, wait a moment, hear me out. I mean, come and live here without any strings. I'm not suggesting that we should . . . well, sleep together, make love, live as a couple in the fullest sense . . . however you want to put it, unless, or until, you're ready for it.'

Laura smiled, a wicked smile that cut through the seriousness of the moment. 'After the last hour, David, I'm not at all sure that would work.'

He grinned back. 'Maybe, but I promise I'd try.'

'I think you'd better take me home now.' Laura glanced at her watch. 'It's going to be after midnight by the time I'm back and I have enough arguments going with my father at the moment without adding to them.'

At Laura's request, David dropped her by the front door of Meadows Reach. It was a dark, velvety night and he was very far from sleep. Back inside the boathouse, instead of revelling in his solitude, for the first time, he felt lonely. Laura's perfume lingered on the air. He touched the indentation their bodies had made on the bed. He poured the last of the wine, not into his glass but into hers, and sat back in a chair gazing up into the night sky through the big picture window, his thoughts whirling. Tomorrow was the first day of his new life, a life he had chosen for himself, free from the constraints of his family, his education and background. Before seeing Laura again, he had been full of energy and excitement. Now he felt oddly listless. How could he be happy and fulfilled in his life, without Laura beside him. Deprived of her presence now, he considered why he had not made love to her – deep down he knew the answer and it frightened him. If they were lovers, it would strengthen their relationship, bind them together – yet he still held back.

It was nearly three by the time he went to bed, but sleep still did not come easily and he could already see the grey streaks of dawn through the window before finally he fell into unconsciousness. A sound woke him. He squinted at the clock by his bed. It was five and almost light. At first, he was not sure what he had heard until the knocking came again – someone in trouble on the river, he assumed. He staggered out of bed, pulled on pyjamas and hopped down the ladder to the side door.

She looked absolutely exhausted. Her hair was rumpled and her face tear-stained. In one hand she carried a small suitcase which she looked about ready to drop. 'Laura, my darling, what on earth's happened?'

'I've taken you up on your offer, if that's alright,' she said, her chin held high, her eyes meeting his. 'Can I come and stay?'

'Of course you can. Come in, here let me take your bag.'

At his words, her resolve crumbled and she burst into tears. In between sobs, David discovered that Bernard had been waiting up for Laura. Powered by David's own bid for independence, she had tackled Bernard about her ambitions and a terrible row had ensued. Bernard had said if that was what she wanted, he would have nothing more to do with her. 'So I went upstairs and packed my case,' said Laura.

'What about your mother, did she try and stop you?'

Laura nodded. A fresh bout of tears poured down her face. 'Yes, she cried and cried and pleaded with my father, but I'd reached a stage when I wouldn't listen to either of them so I just ran out of the house.'

'And you *walked* here?'

Laura shook her head. 'No, I thumbed a lift, from a lorry driver.'

'You shouldn't have done that,' said David, reprovingly.

'He was terribly kind. I explained I was running away from home and he was very sympathetic.' Her voice faltered.

It was no time to think out the implications of what had happened. David took charge. 'You look exhausted. We're not going to talk any more now. I'm going to organize you – alright?'

Laura smiled through her tears. 'Yes, please.'

David gave Laura one of his clean shirts and told her to put it on. She undressed in the bathroom, washed the tears from her face and slipped into David's shirt. Tenderly he tucked her up in his bed and handed her a steaming mug of hot chocolate. 'It has a tot of brandy in it,' he said. 'Drink it all, that's an order.' When she had done as she was told, he took the mug from her and then climbed in bed beside her. They lay very close together, in one another's arms – Laura's head on David's shoulder – and in seconds they were both asleep.

The telephone forced its way through David's consciousness. Gently slipping from Laura's embrace, he staggered out of bed and hopped to his desk. 'Hello,' he said, his voice thick with sleep.

'Is that David Lawson?' He knew the voice instantly, and it snapped him awake.

'Yes, it is,' he said, cautiously.

'This is Bernard Beecham. Have you got my daughter there?'

There seemed little point in lying. 'Yes, sir, Laura is here. She's quite safe. She arrived about five o'clock this morning. Actually, she's still asleep at the moment.' He glanced at the bed. The hump in the bed that was Laura did not stir.

'It's you I want to speak to, Lawson. I hold you entirely responsible for what's happened. It's you who put Laura up to this, don't think I don't know it. I gather you have some scheme to start a boat-building business. If you imagine for one moment that becoming involved with my daughter will mean I'll help you in any way, you couldn't be more wrong. Taking a girl, at only seventeen, away from her home, her parents and the career that's mapped out for her, is quite bad enough, but bearing in mind who and what you are, I can think of few more dreadful things to do to a beautiful young girl's life.'

David was bewildered. 'I – I don't know what you mean, sir.'

'You're a cripple,' said Bernard. 'Crippled in body and obviously crippled in mind, too. I don't know how you dare associate with my daughter. Don't delude yourself that she loves you. If she feels anything for you at all, it's pity. She always was a kind-hearted child – you fit into the same pattern as the bird with a broken wing, the stray cat and all the other nonsense we had to put up with from her over the years. However, unlike them, you have a mind. You've had a decent education, you come from a decent family and you should know better. I don't know what your aim is, but in your condition you can't seriously expect to have a full adult relationship with Laura. It's repulsive, repugnant, utterly unacceptable – a criminal thing to do.' There was silence – Bernard was overcome by emotion and David was too shocked to speak. After a moment, Bernard seemed to gain control of himself, for his voice sounded icily calm, when he spoke again. 'You can tell Laura that whilst she remains with you, I never want to see her again. As for you, if I ever catch sight of you, I swear to God I'll kill you.' For a long time, David stood staring down at his hand, which still held the receiver. 'That was Pop?' Laura asked, in a small voice, from the bed.

David found he could not reply. In what had been no more than a two- or three-minute telephone call, Bernard had put into words all the fears that David had ever harboured about what people truly thought of him. He had never made love to a woman because he was afraid to reveal himself naked, to show his thin, withered leg. He knew women were attracted to him, he knew he had charm and he also knew how to use it, but Bernard's words had struck at the very core of his insecurity, and confirmed his worse nightmares.

Laura, sensing something was terribly wrong, jumped from the bed and came to him. Standing behind him she slipped her arms round his waist, but he stood rigid, resisting her. 'David, David, what is it?'

'It's nothing, it's alright.' He pulled himself away. 'Come on, you'd better get dressed, we have a lot to do today. To start with, we must find somewhere for you to stay permanently – somewhere in Maidenhead would be sensible, unless that is you've changed your mind about the job. To be honest, it doesn't sound up to much, and you're still very young to leave home . . .'

Laura stood very still. 'David, I don't know what he said to you, but judging by the way he was talking last night, I can guess. Look, I love you with all my heart and soul, I love you as you are, I don't want you any different. You're my friend – I can say anything in the world to you. You make me laugh and when you kiss me, I never want you to stop. I can't put it any plainer – I want you David, I want to make love to you. I want to wake up every morning to find your head on the pillow beside me. Is it – is it possible that you might want that too?'

David turned slowly to face her, and to his horror he began to sob.

It was Laura who led David to the bed this time. 'No, it's not right.' He tried to pull away.

'It is right.' In one swift movement, Laura pulled the shirt she was wearing over her head, so that she stood before him completely naked.

He gasped at the sight of her, and before he could stop her, she slipped her arms round his neck, pressing her body to his, and began kissing away the tears which still ran down his face.

'Laura, *Laura*!' He pushed her away, roughly, his hands bruising her arms. 'Listen to me a moment, dammit, will you stop this.' She stood before him. He tried not to look at her beautiful young body. 'Laura, I've never made love to anyone before, I . . .'

Laura smiled, a woman's smile of warmth and understanding that was as old as time. 'Neither have I, David, so we're just going to have to work it out together.'

Lying beside one another on the bed, Laura slowly unbuttoned David's pyjamas, kissing him and telling him how much she loved him as she did so. He did not fight her, he just lay impassively as she stripped off the pyjamas. When he, too, was naked, she stopped kissing him and looked at him in silence for several moments. 'You're beautiful,' she whispered. 'I've never seen a man naked before – I'd no idea, I . . .'

'Don't humiliate me, Laura.' David's voice was rough with anguish. 'We've always been honest with each other, you and I, don't spoil everything.'

At seventeen, Laura had no experience to draw on. She had offered herself to him, told him how much she loved him, and yet it was still not enough to break through the protective shield he had built around himself. She was desperate not to let him down at this moment, knowing instinctively that failure now would influence his life for years to come . . . if not for ever. She was in a foreign country, trying to play a game without knowing the rules. She felt hurt, vulnerable and terribly naive, and there was no time to think things through. So, she reacted from the gut, and in doing so, took the most terrifying gamble. 'It's not me who's spoiling everything, it's you, David. It's not fair to be angry with me. If you're not capable of going ahead with this, why don't you just admit it? I'd understand.'

He raised himself on one elbow and stared down at her. 'Not capable?'

Her heart was beating wildly. 'I'm sorry, I don't know much about this sort of thing, but presumably that's the problem?'

'How dare you!' David shouted before his lips crushed on to hers.

They had eight glorious, unclouded months together. They invented love – they were Romeo and Juliet, Anthony and Cleopatra. Love forbidden and therefore heightened in intensity by the knowledge that they were breaking all the rules and flying in the teeth of opposition. Laura kept in touch with her mother. They met occasionally in Maidenhead or Henley for lunch, when Katrine cried a great deal and they both drank too much wine. Other than these excursions into the less palatable aspects of reality, they seemed to lead a charmed life. David's prototype boat was an instant success and orders followed for more. Laura loved her job on the *Maidenhead Advertiser* and progressed from making coffee to writing small articles. Bernard Beecham had always enjoyed the fruits of his labours, and at the tender age of seventeen, Laura had already experienced eating in most of the world's top restaurants. A review of a new restaurant opening in Windsor so impressed the editor, he allowed her to specialize on articles about places to eat. This quite often involved she and David having a night out on expenses, which they much needed as money was very tight.

Autumn passed into winter. The cold never worried them, nor the poverty, nor the discomfort – they had each other and it was enough. When spring came, they were still riding the crest of a wave until one morning, a letter arrived for Laura. It was a letter from the editor of *Opinions Magazine*, a new upmarket magazine for young women. The editor had read one of Laura's articles. She was recruiting new, young journalists and she had a slot for a food and drink editor – would Laura care to attend an interview in London, she wondered.

'Well done, Darling,' said David, cheerfully. 'Still, there's no point in going, is there?'

'But David I have to, it's a wonderful opportunity.'

He stared at her. 'But you wouldn't take a job in London, would you?'

She by-passed the question. 'Well, I'm hardly likely to get it. Heavens, I'm only just eighteen and there must be far more experienced people than me after it. *Opinions* is getting an awful lot of publicity, David, it's going to be quite a prestige magazine.'

'Well, go if you want to,' said David, dismissively. 'It has to be good experience in any event.'

Despite his apparently casual attitude to the interview, David was nervous all day Laura was in London. When she came home, bubbling with excitement to say the interview had gone well and she had almost certainly been promised the job, he was frankly terrified. Two days later, the appointment was confirmed.

'I have to do it, David, you must see that – it's a wonderful opportunity.'

'But what about us?'

'Why not move to London? I'm sure you could find somewhere on the Thames to build your boats. We can live in a barge, it would be great fun. Oh come on, David, don't be an old misery.'

'I don't want to live in London. My life, my business is here – this is where I have the contacts – both customers and suppliers. I can't start again so soon in the business's life. You must see that, Laura.'

'You could, if you loved me enough.'

'If you cared about me enough you wouldn't even contemplate taking this job. No, no – that's the wrong thing to say, I'm sorry, you goaded me into it.' He sighed. 'You give the job a try. Find some digs during the week and come home to me at weekends. Let's see how that works out.'

The arrangement was doomed from the start. *Opinions* worked Laura hard and she often had to cover stories at weekends. She slept on the floor of a flat rented by some old Wycombe Abbey girls and when one of them left, she moved into the flat permanently. She began coming home for the weekend less and less and when she did, she seemed preoccupied and restless. David tried weekends in London, but he hated the constant stream of people through the flat which meant he and Laura were never alone. Worse still, these Hooray Henry's – the fledgling bankers, accountants and solicitors – who trooped relentlessly to the girls' door, Laura seemed to find highly amusing.

In the circumstances, inevitably, it was only a matter of time before he lost her. He had known that from the beginning. When, during a particularly fraught telephone conversation one evening, Laura mentioned casually that she had been out to dinner with an old school-friend of his – Francis Melhuish – it was the final twist of the knife. He packed the few belongings she had left in the boathouse into a small cardboard box, exorcizing every last reminder of her, and sent it to her flat without a note. She did not even acknowledge the parcel.

'David, David. Are you deaf or something? There's a phone call for you.' Eric Anderson, David's chief designer, shouted at him from the top of the loft steps. Long ago, the loft had been converted into the general office of Lawson Boat-Builders. David now lived in a cottage a few miles away.

'Who is it?' David asked.

'Turners. They've got a query on that order for davits you put in.'

'Tell them I'll ring them back,' David said, 'I'm going home for a while – I'll be back after lunch.'

'Are you alright?' said Eric, his face creased with concern. He was very fond of David, as an employer and as a friend.

'Yes, I'm fine. Don't worry, I'll pull my weight this afternoon, I promise.'

'You always do that, boss. See you later then.'

David bent the Jaguar far too fast around the narrow lanes, on his way up to Turville Heath. The car was an extravagance, but hell why not, he had nothing else to spend the money on. He turned down the lane that led to his cottage and pulled up sharply in the drive, sending gravel in all directions. He jumped out of the car, unlocked the front door, slammed it behind him and walked straight to the telephone. If he hesitated, he knew he would funk it.

He recognized Katrine's voice immediately, even after so many years. He was surprised – the newspapers had said she was staying in Greece while the search for her son-in-law continued. 'Good morning,' he said. 'Could I possibly speak to Laura Beech . . . Laura Melhuish?'

'I'm afraid she's not here.' Katrine's voice was far from friendly.

'Oh. When are you expecting her back?'

'I am not, she is gone.'

'Gone!' There was a silence, and suddenly David realized Katrine must think he was press. 'I'm not a reporter – I'm an, an old friend.'

'Ah, I see. Laura's still not here . . . she's in London.'

'Then I wonder if you could possibly give me her address.'

'I suppose so.' Katrine gave him the address. Her voice sounded choked, as if she had been crying.

'Thank you very much,' said David, preparing to put down the telephone.

'It's – it's David, isn't it – David Lawson?'

He was astounded. 'Yes, it is, Lady Beecham. How on earth did you know?'

'I remember your voice. I know we only met that once but we spoke on the telephone often enough. It should have been you who married her, David – not Francis Melhuish.'

Her words made his stomach churn, but he forced himself to speak in a light tone. 'I thought so, too, at the time. H-how is she? Is there any news of Francis?'

'No, none, it's why I've come back, I'm afraid Laura isn't taking things very well, David. She's in a dreadful state, and to make matters worse, she and her father have had a terrible row. Oh, my poor Laura, I don't know what to do. It seems she always swims against the stream of life.'

'Is that why she's not with you, because of the row with her father?'

'Yes. Go and see her, David, go and cheer her up, if you can. She needs friends at the moment, particularly a friend like you.'

'I will,' David promised. 'Don't worry, Lady Beecham, I will.'

CHAPTER SIX

In an increasingly unfamiliar world, the normally repellent, dismal staircase, leading to the first floor of Oakwood House, Gray's Inn Road, seemed positively attractive to Laura. It was Monday morning. The grimy linoleum underfoot and persistent drizzle outside all smacked of reassuring normality. It was almost possible to believe that nothing had happened.

Laura opened the door into the offices of *Opinions Magazine*. Mandy, the receptionist, was already at her desk. Looking up, she let out a cry and jumped to her feet. 'Laura!' Her surprise was evident.

Laura smiled, thinly. 'Why look so surprised, Mandy. I had to come back sometime.'

'Yes, but I thought . . .'

'How are things, is everyone alright?'

'Well, yes but . . .'

'I expect I've a mound of stuff on my desk,' Laura said. 'Tell Geoffrey I'm in, could you?' The first hurdle over, awkward questions avoided as planned, Laura hurried down the corridor and turned into her office. A figure swung round as she entered, a figure sitting at her desk. It was Jill Reynolds from the Features Department. 'Hi Jill. What are you doing in here?'

'Laura! How good to see you. How are you? I'm so sorry about what's happened.'

Again Laura sensed an awkwardness – still, it was not surprising. 'Don't let's talk about it, Jill. Have you been deputizing for me while I've been away?'

'Well, yes, sort of.'

'That was kind,' said Laura. 'Still, I'm back now and what I need most is hard work. Just point me to the piles and I'll start wading my way through them.'

'I – I think you'd better see Geoffrey first,' Jill said, awkwardly.

Laura noticed she was avoiding her eye. 'Is there something wrong Jill?'

'No, no,' said Jill. 'It's just that I'm sure Geoffrey will want to see you before you start. Hang on, I'll tell him you're here.' She was gone before Laura could protest. Moments later she was back. 'Yes, Geoffrey's free. He would like to see you.'

Laura did not like the new editor, Geoffrey Richards. She had greatly admired his predecessor, Audrey James, who had been editor when Laura originally joined *Opinions*. Audrey had founded the magazine and after years of confirmed spinsterhood, had suddenly met and married a fellow journalist, James Goodwood, in the space of three weeks flat. To everybody's amazement this first development was quickly followed by another. At the age of forty-four, Audrey produced a bouncing son and decided her career as a journalist was over, at any rate for the time being. The parent company owning *Opinions* had replaced her, not with an editor as Laura understood the term, but with a businessman whose background was in commerce. Geoffrey knew nothing about running a magazine and his decisions always had a totally commercial bias. All the staff, including Laura, had resented his arrival, and the fact that the magazine had prospered considerably under his editorship was of little consolation to them. In their view, they were producing a vastly inferior product, and whilst they enjoyed the increases in salary and the growing notoriety of *Opinions*, being the breed they were, it did not compensate, in their minds, for the lowering of standards.

Geoffrey – greased-down thinning hair and dark suit cut a little too tight – stood up with an ingratiating smile when Laura entered and held out his hand. 'Welcome back, Laura.'

'Thank you, Geoffrey.' She took his hand and gave him a cool smile. 'How's business?' she asked, sitting down opposite him.

'Mustn't grumble – the circulation was up again last month. More important, though, how are you?' His cool, grey eyes appeared alive with interest, but there was no warmth in his smile.

'As well as can be expected in the circumstances. I'm surviving – just, and what I need now is to get back to work.'

'Well, I think I can safely say we can provide you with plenty of that.'

'Good, I'm glad to hear it,' said Laura. 'Obviously, I have a lot of catching up to do in the next couple of weeks in order to complete October's columns so, if you will excuse me, I'd better get down to work.' The least time spent in the odious man's company, the better – she stood up to leave.

'No, wait a moment, Laura.' Geoffrey flashed another charmless smile. 'We've done a little re-organizing while you've been away. I've put Jill in charge of the food and drink columns, and what I'd like you to do instead is to join Features. We need some new blood there and . . .'

'What!' said Laura. 'What did you say?'

Geoffrey's expression hardened. 'You heard me, Laura.'

'Geoffrey, I built up those columns from scratch. When I joined *Opinions*, there was nothing at all being written about eating out. Now we have an eating-out guide, a wine guide and a home catering guide . . . I have the readers' following, you can't possibly take me off those columns – they are *me*.'

'I'm sorry, Laura, but I don't agree. I think we've all been getting a little stale. I'd like you to start thinking in more general terms. You're a very imaginative journalist and I'm sure you have a great deal to offer the general Features Department.'

'I have nothing to offer the general Features Department,' said Laura. 'I already have a job and I have no intention of giving it up.'

'It's not a question of giving it up,' said Geoffrey. 'When you didn't come back from your holiday, I had to make arrangements to replace you, which I've done. So far as I was concerned, I didn't even know if you were ever coming back.'

'I rang Mandy the moment I arrived back in England and asked her to tell you I'd need an extra week to recuperate. Geoffrey, you've read the papers, you know what I've been through. Any doctor would be prepared to give me a note for last week – I needed that time.'

'I'm afraid I never got the message,' said Geoffrey, blandly.

'As far as I was concerned, you'd experienced this dreadful trauma in your life, and for all I knew, we'd seen the last of you. I have a magazine to run so I had to make alternative arrangements. It was the only thing I could do.'

Laura stood up, her eyes blazing. 'You could have lifted the telephone, Geoffrey, and simply asked me what was going on.'

'I considered it was your place to tell me.' The grey eyes were brittle now.

'I did tell you. I rang your receptionist. I couldn't speak to you in person because it was four o'clock in the afternoon, and surprise, surprise, you hadn't yet returned from lunch.' It was a remark calculated to cause offence, and it did.

'I'm sorry, Laura, I'm afraid my decision is final. There will be no change in salary, of course.'

'Stuff it,' said Laura.

'I beg your pardon?' said Geoffrey.

'You heard. Stuff it, stuff your job. If I can't have my columns back, I don't want any part of this magazine.'

'Laura, I think you're being very hasty – you're grossly over-reacting.'

'I'm doing no such thing,' said Laura. 'I don't know if this is what you wanted me to say, if you hoped you could goad me into resignation. Well, if so, congratulations.' She did not stay long enough to see the expression on his face, to learn whether he was shocked or satisfied with his morning's work. She simply turned on her heel and left his office.

When she reached reception, Mandy was hovering anxiously around her desk. 'You did give him the message last week, didn't you, Mandy?'

'Laura, I . . .'

'It's alright, Mandy,' said Laura, 'I don't want you to lose your job, too, but I have to make sure I'm not going mad. The last two weeks have been somewhat confusing, as I'm sure you can appreciate.'

'Oh Laura, I'm so sorry. Yes, of course, I gave him the message.'

'That's all I wanted to know. See you sometime.'

Laura took a taxi back to her flat and as they turned into

Chelsea Manor Street, she hurriedly asked the taxi driver to stop.

'Number 82, I thought you said, love?'

'Y-Yes I did, but there's what looks like a crowd of press outside the flats.'

'Must be expecting someone famous.'

'No,' said Laura, 'I think they're expecting me.' The driver turned round and stared at her curiously but she was oblivious to his interest. 'I wonder, if I paid you now, would you be kind enough to drive up to the door as fast as you can and then throw me out. I don't want to talk to them, you see.'

'You're the lady whose husband's gone missing, aren't you?' the taxi driver said. Laura nodded. 'Then I'll do better than that, love – I'll see you right into your front door. I hate bloody reporters.'

Gaining the privacy of her flat, Laura wandered from room to room. The previous evening she had arrived late and tired from the row with her father and earlier that morning she had been in too much of a hurry to get to work to really take in her surroundings. Now, for the first time, it slowly dawned on her how the place was going to feel without Francis – it seemed so big, so uncluttered. Because they had been on holiday, the flat was unusually neat. Their daily help had been in while they were away, cleaned throughout and caught up on the washing and ironing. The result made it feel almost a stranger's flat. It smelt of Johnson's Wax Polish, Francis's discarded clothes were not lying in a heap in the bathroom, nor was his towel draped over the chair, nor were his papers strewn all over the dining room table. Everything was ordered . . . and sterile.

The telephone rang, making her jump. She walked into the sitting room and lifted the receiver. It was a reporter requesting an interview. She dismissed his request curtly and then left the telephone off the hook. With the crowd of reporters outside the flats, and now the invasion by telephone as well, she suddenly felt under siege and recognized that here in London, she was far more vulnerable than she had been at Meadow Reach. It made her feel slightly panicky. For something to do, Laura walked into the kitchen and opened the fridge. Mrs Bell, the daily, had left some basic provisions. It was nearly lunchtime, but though she had eaten nothing the night before, she could not face food. Instead, she went to the drinks cupboard and poured herself a whisky. She took a sip – it coursed down her throat, hit the bottom of her stomach and sent out an immediate warmth which eased her jangled nerves. She sat down, realizing as she nursed her whisky, that being alone was a mistake. She regretted walking out of the family home, when her parents had been so supportive in Rhodes, but Bernard had been insufferable ever since they had returned to England. There was a smugness about him and the words 'I told you so' seemed to hover in the air, for he had never approved of her marriage. It was also quite clear to Laura that now Francis had disappeared, Bernard had assumed he was back in charge of her life. He had spoken confidently about her leaving London, coming back to live at home and perhaps taking a little job in Beecham's Stores. It was the same old story, the same basic argument which had driven her away before, only the circumstances were different. Last time she had left, it had been to go to David, to embark on a life of her own. This time it was to meet head on the terrible guilt she felt about Francis's disappearance. She knew it was a burden she was going to have to carry for the rest of her life – whatever had happened to Francis was clearly her fault. There was no point in hiding from that fact. How to live with it was another matter.

The telephone rang again – damn the reporters, would they ever leave her alone? Then she remembered she had taken the phone off the hook, and realized that it was the house telephone ringing. It was Charlie, the concierge. 'There's someone to see you, Mrs Melhuish.'

'Charlie, I don't want to see anyone, anyone at all.'

'I know, Mrs Melhuish, but it's not a reporter and he's being most insistent. He's an old friend, he says.'

'Who is it?' Laura asked, wearily.

'He says his name's David Lawson.'

David! She hesitated for only a second. 'Ask him to come up, would you, Charlie?'

She waited for him in the hall, staring at the front door,

which represented the only obstacle separating them now. Was she wise to remove it, to let David back into her life? It was five years since they had parted. Still, what did it matter, nothing really mattered any more.

He had changed a great deal, she realized immediately. In appearance, he still had the same boyish good-looks but his face had matured and thinned down and even before he spoke, she saw another, greater difference. He had made a success of the intervening years, and it showed. He confidently met her eye, he was in control, almost relaxed, as she ushered him through the door and they exchanged feckless greetings. The change in him immediately intrigued her but she knew she would have to think about it later. Now she was caught up in the social requirements of the moment. She offered him a drink, told him to sit down and asked him how he was.

David watched in silence while Laura poured him a whisky and replenished her own. She was slightly drunk, he could tell immediately and – he searched for the word – somewhat dishevelled, a description never for one moment would he normally have associated with Laura. Her hair had the same rich lustre, her eyes were still that incredible blue, her skin smooth and brown from the recent sun, but she seemed disjointed, unstable and he could feel the tension flow in her as though it was a tangible thing. He accepted the drink and sat down. 'You must think it rather odd of me appearing in your life like this, out of the blue,' he said. She made no comment and so he pressed on. 'I read about . . . about Francis's accident in the papers and so I telephoned Meadows Reach.'

'That was brave of you.' She gave a short, sharp laugh, which unnerved David so much that for a moment he was silent. 'So, what sort of reception did you get?' she asked, impatiently.

'Luckily, it was your mother I spoke to. She told me that you and your father had argued yet again, and that you had gone back to London.'

'Did she realize it was you?' Laura asked.

David nodded. 'She . . . suggested you could use a few old friends at the moment.' He shrugged his shoulders. 'So, here I am.'

'On a mercy mission?' Laura's voice was ugly with contempt.

'No,' said David. The meeting was not going at all how he had planned it, Laura's reactions were so utterly unpredictable. 'I just imagined that what you are going through at the moment must be dreadful and I was hoping there might be something I could do to help.'

'Dreadful for me, is it?' said Laura, slurring her words, slightly. 'And how would you know? How many people disappeared out of your life, David? Francis may be dead, he just possibly may be alive – either way, I'll probably never know.'

Her face, he realized, wore a haunted look. For some reason, she is blaming herself, he thought. He tried to reassure her. 'Laura, Francis has always been an oddball. I've known him since I was seven, remember. Whatever has happened to him, whatever his fate, it is a direct result of the kind of person he is, or was. You can't blame yourself.'

'Oh, can't I?' said Laura. 'What on earth gives you the right to make that judgement? I know there was no love lost between you and Francis, and no doubt, like everyone else, you thought I did the wrong thing marrying him, but that doesn't give you the right to play judge and jury over my feelings towards him.' She stood up abruptly and went over to the drinks cabinet, to refresh her glass. Discreetly, David glanced at his watch. It was still only a quarter past twelve – he wondered how long she had been drinking whisky – perhaps it was just a temporary thing caused by Francis's disappearance. 'Top up?' Laura said, as if reading his mind.

'No, no thanks,' said David, hurriedly.

'I suppose you think that not only did I marry the wrong man but that now I'm turning into an old drunk. I expect you're really here to gloat – is that right, David? What? Aren't you even going to deny it? Shame on you. Well, I tell you this – I don't want your pity or your advice, nor any moralizing lectures or cheering words. What's happening to me right now is frankly none of your damn business.'

David was unspeakably hurt. This Laura, this new Laura, bore no resemblance to the girl he had loved and lost. 'Why are you trying to sour my motives for coming to see you?' he asked quietly. 'Laura, I've known you since you were fourteen years old. Alright, because of the circumstances, we haven't seen much of one another in recent years, but once we were friends, good friends, close friends, and all I'm trying to do now is to extend that hand of friendship, and to offer help if help is needed.'

'I don't need help,' said Laura, 'from you, or anyone.'

David looked at her whisky glass, now nearly empty again, and then into her eyes – too bright, already slightly glazed. Her hands shook and she was looking at him with naked dislike in her eyes. This Laura he did not want to know – she was destroying the image, breaking the dream. The Laura he had loved was perfect – this woman was out of control and did not care a jot for him any more. Instinctively, he knew that if he stayed any longer she would say something that would hurt him so badly he might never recover. He stood up and straightened his caliper. Reaching into his jacket pocket he drew out his wallet and from it extracted a business card. 'I bought a cottage in Turville Heath about eighteen months ago,' he said. 'The business number is the same as it ever was, but my home number is on here too. Ring me if you need me – I mean it, Laura.'

'I won't be needing you,' Laura said. Her voice was thick with aggression and it cut him to the quick. She made no move to take the card so he placed it on the table beside his empty glass.

'As you wish. Well then, there's not much else to say but goodbye, is there?' he said. 'Don't bother to see me out.'

Five minutes later David was in his car, heading for the M4. He drove as fast as the traffic would allow, wanting to put as much distance as he could between himself and Laura. He was profoundly shocked by her reaction to him. He tried to understand by imagining himself in her position. She had married Francis, so presumably she loved him, and he had gone missing in mysterious circumstances, only two weeks before. Was it surprising that she was enormously upset – no, of course not. Yet, it was the vindictiveness with which she had spoken to him that had shaken him. Her callous disregard for any feelings he might have had been clearly evident. She was locked in her own prison . . . of misery? Was it misery?

Certainly there were strong emotions at work, but it was hard to put a name to them.

He swung the Jaguar round the last bend of South Kensington and stopped at the T-junction with the Cromwell Road. Ahead of him was the Natural History Museum. He stared at it, with unseeing eyes, as the most amazing revelation hit him – Laura's reaction to him today had freed him – quite suddenly. Five years of living in limbo, in the shadow of their lost relationship, were over. Deep down he had always believed it would be only a matter of time before the marriage to Francis Melhuish broke up. He knew the man was rotten to the core, for all his apparent charm. Whilst it pained him that Laura must suffer in Francis's hands, he had believed that in the end her poor choice of husband would bring her back to him, that she would return to him for comfort and that their love would blossom again . . . but not any more.

A car hooted behind him making him jump, and he realized he had been stationary at the junction for some time. He waved an apologetic hand and moved off, turning left into the Cromwell Road. 'Free,' he said the word aloud and instantly his mind went to Serena James. Serena was a freelance computer consultant. David had met her at a party a year before and had ended up in bed with her, within hours of their first meeting. At thirty-two she was older than him and had clearly lived a very full life. Judging by the little anecdotes that would come out from time-to-time, her lovers had been both diverse and plentiful. Certainly she was very good in bed, with few inhibitions and an amusing lighthearted approach to sex which he found refreshing. She was excellent company, with a wicked sense of humour, and they shared a mutual love of music, the theatre and long walks in the country. They were both entrepreneurs and understood that work always had to come first. He also knew that in her own way Serena loved him, but he had never thought of taking the relationship further because of his unspoken commitment to Laura. Suddenly, everything seemed very clear. It was obvious, he should have done it months ago. He would ask Serena James to marry him.

*

The following morning, somewhere in the no-man's land between sleep and full wakefulness, Laura formed a single conscious thought – she had to get to the bathroom fast. She was violently sick – it left her trembling and cold and she crawled back to the warm cocoon of her bed again, full of self-disgust. Of the previous day, she could remember little, beyond walking out of her job and the arrival of David on the doorstep. She knew she had behaved badly, very badly, but at the time his visit seemed like that of a social worker. She felt sure he had come out of curiosity and she strongly resented his intruding on her at this moment in her life. She wanted privacy, not the inquisitiveness of so-called friends, even friends who had once meant as much to her as David had done. It was seeing him standing on her doorstep, so evidently confident and successful, and yes, so very attractive, which had incensed her. She was vaguely ashamed of the emotion, but it angered her that having rejected him, he clearly was making more of a success of life than she. There was no point in ignoring the fact that they were strangers now and her words of yesterday could only have served to drive them still further apart. She rolled over in the bed, as if to escape the memory. The movement brought the nausea flooding back and sent her staggering to the bathroom again.

For three consecutive days, Laura woke to sickness and nausea, but it did not occur to her that it was anything other than the side-effects of acute and unaccustomed alcohol poisoning. During the day, she did nothing but wander listlessly around the flat, creeping out only for a newspaper and a little food, when Charlie gave her the all-clear that there were no reporters about. The newspapers continued to feature the Francis Melhuish story, but since neither a body nor the man himself had been found, the story was losing momentum. There were various sightings, of course. He had been seen in London, Sydney, New York, Paris and all stations in between.

It was not until the fourth morning that Laura, having returned to bed after being sick yet again, began to wonder at its cause. She had eaten nothing that could have possibly disagreed with her – in fact, she had hardly eaten at all and she had not touched a drink since the visit from David. During the day, apart from feeling a little tired physically, she was in reasonable shape – it was just the mornings. The word 'pregnant' slipped insidiously into her mind. She tried to ignore it but the more she thought about it, the more of an obsession it became.

On Thursday afternoon, she finally telephoned the doctor and made arrangements to drop a sample into Chelsea Women's Hospital. They agreed to ring her when the results came through, but a long day, followed by an even longer night, had her pacing the flat like some caged animal. Finally, in desperation, she rang her doctor again. Clearly he was a man who did not read the papers, judging by his confident assumption that he was the bearer of good news. For while no one apparently knew whether Francis Melhuish was alive or dead, there was no doubt about the fact that Laura was carrying his child.

THE END OF THE BEGINNING:
Oxford, August 1968

CHAPTER SEVEN

The A40 was crowded with Friday evening traffic and the tail-back from the Oxford Ring Road roundabout was over three miles long. It gave Laura too much time to consider whether she was doing the right thing. On impulse that morning, she had rung the Berrys. While still in Rhodes, both Eleanor and Chris had been adamant that Laura should come and stay with them as soon as she felt able. Although, of course, she had friends of far longer standing, somehow because they had been so involved in the drama of Francis's disappearance, at this particular time, she craved the Berrys' company more than anyone else's. She was also aware that Eleanor was a doctor. While sitting in the queue of traffic, Laura came to a decision. She would ask Eleanor's advice on abortion – it clearly was the best and only answer.

The Berrys' home proved to be a big, Victorian family house in North Oxford, in a quiet, leafy street just off the Banbury Road. Laura parked her car in the road, a few yards beyond the entrance and well out of sight of the house. She fumbled in her bag and began, distractedly, making up her face, knowing she did not need to, knowing she was putting off the moment when she would be absorbed into the Berry household. Eleanor had sounded genuinely enthusiastic when Laura had rung and invited herself for the weekend. Now though, sitting outside their house, she realized that the Berrys were little more than strangers. What was she doing here? The temptation to drive off was enormous but the image of her lonely flat came into her mind – anything had to be better than that. She climbed out of the car.

'Laura!' Eleanor's smile was warm and welcoming. She held out her arms and gave Laura a quick, awkward hug. 'Dump your suitcase and come into the kitchen,' she said.

'What shall we have – a cup of tea, or would a glass of wine be better; after all, it's almost six o'clock.'

Eleanor's kitchen was vast, full of colour and activity. Eddie sat in a highchair, wiping Marmite fingers round his face. His brother Thomas, seemed to be involved in some sort of complicated wrestling match, with a benevolent golden labrador. A large, marmalade cat sat on the window ledge in the evening sunlight, watching proceedings with disdainful detachment. Drying herbs hung from the high ceiling, and the walls were covered with the children's pictures. Laura gazed around her, feeling her tension and loneliness drain away. She instantly felt at home, and after greeting Eddie and a preoccupied Thomas, she sat down in one of the two old tapestry rocking chairs, pulled up in front of the Aga. 'This is lovely . . .' she began.

Eleanor smiled as she handed Laura a glass. 'Yes, I love this room – we all do, which is just as well really, since we literally live in it. With the children the age they are, they're not really ready for civilized living.' She raised her glass. 'Cheers.' There was a moment's silence between the two women, the obvious question hanging in the air. 'No news then?' Eleanor asked, gently.

Laura shook her head. 'Absolutely nothing, it's as though he never existed, Eleanor, and worse still, everyone's losing interest. While the press were still hounding me, horrible though it was, at least I felt . . .,' she broke off. 'In the last few days, the reporters have just drifted away – Francis is yesterday's news, which I suppose is hardly surprising considering all the trouble in Paris with the student riots.'

'Yes, he's certainly not front page any more. Still, perhaps it's as well. At least it takes the pressure off you, and honestly Laura, you're not really looking very well,' Eleanor said. It was clearly a professional appraisal.

Laura shrugged her shoulders. 'I'm alright, I'm not sleeping much and I don't like being on my own . . . it's just that everything seems to have gone wrong at once – I've lost my job and I've fallen out with my parents.'

Eleanor looked shocked. 'Lost your job, why – and why have you fallen out with your parents? I adored your mother, such a character, and your father seemed solid as a rock – the ideal person to lean on in a crisis.'

'Oh he is, he is,' said Laura. There was a despair in her voice which Eleanor did not like.

'You sit here and keep drinking. I'll just throw these two monsters in a bath and then we can have a good chat. Chris won't be home until late tonight.'

Later, while Eleanor cooked supper, Laura told her everything – about her job, about her parents, about David's visit – everything, that is, except the baby. 'I suppose it's me,' she said, at last, 'I'm the one who's causing all these rows. Certainly, I do seem to have the unique ability to upset people at the moment.'

'It's hardly surprising you're tense,' said Eleanor, 'you're in such an impossible situation. You don't know if you're married or not, whether to mourn your husband or not, and, in the long term, you don't know whether you can, or should, start a new life without him. It's an absolute sod, I feel so very, very sorry for you.' She hesitated. 'Have you tried to make any plans?'

Laura shook her head. This was the moment to mention the baby but she knew she was not ready to do so. 'I just can't, not at the moment.' She shrugged her shoulders. 'After all, it's barely been four weeks.'

Eleanor, stirring the sauce, paused for a moment. 'Losing your job doesn't matter a damn, you can easily find another, and as for falling out with an old boyfriend, I'm sure that's no great hardship. It's a pity about your parents, though, Laura. It seems to me that you could do with some sort of major stabilizing influence in your life at the moment.'

'I've managed without their support before and I'll do it again,' said Laura, defiantly. 'I'm not a child, Eleanor. Surely you understand I have to work this out for myself, without Pop hovering over me, playing Mr Fix-It and telling me how to run my life.'

Chris, when he arrived home, was bone weary. He'd been at a representatives' conference in Eastbourne. He greeted Laura warmly and then turned to Eleanor. Their obvious delight at seeing one another both touched and saddened Laura. The warm, caring relationship that existed between the Berrys, Laura knew, had never been a part of her own marriage.

It was not until after breakfast on Sunday morning that Laura had another chance to talk to Eleanor alone. As if sensing that she had something on her mind, Eleanor suggested that they took the dog for a walk in the University Parks, leaving Chris to cope with the boys and mind the joint. The gentle stroll, through quiet streets to the Parks, did nothing to calm Laura. She had built herself into a considerable state of tension, trying to find the right moment to talk to Eleanor, and now that the situation had so obviously presented itself, she was uncertain how to begin. As it happened, Eleanor did the job for her. Once they had entered the park gates, Eleanor slowed her pace. 'Laura, there's something on your mind, isn't there? Something you've been trying to say but haven't been able to.'

Laura kept her eyes firmly on the path ahead of her. 'Y-yes,' she said, 'but it's something I had to talk to you about alone and there hasn't really been an opportunity.'

'Well, we have an opportunity now, don't we?' Eleanor said. 'Come on, spit it out, it's no good letting it fester.'

'I'm pregnant,' said Laura. Saying the words aloud for the first time, gave her predicament an immediate sense of reality. 'I'm pregnant,' she said again. 'I'm expecting Francis's child.'

'I see,' Eleanor said, cautiously. 'How do you feel about it? Are you pleased?'

Laura stopped walking and stared at Eleanor, pushing her hair back from her face with a nervous gesture. 'Pleased. Are you mad? Of course I'm not pleased.'

Eleanor looked and felt confused. 'I'm . . . sorry, I was just trying to put myself in your shoes. Whilst I appreciate bringing up a child alone is no small task, I think, in similar circumstances, if I thought Chris might be dead, I'd . . . well, I suppose I'd welcome the opportunity of having his child. No, more than that, it would be a lifesaver for me.'

'Your marriage to Chris bears very little resemblance to mine with Francis,' Laura said, bitterly. 'I haven't said this to you before, Eleanor, because it wouldn't have been right after he disappeared, but we weren't at all happy. He was such an impossible person to live with. He couldn't tell the difference between truth and lies, he never worked, what little money we had he spent, and of course there's this trouble with the police. I wouldn't have stayed with him as long as I did, but for the fact that I didn't want to admit that all the warnings people had given me about him were right.'

'But you obviously had some kind of feeling for him, for each other,' Eleanor said quietly, 'or you wouldn't be pregnant now, would you?'

'Oh yes,' said Laura, 'but it wasn't very . . . it was lust, not love. We were still attracted to each other, that's true, but without true friendship and caring, it was all fairly meaningless – no better than animals really, I'm ashamed to say.'

'Are you sure you're not saying this to protect your feelings and stop yourself missing him?'

Laura shook her head. 'I didn't love him, Eleanor. I may have done once but by the time he disappeared, I neither loved nor respected him any more.'

'Which brings us back to the baby,' Eleanor said. They had reached the banks of the River Cherwell. The river, with its willows and slow-moving, brown-green water, reminded Laura, suddenly, of the day she had first met David. She closed her eyes for a moment, pushing the memory away. Eleanor saw the expression on her face, misunderstood it, and tentatively touched her arm. 'Let's sit down on the river bank for a moment, Laura.'

Laura did as Eleanor suggested and took a deep breath. 'Eleanor, I don't want this baby, I really don't. I can't cope with it. It's . . . it's one of the reasons I came to see you – I thought you might be able to help me arrange an abortion.'

Eleanor was silent for a long time. When at last she spoke, Laura noticed instantly the change in her voice. She had somehow distanced herself and, quite literally, had turned professional. 'I think it would be very wrong to take such a step,' said Eleanor, 'at any rate, certainly to rush into it. Your life is lacking any kind of direction at the moment, because of the circumstances. I appreciate you've lost your job, I know your future is uncertain, but having to care for and support a child might be the very thing you need to give yourself some sort of purpose in life.' She relented a little and smiled. 'Certainly, with a baby howling for food every three or four hours, you wouldn't have much time to feel sorry for yourself.'

'But it's not just *a* baby is it?' Laura bit back. 'It's *Francis*'s baby.'

Eleanor was clearly exasperated. 'So, it's Francis's baby – is that so terrible? After all, he was – perhaps, still is – your husband. It's not as though you've been raped. You may have fallen out of love with your husband, but is that any reason to kill his child?'

'Stop it, stop it,' said Laura, jumping up.

The dog, sensing trouble, came nosing up to Eleanor, licking her face and prodding at her with one muddy paw. She was forced to stand up, too. 'No, I won't stop it. You think you have problems now, Laura – believe me, they're nothing compared to the ones you're likely to have if you go ahead with this abortion. Very few caring, relatively intelligent women walk away from an abortion unscathed, in any circumstances, let alone yours.'

'I don't want it, Eleanor, I've simply no maternal feelings towards it at all.' Laura was flushed, but she was dry-eyed and clearly determined.

'Let me ask you a question,' said Eleanor. 'What happens if Francis isn't dead? What happens if he turns up like a bad penny, in a few weeks' or months' time? How will you feel then?'

'I don't see that it's relevant,' Laura snapped. 'The decision I am taking is based on the facts as they stand now.'

'You're being very businesslike about it,' said Eleanor, 'and making it sound so simple, but a year from now, I can promise you this, Laura. You'll be walking in a park, this one perhaps, or one very like it, and you'll see a woman pushing a pram. Suddenly you'll realize that small bundle could have been your son or daughter, if you hadn't killed it. I'm talking to you now as a doctor. We, the female of the species, carry hormones in us to ensure that the breeding instinct is strong enough to guarantee the continued survival of mankind.

Exhausted and confused as you are now, understandably you're suppressing your natural instincts. But when the deed is done and you've had time to reflect, I'm certain that you'll regret it. By then, of course, the tragedy is it will be too late.'

'I resent you preaching to me like this. What the hell do you know about it? You're happily married with two much-wanted babies – you've no idea what it's like to have to make this kind of decision.'

'That's where you're wrong,' said Eleanor. She turned abruptly away and whistled to the dog. 'Come on, we had better be heading back now or the joint will be over-cooked.'

Something in Eleanor's face told Laura she should let the remark go, but she was in no mood to tread gently with other people's feelings. 'What makes you say that?' she asked, aggressively.

'I became pregnant when I was in my last year at medical school,' Eleanor said. 'I was in love with a fellow student. He was enormously charming, a little younger than me and light years away from being ready to settle down with a family. I wasn't prepared to waste six years of my life without qualifying and nor was I prepared to force Victor into marrying me. So . . . I didn't tell him or anyone, I simply had an abortion. It was a girl – I asked to be told – she would be seven, nearly eight now and I see her face in every little girl of a similar age, and always will. I even wonder, sometimes, whether it's some sort of divine retribution that I've had two sons. We can't afford any more children, but I'd have loved a daughter.' Surreptitiously, Eleanor wiped away a tear, walking so briskly now, that Laura had to almost run to keep up with her. 'There, I've told you,' said Eleanor, 'and it's something I've never told anybody else, except Chris, of course. However, it does prove I'm in a position to say – *don't do it, Laura.* Please don't do it.'

Eleanor's admission temporarily stunned Laura, but not for long. 'Don't you think your experience may have coloured your attitude to the subject?' she said. 'I'm sorry, Eleanor, I'm really very sorry and thank you for telling me about it, but you can't inflict your own feelings on to me. I'm clearly not a particularly maternal person. It had never entered my head that Francis and I should start a family – it was just a freak accident.'

'Some might say a freak blessing,' Eleanor suggested.

'Oh, come on now, you're being whimsical.'

'Whimsical, am I?' said Eleanor, angrily. 'We're talking about a human life. There's a person growing inside you, Laura.'

'Not yet there isn't,' said Laura, 'it's just a few cells, nothing more. Honestly, Eleanor, you're just not making any attempt to understand. I don't know why I came to you for help.'

'You came to me for help because I'm the only doctor you know well enough. Certainly, I can give you the name of a gynaecologist who will terminate for you, if that's what you want. However, I will not give you his name for another month – you must have more time to think.'

'Do you enjoy playing God?' Laura asked, angrily.

'I'm not playing God. You don't need me. If you are determined upon this abortion, you can go to your GP, who'll soon fix things for you, in the circumstances. I'm simply asking you to wait. The next few weeks aren't vital in a physical sense, but emotionally, they most certainly are. There is another thing, too – from Francis's point of view, you ought to give it more time.'

'What do you mean, *from Francis's point of view*?'

They had reached the Berrys' front gate and Eleanor hesitated. 'As I said just now, he may turn up, Laura. Supposing, for a moment, he had simply funked facing the police, which is why he disappeared. Once he's run out of money and hope, he may give himself up.'

'So what if he does?' said Laura.

'The baby you're carrying is your husband's, too.'

'He gave up all rights to the child the moment he disappeared.'

'I disagree,' said Eleanor.

'Then there's really nothing more to be said,' said Laura. 'I won't stay for lunch, I'll just go upstairs and pack.'

Eleanor put a restraining hand on Laura's arm. 'Laura, don't . . .' she began.

Laura shook off the hand impatiently. 'I came down here

for help, not a moral lecture. I don't want to sit through lunch while you parade your babies in front of me, showing me what I could be missing. You can't stop me going – it's what I want to do.'

The M40 was uncharacteristically deserted – everyone was clearly involved in Sunday family lunches, Laura thought sourly. She drove ferociously, but the nearer to London she came, the more overwhelming was her feeling of isolation and loneliness. Everyone seemed to be turning against her – her father, her boss, David, Eleanor . . . the expression 'kicking someone when they were down' had never seemed more apt.

Laura passed the Marlow/High Wycombe junction and thought briefly of her parents. It was tempting to drop in and see them, but pride would not allow it. She pressed harder on the accelerator, yet the thought of London continued to appal her. Suddenly, the sign to Beaconsfield flashed past and on an impulse, she veered off the motorway. There was no conscious plan in her head. She had never been to Campling Hall, though she knew it was somewhere near a village called Coleshill, which in turn was near Beaconsfield. On the outskirts of Beaconsfield, she took the Amersham road, and when the signpost to Coleshill came up she was not surprised although she had never knowingly been given directions. On the bend of a narrow lane, less than a mile from the main road, the park gates confronted her. There was no sign, but she knew at once it was Campling Hall for the gateposts were unmistakable. In the bedroom at the flat, there was a photograph of Francis and his brother, Anthony, little boys on bicycles, standing by the gates. She slowed the car to a halt and stared up the long driveway. There was a squeal of brakes behind her, followed by violent flashing and hooting. Looking in her mirror, she saw a man gesticulating angrily at her from a Landrover. As she really had no choice in the matter, she indicated right and turned in through the gates.

Francis had spoken fondly of his ancestral home but nothing could have prepared her for the sight she saw. The driveway wound through parkland. To the right there was a large lake, into and out of which flowed a river. To the left, beech trees formed a vast wood which rose steeply from the edge of the park. A herd of deer wandered across the drive in front of the car, sheep grazed nearby. Apart from the tarmac of the drive itself, the scene could have been hundreds of years old, Laura thought. The driveway suddenly turned and opened out and there stood the house – a strange mix of the centuries. It had been built originally in the 1300s, Laura knew. Since then every period had wrought some influence, yet somehow the strange combination of architectural styles suited it, and Laura warmed to it immediately. Several cars were parked in the drive and Laura drew up alongside them, feeling very stupid and confused by what she was doing. She looked at her watch. It was half-past one, a time when most people would be in the middle of lunch. Her arrival was an imposition and ill-timed. What was she doing here, anyway? Logic told her the answer – in her womb she carried a child who belonged to this place. It was somehow intended that she should come – choice seemed to have played very little part, and it was this thought which gave her the courage to finish what she had started. Dressed casually, in jeans and a shirt, she stepped self-consciously out of the car and walked the short distance to the front door. She rang the bell and listened to it echo through the house. There was still time to go, if she ran to the car now . . . but she seemed unable to move.

The man who opened the door was vaguely familiar. He was short and dark with a kindly open face. She had expected a servant, which clearly this man was not, and, momentarily, it threw her, leaving her tongue-tied. The man smiled. 'You probably haven't a clue who I am, but I know who you are.' Laura stared at him, amazed. 'You're Laura. I saw the wedding photographs and of course, recently . . .' he let the sentence tail off. 'I'm Anthony Melhuish, Francis's brother.' Of course, the little boy on the bicycle. Laura took the outstretched hand offered and smiled into his eyes. He was like Francis in some respects – his features were not dissimilar, certainly – but the eyes that met hers were warm, kind and intelligent. There was none of the shiftiness she associated with Francis. Anthony, Laura knew, was only three years older than his brother, but to Laura he appeared much more than that. He seemed quite definitely middle-aged and, because of it, oddly comforting. 'My father will be thrilled that you've come,' he said, as though she was actually expected for lunch. 'We're having drinks in the drawing room, do come in.'

'I'm not really dressed . . .,' Laura began, and then she noticed Anthony's mud-splattered jeans and old sweat shirt, and they both laughed, easing the tension between them.

There were four people in the drawing room as Laura entered. 'Father, I have a lovely surprise for you,' Anthony said.

Lord Campling turned, and for a moment his expression showed surprise. Then he smiled hugely, and coming forward, gripped Laura by the shoulders and kissed her. 'Laura, my dear, this is wonderful. I'm so pleased to see you. I was hoping one day you'd come, but . . .' he shrugged his shoulders. 'Come and meet everybody.'

A tall, fair, rather horsey-looking girl was introduced as Lavinia, Anthony's wife. She pumped Laura's hand enthusiastically and any moment, Laura expected to be slapped on the back as well. She was taller than Anthony and very noisy, but the friendly expression on her face was reassuring. The other couple present were introduced as Colonel and Mrs Featherstone, a faded elderly couple who both seemed very confused by Laura's appearance, clearly not having the least idea who she was. 'You'll stay to lunch, Laura?' said Lord Campling.

'Well I . . .'

'Please, my dear, for me.'

'I'd love to, thank you,' said Laura.

After a couple of sherries and plenty of wine, Laura began to relax. Extraordinarily, she felt entirely at home among these people. It left her wondering how Francis could ever have gone away. After a generous meal of roast pork, followed by chocolate mousse and cheese, they returned to the drawing room for coffee. Brandy was circulated and Lord Campling drew Laura to one side. 'I'd like to show you around, assuming you'd be interested, my dear. If you're agreeable, we'll leave the others to their brandy and Sunday papers.'

He gave her a thorough conducted tour of the house and then they wandered out into the afternoon sunshine. It was a beautiful day with a golden quality to the sun which suggested that autumn was not far away. They ambled across the grass, towards the lake. 'So why did you come, Laura?'

'I – I don't know.' Laura hedged.

He smiled at her, his wise, hooded eyes wrinkling at the corners. 'Don't think you're not always welcome to come here. I hope this is the first of many visits you'll make to Campling Hall, but on this occasion, I know you came for a quite specific reason. Tell me what it is.' His candour was totally disarming.

'I'm pregnant,' Laura blurted out.

'I wondered if you might be.'

'Really?' Laura looked at him in astonishment.

Lord Campling smiled. 'Margaret, my wife, only had two living children – Anthony and Francis – but, poor darling, she had five miscarriages, and so you see, I'm rather good at recognizing the signs of early pregnancy.' Laura, not sure how to react, said nothing. 'And so,' Lord Campling continued, 'you've come here hoping it will help you decide whether to have the baby, or have an abortion.' His ready grasp of the situation shook her so much that she remained tongue-tied, neither agreeing nor disagreeing. 'Come now, my dear, don't look like that – you young things have the choice these days and you'd be foolish not to consider an abortion, given all the circumstances. You have a career, you're young, you'll marry again one day and what you have to decide is whether you want to be saddled with a child from a former marriage. Believe me, I do understand.'

'Of all people,' Laura said at last, 'you are the last person I would have imagined to have reacted as you have just done.'

'Because I'm such an old fuddy-duddy?'

Laura blushed. 'Well . . . yes, I suppose so.' They both laughed.

'Laura,' Lord Campling held out a hand and she took it, 'a number of questions.' She nodded, bracing herself. 'Firstly, will you call me William? We're far more likely to be friends that way than if we continue to struggle with this wretched title,' he smiled, charmingly.

'Of course, William.'

'Good. Now secondly, do you still believe that Francis is alive?'

'I don't know,' Laura said, 'I honestly don't.'

He squeezed her hand. 'No more do I. I think the workings of Francis's mind have been something of a mystery to us both.' Laura nodded. 'As you can imagine, although Francis and I have had our differences, he is my son and I have thought long and hard about him over the last month. I have come to the conclusion that for my own sanity, I must assume he is dead and I rather think you should do the same. Whether in reality Francis is alive or not, so far as we, his family, are concerned, he wishes us to believe that he is dead. It all amounts to the same thing – he does not want us to think of him as a living person, as somebody who will come back to us, so whether he is alive or dead is only relevant because we would like to feel he is alive and unhurt for our own comfort.'

'I hadn't thought of it like that,' said Laura.

'Well, think about it like that now.' He paused a moment. 'I'm saying this for one quite specific reason, Laura. Whatever decision you come to about the child you are carrying, make your decision selfishly. Consider only your own feelings, your own ability to cope, the responsibility of single parenthood and the implications the child will have on your future. Don't let Francis influence you in the slightest, nor me, nor anyone.' Laura stared at him incredulously. She felt a tear slide down her cheek but made no attempt to brush it away – somebody understood her at last. 'Having said all that,' he continued, 'obviously, if you decide to have the child, I will do everything to help, everything you'll let me, that is – financially, emotionally, in any way at all. Just don't panic, my dear, take your time.' He patted the hand he still held and then tucking it through his arm, he turned them round so that they began walking back towards the house.

'We had never talked about a family,' Laura said, almost to herself. 'Francis was so tied up in his own affairs, it was simply a subject that never came up. I don't know how he would have reacted.'

'As I say, I honestly don't think it's relevant. Tell me, have you talked this through with your parents?'

'No,' said Laura, 'no, I haven't. I've confided in a girlfriend who is a doctor, but no one else.'

'Then I feel very flattered that you've come and spoken to me about it, though I don't expect I've been of much help.'

'You've been of more help than you can possibly know,' said Laura.

The flat was not so hostile as Laura had imagined it would be – in fact it was almost a relief to be inside her own four walls again. Wearily, she dumped her case in the hall, went through to the kitchen and plugged in the kettle. It had been a long day, a long, emotional day. She had talked so much she felt drained and the thought of being alone now seemed a blessed relief, rather than the purgatory it had been in previous days. She took her coffee into the bedroom, went through the motions of removing her makeup, brushed her hair and then she slipped between the sheets. She felt them cool and soft against her skin and pulled them up to her chin. Involuntarily she glanced at the pillow beside her as if to check that Francis was not there. Then she turned out the light and lay staring into the darkness. Although her mind was too tired to function properly, certainly to make any major decision, she felt more at peace. She would ring Eleanor tomorrow and apologize, and as for William Campling – his understanding had touched her deeply.

Dawn over Campling Hall the following morning was a laborious affair. The sky was thick with cloud, the atmosphere heavy with the threat of a storm. The light, when at last it came, was thin and insipid. William Campling sat in his study looking out over the park. How he loved it. He knew every inch of it, every blade of grass it seemed, and except for his time at Eton and a period in the army during the war, he had never been away from it and now, certainly, he never would be again. He glanced at his watch – 6.45 – and then found himself glaring at the telephone. It was stupid. Laura had promised him that she would ring as soon as she had made up her mind and it was he who had pressed her not to be hasty and to take as many days or weeks as she felt necessary to make the right decision. Yet, within minutes of her departure, he had begun fretting. He must pull himself together – clearly it was ludicrous to expect to hear from her so soon. He considered the options open to him – a bath and a shave, a walk or a ride, a drive to the village for the newspapers – none of these simple tasks held any of their normal appeal. He sat slumped in his chair, an unusual pose for him, his chin resting on his chest, his eyes sombre and brooding. As a man used to taking decisions and putting plans into action, he found the impotence of the situation quite intolerable.

The shrill sound of the telephone, when it rang, made him jump. No one normally telephoned this early. With a beating heart, he picked up the receiver. 'Hello,' he barked.

'William?'

He recognized her voice instantly. 'Laura, it's you. I knew you'd ring this morning, just knew it.'

'Did I wake you?' she asked.

'No, no. I've been up for hours – didn't sleep well, actually.' There was no harm in hinting at his feelings.

'Oh William, I'm sorry. It wasn't fair of me to burden you as I did yesterday.'

Damn the girl, why couldn't she come to the point? 'It's alright,' he said, with just a hint of impatience, 'it's what father-in-laws are for, I think.'

'William, I thought I'd let you know right away, I've made my decision . . .'

There was a roaring in his ears so loud he could barely hear her voice. 'Yes, yes,' he said faintly.

'. . . and I've decided I'm going to have the child.'

He seemed to have difficulty breathing. 'You are, Laura, truly?'

'Yes. I don't know what changed my mind, exactly. Yesterday morning I was quite sure I couldn't go through with it, but now, somehow, having talked to you . . .'

'You've made the right decision,' he said, hastily, impatient now to tell her everything. 'You see, Laura, I wasn't being quite straight with you yesterday.'

'How do you mean?' She suddenly sounded very young and

vulnerable. It was a brave decision to take alone and it was vital to reassure her.

'Don't misunderstand me. Everything I said to you yesterday was what I truly believe, but I left out just a few pieces in the jigsaw because I didn't want to bring too much pressure to bear on you.'

'What pieces?' Laura's voice was suspicious.

William slumped back into his chair, he was really feeling very strange and light-headed. 'Laura – my son, Anthony, and his wife, Lavinia, are very devoted to one another. I am sure theirs will be a long and happy marriage but the fact is, they can't have any children.'

'*Can't* have?' Laura said. 'Are you sure?'

'Quite sure,' William said. 'It's Anthony who has the problem. He was very ill as a child – some sort of virus – and they think it's that which has left him with a virtually non-existent sperm count. Sorry to be technical, my dear, but that's the fact. So you see, with Francis missing, presumed dead, your baby is the Camplings' last chance.' There was a lengthy silence on the other end of the phone which William felt obligated to fill. 'Whether it's a girl or a boy, I will make your baby my heir – after Anthony, of course – and if it's a boy, he will inherit the title in due course. You see, Laura, without your child, the family was going to die with Anthony, and the title with it. As it is, even if your child is a girl, her son can still inherit.'

'I don't know what to say,' said Laura.

'Don't say anything, my dear. The only words appropriate at the moment are mine – to thank you, to thank you with all my heart. I cannot tell you how much this means to me. It has been dreadful having to face the fact that everything I am doing for Campling Hall might be for the benefit of a stranger. At a stroke, you've given me a future again.'

It was not until William had replaced the receiver that he realized his face was wet with tears. He was not used to crying. The only other time he could remember crying in his adult life was when his wife, Margaret, died. Self-consciously, he mopped himself up. His heart was still beating unnaturally fast. Steady on, old boy, he thought to himself – you'll give yourself a heart attack, which will never do when you've such a lot to teach that child. More composed now, he let his gaze wander towards the park again. He stood up, walked to the window, unlocked it and threw it wide open. The scent of the morning rushed in to greet him – the damp, earthy smell he loved so much. The world was suddenly a very different place, and he smiled with delight as he watched a thin ray of sunshine force its way out from between the clouds, bathing the park in sudden light. Nothing at that moment could have been more appropriate.

CHAPTER EIGHT

Harry Sutherland was nursing what he sincerely believed had to be the worst hangover of his life. The previous evening had begun innocently enough with a publisher's summer party. He had started well by being suitably ingratiating to an appropriate number of editors and seeing to it that his authors had a good time. Indeed, in his own eyes he had behaved like the perfect literary agent. However, by nine o'clock, he felt his duties were over. He drifted from the party to a pub with a couple of designers he had met. After a fairly hefty session, they had gone to a cheap Greek restaurant, where they had unwisely drunk a vast quantity of ouzo. From there, they progressed to a girl's flat, where grass had been substituted for booze. He had woken up in the early hours of the morning, beside a woman who, so far as he knew, he had never set eyes on before. His head felt like it had been beaten in by a sledgehammer and his mouth tasted like the bottom of a parrot's cage. The woman had been most affronted when he had tried to leave, and so he had allowed himself a little dutiful copulation, which had left him prey to both exhaustion and self-disgust. Now, back in the hallows of his office, he was facing a mountain of paperwork, the usual pressure from Judy, his secretary, and the knowledge that he was having lunch with one of the most insatiably alcoholic authors in the business. Judy was speaking and he tried to concentrate his mind on what she was saying.

'She says it really is most urgent, Harry, and you do have time to see her. Come on, you've earned quite a decent screw from her over the years. It won't kill you to do something in return for once – particularly in the circumstances.'

'What are you talking about, Judy?'

'Jesus, you never listen to a bloody word I say. Why I stay in this job I just can't imagine. You're a good-for-nothing, lazy, lecherous old bastard. God knows why your authors put up with you.'

'Because I bloody well keep them in work, that's why. Now, sod off, and leave me in peace.' While to an outsider their exchange might have sounded somewhat extreme, it was standard repartee for Harry and Judy.

'If you don't see her, I'm leaving,' Judy said, firmly.

'Who, for Christ's sake, who? You haven't told me yet.'

'I've told you a million times but you just don't listen – Laura Melhuish.'

'*The* Laura Melhuish?'

Judy looked mildly surprised, 'Well yes, *the* Laura Melhuish, if you mean Laura Melhuish the food writer.'

'I don't mean Laura Melhuish the food writer, I mean Laura Melhuish whose husband did a bunk.'

'One and the same thing,' said Judy, dismissively.

'Well, why the hell didn't you say so before? Of course I'll see her. Is she willing to write about it do you think?'

'I don't know,' said Judy, 'but go easy, she looks pretty shell-shocked.'

'I will, you know me, the soul of tact. Well, why are you standing there, girl, wheel her in? No, on second thoughts, coffee and aspirin first, Laura Melhuish second.'

'Laura!' Harry rose from behind his desk and came forward to greet Laura.

They were both surprised by one another's appearance. Laura had been pre-warned by Judy that Harry had the mother and father of a hangover, yet it was hard to believe. His florid, handsome face was as cheerful and apparently healthy as ever. His dark hair looked carefully groomed, the bow tie and sports jacket – an odd combination which was his hallmark – looked terrific on him as usual. Laura knew Harry to be well into his fifties but he certainly didn't look it.

Harry, by contrast, was disappointed with what he saw. He had not seen Laura in more than a year but he had always thought of her as being a pretty little thing. The wild, black hair was as he remembered, but her face had a thin, pinched look. There were dark circles under her eyes, which seemed bigger than ever and were full of pain. He kissed her on both cheeks and summoned a glass of champagne. This was breaking the rule of a lifetime in the business – he never gave champagne to authors who earned him less than five thousand a year, but this girl looked like she needed it.

'Well, my darling, what can I do for you?', he said, at last, having exhausted the ritual pleasantries. 'I must say, apart from receiving my cut for the odd freelance article you've done in the last year or so, it seems your old literary agent hasn't been pulling his weight. Still, I don't suppose you've had time to do much work, outside the magazine.'

'Well, now is your chance to pull your weight,' said Laura, startling Harry by her directness. 'I need work, Harry, and lots of it, right away.'

'What sort of work?' Harry asked.

'Anything. I'm a journalist, I can write on any subject. OK, so I've specialized in food and wine, but I've had good all-round experience on both newspapers and magazines, and I'm not too proud to do anything that will pay.'

'You're suggesting I try to place your freelance articles?' Laura nodded. Harry lit a cigarette, leaned back in his chair, inhaled deeply and watched the smoke curling up to the ceiling. 'The fact is, Laura, it's simply not worth my while representing your interests, or indeed anyone's, when it comes to selling articles. *Books* are *my* business.'

Laura's anger flared. 'Then why have you been quite prepared to sit back and take 10 per cent from my articles in the past, if, as you say, books are your business?'

'You're a food editor on an increasingly popular magazine,' Harry said, mildly. 'It's only a matter of time before someone will ask you to write a book on the subject – but not yet, your name's still not well known. You need another year or so, a little more exposure and then you'll be ready for that book.'

'I can't wait that long.'

The girl, Harry noticed, was trembling slightly and was very, very close to tears. He felt a rush of genuine concern. She hung her head, her hair falling forward in a curtain which obscured Harry's view of her face. 'What's up, love,' he said, gently. 'Tell Uncle Harry – I know all about your husband going missing, I wrote to you at the time, if you remember. Has he turned up?'

Laura shook her head. Her shoulders were heaving, she was obviously crying hard, and just when Harry was wondering what on earth to do with an hysterical young woman in his office, she managed to collect herself, straighten up and raise a tear-stained face to meet his eye. 'It's just that things have gone from bad to worse since my husband disappeared,' she said. 'Firstly, I lost my job . . .'

'Lost your job! Why?'

'It's a long story, but let's say I fell out with the editor.'

Harry smiled, trying to lighten the mood. 'Not a good policy, though Geoffrey Richards is a little tick, I'll grant you.'

Laura was not to be side-tracked. 'Then, well, then I found I was pregnant.' Harry said nothing, there seemed to be nothing he could say. 'And then . . . it seems likely that I'm going to lose my home.'

'Good God – tell me how that's come about?'

She hesitated and then plunged on. 'My father gave us our flat as a wedding present, mortgage-free,' Laura said. 'When I finally caught up on our mail which had accumulated while we were away, I found a letter addressed to Francis saying our mortgage repayments were overdue and that the building society would have to foreclose unless payments were brought up to date.' Her complexion paled at the memory. 'I went along to see the society and they told me that my husband and I had taken out a 90 per cent mortgage on the property just over six months ago.'

Harry stared at her. 'You mean you didn't know?' Laura shook her head. 'But surely the property was in your joint names?'

'Yes,' said Laura patiently. 'I went to see my solicitor, of course, and he tracked down the original application and the signatures on the mortgage document. The man at the society who handled the application said a woman had come in with Francis to sign the mortgage document and that as far as he remembers she looked exactly like me. The signature on the document is a very good likeness to mine.'

'Are you suggesting you're suffering from amnesia?'

Laura shook her head. 'Oh no, there's no question of that. The woman who went with Francis to sign that document was not me and the signature on it is not mine.'

'Well then, surely it's just a question of getting a handwriting expert in to prove it.'

Laura nodded. 'My solicitor says there is a chance that might work.'

'A chance!' said Harry, jumping to his feet. 'It's monstrous, you can't let the building society get away with this. It is their job to protect your property, not lose it for you.'

'Maybe, but I can't face a court case at the moment. Just imagine the publicity,' said Laura. 'In any event, I may not even win – it's just my word against the man at the building society, and he's certainly not going to change his story now. Anyway, I don't want to talk about it any more. The decision's made and I'm just going to grit my teeth and pay the mortgage. My solicitor has persuaded the building society to waive back-payments and tack them on to the end of the repayment programme, so, I only have to earn enough money to make future payments.'

'How much?' Harry asked.

'Approximately £300 a month.'

'Jesus,' said Harry, 'that's going to take some finding.'

'I know, it's why I'm here,' said Laura. Her voice was steady now, and she looked at Harry expectantly.

He decided not to mince his words. 'There is a way you could earn some money – a great deal of money.'

'How?' He saw hope wash across her face.

'Write your story, your own story.'

'How do you mean?'

'Write about your husband's disappearance and what's happened since. It's a sod that we can't catch the Christmas market now, but it would be a good subject to publish in the spring. It's soon enough that the punters will remember the headlines – in fact, thinking about it, maybe spring's better anyway.' He grinned. 'It will certainly concentrate every woman's mind on looking after her old man on holiday this year.' He saw the stricken expression on Laura's face and hurried on. 'And I can get you a fat advance – £5000, maybe £6000.' He paused for a reaction. He did not have to wait long.

'No,' she thundered, 'no, not under any circumstances.'

'But why?' said Harry. 'You certainly don't owe the guy anything. He's walked out of your life, stolen your flat and left you . . .' his voice softened, 'left you to bring up his child alone. Think of the child – you want the best for it – and I tell you, Laura, this is the way to get the best. Jesus, it might even make a movie.'

'I said no, Harry, and no is what I mean. I am not prepared to sell my husband's tragedy, cheapen myself and destroy his family, just to solve my financial problems. Would you do the same if your wife went missing?'

Harry grinned. 'Currently, all my wives are ex-wives, and considering the amount they're costing me, I wouldn't hesitate to write about any or all of them. I just wish at least one of them would do something sufficiently sensational to justify a story.' It was an incredibly tactless remark, and he regretted it immediately.

'You have your problems, I have mine,' said Laura, coolly. 'Can we come back to the subject of food, for a moment. How about a book on famous restaurant recipes?'

Harry shook his head. 'The market's absolutely flooded with recipe books. The only way you can break into that market these days is to be a name, and you're not a name, Laura.'

'What about vegetarian cooking?' Laura suggested. 'Since I've been pregnant, for some reason I've gone off meat. I'd be quite interested in exploring vegetarian recipes.'

'Vegetarian food!' Harry said. 'Who wants it? Ruddy CND, Women's Lib fodder. You might get a few cranks buying the books, but that's all.'

'More and more people are going off red meat,' Laura said, patiently. 'I am sure there will be a lot less meat eaten in the next few years.'

Harry shook his head. 'There's no book in it, Laura, truly.'

Laura could see his prejudice was hopelessly ingrained. 'So where does that leave me?' she said, exasperated.

Harry looked at her tiredly and smiled. 'It leaves me playing Father Christmas I suppose,' he said. 'I'll try to help you find some freelance work. Tell me, when is your next mortgage repayment due?'

'In a week's time,' said Laura.

'Can't you touch your parents or your husband's parents?'

'No,' said Laura. She was clearly not to be moved.

'It seems a little short-sighted, particularly bearing in mind the baby,' Harry tried, lamely.

Laura stood up abruptly. 'No lectures, Harry. Do what you can, alright?'

'I will,' he said. He showed her to the door and then returned to his paperwork. The headache, temporarily forgotten, returned with a vengeance. He would put out a few feelers because he had promised the girl, but he did not hold out much hope of finding any regular work and neither, he suspected, did she. It was a last ditch attempt to save her home. He felt sorry for her, but as she had said herself, he had problems of his own without getting involved with hers.

The interview had done nothing to lift Laura's spirits. She cut through the back streets out on to High Holborn and joined a long queue to wait for a bus. She stood there, as if in a trance, thinking back over the years. Until the last few days, she would never have considered travelling any other way than by taxi. She had taken her lifestyle so much for granted, she realized. When she was a little girl, her father used to tell her of riding the trams in the early morning smog of Manchester, half freezing to death. It had meant nothing to her until now for she had never wanted for money – not for a single moment of what, to date, had been a charmed life. Now though, it was different. The facts were that she had a £300 overdraft, an electricity and telephone bill due and just over £5 in her purse. Such a situation did wonderfully concentrate the mind towards thrift.

Just fleetingly, Laura let her thoughts flirt with the idea of asking for help, either from her parents or from Lord Campling. Pride saw to it that her parents were out of the question, and so too, she felt, was William. When, three weeks ago, she had telephoned him with the news that she had decided to keep his grandchild, his pleasure had come as no surprise. Indeed, she had almost made the decision for his benefit because she felt that at long last she had found somebody who fully understood what she was going through. However, her faith and trust in her new-found friend had disappeared the moment he had told her his plans for her unborn child. Clearly, William had not been interested in Laura, the person, other than in her role as incubator for perpetuating the Campling dynasty. With his revelation as to her baby's future, the growing sense of friendship she had felt, instantly disappeared. She could not go back on her promise to have the child but she would do it without his help, or anyone else's. It was her baby and her life and from now on she would cope with both – alone.

It was a brave decision but the consequences were dire. By the following Thursday, when payment was not forthcoming, the building society foreclosed. Calmly, Laura divided the possessions that she and Francis had accumulated into three piles – the good stuff for the auction rooms, the junk for a local scrap dealer and the rubbish consigned to an incredible number of black dustbin liners. Francis's clothes she sent to Oxfam and what was left after this purge fitted comfortably into two medium-sized suitcases. She worked in a dream and, strangely, found the whole experience cleansing rather than distressing. Her solicitor negotiated for her to stay in the flat until the end of September, but the moment she received a £700 cheque from the auction rooms, she had itchy feet. It was time to move on and away – fast. She already knew that by the time the flat was sold there would be nothing left over – fees having more than absorbed any surplus. She was reduced to two suitcases and, having paid off her overdraft, she had approximately £400 pounds. It was not such a bad start, she thought, until she began flat hunting.

Laura was not prepared to share with anyone. She wanted a quiet little self-contained flat where she could sit and wait for her baby to be born, in peace and solitude. It was easier said than done. Although she was still as thin as a rake, landladies seemed to sense she was pregnant. 'No children,' they said, staring pointedly at her stomach which displayed only the faintest curve. In any event, the flats were all gloomy, with unspeakably depressing furniture and either noisy, dirty or too expensive.

One glorious, golden September day, Laura woke with an overwhelming desire for the country. The thought of another day's flat hunting depressed her beyond belief. Instead she took a bus to the Embankment and boarded one of the river steamers for a round three-hour trip. The river soothed her. She thought of it rolling past the end of her parents' garden, past David's boathouse, curling through Oxford, just across the Parks from Eleanor and Chris – all people she had turned her back on, but there were no regrets.

At Greenwich they were herded off the steamer to view the Cutty Sark. An hour with her fellow passengers had been more than enough for Laura. She left them exclaiming over the ship and walked up the hill into Greenwich itself. She realized suddenly that, having had no supper the night before nor any breakfast, she was hungry, and on an impulse she wandered into a wine bar. It was a pleasantly relaxed place with sawdust on the floor and old pine furniture dotted about. She ordered a glass of wine and a chicken salad and while she stood waiting for them to be served, her eye was caught by a display board of advertisements.

'One-bedroom flat to rent, overlooking Greenwich park. Enquire at bar for details.'

'Interested in the flat?' the barman's voice broke into her thoughts.

'Yes, I am,' she said, 'at least I think I am. I have to admit it never occurred to me to live as far out as Greenwich.'

'Greenwich isn't far out at all. Twenty minutes to the City, half an hour to the West End – it can take that from Fulham on a bad day.' Laura laughed. He was an attractive man, and looked to be in his late thirties, tall and thick-set with dark, overlong, unruly hair. He wore a guernsey with holes in the elbows. 'Perhaps you should see it,' he suggested.

'Perhaps I should,' said Laura.

'Drink your wine and eat your salad. I'll get somebody to

hold the fort at the bar and then I'll show it to you, it's only five minutes' walk from here.'

'You own it?' Laura asked. She couldn't keep the surprise out of her voice. Somehow he didn't look the sort of person to own property or anything else much.

'Yes, my partner and I do.' He held out a hand. 'My name's Charlie Robins. I'm the uncouth, uneducated but practical member of the partnership. Giles Latham, my partner, is the suave, sophisticated one with all the money. We dabble in property, we dabble in antiques and this is our latest venture – dabbling in wine bars.'

'How enterprising,' said Laura, genuinely impressed. 'My name's Laura Melhuish.' Charlie frowned. Clearly the name was familiar, but mercifully he appeared not to know why.

The flat was perfect. It was on the first floor and in the sitting room, there was a deep bay window overlooking Greenwich Park. The rest of the flat consisted of a double bedroom, a bathroom and an adequate kitchenette. 'How much?' Laura asked.

'Twenty a week,' said Charlie.

'Twenty!'

He shrugged his shoulders. 'OK, fifteen to you, but not a penny less – it is in a unique position.' Laura walked to the window and gazed out across the park. The leaves were just starting to turn, the colours quite exquisite. It was a beautiful setting. For a moment she tried to envisage herself pushing a pram through the park, but as yet the realities of having a baby were unimaginable. 'It's a quiet house.' Charlie was saying, 'A retired naval man lives above but he spends most of his time in the museum. Below you there's a university don, a woman – in her fifties I should think. She works from home mostly. What do you do?'

'I'm a freelance journalist,' said Laura.

'Then that should be ideal for you all – perfect peace in which to work.'

It would have been easy to let the remark go, but somehow Laura could not. 'There's something I ought to tell you,' she said and hesitated.

'Go on then,' said Charlie, with an engaging grin. 'Tell me

the worst. No, let me guess – your hobby's playing the trumpet.'

'Not quite, you see I'm pregnant.'

'Ah.'

'The rule is, no animals and children, right?' He nodded. 'The baby's not due for six months.' Laura tried not to sound pleading. 'Perhaps I could stay here until then.'

Charlie shook his head. 'That's not very satisfactory from your point of view. Look, I'll have a word with Giles. Who knows, if you can endear yourself to your co-tenants, they may not mind the baby at all.' He hesitated. 'You've no husband then? Sorry to be inquisitive but I need to give Giles some background.'

'Separated,' said Laura.

'No hope of reconciliation?'

'None.'

Charlie smiled. 'Poor old you. Never mind, I'll see what I can do. Have you a phone number where I can reach you tonight?'

In fact, it was two days before Charlie Robins contacted Laura again, by which time she was in despair. 'Sorry to be so long coming back to you, but the flat is yours if you would like it.' There was a lot of singing and shouting in the background – he was clearly speaking from the wine bar.

'Marvellous!' said Laura. 'To be honest, I'd just about given up hope.'

'Me, too,' said Charlie, cheerfully. 'Giles said absolutely no baby, so I had to work on him. He got pissed as a newt last night and while he was on cloud nine I made him agree to your taking the flat, baby and all. This morning, I told him I'd rung you last night on the strength of his agreement and so he couldn't go back on it. He's angry now, but he'll soon calm down.'

It sounded a far from ideal situation. 'Are you sure I should come,' said Laura, doubtfully.

'No sweat,' said Charlie, 'move in as soon as you like, but I really need a month's rent in advance. Can you manage that?'

'Yes, no problem,' she said, brightly. 'Can I move in tomorrow?'

'Why not?' said Charlie.

The following morning, Laura packed her two suitcases and, for the last time, walked out of the home she had shared with Francis Melhuish. She did not have one last look around the flat, nor even glance over her shoulder, as she left. She closed the door behind her with relief – anxious to get away, to put distance between herself and the shell of their marital home, where guilt and accusation seemed to shout from the very walls.

'I caught sight of your little waif and stray for the first time yesterday,' Giles said. He was totally blocking the light from Charlie who was trying to fix the innards of a rather dilapidated grandfather clock.

'She's not *my* little waif and stray,' Charlie said, irritably. 'Oh, for Christ's sake, Giles, get out of my light, I can't see what the hell I'm doing here.'

'Sorry, old boy, I rather thought she was. What about all these visits you make to her? You must have taken a shine to her, because you're certainly overdoing the caring landlord bit – Rachman, eat your heart out!'

Charlie raised his head and glared at Giles. As usual, he was immaculately turned out in sports jacket and cavalry twills. His fair hair was cut very short, and he sported a small military moustache. He looked considerably older than his thirty-six years – in fact, his appearance was more suited to his father's generation than to his own. 'The trouble with you, Giles, is you can only see relationships between a male and female on one level.'

'Is there more than one level?' Giles asked, affecting an innocent smile.

'Piss off. Look, go and have a drink, go for a walk, do anything but stop pestering me and let me get on with this job. You're worse than having a bloody kid about the place.'

'It's just that she's not your type – you like them blonde and buxom,' Giles persisted. 'You've rather a crude taste in women, actually, but that's fairly appropriate, I suppose, given the type of bloke you are. *She*, however, is definitely not conforming to the pattern.'

'Thanks a bunch,' said Charlie. 'Sod, now look what you've made me do – I've dropped the bloody screw.'

'Small, dark and pregnant, quite out of character, unless . . . the baby's not yours, old boy, is it? You haven't knocked her up.'

'No, of course I haven't,' said Charlie, 'the baby is her husband's – he disappeared.'

'Disappeared! Still, not surprising really, she looks fairly dreary to me,' Giles said, sagely.

Charlie abandoned all hope of mending the clock and sat back on his heels. 'It's not a very pleasant story actually. You may have read about it in the papers a few months ago. Her husband, a titled gent, Francis Melhuish, his name was, disappeared off their yacht one night. They were sailing in the Greek islands, and he was wanted by the Fraud Squad.'

'Good lord, yes,' said Giles, 'I remember the story. You mean this is the wife?'

'The same,' said Charlie. 'She told me about it the other evening.'

'Then you steer well clear – her husband might come back and knock you into next week, if he finds you're dabbling with his goods.'

'I wish you wouldn't speak about her like that, Giles. She's genuinely not my type, as you say, but I do like her – she has a lot of guts. I just wish she'd show some enthusiasm.'

'For what,' said Giles, 'your carnal desires?'

'No, I've told you, there's nothing between us – enthusiasm for anything, really. She drifts from day to day, and apart from the size of her stomach, everything else about her seems to shrink, and I don't just mean physically – her mind seems to be shrinking, too. She's losing interest in everything and everyone. It's as though she has withdrawn from life, because it's too painful for her, I suppose.'

'Listen Charlie, old boy, this really isn't your problem. Why don't I give Diana a ring, see if she can produce an extra girl and the four of us can go out on the tiles tonight. What do you say?'

'No thanks,' said Charlie, 'I'll still be working on this sodding clock I should think, unless you give me a bit of peace.'

*

Giles Latham had always liked his women to play the dominant role, both in and out of bed. It was for this reason Diana ffinch-Mason suited him perfectly. He lay now on his back, as she hovered above him. She knew just how he liked it. She was on all fours, moving her pelvis up and down slowly, tantalizingly slowly, until he was begging her not to stop, to go faster, faster . . . His hands grasped her buttocks and he pulled her down on to him again and again. They came together, they always did, shouting, laughing, collapsing in a tangled heap, bathed in sweat and gasping for breath. No woman had ever made him feel like this, and the last spasm had barely died away, it seemed, when he felt her hands on him. The whole delicious ritual was starting again.

Some hours later, Giles eyed Diana through a haze of cigarette smoke as she brushed her marmalade hair. The sun, slanting through the skylight, played with the different shades that combined to make up its extraordinary colour. He watched her in silence, fascinated. In Diana's case her hair was truly her crowning glory. His sense of well-being for some reason made his thoughts shift to Charlie. 'Di, you haven't got a blonde, buxom, unattached girlfriend in your life at the moment, have you?'

Diana turned and gave him one of her brittle, ironic smiles. 'Darling you're not suggesting I'm swinging both ways, are you? I thought I'd just demonstrated to your apparent satisfaction that I am entirely heterosexual.'

She shocked him sometimes. 'No, no,' he said, hurriedly, angry at being embarrassed. 'I'm thinking of Charlie. He seems to have developed an unhealthy obsession with one of our tenants. She's totally uninterested in him and seems to be suffering from the rather unfortunate combination of being both pregnant and anorexic. He says it's just platonic friendship, but I've never known old Charlie have a platonic relationship with a woman yet – he's just not that subtle, bless him.'

Diana continued to brush her hair, thoughtfully. 'I can't honestly think of anybody particularly suitable at the moment, darling,' she said after a pause, 'but why all the fuss? Charlie's a big boy, he can look after himself.'

'I suppose so,' said Giles, 'it's just that with her past, I find her rather sinister.'

'Past, what past?'

'Her husband disappeared in mysterious circumstances.'

Diana laughed. 'So what are you suggesting, she's a pregnant, anorexic husband-killer? It does sound a little far-fetched.'

'No, no, though come to think of it, nobody's ever suggested she murdered him, as far as I know, and it does seem the most logical explanation.'

'Murdered who? I don't know what you're talking about, Giles.'

'You must have read about it at the time. They were on holiday in the Greek islands and the husband, a son of William Campling, disappeared overboard one night and they never found him.'

'Laura Melhuish,' Diana said, immediately.

'Yes, yes, that's right,' said Giles, 'what a good memory you have.'

'No prizes in this case,' said Diana. 'I know Laura – in fact I knew her very well, at one time. What an extraordinary coincidence.'

'Did you? How fascinating. *Could* she have murdered her husband?'

'No, of course not – you are a ghastly man sometimes, Giles.'

Giles shifted himself into a more upright position. 'So, don't stop now – tell me all the gossip about her. You know I love a scandal.'

Diana turned back to the mirror. 'You say she's pregnant?'

'Yes. Charlie says the baby is her husband's, but that could be a story for Charlie's benefit.'

'And she's living in one of your flats, you say?'

'Yes, has been for some weeks, now.'

'I wonder why?'

'Well why not? Our flats are very nice.'

'They're not very nice at all, not the ones I've seen in any event, and you charge far too much rent.'

'The one your chum Laura has is extremely nice. It's in Nelson Street, overlooking the park.'

'It'll be damp, dreary and entirely suitable for a demolition order, if I'm not mistaken,' said Diana. She sighed. 'It just seems such an extraordinary thing for her to do.'

'Why?' said Giles. He climbed out of bed and wandered into the bathroom.

Diana watched his naked form disappearing through the door. She felt her body stir at the sight of him and not for the first time she wondered at her obsession for Giles Latham. It was not love, at least there was no sentiment, yet the need for him grew daily, hourly even, and she could not deny the growing bond of friendship between them – she was becoming dangerously close to him. Diana forced her mind back to Laura, and shouted through the bathroom door. 'It's *who* she is that makes it so extraordinary – she's the only child of Sir Bernard Beecham. She could be living in a penthouse suite in Mayfair if she wanted.'

'Obviously she doesn't want,' Giles called back. 'Mind you, I'm not surprised she prefers one of my flats . . .'

Diana considered the Laura she knew for a moment – pretty, vivacious, sparkling with good humour and fun. It was a very different picture from the one Giles had so glibly described. 'I'll go and see her,' she said firmly, 'just to check she's OK.'

Giles emerged from the bathroom dripping, a towel round his waist. 'Oh no,' he groaned, 'not you as well. Why does everybody feel this tremendous urge to befriend the wretched girl.'

Diana looked at Giles thoughtfully and took her time over her reply. 'Because Laura was very good to me once – it was a long time ago, but at the time I desperately needed a friend and she was there. I've never forgotten it, I never will.'

'Ooh,' said Giles, coming up to Diana and gently raising her to her feet, 'do tell me more.'

Diana did not answer. She leant forward and kissed him on the lips, moving her hips against his. 'You wouldn't want to hear about it, darling, it was just a schoolgirl prank and I've done a lot of growing up since then.'

Giles ran his hands down the centre of her back and over the curve of her hips. 'So you have,' he said, his breath already uneven.

CHAPTER NINE

Diana ffinch-Mason had never known who her father was. Her early childhood was a confusion of memories – she and her mother together, always on the move, practically living out of a suitcase, their lifestyle gyrating wildly between poverty and luxury. A penthouse suite at the Ritz one week, a draughty, rented cottage in Wales the next. The governing factor seeming to be a series of 'uncles' who flitted in and out of her mother's life. Her mother, Betty, who had started out in life with everything – extraordinary beauty, a privileged upbringing, wit and intelligence – had somewhere, inexorably, taken a wrong turning, which in later life, Diana realized, must have been connected with her own birth. Certainly with hindsight, by the time Diana was three or four, Betty had become little more than an upper-class whore. The instability, the uncertainty, the midnight flits, the bounced cheques, the uncles – some kind, some downright cruel – might have gone on for ever but for Simon ffinch-Mason, who walked into Diana and Betty's life one day, when Diana was seven, and overnight created order, stability and an entirely new emotion for Diana – love. For Simon married her mother and took to his heart his little step-daughter. It was Diana who had insisted on changing her surname to his, and, of mother and daughter, it was Diana who truly loved him.

From the moment Simon ffinch-Mason became her step-father, Diana's education was taken in hand. She was sent to a good preparatory school, from where she passed Common Entrance with flying colours and was offered a place at Wycombe Abbey. Initially, she was very happy at boarding school. She missed Simon, but the ordered, routine life suited her very well and made her feel secure. However, Diana going away to school heralded the beginning of the end for her parents' marriage. Betty had always drunk heavily and when she was drunk, she did foolish things. After five years of marriage to Simon, the foolish things included a public and very messy affair. Simon stuck it out for as long as he could, but with Diana away at school, he and Betty were thrown together. With no one to act as buffer, the cracks that had shown for a long time began to split and tear.

It was Simon who told her, of course, Simon who realized the importance of explaining precisely what was happening and why. He collected her alone, for a going-out day, which in itself was not unusual – Sunday mornings were not a good time for Betty. Instead of taking her to their usual favourite Italian restaurant in Windsor, Simon had driven out into the country. Together they had walked over the fields . . . and as Simon talked, despite the loving care and thought he put into explaining the situation, he broke Diana's heart. He had tried to stay with her mother, he explained, but he really could stand it no longer. In fact his very presence, he felt, was actually detrimental to Betty's stability – when he was around, she had to behave badly in order to provoke him. Diana was not to worry, it would affect her very little. He was her father, he would continue to pay her school fees, love and protect her, and as long as he had breath in his body, she could absolutely rely on him – always.

'But when will I see you?' Diana had said. 'Please give it a little more time, please. I'll leave school, I'll come home. If I'm there to help with Mummy . . .'

No, Simon had insisted, it was over. Diana could come to him whenever she liked, but he could no longer live with her mother. He succeeded in drying her tears, soothing her anxious inquiries and returned her to school in the belief that he had done as good a job as was possible in the circumstances. What he did not, or could not, have known was that he had left her with the unshakeable conviction that the breakdown of her mother's marriage was entirely her fault.

It began with a chocolate bar – a strenuous game of hockey, followed by an extra music lesson, had left Diana both ravenously hungry and too late for tea. Jane Richards, the girl who had the locker next to hers, had a secret supply of Mars bars, sent to her, with great subterfuge, by an indulgent elder sister. The locker, when Diana looked in it, contained four Mars bars. She helped herself to one, telling herself she would pay back Jane at the weekend, when they were allowed to go to the shops. Jane never noticed the missing Mars bar and somehow Diana never got round to telling her about it.

After the Mars bar, Diana found it was convenient to borrow things on a regular basis – a biro, a rubber, some notepaper – nothing of any real value and nothing she could not have perfectly well afforded to buy herself. Stealing meant taking things you could not get any other way, Diana reasoned, whenever she queried in her mind why this habit had developed. Besides, it could not be so terribly wrong since no one ever seemed to notice. It was the fountain pen which changed things and it was Jane again from whom she 'borrowed' it. It was silly really because once the pen was in her possession she could not use it when anyone else was around, and how could she have been expected to know that the pen was special. It had been given to Jane by her godfather. It was a new sort of Parker and all the trimmings were in real gold-plate. There was quite a fuss about it. The headmistress mentioned it at assembly, their form mistress – a hideous woman with a bun and buck-teeth, named Miss Child, highly inappropriately for the woman could never have been a child – issued dire threats and the suggestion was made that the pen had not been lost, but stolen. Only Diana knew the pen had not been stolen – simply borrowed.

When by half-term, the number of missing personal possessions from the girls of Form Upper 4 had reached almost epidemic proportions, a note was sent home with the children to their parents, asking that all valuables should be kept at home for the second half of term, until 'this little problem is resolved'. During that dreary half-term, in between bouts of drinking, Betty had actually read the note. 'I really don't understand it,' she said, 'I spend all this money on your education, sending you to one of the top girls' schools in the country, only to find you're mixing with a lot of juvenile delinquents.' Diana was tempted to point out that in fact it was Simon who paid her school fees, but it would have involved a screaming match, and she frankly felt too weary to start all that.

It seemed that parents had not taken much notice of the note, for in the first week after half-term, Laura Beecham left her gold religious medallion and chain in the cloakroom after swimming. Diana had always wanted a St Christopher and this was a particularly fine one, which was not surprising really because everyone knew Laura's parents were stinking rich. Diana wore it, carefully concealed under her vest and no one noticed. It was an odd sensation, when Miss Child made the announcement about the missing medallion, to feel it lying cool and unnoticed between her budding young breasts.

In the end, of course, it was Miss Child who caught her red-handed. On Saturday morning, the girls were allowed to draw out pocket money for their weekend's activities. On this particular Saturday, Susan Young had been allowed to draw £1 – a fortune – to buy some new wellington boots, since hers had been lost. Susan's wellington boot saga was on the way to becoming a well-established school legend. It had involved a nature ramble and a pond, and Susan wading into the pond against specific instructions not to do so, and having to be dragged out by the fire brigade, minus her boots. Everyone knew, therefore, that she was allowed to draw extra pocket money and when the girls went out to break on Saturday morning, Diana stayed behind. She was just extracting the £1 from Susan's desk when Miss Child slid slowly round the door . . .

The ensuing scenes at the time appeared to have very little effect on Diana. She was hauled before the headmistress, her belongings were searched and most of the inedible missing treasures found. Her mother was sent for, arrived and threw hysterics. Diana was moved out of her dormitory and into the sick room temporarily while her future was decided. Just when the turmoil seemed at its height, Simon arrived and calmed down her mother, persuaded the headmistress to take no further action, and then sat and talked quietly to Diana for a long time. He did not ask her stupid questions, like why she had done it. Instead he told her that the bravest and most difficult thing she would ever have to do in her whole life was to stay on at school and face her peers. He also told her that if she was ever tempted to do such a thing again, she was to call him and he would come to her from wherever he was.

In anticipating her suffering, Simon had been chillingly accurate. Diana was sent to coventry, everyone sniggered at her behind their hands and no one would be her partner. The staff, in a far more subtle and cruel way, clearly demonstrated their view that the headmistress had acted wrongly and Diana should have been expelled. Her work suffered and she found she could not eat without feeling sick. In her mind's eye, Diana saw herself as being permanently excluded from society, a freak, a social outcast . . . and then a miracle happened – Laura Beecham decided it was time Diana had a friend. It was extraordinary really. Without doubt, Laura was the most popular girl in the form – bright and funny, clever at work and games. Diana had always liked her but Laura was in a different league from herself. As always, with Laura, there was no beating about the bush. She came up to Diana in the junior common room one evening and suggested they go for a walk round the grounds, after supper.

'Who me?' said Diana. No one had spoken to her for three weeks and she just could not believe Laura was serious.

'Yes, of course you,' said Laura. 'See you later, by the chestnut – about seven?'

'I've thought a lot about it,' Laura said, later, as they walked over the newly cut lawns. 'I think everyone's being beastly to you. You've been punished enough and, well . . . I'd like to be your friend.'

All her life, the smell of a newly mown lawn on a summer's evening was to bring Diana a sense of warmth and well-being, and it stemmed from that moment. First, though, there had been her pride to overcome. 'No, it's alright, I don't need anyone,' she said, 'I'm getting used to it.'

'You must have a friend, everyone needs a friend, it's miserable without one. I didn't have any friends when I first came into the junior school, and I hated it. I was so miserable and homesick.' Laura sounded quite sincere, but Diana remained unconvinced.

'Were you?' She said. 'I don't remember – you've always seemed very popular to me.'

'Oh, that's only recently. I had a long period of feeling lonely. Look, Diana, if we started going around together it will only be a few weeks before everyone forgets all about . . . the stuff that went missing. It's because you're moping around on your own all the time, that everybody remembers why.'

'They'll never accept me,' said Diana, 'not after what happened.'

'Of course they will, and anyway I'd like to give you something – just to show at least I don't bear grudges.' Laura stopped walking and opened her hand. In it was clasped the gold St Christopher that Diana had taken.

'No, no, I couldn't possibly.' Diana turned away.

'Please, Diana, I'd really like you to have it and I think it would help. I'll tell everyone I've given it to you, as a kind of peace offering. Miss Child told us that your parents have recently divorced – things must be awful for you at the moment. Please, wear this – it'll maybe bring you luck.'

Watching Giles climb out of bed for the second time that afternoon, Diana fingered the medallion. She had worn it always, from that day to this. Laura had been right. Within a few days, or so it seemed, she was an accepted member of the form again. Her work improved and by the time she reached the Sixth Form, she was a respected and highly praised pupil, with an excellent academic record and a prefect's badge. Simon and Laura between them had saved her – she would never have made it alone, she knew that.

Laura and Diana had remained friends after school. Laura, of course, soon began living with David Lawson, while Diana took a flat in London with some other girlfriends. They kept in touch and when Laura landed the job on *Opinions*, naturally Diana offered her a place in her flat. They had shared the flat together for about six months, during which time Diana had been privy to all Laura's heartsearching about leaving David. Inevitably, David had assumed that *all* Laura's London friends were responsible for driving the wedge between them. In fact, Diana had been a considerable champion in his fight to keep Laura, but to little effect.

It was also during this period that something happened

which changed Diana's life yet again – Simon died. She would always remember the reading of his will with a mixture of pain and amusement. Diana, her mother and Simon's sister, Angela had been summoned to the solicitor's office, much in the manner of a Victorian melodrama. They had all been aware that Simon was a successful businessman, but no one had been prepared for the extent of his wealth. He left his sister a comfortable annuity for life, Betty the same – which was very generous in the circumstances – but the rest of his considerable fortune went straight to Diana, with the simple instruction – 'Be Happy'. God knows, I've tried my best, Diana thought, watching Giles as he dressed. He was talking earnestly about something, but she was not listening.

With her new-found wealth, Diana fulfilled a long standing ambition to travel, and she had been on the move now for four years – the States, Australia, the Far East, Europe – she had seen it all. It had been a wonderful experience, it had matured her and given her confidence. She had also grown into a strikingly good-looking woman, who used her money well to show off her appearance to best advantage. She was always beautifully dressed and impeccably groomed. She was a natural party host, the perfect guest. She had a delicious dry wit and a genuine interest in people, which made her equally popular with men and women. Yet she still felt empty inside. Betty had died two years before, of cirrhosis of the liver, and whilst her death had relieved Diana of the guilty dislike she had always felt for her mother, it had also left her entirely rootless. At present she was living in the Dorchester, and the affair with Giles – whom she had met the previous year in the South of France – was enjoyable but it was hard to imagine it having any kind of future. Giles was not the type for settling down, and nor in fairness was she.

Diana, of course, had read about Laura's troubles in the newspapers and had meant to contact her at the time. Now, this extraordinary coincidence seemed like a signal. Laura was in trouble, and Diana always settled her debts.

The two young women stared at one another with mutual astonishment – Diana, of course, had been prepared for the meeting, but she had not been prepared for the change in Laura. She stood hesitantly by the front door. She was heavily pregnant, but painfully thin. Her face was very pale, there were dark smudges under her eyes and her clothes were shabby and creased. However, it was her eyes which worried Diana most. She remembered them bright blue and merry – now they were full of pain – pain and something else, hopelessness. 'Laura . . . it – it's lovely to see you.' There was a catch in Diana's voice and she leant forward, awkwardly, over Laura's stomach to kiss her on the cheek.

'Diana, what an extraordinary thing! How on earth did you find me?'

Although it was a question, Diana had the feeling that Laura was not particularly interested in the answer. 'Darling, it was a complete coincidence. I have to admit to be currently indulging in a quite delicious affair with your landlord.'

'Charlie?' There was just a flicker of interest there.

'No, no, not Charlie – Giles.'

'Oh, I see,' said Laura, 'I haven't met Giles.'

'Darling, it's freezing. Do we have to stand here on the doorstep, gossiping?'

'No, I suppose not, come in,' said Laura, a little grudgingly. She led the way up a narrow flight of stairs into the first floor flat. Judging by Laura's appearance, Diana was prepared for anything, but the flat was neat and clean and well-tended plants were grouped around the windows. It was excruciatingly cold however. 'Would you like . . . some tea,' said Laura. 'I'm sorry, I haven't any coffee, tea's cheaper.'

'Tea would be fine,' said Diana. She followed Laura into the tiny kitchen. 'It's absolutely freezing in here, Laura, haven't you any heating?'

'Oh yes, there is heating – electric radiators – but they're too expensive.'

These immediate references to shortage of money were too much for Diana's curiosity. 'Darling, are you saying you're stuck for cash?'

'Well . . . yes, pretty much. Social Security doesn't go very far, and although I had a few hundred pounds left over from the selling of the contents of our flat, it's more or less gone.' Although reciting the facts, Laura did not sound particularly interested in her circumstances.

'But that's crazy,' said Diana. 'Why aren't your parents helping you, particularly at the moment?' She glanced meaningfully at Laura's bump.

'I'm managing without their help quite well,' Laura said, in a tight little voice.

'But why, darling?'

Laura poured boiling water into the teapot, concentrating in silence for a moment. 'It's time I went my own way,' Laura said at last. 'In the past, I've relied too heavily on my parents, on their position and their money. In fact, I've relied too heavily on everyone – I've always had a prop. Now, at last, I'm doing things for myself.'

'But living in a sleazy flat on Social Security isn't exactly doing much for yourself, is it?' Diana said, not unreasonably.

Laura's head jerked up. There were two high spots of colour in her cheekbones and her eyes blazed. 'It's a start. Don't tell me that you, of all people, have let your money divorce you from the realities of life. This . . .' she gestured round the flat, 'this is how most people live – in fact this is the lap of luxury compared with the conditions in which many people are forced to exist.'

'But why choose this moment, of all times, to make your stand?' Diana said, exasperated.

'I suppose because of what happened to Francis. It's made me realize how futile and spoilt my life has been when compared with the realities of life and death.' There was a silence between them while Laura poured out the tea.

'It's guilt, isn't it?' said Diana, with a sudden flash of inspiration. 'You're feeling guilty about what happened to Francis and so you're trying to punish yourself by living like this.'

'Don't be ridiculous,' Laura snapped.

Diana could feel hostility radiating from her. 'Don't clam up – please talk to me,' she said. 'Let me help you, Laura – you really look like you could use some help right now.'

'I don't need help,' said Laura. 'I'm fine. This is the way I want things to be, so if you've come here hoping to play Lady Bountiful, forget it.'

'I let you help me once,' Diana said, gently. 'You know, Laura, I've been round the world at least twice. I've been made love to at one extreme by a Greek peasant on a beach, and at the other by an Arab prince in a palace. I've had more experiences than you would believe possible, yet through it all, I have held on to one consistent thing.' Diana pulled the little medallion through the opening of her shirt. 'This,' she said, holding it out for Laura to see. 'It stands for something, Laura – for trust, friendship and new beginnings. Please let me help you as you once helped me.' Her own words had brought Diana to the point of tears, but when she looked at Laura, an extraordinary thing happened. It was as though the door to her very soul slammed shut. She appeared neither angry nor sad – indeed it looked as though she had not even heard what Diana had said. Her expression was quite blank.

'I can only repeat, Di, I don't need help,' she said at last. 'Come on, let's go into the sitting room.'

In the sitting room, conversation between them was stilted and awkward. It was a ridiculous situation. They had been as close as two people could be as children, yet now Diana's mind was reeling from the effort of trying to make conversation. 'Tell me about Francis's accident, it must have been awful for you,' she said, in a last ditch effort to get through to Laura.

'Far more awful for him,' said Laura. 'One has to assume he is dead, in which case he died from drowning which must be a dreadful thing.' There was no emotion in her voice.

'And the baby,' said Diana, carefully, 'it's his, I presume?'

'Of course,' said Laura, 'you don't imagine I'd go off and have an affair as soon as my husband went missing. I'm not like you, Di – it's always been one man at a time for me.'

Diana ignored the insult. 'I'm sorry, Laura, but because of my travels, we've drifted apart and I suppose I feel I don't know you very well any more.'

'There's no harm in that,' said Laura, 'people change, drift apart, there's no reason why childhood friends should be friends for life.' She smiled for the first time. 'In a way we've reversed roles – funny isn't it?' She gave a hollow laugh.

'You sound so bitter,' said Diana.

'Bitter! Do I? I don't feel bitter.'

'But surely, if you've cut yourself off from your family and your friends . . .'

'I'll make new friends,' said Laura, 'when I'm ready, besides I do have friends. I'm going to Oxford for the birth of the baby, to stay with some people who were very kind in Rhodes, when Francis . . .' her voice trailed off.

'That's good. Anyone I know?' Laura shook her head. There was a lengthy pause. 'David Lawson has married, you know.' The moment she spoke the words, Diana regretted them. She had blurted them out, partly to change the subject and partly, she knew, in the hopes of getting some sort of reaction from Laura. For a moment, she was rewarded by a flicker in Laura's eyes. Then they went dead again.

'He's married a girl called Serena,' Diana continued, desperately. 'Well, I say *girl*, more a woman really. She's quite a lot older than David. Still, I suppose, it's a good thing for the poor old love. I was beginning to think he would never get over you.'

'He came to see me, you know,' Laura said. Her voice had an almost dreamlike quality – it was so devoid of feeling. 'He came to the flat just after Francis disappeared.'

'Did he?' said Diana. 'That was kind of him.'

'Yes, I suppose it was, though I don't think I was very kind back. I'm afraid I'd drunk too much. I sent him away with a flea in his ear.'

Poor David, poor Laura, Diana thought – they had fallen in love too young to sustain a permanent relationship and now the only power they had over one another was the ability to hurt. There was another long silence. 'Will you stay in Oxford when the baby is born?' Diana asked.

'No, of course not, I'll come back here, though it's only on a trial basis – Charlie says that if the neighbours complain, I'll have to go.'

There was no hint of concern in her voice. In fact, Diana realized, quite the reverse. It almost sounded as though Laura wanted to be thrown out on the street with her baby. She's wearing sackcloth and ashes, Diana thought, and she's blaming herself for everything that's happened.

The tea was drunk, the conversation was at an end. There was nothing more Diana could do but leave – Laura was certainly not making her welcome. She stood up. 'I'll go now, Laura, but don't think you're going to get rid of me this easily. I'll be back, and meanwhile, I have my spies to check up on you and see you're looking after yourself properly.'

'Do you?' said Laura wearily. She hesitated. 'You asked just now, Di, if there was anything you could do to help. Well, there is. What I want you to do is leave me alone, and to make sure that all the other so-called well-wishers from my past follow your example.'

CHAPTER TEN

In the flat above Latham Antiques, Giles sprawled on the sofa before an excellent bottle of claret, watching Charlie's inadequate attempts to iron a shirt. It was unheard of for Charlie to wear a shirt and tie and it only served to heighten Giles's sense of unease with regard to his relationship with Laura Melhuish.

'OK, Charlie, so these days your idea of a truly exciting date is to take out a woman who is eight and a half months pregnant with somebody else's child. Fair enough, I accept that, but why the shirt and tie?'

'We're eating at the Spread Eagle.'

'So?'

'So, it's the kind of place where you're expected to dress up a bit. Besides which, I want to make it a special occasion for Laura.'

'Why?' said Giles.

'Because it's her birthday.'

'How old is she?' Giles asked.

'Twenty-three.'

'Twenty-three? Good God, is that all? Still, she is a contemporary of Di's, I suppose. Did I tell you about Di going to see her?'

'Several times,' said Charlie.

'Di thinks Laura is deeply psychologically disturbed.'

'I don't,' said Charlie. 'It's just that she is trying very hard to make a life for herself and she's frightened that anyone from her past will undermine her independence. It's why she trusts me, because I'm nothing to do with what happened before. All that is really wrong with her is she doesn't eat enough – she's *so* thin. Still, perhaps she'll eat properly tonight.'

Giles set down his glass slowly and studied Charlie in

silence, as he bent his large frame over the ironing board, a frown of concentration puckering his brow. Charlie was such a straightforward, honest, simple soul – he liked his beer, the odd woman and above all, his work. Since Laura Melhuish had appeared on the scene, however, he had drunk far less, apparently given up women and even his beloved work had suffered. Instead of spending long hours in the workshop in the evenings as he used to do, followed by a session at the pub just before closing time, he had taken to going round to Laura's for a chat – God knows what they talked about night after night, and now it was a shirt and tie . . . 'You're in love with her,' he said, suddenly.

His remark caught Charlie off-balance. 'No, of course I'm not.'

'I think you are, Charlie old boy, even if you don't know it yourself.'

Charlie thought about the remark as he walked up the hill to Laura's flat. It was hard to define his feelings for her. They certainly were not purely brotherly and yet, perhaps because of her pregnancy, they did not appear to be sexual either. He did recognize, however, that he revelled in her vulnerability. He enjoyed being able to do things for her and because he knew how difficult it was for her to accept help, he had developed a degree of subtlety in his approach to her, which was quite out of character with his normal uncomplicated brashness . . . but then Laura reminded him of his mother.

Charlie Robins's childhood was an entirely uncomplicated blur until shortly after his seventh birthday. He lived with his parents, Pete and Doris, in a small terraced house in the Norfolk town of Fakenham. The house was always spick and span, indeed meticulously neat, and Charlie was always the best-dressed boy at school. He took for granted that he was the apple of his parents' eye, and assumed that the world revolved around him – not in an unpleasant, arrogant way, but because he had never known anything different. Then one day, as a birthday treat, his father announced that he was taking Charlie to Norwich and that it was to be a boys' outing from which Charlie's mother was excluded.

While Charlie was much closer to his mother than his father, the prospect of spending a day alone with his father thrilled him. He did not know him well but he did appreciate the fact that his father did not baby and fuss over him, as did his mother. He was to remember always, walking down the street, hand-in-hand with his father, and turning at the street corner to wave back to his mother, who stood neat and, in his eyes at any rate, very pretty, in her flowered apron, her eyes gentle, tranquil and full of love.

They took the train to Norwich, Charlie had only been on a train once before and he revelled in the experience. He and his father spoke little on the journey and years later, thinking through the episode, Charlie was to wonder how he could ever have managed to talk at all. From Norwich station, Pete led Charlie through back streets to a hot, steamy little café. He went straight up to a table where sat a large, pleasant-looking, fair-haired woman, with a healthy country face and an open smile. On her lap sat a fat baby, by her knee stood a toddler, a boy, and sitting on the chair beside her was a little girl of perhaps four or five. At the sight of Charlie and his father, the little girl jumped up excitedly. 'Daddy, Daddy, we're here,' she called.

Charlie's father smiled and scooped the little girl into his arms, hugging her to him. Her words riveted Charlie – why was this child calling his father, Daddy? He stood stock still, shocked and bewildered.

The woman leaned forward and touched his arm. 'Hello, Charlie, my name's Hilda.' She bounced the baby on her knee 'This here's Tony, one size up is Joe and that one over there is Mary.'

Encouraged by her friendliness, Charlie found his voice. 'But, who are they and who are you?'

'These are your brothers and sister,' said his father, 'and this is your new Mummy.'

In the confusing hours that followed, Charlie learnt that he was to live with his father and the Hilda woman in future. Hilda and the children lived on a farm and Pete had apparently given up his job to work on the farm, too. These children appeared to belong to his father, yet he and the Hilda woman were not married. Charlie could not understand how this was possible. He would not be going home, they told him. They took him shopping and bought him new clothes and *everything* –pyjamas, slippers, a toothbrush, new toys and his first proper bicycle. Then, sitting him in the back seat of a Land-rover, between Mary and Joe, they drove him to Blandings Farm, which was in fact to be his home for the next ten years.

The farmhouse intrigued him immediately – it was so unlike the home he knew. The kitchen was full of dogs and cats, and chickens wandered in and out freely. There was colour, noise and laughter everywhere. Nobody seemed to mind about table manners, or washing your hands before a meal, and everyone was very kind to him. Tea was a feast – cold ham, salad, scones, cream, jam and homemade lemonade. 'It's nice here, isn't it, Charlie?' Pete said, encouragingly. Charlie nodded, his mouth too full to speak.

After tea, the Hilda woman took him up to his new room and helped him unpack all the shopping and put it in a chest of drawers. He was sharing a room with Joe but Joe had been told not to go into Charlie's end of the room – '. . . not without permission,' Hilda said, sternly. As Hilda unpacked, Charlie gazed out of the dormer window. The fields stretched as far as the eye could see, in the soft evening light. It seemed wonderful compared with the narrow street, which was the only home he had ever known. He turned to Hilda. 'What about my Mum, will she be coming to live here, too?'

Hilda hesitated, not meeting his eye. 'No, Charlie.'

'But that means she'll be all alone?'

'I think perhaps you'd better talk to your Dad about it,' said Hilda. 'But don't you worry your head, love, you'll be happy as a lark here with us. I'll look after you as well as my own, you can be sure of that. Look, I'll go and fetch your Dad directly.'

His father deposited his large frame awkwardly on Charlie's little bed and put an arm round the boy. 'We're going to be really happy here, Charlie. It's a wonderful life for a boy, growing up on a farm, with brothers and sisters.'

'But what about Mum?' Charlie persisted.

'She'll be alright. She'll probably marry again one day. She's still a young woman, you know.'

'Marry again? You mean . . . you and Mum are going to stop being married?'

'Yes.'

'But what about me? Doesn't she want me any more?'

His father hesitated. 'It's not a question of not wanting you, Charlie, it's just that this is the best place for you.'

'Does she know I'm here, then?'

Again, his father hesitated. 'Not yet, but I'm going round to see her later this evening to explain.'

'She won't like being all alone. Can't she come and live here?' Charlie began to cry.

'No, Charlie, she can't.'

'Then can I go and see her often.'

'Of course, of course.' Pete patted Charlie's arm reassuringly and then helped his son into bed.

It was right at the beginning of the summer holidays and one golden day followed another. Charlie revelled in life on the farm, and being the eldest child, he was given special responsibilities, which in turn gave him a sense of importance. He was allowed to help round up the cows, bring in the eggs and fill the milk churns. His tiny brothers revered him and his sister, Mary, positively doted on him. The life was irresistible, and even Hilda he could not but warm to, which was made easier by the fact that she was so very different from his mother. At bedtime each night, the dry, light kiss he remembered, was replaced by a bone-crushing bear-hug as Hilda scooped him into her arms. He liked the feel of so much demonstrative love. He was shy of it, but he enjoyed it, and as each day passed, he thought less and less of his mother, until each night he fell into an uncomplicated slumber, without even shedding a single tear on her behalf.

In fact Charlie never saw his mother again. The next contact he had with her was at the Crematorium, when he was ten years old. His mother had died, was all his father told him. They sat apart from the other mourners, but Charlie could feel their accusing eyes boring into his back, and he and his father left immediately after the service was over and hurried back to the cosy comfort of Blandings Farm.

Strangely, once his mother was dead, Charlie found he

thought about her far more often, and he had reached the age of questioning the decisions of others. Why did his father have two families? Why had he left his mother to live with Hilda? The less satisfactory the answers and the more he became aware of the discomfort his questions caused, the more he persisted with them. It gave him a strange sense of power which he revelled in.

One night, when Charlie was fifteen, and struggling with a difficult homework late into the night, he went downstairs to fetch himself a drink. Halfway down the stairs he heard raised voices. It was unusual for Hilda and his father to argue – even in his current frame of mind, Charlie had to concede they had a good relationship. 'But sometime he's bound to find out,' Hilda was saying. 'It's amazing nobody's told him already. You've got to tell him, Pete, he needs to hear it from you, not from anyone else.'

'I can't tell him, I just can't. Put yourself in my position.'

'It's not your position that concerns me,' said Hilda, 'It's Charlie's. You and me made our decision, knowing at least some of the problems it would cause, but Charlie, he had no part in it – he was not responsible. Don't you see how important it is he recognizes that what happened was not his fault.'

Charlie could contain himself no longer. He burst through the kitchen door. 'What's not my fault?'

His father turned on him, shocked and angry. 'What the hell are you doing skulking outside the door. Eavesdropping now, is it – you should be ashamed of yourself.'

Charlie ignored him and turned to Hilda. 'What isn't my fault, Hilda?' he asked, quietly. His eyes held hers, willing her to speak.

She could not deny him. 'Your mother, Charlie. The way she died – you see, she committed suicide.'

His mind reeled. 'How?' he managed.

'Oh for Christ's sake, does it matter?' his father burst out.

'Yes, of course it matters,' said Hilda. 'A gas fire, she left the gas on, shut all the windows and blocked up the door.'

'In which room?' Charlie asked.

'The dining room.'

Charlie had a vision of the neat, little dining room, with the polished table and bowl of roses in the centre. He tried to imagine his mother lying in front of the gas fire while her life ebbed away.

His father made an effort. 'Look, old lad, I should have told you about this before but I thought you were too young. Hilda's right, though, you're old enough to know now. Your mother wasn't right in the head, Charlie, that's the truth of it.'

Charlie stared at him. 'There was nothing wrong with my mother until we left her,' he said, his voice suddenly choked with tears. 'She killed herself because of us – didn't she, didn't she?'

'No, of course not,' said Charlie's father, but he turned away, shrinking from his son's anger as if he had been struck.

'Yes, she did,' Charlie shouted. 'She didn't kill herself, *we killed her*.' He turned and ran out of the kitchen door, slamming it behind him and flying up the stairs, to throw himself on his bed and sob as if his heart would break.

From that moment, Blandings Farm was finished for Charlie. He had no right to enjoy it, his easy seduction had cost his mother her life. They all tried with him, the children and Hilda especially, but as soon as he turned seventeen he left home. He was not angry with Hilda nor even his father, because the way he saw things it was not really their fault. His mother had not killed herself because his father had left her for another woman – another woman by whom he already had three children. She was a sensible woman, she would have accepted the situation. No, Doris Robins killed herself because her only child had abandoned her.

The knowledge had left him with a burden of guilt he would carry for the rest of his life. It also gave him a unique understanding of the anguish of mind to which Laura Melhuish was subjected following her husband's disappearance. He had failed his mother, but he was determined not to repeat the mistake with Laura. Helping her seemed to ease the tortured meanderings of his mind.

Charlie let himself through the main front door of Nelson Street with his landlord's key, bounded up the stairs, tapped on the door to Laura's flat and burst into a horrendous rendering of 'Happy Birthday'. She opened the door immediately. 'I heard you on the stairs,' she said, smiling.

'I can't think how you knew it was me!' said Charlie.

'Nobody bounces up the stairs like you, Charlie – you do everything at full speed, and as for your singing . . .' Her hair was newly washed and it hung in thick dark curls to well below her shoulders. For once she had put on a little makeup and it suited her, as did the long, blue woollen dress which, although tent-like to contain her bulk, enhanced her colouring. She was wearing a light perfume and the smell intoxicated him. Standing there, so close to her, it was all he could do to stop himself taking her in his arms. She shrugged her shoulders and smiled at him, charmingly. 'I'm awfully sorry, I'm afraid I have nothing to offer you to drink.'

'That's alright, we'll have a drink at the restaurant. Have you a coat?' She shook her head. 'Silly girl, we'll just have to walk fast then, it's a cold night.'

The evening was a considerable success. It was the first time Laura had been out with a man since Francis's disappearance, and several times, while waiting for Charlie to arrive, she had nearly telephoned to cancel their dinner. Now she was glad she had come. Charlie was a kind and considerate host, and she found his company both stimulating and revealing.

They had talked so much about her problems in the weeks they had known one another, she tried to persuade Charlie to, for once, tell her about himself and his family. Of his family he would say nothing at all, but she learnt that his life since leaving home had been colourful, to say the least.

'I left home at seventeen,' Charlie said, 'And I suppose you could say became an embryo terrorist. I lived in squats and joined in every bit of trouble.'

'You!' said Laura. 'I don't believe it – you're not the type at all.'

'I fell in with a crowd – CND, international socialists, anti-Vietnam . . . I've been involved in the lot – still am now and again for the odd demo or sit in.'

'Good heavens, I'm sorry to sound so surprised, Charlie, but how do you relate your beliefs to, well, being a blatant capitalist – a landlord, an entrepreneur – hardly good bedfellows with anarchy, surely?'

'No, perhaps not, but the business is Giles's really – it's his money, his flair, his ideas – I just do all the work.' His words sounded bitter.

'Alright, but what changed the anarchist into a respectable member of society?'

'Prison,' said Charlie, bluntly.

His words stunned Laura. 'Oh, I see,' she said, lamely.

Charlie grinned and refilled their wine glasses. 'No you don't see. Look at you – now you're thinking I might have robbed a bank or murdered my granny. I was only sent down for five weeks – a breach of the peace, that's all. I had a scuffle with a policeman but it was my first offence so they went easy. It sobered me though – being inside's no picnic.'

'I can imagine,' said Laura, thoughtfully. 'So what happened when you came out?'

'Hopeless,' said Charlie. 'I couldn't get a job with my record. I bummed around and then one day I met Giles in a pub. I needed a job, he needed a work horse – it was as simple as that. In the early days, he couldn't afford to pay me so I lived free in his flat, and simply took a cut of whatever came our way. The partnership grew from there – we've been together five years now.'

'Yet despite the time you've worked together, I sense you don't really like him – is that right, Charlie?'

Charlie considered the question. '*Like?* Well, we get along alright, I suppose, but I don't approve of what he stands for – the arrogance of his class and the natural assumption that it's OK for him to give all the orders. I'm still a fully paid up member of the Communist Party – I believe in what the Party stands for, and that's light years away from how Giles Latham conducts his life.'

'You're a dark horse, Charlie,' said Laura smiling.

'So are you,' said Charlie. 'Here's to dark horses, everywhere.' They raised their glasses and drank a silent toast.

'Why are you so kind to me?' Laura asked, suddenly.

Charlie shrugged his big frame and as he made no attempt to answer the question, Laura was forced to persevere.

'Charlie, this is awfully presumptuous of me, but you know there can be nothing between us, don't you? I'm not a fit person for anyone to get fond of at the moment, I'm still far too much bound up with Francis and his baby.'

There was a sudden cold, tight knot deep in Charlie's chest, but he smiled brightly. 'I understand all that, Laura. We're friends, I'm not expecting anything more.'

But he was expecting more, and at that moment he knew it with an unshakeable conviction. He had been biding his time, waiting until the baby was born, until Laura was strong again, and then she would be his. It was all so obvious, he wondered why on earth he had not realized it before. 'Come on,' he said, frightened lest his amazing revelation should be apparent to her as well, 'I'd better take you home.'

After Charlie had left, Laura felt restless despite the late hour. Although she had eaten and drunk sparingly, it was a vast meal by her normal standards. She felt vaguely sick and uneasy, and made a cup of tea only to find she could not drink it. Instead, she wandered aimlessly about the flat. She was due for a checkup at the clinic the following day, and after that, she decided, she would move to Oxford. The baby was due in less than two weeks and Eleanor had arranged everything – a bed in the John Radcliffe hospital and the transfer of her papers to a local gynaecologist. Considering how badly Laura had behaved at the time they had discussed abortion, Eleanor had been very forgiving. She had even insisted that Laura should return to her house after the birth for a few weeks, before taking up the threads of life alone again. Laura had eventually written and told her mother about the baby. Katrine had begged her to come back home, but Laura had been adamant – she had to make a life of her own.

At last, the pacing wearied her. She undressed and sank into bed. Her back ached, she could find no comfortable position in which to lie and she was also very cold. The wind was whistling outside, the weather forecast earlier had threatened snow. She must have slept for suddenly she was aware of being forced awake. For a moment she thought it must have been a noise she had heard, and then she realized it was not a noise but pain. At the same time, she was aware of a wetness between her legs – the baby was coming early.

She was terrified – this was not supposed to happen, she was supposed to be with Eleanor. Competent Eleanor – a doctor, a mother of two, who would know what to do. To be alone here, in this cold, damp flat was no longer a challenge, it was a threat – a threat to survival. She knew she should call the hospital but a feeling of hopelessness spread over her – she did not know the number and she had not even packed a case yet. The pain came again, grinding, gnawing. She cried out, more from surprise than anything. It faded, as quickly as it had come and she knew, before the next one, she must reach the phone. She climbed gingerly out of bed, feeling for the light.

Somehow it was not where she expected it to be, she felt so disorientated. She groped her way to the bedroom door, out on to the landing and began feeling her way along the corridor.

It was the rubbish bin that tripped her up – a small bucket put out for the morning. She stumbled over it and began pitching forward. She was almost at the entrance to the sitting room and as she fell, her temple struck the little sofa table just inside the door. As the blackness came, she had one single moment of lucid thought – this fall was going to kill Francis's baby, and the baby's death would be her fault just as surely as his father's had been hers, too.

Charlie did not go straight home. Despite the biting cold wind, he buttoned his duffle coat around him and walked down to the edge of the river. The coldness of the night gave the atmosphere an incredible clarity. He looked upstream towards the West End, the whole sky was bathed in orange. There was no one about, it was as though he was the last person left on earth. His footsteps echoed as he walked along the towpath – Laura, Laura – her name rang in his ears. He loved her, he knew that now. After his mother, she was the first woman he had ever loved, and, with a sickening clarity, he knew she would be the last – an enigma, a one-off – the only person who could inspire these feelings. He was used to straightforward desire – that he could handle, but this emotion flummoxed him. The most important thing in the world to him at that moment was Laura's happiness, health and well-being – his own needs were of no consequence. He longed to see laughter in her face, to see her eyes sparkle, and somehow he had to find a way to achieve that. He was not a man who had a way with words – Giles could have handled her better, he thought, without envy.

Somewhere, a clock struck one, the cold was eating into his very bones. Charlie turned for home, the wind mercifully at his back. Yet when he reached the shop and saw from the lights in the flat above that Giles was still up, he knew he could not face going in. Giles with his questions, his ridicule, his thinly veiled criticism. On an impulse, Charlie kept walking, back up the road towards Laura's flat. It was not until her window was in view that he realized he had been hoping she would be still awake. Clearly she was not for there were no lights. He realized, too, that he had already formed an excuse for calling back – she was getting near her time now and she ought to have his telephone number in case the baby started while she was alone. She had the shop number, he knew, and the wine bar, but not the flat number. He stared up at the darkened windows momentarily undecided as to what to do. He would call round tomorrow morning with the number, that was best. He turned and began walking down the hill again. Then he stopped. The force of the wind blowing in his face seemed to be trying to tell him something. Cursing himself for his own stupidity, he returned to the flat and hovered outside the front door for a few moments. Finally, it was sheer cold that forced a decision on him. She would not like the idea of him using his pass key to enter her flat, particularly when she was asleep in bed. However, if he crept in quietly and left his number by the telephone, he need not disturb her and then at least, hopefully, he would be able to sleep himself.

Before he even heard the sound of her whimpering, he knew something was wrong. Standing by the flat door, fumbling with his key, he experienced, as an animal experiences, the twin sensations of danger and fear. Without hesitation he snapped on the hall light and saw her lying sprawled on the floor. So this was why he had come back, why he had been unable to sleep. He ran to the telephone and began dialling 999, thanking God he had not denied his instincts.

Francis Charles Melhuish took fourteen hours to make his debut on to this earth – fourteen hours which exhausted his already frail mother to the point of becoming life-threatening – fourteen hours which did at least enable his future godmother, Eleanor Berry, to drive down from Oxford through the rush hour traffic to Blackheath and make it in time to hold his mother's hand during the last agonizing moments of birth.

Before passing into an exhausted sleep, Laura caught a brief glimpse of her son. He was his father's child in features and colouring. Even the tiny, but long-limbed body seemed familiar. The resemblance did not bring pain, in fact quite the reverse, it brought a profound sense of relief. Francis's replica lived even if he, himself, was dead. When, hours later, she woke and had her baby son placed in her arms for the first time, the likeness to his father had already faded a little, and he began to establish himself as an individual in her eyes. She examined him carefully, his toes, his fingers. She gazed into his blue eyes, which she realized were her own, not Francis's. She felt the burden of responsibility, of inadequacy, of guilt take hold of her – the burden that all parents feel. With it, though, came something else. As she watched the tiny, sleeping face, for the first time she knew what it was to love someone unreservedly. She hugged the tiny body to her. She was no longer alone – there were the two of them against the world now.

CHAPTER ELEVEN

During Laura's protracted labour, it soon became evident to Eleanor that she had two patients on her hands – the other was Charlie. He paced the hospital waiting room in an appalling state of agitation. He had convinced himself that Laura was dying and nothing Eleanor could say would convince him otherwise. In truth, his fears were far from groundless. As Dr Edwards confided to Eleanor, Laura was hopelessly underweight, very weak and apparently had no desire to fight. It was touch and go.

It was because of the seriousness of the situation that Eleanor broke all the rules of friendship. She had faithfully promised Laura not to contact her parents, but in the circumstances it seemed criminal not to do so. She gave Charlie both the Beechams' telephone number and that of William Campling. 'Don't frighten them,' she said to Charlie, 'but tell them Laura is having a difficult time and I think it would be sensible for them to come.' Seeing the stricken expression on his face, she added, 'By the time they get here, Charlie, the baby will be born. Now for heaven's sake remember, they're fairly elderly, so be tactful or they'll go and pile themselves up on the motorway.'

Contrary to what Charlie had expected, the telephone call to Lord Campling was the easier of the two. Bernard Beecham was both aggressive and suspicious when Charlie made his call. 'Who are you anyway?' he demanded.

'A friend of your daughter's,' said Charlie.

'A friend?' Bernard made it sound like an accusation.

'Well, actually I own the flat in which Laura lives.'

'I see . . .' Bernard's hostility seemed to be crackling down the telephone line towards him.

'I'm just her landlord,' Charlie felt compelled to explain. 'I found her this morning in the early hours. She'd already started having the baby. Eleanor Berry, you know, the doctor friend of hers, says it's due any time, but it's not an easy birth, sir, and Eleanor suggests you and your wife should be here.'

'We're on our way,' said Bernard.

As it happened, Eleanor was right. By the time the three grandparents arrived, Francis was safely delivered and bawling his head off. Laura, mercifully, was asleep and therefore did not witness the scene in which her father demanded that she be moved into a private room and that a private paediatric nurse be employed to look after his grandson. 'I'm not having the boy in the nursery,' Bernard said, in response to Eleanor's attempts at intervention, 'he might catch something.'

The scene reached the ears of Dr Edwards, who appeared like the wrath of God. He marched Bernard and an almost hysterical Katrine into the waiting room, together with Lord Campling and Eleanor. Dr Edwards did not mince his words. 'Your daughter, among other things, Sir Bernard, is suffering from severe malnutrition. Her will to live seems non-existent and she is so exhausted, it will take her weeks, if not months, to get over this birth. I don't know why a twenty-three-year-old girl – who, I understand from Dr Berry, is almost certainly a widow – should have been allowed to get in this state, when she has such obviously influential and wealthy relations. However, since you have let this happen, I must insist that you follow, precisely to the letter, my instructions for getting her well again.'

At his words, Katrine burst into a storm of tears. 'I'm so sorry, Doctor, but she wouldn't let us help. I tried but she would not even see me. She said she wanted to live her own life, to be independent of us.'

Dr Edwards looked directly at Bernard. 'Judging by the way you have behaved in this hospital during the last half hour, I'm not entirely surprised.'

'Now look here . . .,' Bernard began.

'I'm sorry, I withdraw the remark, we're all overtired, but I am very concerned about your daughter. I am happy for her to stay in a private room because she needs rest above everything else and it will ensure that she has peace and quiet. However, I do not want your grandson taken out of the nursery away from the other babies. In a couple of days, I want Laura up and about, and then I want her mixing with other mothers. I don't know your daughter well, Sir Bernard, she didn't become a patient of mine until the early hours of this morning, but in my view she's deeply disturbed and contact with other young mothers is vital at this stage, when all women feel rather emotional.'

'If she's as ill as you say, then she shouldn't be expected to look after the baby.' Bernard's expression was stubborn.

'Sir Bernard, you must allow me to judge what your daughter should or should not do. I have to say that if you're not prepared to follow my advice then I suggest you move both your daughter and grandson to another hospital, a private nursing home perhaps, where what you are prepared to pay may influence the attitude of the medical staff to your demands.'

Eleanor blanched. What Dr Edwards was saying was right but she braced herself for the explosion. It did not come. Bernard remained mulish, but miraculously silent. 'Please, darling,' said Katrine, placing a hand tentatively on his arm. 'I'm sure Dr Edwards knows best. After all . . .' there was a sob in her voice, 'we haven't seen Laura for nearly nine months so how can we judge how ill she really is.'

'Alright,' said Bernard, standing up, 'have it your own way but I expect nothing but the best of care for my daughter. Is that clear?'

'I do my very best for all my patients,' Dr Edwards said, uncompromisingly.

'I'm going for a walk,' said Bernard, 'hospitals make me feel claustrophobic.'

'I'll come with you,' said William Campling, and much to everyone's surprise, Bernard did not argue.

After the men had left the room, Dr Edwards visibly relaxed. 'Look, Lady Beecham, do you mind me talking frankly to you in front of Dr Berry?'

Katrine smiled at Eleanor. 'No, no of course not, Eleanor is a good friend of my daughter's.'

'Sadly, I see hundreds of cases like your daughter's – young women come in here to have a baby, a baby they usually do not want. The birth of their baby makes them single parents, they have been existing on Social Security, perhaps all their adult life and pregnancy and childbirth are the final straw. They're trapped, they have no hope, they are ill in mind and body, and all set to bring up their child to make exactly the same mistakes as they themselves made. It's a sad and vicious circle.' He hesitated. 'In most cases there is no remedy, we do the best we can for them and then cast them adrift again – it's all we can do. However, Laura's case is different. Somehow you have to persuade her to accept help from you. She urgently needs a better home, a better diet and emotional support, too – for herself and her baby.'

'She won't accept anything from us,' Katrine said, almost in a whisper. 'It's my husband, you see, he tries to take over her life.'

'I understand,' said Dr Edwards, 'but this is one battle you must win. You're going to have to be an immensely clever diplomat, Lady Beecham,' his eyes twinkled, 'but I'm sure you're up to the job. Make it easy for her to accept a little help from you – don't flood her with gifts, just a little help here and there to ease the load. For example, find out what she already has for the baby. Say you want to give him a present and buy some of the vital things she needs. Don't frighten her off, or you'll lose her for good.'

'You're a very wise man, Dr Edwards,' Katrine said. 'I will try very hard to take your advice. The most pressing problem is where she goes when she leaves hospital. She certainly mustn't go back to her flat, and I don't think she will come home with me and her father.'

'She's coming home with me,' said Eleanor, 'it was arranged before the baby was born. She can stay as long as she likes.'

'It's awfully good of you,' said Katrine. 'I'd so love her to be with me but in the circumstances . . .'

Laura stayed with the Berrys for three months, three months during which her son turned from the delicate baby, with whom she had first fallen in love, into a chubby, noisy, rip-roaring character. Physically, he still looked heartbreakingly like his father, yet to Laura's growing relief, there the similarity seemed to end – baby Francis did not take himself, nor life too seriously. The blue eyes that met hers were merry and everything that happened to him he took in his stride. He adored Eddie and Thomas, the dog, the cat, and every new person he met seemed to give him pleasure.

Laura slowly improved – physically at any rate. However, her listless acceptance of each day as it came, without apparently having any plans for the future, worried Eleanor far more than her lack of weight and pale face. It soon became clear that the flat at Greenwich could be re-let, since there was no way Laura was ready to cope alone. Charlie packed up her belongings and stored them in his own flat, and although her possessions were pitifully few, Giles was characteristically difficult about the amount of space they absorbed. 'I suppose you think that now she's had the baby, you'll have a chance of getting your leg over,' he said to Charlie. 'From what I hear, old boy, you're way out of line. The last thing women have on their mind when they've had a baby is a bit of nookey. It'll be months before she'll even look at you . . . if at all.'

'Belt up, you stupid bugger,' Charlie said, viciously, and even Giles recognized it was time to do just that.

Giles Latham was not the only person less than happy with Laura's impact on their lives. After three months, Chris Berry felt Laura had been with them long enough. 'She's got to go,' he said to Eleanor one night. They were lying, side by side, in bed but not touching. Their relationship had been strained for some weeks.

'Chris, we've been through it a hundred times, I'm not throwing her out of the house.'

'If you don't, I will.'

'You're being terribly unfair, Chris. The baby's no trouble –he's absolutely sweet.'

'It's not the baby who upsets me, it's Laura. She has a dampening, depressing effect on the house, and far more important, we're never alone these days.'

'We're alone now,' said Eleanor.

'Yes, alright, in bed.'

'Well, surely that's the only place where we actually need to be alone.'

'Don't you remember our nights together in the sitting room?' Chris said. 'The roaring fire, you and me and . . .'

'Yes, yes,' said Eleanor, 'of course I do, but this is only a temporary phase. Besides which, it's June – nobody has a roaring fire in June.'

Chris sat up in bed, snapped on the light and turned to study his wife. She looked tired and strained, he noticed. A full-time job as an anaesthetist, two preschool children, a neurotic friend and her new baby, and him griping all the time . . . it was taking its toll, and for a moment he felt guilty for being so contentious. Then he hardened his heart – Laura and Francis were the cause of the strain. Without them, the family would be able to cope far better. 'Darling, Laura's father is one of the richest men in the country. Laura's mother adores her and would give her right arm to have her daughter living at home. Laura's father-in-law is a man of influence and power who is desperate to steep his grandson in the Campling tradition, and would do anything in the world for Laura to further his ends. And that leaves us. This time last year, we'd only just met Laura. She's not a lifelong friend. It just so happened that the taverna she chose to collapse in was the one in which we were having a hard-earned holiday.'

'She is a good friend,' said Eleanor, defensively, 'at least she's a good friend of mine.'

'And of mine,' said Chris. 'I like her, genuinely, but this is our life, our marriage, our home and I want to be alone with my wife and children again. Besides which, I don't even think you're doing her any favours by letting her opt out of life like this – it's time she got back into the swim of things.'

'She's no home, no job . . .'

'She has a bloody sight more on offer than most people. No, I'm sorry, darling, I'm not prepared to play nursemaid to Laura Melhuish any more. I just don't feel that sorry for her – perhaps I should, but I don't. I do feel bloody sorry for us, however. You can have tomorrow in which to tell her she must leave and if you haven't tackled the subject by the time I come home, I'll talk to her myself.'

'I'm working tomorrow,' said Eleanor.

'Then you'll have to get up early and speak to her before you go to work.'

'There isn't time, the children . . .'

'Then you'll just have to make time.'

'Chris, why are you being so horrible? You didn't used to be this hard, you've changed recently, you really have.'

Chris shook his head. 'No, *I* haven't changed, it's just our circumstances which have changed. We're all under too much pressure and the strain is starting to show. If Laura were destitute then I agree we would have to think out this decision a little more carefully, but she's not, she has choices and so, by God, do we. You or I, Eleanor – I don't mind which – are going to tell Laura that she has to find somewhere else to live – fast.'

As it happened neither of them had to issue Laura with the ultimatum. When Chris got up the following morning to make early morning tea, he found Laura already in the hall. Neatly stacked were her two suitcases, pram wheels and Francis asleep in his carrycot. She looked pale and strained but quite composed. 'Going somewhere?' said Chris, lightly.

'Yes, I'm leaving.'

'Leaving! But why?' He tried to introduce a note of regret into his voice but with little success.

'I'm sorry, Chris,' said Laura, 'there's nothing more despicable than eavesdropping, but I was in the bathroom last night when you and Eleanor were talking and I couldn't help but hear what you said. You were . . . well, you were rather agitated and your voice carried.'

'I see,' said Chris.

'I do understand how you feel, Chris, I really do, and of course, you're absolutely right, Francis and I being here must have put a strain on your marriage. The trouble is I've been so wrapped up with myself and my problems, I've been too preoccupied to notice. What you said to Eleanor last night was exactly what I needed to hear. I've been awake most of the night thinking things through, and I have a plan. I'm just sorry it's taken me so long.'

The relief was evident on Chris's face. 'I must say, Laura,

it's very decent of you to take it like this. Mind you, I thought you would, as a matter of fact, which was why I was so cross with Eleanor for not talking to you about it before.'

'Well now she doesn't need to. It's why I'm leaving so early so as to avoid embarrassment. I've called a taxi and I've left a cheque by the telephone. It's not much, but it must just about cover what Francis and I have eaten. I hope it's OK.'

'There's no need for that,' said Chris.

'Yes, there is.' Laura's eyes sparkled, her small pointed chin held high.

You're better, Chris thought, you're better than I've ever seen you. This must be the sort of person you were before Francis Melhuish disappeared. They were staring at one another in silence when, outside in the street, they heard the peep from a car horn. 'That'll be the taxi, I'll help you with your stuff,' said Chris. In a moment Laura and Francis were stowed into the car. Chris kissed her on both cheeks. 'Good luck,' he said.

'Thanks, and thank you for everything.' Laura hesitated. 'Not just for your hospitality, but for making me realize that I must start a life of my own.'

'I bet you think I'm an awful sod,' said Chris.

'No, I don't, quite the contrary, I think you're a very nice man and Eleanor's very lucky to have you.'

It was a sentiment Eleanor did not share, when a few minutes later Chris told her Laura had left. 'What do you mean, she's gone?' Eleanor demanded.

'She took a taxi just now, to the station. She overheard our conversation last night and recognized it was time to move on, so that's just what she has done.'

'And you let her go?' said Eleanor. 'Chris, how could you? You must stop her, drive to the station, there's probably still time.'

'I'll do no such thing,' Chris thundered, 'she wants to go and she's grateful for having been brought face-to-face with reality. She actually said that, Eleanor.'

'It's bad enough that you've driven her away,' said Eleanor, 'without congratulating yourself on what you've done. I hope to God you're never in trouble, and needing a friend, Chris, because after the way you've treated Laura, you don't deserve to have anybody to help you.'

'You're wrong about this, Eleanor, you're over-reacting.'

'I'm right and you know it. Where is she going, anyway?'

Chris looked startled. 'I – I've no idea.'

'You mean you didn't ask? You let her go off as she is, still very weak, with that new-born baby, without knowing where she is going?'

'Francis is not a new-born baby, he's three months old as we know to our cost. He is thriving well and Laura's a very good mother. She won't do anything to jeopardize Francis's well-being.'

'But she could be anywhere.'

'She'll be in touch,' said Chris, 'when she's good and ready.'

'Up until now I've always thought that you and I shared the same views on all major issues, but over this, I just don't understand you, Chris. These days I feel I'm living with a stranger.' Eleanor's voice was full of despair.

Eleanor and Chris never did quite go back to their old ways, like making love in front of the sitting room fire and sharing the easy camaraderie of their early married life. There was no way it was right to hold Laura responsible for the gradual disintegration of their marriage, but for some reason her protracted stay had acted as the catalyst. When, four years later, their marriage finally collapsed, Eleanor looked back to Francis's birth as being the moment from when things started to go wrong.

Giles and Diana were sharing the luxury of a sunken bath. Diana, tired of hotel life, had taken a temporary lease on an apartment just off Park Lane. It belonged to a wealthy Arab and everything about the flat was luxurious to the point of decadence – particularly the bathroom which was all marble and gold-plate. Giles was painting Diana's toe-nails, her feet propped up on the edge of the bath, out of the way of the water. They were both drinking champagne. It was their second bottle and the combination of the steam, the alcohol and Diana's toe-nails – which were being painted gold to match the bathroom – had them in hopeless hysterics of laughter. It was while they were in this parlous state that the doorbell rang. 'You'll have to go, darling,' Diana said.

'How can I?' said Giles. 'The spectacle of me answering your door naked, with a bottle of champagne in one hand and gold nail polish in the other, won't do anything for your reputation.'

'My reputation is already beyond repair,' said Diana. 'Besides which, you could always wrap a bath towel round you.'

It seemed a reasonable suggestion, but Giles was not at all certain he could stand up. 'You could go instead,' he suggested. 'It is your flat, after all.'

'Ah, but we have to consider my toe-nails,' said Diana. 'If I smudge them, you'll have to start all over again.'

'That, I am not doing,' said Giles.

'Then, my darling, you'd better go and open the door.'

Although they had never met, Giles and Laura recognized one another instantly, with a degree of mutual suspicion and preconceived dislike. Most of the dislike stemmed from their entirely opposing views on the subject of Charlie. While Giles felt that Laura was turning his easy-going, uncomplicated partner into a neurotic wimp, Laura favoured Charlie's view that Giles exploited him, leaving him to do all the work while Giles took most of the money. There was sufficient justification in both points of view to make their expressions of righteous indignation, at this their first encounter, almost identical. Giles also could not help noticing the suitcases, the pram wheels and the sleeping child in the carrycot. 'You're Laura,' he said, making it sound like an accusation.

'And you have to be Giles,' said Laura, allowing her gaze to wander over his dripping form. It was not a displeasing sight – Giles was broad-shouldered and muscular and modesty was saved only by a minute bath towel.

Giles raised an eyebrow. 'You're moving in, I take it?'

'Just for a few days,' said Laura, 'assuming Diana will have me. I have plans you see, plans for her and me.'

'Oh you do? Well, I suppose you'd better come in. She's currently in the bath, drinking champagne but no doubt you won't mind waiting . . .' He glanced at the carrycot, '. . . either of you.'

CHAPTER TWELVE

'Di, it's Laura!' Diana let out a shriek and there were hectic sounds of splashing as she erupted from the bath. 'Oh God,' said Giles. 'Mind your toe-nails.'

'Whilst you may not altogether approve of me,' Giles said, 'I can assure you I have not been pulling her toe-nails out one by one. I was simply painting them for her in the bath.' Laura laughed and the tension between them eased a little as Giles found himself smiling back. Watch it, old son, he thought. This girl has a strange ability to attract people and I have more than enough complications in my life. He secured the bath towel more firmly round his waist. 'Let me help you bring in your stuff,' he said, graciously.

'No, it's alright,' said Laura. 'I'm not sure Mayfair can cope with you in a bath towel.'

Giles ignored her and grabbed the carrycot in one hand and the wheels in the other. Francis did not stir as he lifted him through to the sitting room. 'A remarkably good baby,' said Giles, 'I thought they always screamed.'

'I've just stuffed him full of milk,' said Laura. 'I thought if I was going to try and persuade Diana to let me stay, it was important to present Francis at his best.'

Giles liked her candour. 'I'm afraid Di and I are pissed,' he admitted. 'We've been drinking champagne since ten o'clock this morning and have missed lunch altogether. There's still half a bottle left – you'd be doing us a favour if you joined in.'

'Darling . . .' Diana burst into the room, looking totally spectacular in a mauve kaftan. She wore a thick, gold bracelet, a heavy gold necklace and large dangling earrings, which, combined with her gold toe-nails, made a truly stunning sight.

'Sorry about the garb, darling,' she said, kissing Laura. 'I realize it's not terribly suitable for a Sunday afternoon but well, we've . . .,' she glanced at Giles, '. . . only really just got up.'

'I hear you've been drinking champagne all morning,' said Laura.

'We have, darling . . . oh, my dear,' she caught sight of Francis, still angelically asleep. 'Laura, he's gorgeous. Can I pick him up.'

'No, you certainly can't,' said Laura, 'the longer he's like that, the better. There'll be plenty of time to juggle him around later,' she hesitated, 'that is, if you'll have me, Diana.'

'Have you! You mean you're coming to stay?'

'If it's alright, just for a few days.'

'Of course it's alright.' Diana glanced at Giles, expecting an outraged expression. Instead, he was busying himself pouring a glass of champagne for Laura and looking almost affable.

Laura accepted the glass and perched herself on the edge of the sofa, beside the carrycot. 'Actually, I'm really here because I have an idea I want to talk to you about, and Giles could be very useful, because we need an unbiased commercial view.' Laura looked at Giles appealingly.

'I take it you're asking for my advice?' he said. 'How very flattering.'

Diana looked from one to the other with surprise. It was a relationship she had imagined would be doomed from the start, yet clearly they were already getting on well. Giles collapsed into an armchair and Diana sat at his feet. 'Go on then,' she said, encouragingly.

Laura addressed herself to Giles. 'I suppose you know a little about me from Charlie and Di.'

'You could say that,' said Giles, dryly. 'One way and another, you're usually the main topic of conversation.'

Laura looked genuinely nonplussed. 'Oh Lord, would you rather not get involved in this?'

'I don't know what *this* is yet, but I'm hopelessly hooked now – you'll have to tell me your plan – I can hardly wait.' There was only a trace of irony in his voice. It provided just enough encouragement for Laura to continue.

'Well, since Francis disappeared, I've been in a sort of state of limbo, incapable really of making even the smallest decision. In fact, when I look back over the last year, I feel very ashamed.' She glanced down at the carrycot. 'I've looked after the baby well enough but, if anything, I feel I've leaned on him rather than the other way round. His birth has been my sort of *raison d'être* – and, he's pulled me through. I honestly don't know how I would have survived without him.' She smiled briefly, 'Awful isn't it, owing one's sanity to a three-months-old baby?'

'Not at all surprising in the circumstances,' said Diana.

'Two things happened yesterday which changed me – quite suddenly.' Laura twisted the stem of her glass. 'The first was the date – it was the anniversary of Francis's disappearance. For a full year now he has been missing from my life, yet I realized when I got up yesterday that I was in exactly the same state of shocked inertia as I'd been in Rhodes. In other words, I had progressed not at all, and most of my emotion is wasted on feeling sorry for myself. The second thing that happened yesterday was that last night Eleanor and Chris – they're friends I've been staying with,' she explained to Giles, 'had a row – horrifyingly, about me. It was a totally understandable row. Chris has had enough of me mooching around the house and he wanted his home back for the exclusive use of his family. Eleanor felt she couldn't let me go out into the big, bad world because I wasn't capable of fending for myself at the moment. It was dreadful to listen to them. They were in Rhodes when Francis disappeared and they were wonderful – incredibly kind and helpful, and obviously, at the time, a very happy couple. To hear them arguing last night, because of me, I just can't tell you how guilty it made me feel. Anyway, I didn't go to bed, I sat up all night, drinking endless cups of coffee, and thought about my future and the future of my son. By this morning I'd come to the conclusion that it's time I started to make my own way in life instead of collapsing all over people. Whether my husband is dead or alive is not relevant, that's how I have to look at it, for it's the only way I'll get back to living again.'

'Bravo,' said Diana, 'that is music to my ears, darling.'

'I know it is, and I'm sorry I've taken so long to come to my senses, and I'm sorry I was so rude to you when you were only trying to help.'

'It must have been dreadful for you,' Giles said, quietly, glimpsing for the first time what Laura must have felt. 'It's the uncertainty that must be so paralysing.'

'Yes, that's right,' said Laura, 'but it's in the past now. What I want to talk about concerns the future.' She took a gulp of her champagne. 'I want . . . independence, but also a sense of commitment, and I also have a living to earn to support my baby and provide a roof over our heads. I thought about freelance journalism but it's too insecure and in any event, it means me working long hours on my own. I think I'm probably introspective and peculiar enough as it is, so I decided a business of my own was the answer.' Laura looked directly at Diana. 'Di, you're really at a loose end – your money's given you freedom, but freedom to do what? You've travelled the world – great – but now what?'

'I don't know,' said Diana, taking a melancholy sip of her champagne.

'So,' said Laura, 'why don't we join forces and start our own business?'

'Doing what?' Giles asked.

'Running a restaurant,' said Laura, without hesitation.

'But do you know anything about it?' said Giles.

'Well, in a way, yes I do. I've had no formal training, though I think I cook well.'

'Very well,' Diana confirmed.

'And I have reviewed restaurants for years. I must know better than most exactly what makes a restaurant successful. I also know, or think I know, where there is a mighty gap in the market.'

'And where would that be?' Giles asked, a little too indulgently.

Laura hesitated. 'Over the last ten years, people have gradually started having holidays abroad – not just the rich but all classes and income groups. It has introduced a whole new range of people to wine and foreign cooking, and also to relaxed and casual eating out – café, bistro style.'

'Go on,' said Giles.

'Even today, eating out always tends to be a big event to celebrate something. No one simply has a meal out because they're tired or don't want to cook. I'm suggesting we open a bistro which offers good basic, home-made food at rock-bottom prices, accompanied by lashings of house wine, fresh vegetables and proper coffee.'

'And who do you see as your customers?' said Giles.

'Everyone, that's the point. I suppose there would be a tendency for it to be aimed more at the young, but not necessarily so.'

'And whereabouts would you run your restaurant?'

'Somewhere round South Kensington, where there is the most rented accommodation. I think we should open evenings only to start with, plus Sunday lunch.'

'I think it's a brilliant idea,' said Diana, 'but I don't honestly see where I come into all this.'

'In every possible way,' said Laura. 'Initially, there's the question of money. If you would put up half the money, a bank will allow me to borrow the other half, so that we can be equal partners in a commercial sense.' Both Diana and Giles fought the temptation to ask why she did not simply borrow the money from her father, but neither dared. There was a pioneer light in Laura's eye – she was in the mood to be listened to, not questioned. 'Then we have to find the right premises, work out the interior, the decorations, the equipment, hire staff, advertise and promote . . . it's not something one person can do on her own, but we could do it together. You're awfully bright, Di, far brighter than me. You have a brilliant sense of colour and design, you're good with people. It's simply a question of our carving up the jobs between us.'

'I'm not sure I'm up to it.' Diana stood up and poured herself another glass of champagne, her movements were jerky, nervous.

'Of course you're up to it,' said Giles, 'and it's a damn good idea, a thundering good idea and it's just what you need, Di. You and Laura would make a brilliant team.'

'He's right,' said Laura.

'But I haven't even decided if I'm going to stay in this country,' Diana protested.

'Of course you haven't,' said Giles, 'because you can never make a commitment of any sort. What you need is an anchor, Di, and this is just the thing.'

Diana turned on him angrily. 'The last thing I need is somebody telling me what I should do with my life. I make my own decisions – right.'

'Then I have to say you're not making a very good job of it. It's all very well lounging around in this place, drinking too much, playing at a love affair with me, but it's not the real world – in fact, it is no more real than the life Laura has been leading in the last year.'

'Stop it, stop it, you two,' said Laura. 'Look, I don't want to cause trouble between you. This was just an idea – forget it.'

'It's a very good idea,' said Giles. 'Look, Di, if you can't have a crack at it for your own sake, do it for Laura. She'd be far better off having you as a partner than anyone else because you know each other so well. You're not going to double-cross each other, or mess one another about. A stranger could lead Laura a hell of a dance, and frankly, she's been through enough trauma, one way and another.'

It was precisely the right thing to say. Unconsciously, Diana fingered the little medallion around her neck. Suddenly, she gave Laura a bright smile. 'Put like that, how can I refuse. It is a good idea – quite a challenge in fact.' She glanced at the carrycot, 'But will you be able to cope with this and Francis?'

'For the time being, yes,' said Laura. 'As he gets older, it will become more difficult, but if the restaurant is a success, perhaps we could open more than one, in which case I could concentrate on administration.'

'More than one!' Giles and Diana chorused.

'Well, why not – if the formula works in South Ken., it should work anywhere.'

'Your father's daughter,' Diana suggested.

Laura frowned. 'If you ever say that again, we're going to fall out.'

'I know,' said Diana, 'I'm sorry, but you must admit it's a fair comment. Who else would think of a chain before we've even got one off the ground?'

'I think there'a a basic flaw in the whole scene,' said Giles.

Laura looked at him, surprised. 'Really! I thought you were all for it.'

'I am all for it, but there is one vital ingredient missing.'

'What?'

'Me,' said Giles. 'It just so happens that I have a property in South Kensington which would be absolutely perfect. It's a defunct pub so there's even a licence on the premises. There's a large flat above which one or both of you could live in, and although the interiors are dreadful, the fabric of the building is quite sound. Of course I could simply sell it to you, and I will, gladly, but what I'd rather do is offer it to you as my investment in the business. I would imagine the value of the property, which is about £25,000, more or less, represents the sort of sum you will be investing in the business. If that's the case, we can form a limited company in which we can all be directors and equal shareholders. As a matter of fact, it would be a great help to me – for example, Charlie and I import our own wine for the wine bar but we could buy in bulk for both premises – the same goes for the food. It would give us far greater clout as a buyer.'

'I think that's a great idea,' said Diana. 'What do you think, Laura?'

'What about Charlie?' Laura asked, 'won't he feel left out?'

Giles shook his head. 'He has more than enough on with our antiques business and the wine bar. He'll help out, of course, because that's his way, particularly as you're involved.'

There was an awkward silence for a moment which Laura broke. 'You know, Giles, I didn't like anything I heard about you, before I met you,' she said, with her disturbing honesty. 'Now I've met you, however briefly, I feel that we could work together, although it is rather a snap decision, for all of us.'

'All the best decisions are snap decisions,' said Giles, 'and I feel exactly the same way. I think the three of us could make a very good team.'

'This calls for another bottle of champagne,' said Diana and dashed off to the kitchen.

Giles took advantage of their being alone to ask the

inevitable question. 'Have you considered involving your father in this, Laura?'

'No,' said Laura. 'I have to make my own way.'

'I understand that,' said Giles, with uncharacteristic seriousness, 'I understand that only too well.'

It would have astounded everyone he knew, particularly Charlie, had the truth of Giles Latham's origins ever been revealed. He had been born in Bingley thirty-nine years before, and the name he had been born with was Ernest Smeeton, the only son of Dorothy Smeeton. His earliest memories were of his mother taking in washing and ironing – her hands red-raw from endless exposure to water and washing powder. Her face was thin and waspish, but with a little more weight on her, she could have been a pretty woman. His father had died before Ernest's first birthday – a combination of a youth in the pits, followed by severe TB. Life had not been kind to Dorothy Smeeton and it showed. She was a sad, exhausted, bitter woman, and the only person around on whom she could vent her spleen was her son. They frankly hated one another, and little Ernest's first conscious thought was to find a one-way ticket out of the life into which he had been born. When he was eight, he began helping out on the market stalls in Bradford on a Saturday, and it was there he discovered an interest in antiques. By twelve he was helping a dealer. By fifteen, already tall and well developed for his age, he left home without even saying goodbye to his mother, leaving her to her washing and her resentment. On the train somewhere between Bradford and Kings Cross, Giles Latham was born, and three years later, Ernest changed his name by deed poll. He invented a public-school education after rooming with a boy from Stowe during his early years in London. He simply learned all he needed to know about that particular school and adopted it as his own. Nature had been kind to him, giving him an elegance and natural grace which supported the upper class image he sought to nurture. His only concession to sentiment was to occasionally fantasize about his father. His mother had spoken only of the inconvenience of his father's poor health and Giles's sole link with his father was a yellowing, faded photograph of his parents' wedding. When sometimes, particularly in the early days, he had felt very alone and insecure in the identity he had created for himself, Giles would imagine the kind of camaraderie he might have shared with his father, had he lived. It was a piece of self-indulgence he pretended to despise.

Long ago, Giles had decided never to confide the truth of his origins to anyone, which meant that there would never be anyone with whom he could be completely honest. In business dealings, however, he was scrupulously honest, aware, as perhaps another more secure man might not have been, that one indiscretion would blow his cover. Banks trusted him, dealers knew his word was his bond, he could not afford to lose that. It was his background that had compelled him to help the destitute youth, Charlie Robins. It was also his background that made him understand Laura's need to escape her family's influence and carve a life for herself.

Diana returned from the kitchen, clutching a fresh bottle of champagne which Giles opened. He refilled their glasses and raised his. 'Partners?' he queried.

'Partners,' the girls confirmed.

CHAPTER THIRTEEN

They were mad weeks, the period between June and September 1969. Giles had been right – the public house, situated at the South Kensington end of Fulham Road, was perfect. The flat above had three bedrooms, a large sitting room, a tiny kitchen and a fairly sordid bathroom. It had little character, not a great deal of comfort but it was more than adequate.

Diana decided to buy a place of her own and found a delightful mews cottage in Chelsea. As she pointed out, if she and Laura were to work together every day, they would need a little space away from each other at night. The purchase of the house also demonstrated her commitment to live in England for a while, which pleased both Laura and Giles.

They were all anxious to open the restaurant by mid-September, to take full advantage of London's slow build-up for Christmas, and because they were spending money like water, they desperately needed an income. Giles was used to the rigours of commerce, but the amount of money involved frightened both Laura and Diana. Often Laura thought of Francis, experiencing for the first time both the thrill and the terror of private enterprise and at last beginning to understand how it had so fatally attracted him.

The restaurant's name was the first hurdle. They all had ideas – but none seemed right. Diana and Giles were in favour of 'Laura's Bistro'. Laura herself thought it unspeakably dull. They tried combining their Christian names, their surnames, they considered the local place names, but that did not seem sensible in case they managed to develop a chain. In the end the garden provided the answer. Laura spent a happy day with Francis in the sun, clearing the nine-foot square patch and planning its future. It was important it looked good since the restaurant windows overlooked what Giles liked to describe as 'their rolling acres'. In the sunniest corner of the garden, there stood a gooseberry bush. It was big and healthy and already a mass of fruit. Laura stood staring at it for a long time one day.

'Gooseberries!' she announced that evening.

'Gooseberries what?' Diana asked. The four of them, including Charlie, were wielding paintbrushes in what was to be the kitchen. Diana, who had never held a paintbrush in her life before, was already covered in paint and hating every moment of the task. Conversation came as a welcome break.

'The name of the restaurant,' Laura explained. 'There's a gooseberry bush in the rolling acres.'

'So?' said Giles. 'There's a worm or two as well no doubt, but you're not suggesting we call it 'Worms', are you?'

'No, of course not,' said Laura crossly, 'but "Gooseberries" is fun and we can use a bunch of gooseberries as our logo. It's a name people will remember.'

'It's crazy,' said Giles.

'I disagree,' said Charlie. 'I think it's a brilliant name.'

Everyone groaned. Since Laura's return to London, Charlie's infatuation with her was a standard joke which no longer rankled with anyone.

'Thank you, Charlie,' said Laura, graciously. 'I'd just like to remind you all that I'm in charge of publicity so unless or until someone comes up with a better name "Gooseberries" it is.'

No one did.

Staff were a problem. They decided on a series of part-time waiters and waitresses until they saw how trade built up, but the chef, they recognized, was all important. They interviewed well over forty candidates, and such are the peculiarities of the profession that when the simple menu was explained, most of the applicants considered it was beneath them to take the job. They were at their wits' end when Jamie Pearson presented himself. He was an imposing figure – six foot three, built like an ox, with great sprouts of red hair and huge, fierce, shaggy eyebrows. He had a square face the colour of mahogany and was utterly ageless in appearance. It turned out he was only twenty-six and this was his first sortie out of Scotland. He studied the menu for some time and then announced. 'Only a Scotsman can make this restaurant of yours pay, lassies. At these prices you're going to have to cost every grain of salt and waste nothing – I'm your man. When do I start?' He had not even asked about the salary.

'Now?' suggested Laura, weakly.

By early afternoon, the same day, Jamie had found himself a room just across the street. 'After a busy night, I've got to be able to crawl to me bed,' he explained. The following day, he set about working his way through their proposed menu, cooking Laura and Diana a different dish at each mealtime. He was perfect, he could take criticism, was prepared to alter everything from ingredients to presentation if the argument was valid, and he was full of bright ideas himself. During a week in which Diana and Laura were quite convinced they must have put on at least a stone, they fine-tuned the menu to the point where it was balanced, attractive, highly profitable and absolutely delicious.

While Diana worked on the decor and organized the purchasing of equipment – mostly with Jamie's advice – Laura concentrated on publicity. They decided to throw a party on the opening night, which they set as a Saturday in late September. Laura contacted all her old journalistic colleagues and offered them free dinners for two. Giles fretted at the cost saying it was going to be a very expensive night but Laura compared it to the cost of advertising. Then he graciously conceded and added a few names of his own.

'We'll need a few friends as well,' said Diana, 'real people as opposed to journalists – people who we can rely on and trust to say they think the place is wonderful, while denying they're our friends. In other words, we need to import some satisfied customers.'

'Good idea,' said Laura. 'Who have you in mind?'

Charlie said he would come, but alone.

'That's ridiculous,' said Giles. 'Dig into your little black book, Charlie, and treat us to one of your buxom blondes. Laura won't mind, will you, Love?'

'Of course I'll mind,' said Laura, smiling at Charlie, 'I'll be wildly jealous but I'll cope – somehow.' Since the inception of Gooseberries, Laura had not seen Charlie alone. Indeed, since the night before Francis was born, they had seen each other very little. Laura regretted their loss of intimacy, but was aware that their relationship during her pregnancy had been formed on a false premise – the quiet, introspective person Charlie seemed to have enjoyed as his friend, was not her true self. She wanted to explain all this to him and to thank him for his support during her dark days, but an opportunity never seemed to present itself.

'I'm coming alone, or not at all,' Charlie said, firmly.

Giles frowned. 'You're not turning gay, are you, Charlie? Is it safe for me to share a flat with you?'

'I wondered how long it would take you to realize,' Charlie said, leering. Everyone laughed but Laura sensed a loneliness in Charlie which worried her, since she felt in some way it was her fault.

Later that evening, Laura and Diana returned to the guest list. 'We can seat sixty couples, which means I need to ask at least eighty, and so far I've only drummed up fifty-odd.'

'What about your friends from Oxford?' Diana suggested.

'Brilliant, of course, I'll ask them to come. It will be a small gesture in repayment for having Francis and me for so long.' She added Eleanor and Chris Berry to the list.

'You're not going to like this suggestion,' said Diana, 'but what about David and Serena?' Laura stared blankly at Diana for a moment. 'David Lawson . . . you know, former man in your life.' Diana grinned.

David and Serena – Laura had never thought of him in those sort of terms. 'No, no, I don't think so,' she said.

'Why ever not?'

'I just don't want to ask him, that's all.'

'Oh come on Laura, you two ought to be friends again. You shared so much of your youth, and now he's happily married and you're . . .'

'No,' Laura said. 'It would be awkward.'

'You're wrong,' said Diana. 'I met David and Serena at a party back in the summer, during Regatta week. He said then how much he would like to see you again and he also said he felt so useless at not being able to help you. Serena's really nice, she's fun, not a bit the sort of woman I imagined David would marry. She's very high-powered, but not frighteningly so.'

'Di, will you stop?' Laura said. 'I'm not asking David and that's an end to it.'

'Will you be angry if I do?'

'Very.'

'I think you're being most unreasonable.'

'Tell me,' said Laura, shrewdly, 'how many of your ex-lovers do you keep in touch with, or indeed would want to ask to this party?'

Diana smiled. 'Point taken.'

Having organized the party and a mailing shot in the local area, Laura turned her attention to making a home for herself and the baby. For the first time, she felt she was really putting down roots, her own roots. When she had married Francis, she had been so blinded by love, so young and naive she realized now, that she had simply let life happen to her. She had accepted her father's offer of a flat without a qualm. Now she wondered whether in accepting his offer, she had already sealed the fate of her marriage with Francis. Perhaps if he had not imagined other such generosities would follow, he would not have been attracted to her. There again, perhaps her father's wealth and success had undermined his confidence in himself. Either way, for the first time, Laura was making the choices.

The upstairs rooms of the pub were mostly small, cheerless and without enough light. With precious little money to throw around, Laura simply painted all the walls and ceilings white and then walked a few doors down the Fulham Road to a little shop called Laura Ashley. There she bought pretty sprigged cotton fabric to make curtains, bedspreads and cushions. For the first time, Francis had a room of his own. She painted the built-in cupboards in bright primary colours, bought light fittings in the shape of a drum and was deeply touched when Charlie completed the little boy's bedroom by presenting him with a nineteenth-century rocking horse, lovingly restored.

'Charlie, you shouldn't have done this, it must have cost a fortune,' Laura said, when Charlie, purple with exertion, finally installed it in Francis's room.

'Not really,' he said, 'it was in a pretty shambolic state when I bought it – it just needed some work on it.'

'How long *have* you been working on it?' Laura asked.

'Since before Francis was born. I finished off the saddle and bridle when I knew the baby was a boy – otherwise I'd have gone for more feminine colours.'

They lifted Francis into the saddle and while Laura supported him, Charlie gently rocked the horse back and forward. The gurgle of pleasure was deeply satisfying to them both. Francis had grown into an extraordinarily attractive baby, with his almost white hair and periwinkle eyes. He awakened emotions in Laura she had never known she possessed, and in an extraordinary way, it was a kind of release. Up until Francis's birth she had been totally preoccupied with the past and everything that had gone wrong. Now, because of the baby, she thought ahead. It was Francis's future that mattered and she was determined to give him the best of all possible childhoods, despite the fact that he was to be brought up in a single-parent family. She was, of course, painfully aware that once the restaurant opened, combining motherhood and a career was not going to prove that easy, yet she shied away from the idea of a nanny. She wanted to be the number one person in her son's life. The problem seemed insoluble, until Bridget arrived.

Bridget walked into the restaurant one day and picked her way over the builder's rubble. Short and slight, with spikey urchin hair, dressed in shabby jeans and knee-high boots and wearing a very sullen expression, she did not immediately endear herself. 'Got any work?' she asked Laura, who was busily checking printers' proofs for the menu and wine list.

Laura barely glanced up. 'No, I'm afraid not, we've taken on all the staff we need.'

'Please yourself.'

It was the aggression in her voice, combined with something else – a fierce pride, which made Laura look up just as the girl turned away. 'Hang on a moment,' she said. The girl turned back to her. She would not meet Laura's eye – instead she gazed down at her boots. Her face was thin and pallid, there were dark circles under her eyes. She wore a baggy sweater over her jeans that was faded and none too clean, but was worn with style. She carried a holdall, slung casually over one shoulder. She couldn't be more than sixteen. 'What sort of work are you looking for?' Laura asked.

'Anything.'

'What's your name?'

'Bridget.'

'Bridget what?'

For the first time the girl met her gaze. 'None of your bloody business. If you ain't got no work, there's no point in asking questions, is there now?'

Laura recoiled from the angry stare. Warning bells sounded in her head, telling her that this was a situation in which she should not get involved. But there was an echo in the girl's desperate aggressiveness, an echo of her own state only months before. 'I might have some work for you, Bridget,' she said. 'Look, come upstairs to my flat and we'll talk.'

'Suit yourself.'

They climbed the stairs to the flat and Laura sat Bridget on a trestle table, which currently was the only furniture she had in the sitting room. 'Coffee?'

'OK. Milk, no sugar.'

'Where do you come from, Bridget?' Laura asked conversationally as she poured the coffee.

'Look, what is this, some sort of interrogation?'

God, the girl was impossible. Laura tightened the rein of her irritation. 'No, it's not. I'm trying to make polite conversation while I organize our coffee. Don't be so suspicious.' The girl said nothing. Laura poured the boiling water into two mugs and came and sat opposite her. 'I'm opening this restaurant with some friends in a month's time. I have a five-month-old baby, called Francis, and I've realized I can't cope with being a full-time mother and running the restaurant, particularly in the early days. I'm looking for somebody who will muck in – help look after the baby, clean the place and be prepared to become a relief waitress if someone falls ill. Someone who will hump the logs in for the fire, wash the glasses and help the chef when he's overworked. Someone who . . .'

'In other words, a dogsbody,' Bridget finished.

'That's right. Is it something you can do?'

'I've been a dogsbody all me bleeding life, that's no problem. What are you paying.'

'Well, before we get on to pay, how do you feel about children?'

'Kids?' Bridget considered the question, 'I like 'em, animals too. It's people I'm not too fond of.'

'Come and see Francis,' Laura said, recognizing that she must be going mad. This creature had walked off the streets and here she was contemplating putting her beloved son in her charge.

Bridget followed Laura on tiptoes into Francis's bedroom. He had woken from his nap but was lying on his back apparently content. Bridget bent over the cot, a smile suddenly lighting her sullen face. 'You're a right little cracker, aren't you?' she said. The baby stared up at the new face. He took his time and then, suddenly, his face broke into a huge smile and he stretched out a hand towards her. Bridget took the little fist in her hand and Laura knew, in an instant, a bond was formed.

'A fortnight's trial,' Laura said, half an hour later, when they'd agreed terms, 'just to see how you and Francis get on.'

'Oh Francis and I'll get along,' said Bridget.

'Are you happy to live in?'

'I've nowhere else to live.'

Laura grinned. 'Are you going to tell me your surname now?'

'Palmer.'

'And how old are you?'

'Sixteen.'

'And where do you come from, Bridget?'

'Does it matter? I've got me national insurance number, that's the only other thing you need to know, ain't it?'

'Alright,' said Laura, reluctantly. 'Now, I don't want you bringing people up here, friends, I mean. OK? They're very welcome downstairs in the restaurant, or in the bar, but not upstairs in your room.'

'What *do* you take me for?'

Laura met her eyes with amusement. 'I don't know, Bridget, I really don't.'

There was a ghost of a smile on Bridget's face. 'Well, we'll just have to see how we rub along then, won't we?'

'Have you got any luggage or personal bits and pieces you will need a hand with? We have a van.' Laura said.

Bridget really smiled this time. 'It's in here,' she said, indicating the holdall, 'and I reckon I can handle that meself.'

Against all odds, Bridget was exactly what Laura needed. She was the final piece in the jigsaw which completed the picture of Laura's recovery – the recovery which had begun with her overhearing the quarrel between Chris and Eleanor. Laura recognized in Bridget a damaged human being, damaged in a way she knew she had never been, coming from a background that she could only imagine. Bridget's stoic attitude to life, her refusal to give in or to be intimidated by anyone, inspired Laura and made her despise her own weak behaviour of the preceding year. The girl proved to be hard-working and reliable, and her devotion to Francis was without question. Laura, in her efforts to provide Bridget with a feeling of family life, found a domestic routine emerging. When Francis was in bed, they would have supper together and over a glass of wine would talk of every subject under the sun, except their past lives. Bridget's youthful energy spilled over into Laura and made her feel more alive than she could remember in a long time. Bridget, with three square meals a day, plenty of sleep, security and an unlimited supply of hot water, changed too. Her appearance remained shabby but she was always clean and neat. Colour came into her cheeks and whilst the haunted look remained in her eyes, it was no longer the dominating feature.

It was because of growing trust between the two young women that in the second week after Bridget's arrival, she told Laura one evening about her father. They had drunk more wine than usual. It was Friday night and only a week away from the opening of the restaurant. They were dog-tired and sitting either side of the trestle table, Bridget opened the subject. 'You got parents?' she asked Laura. Laura simply nodded, not wishing to disclose the identity of her father.

'They don't see much of their grandson, or you either, come to that.'

'We're not very close,' said Laura. 'It's my fault – I've distanced myself from them. My father's a rather dominant character – I can't cope with him.'

'Got lots of brothers and sisters, have yer?'

'No, none,' said Laura.

'You mean you're their only child?' Laura nodded, squirming slightly under Bridget's candid stare. 'What have they ever done to cause you to act like this then?'

The question surprised Laura. 'Nothing. They're good, kind people, it's just that they're too smothering.'

'Not surprising, is it? You're their only baby, you and young Francis, of course. Where do they live?'

'In Oxfordshire,' Laura said.

'Oh, a long way then.'

Laura laughed. 'No, not really – only about an hour in the car from here.'

'Blimey. Well, I must say, I don't understand you, Laura. Poor old buggers – at least, you ought to ask them to your party next week.'

'No,' said Laura.

'Why not? They'd be proud of you and it would give 'em a bit of pleasure. Go on, I'd like to meet them anyway, and so would Francis.'

'Tell me about your parents,' said Laura, anxious to change the subject.

Pain suddenly clouded Bridget's eyes. 'Nothing much to tell about my parents. Me Mum's dead, anyway.'

'What about your Dad?'

'Me Dad's a sod – I don't see him no more.'

'Well, you're a fine one to lecture me, aren't you?' said Laura, only half serious. 'Fancy taking me to task for not seeing my parents very often when you don't see your Dad at all.'

'Fill up me glass,' Bridget said, her tone sombre, her eyes shifty. The tiny hand that held out the glass shook slightly. 'It's different, you see. He . . . he abused me, me Dad did. The first time was when I was seven and after that he never really let up.'

'Abused . . .,' Laura began. She stared at Bridget, 'You mean sexually?'

'Yeh. He didn't rape me, mind, not 'til I was eleven. Thoughtful of him, wasn't it?'

'Oh Bridget, I'm sorry, I didn't mean to be flip just now, I – I just had no idea.'

'No, well, people like you don't.'

'But why did he do it?'

Bridget shrugged her shoulders. 'I'm the only daughter. There's five boys and me in our family – four older, one younger. Me Mum died giving birth to Tommy, he's my little brother. Well, Dad was left without a woman, wasn't he, so I suppose it wasn't surprising he turned to me.'

'You must have been so frightened,' said Laura.

Bridget shrugged her shoulders. 'No, it was just me Dad. When I was little I . . .,' she hesitated, her eyes briefly met Laura's and then shied away again, '. . . I quite liked it. It was comforting, I missed me Mum then, you see.' The silence was heavy between them. 'And then,' said Bridget, 'me Dad met Shirley,' her voice hardened. 'She's my step-mum, fat cow, lazy slut – not a bit like me Mum. Anyway, Dad left me alone for a bit then one night he and Shirl had a fight, after a session in the pub. He hit her a bit and she locked him out of the bedroom – so he came to me. That was when . . . when . . .'

'Oh Bridget, I'm so sorry. Did it happen more than once?'

'Pretty regular after that. When I . . . when I started me periods, I knew I'd better go, otherwise I might get pregnant, so I left home.'

'When was that?'

'Nearly two years ago.'

'And what have you been doing since?'

'This and that,' said Bridget.

'Are you going to tell me what "this and that" is?' said Laura.

'No, but I got by.'

'You make me feel very humble,' Laura said, after a pause.

'I do! Why?' Bridget asked.

'Because I don't know what having troubles are, not compared with you.'

'There's a thing we learnt at Sunday School once. This vicar, poor bugger, he used to round up us kids off the streets on Sundays. Thought he could bring us to God, he did, and change our lives, but we used to go 'cos his wife gave us squash and biscuits after.' Bridget hesitated, her mind obviously turning over the memory. 'Anyway, he said something I've always remembered.'

'What's that?' Laura asked, fascinated.

'Well, something about "the wind being tempered to the shorn lamb"; in other words,' said Bridget slowly, as if explaining to a child, 'you only get troubles what you can cope with, and some people can cope with bigger troubles than others. Me, well, obviously, if there's a God up there, he thinks I can cope with the bloody lot.' She gave a hollow little laugh.

'Don't get too tough, Bridget,' Laura said, gently.

Bridget stared at Laura, a thousand years of living in her eyes. 'Don't give me that,' she said, 'tough's why I've made it to this place – nice job, nice kid, you're not so bad. Whatever happens in this life, the only way to cope with it is to pick yerself up and start again. That means being tough.'

'You amaze me,' said Laura, 'and I tell you what I'll do. Just to prove I do take notice of what you say, I'll ask my parents to the party next week and Lord Campling, Francis's other grandfather.'

'A flipping lord! You're related to a flipping lord, then why aren't you a lady?'

'Because my husband wasn't the eldest son.'

'Wasn't,' said Bridget, 'is he dead?'

It was then that Laura told Bridget her story.

Seventy-three people attended the opening party, of which over forty were journalists of one sort or another. It was a personal triumph for Laura and the highlight came in the middle of the evening when a white Rolls Royce drew up right outside the door and out stepped none other than Fanny Cradock and her husband, Johnnie – naturally bringing up the rear and carrying her handbag. After some very shrewd questioning, a spirited interview with Jamie and a taste of every single dish on the menu, she announced that

Gooseberries would make her Bon Viveur column in the *Daily Telegraph* the following week. It was that article, and that article alone, which Laura always believed, put them firmly on the path to success.

Laura's parents were fulsome in their praise of Gooseberries and Bernard and Lord Campling spent much of the evening talking together, something which a year ago, Laura would never have believed possible. Katrine divided her time raving over the twin glories of her grandson and her daughter's restaurant. She was in seventh heaven – it seemed her daughter was back amongst them again, bringing little Francis with her.

It was after three before the last people left. Laura, Diana, Giles, Charlie, Jamie and Bridget sat around in the chaos, finishing up the last of the wine. They were on such a high, sleep was the last thing on their minds. 'Of course,' said Giles, normally the most sanguine amongst them, 'it will be tomorrow before we know whether we have a success on our hands, or not. All these people here tonight had a wonderful evening but they didn't have to pay for the privilege. However, tomorrow's lunch is for real, and Sunday lunchtimes are always a gamble in London – sometimes they work, sometimes they don't.'

'It'll work,' said Jamie, confidently.

Giles eyed him sceptically. 'How many bookings do we have?'

'None, because we only opened tonight,' said Laura, hurriedly, 'but really, Giles, I think you're being unnecessarily pessimistic.'

'He's always the same,' said Charlie, 'no deal he ever does is quite good enough.'

'That's not true,' said Giles, 'and I will admit to being cautiously optimistic about this venture. I'm just trying to prepare you all for the fact that tomorrow's lunch could be a disaster, despite Laura's excellent publicity. Things will pick up, I'm sure, but we really can't judge anything from tonight.'

'I tell you what,' said Diana, 'why don't *we* book a table for ourselves tomorrow, and then at least Jamie will have someone to cook for.'

'Can me and Francis come?' said Bridget.

'Of course you can come,' said Diana. 'A real family party. What do you say, Giles?'

'Sounds alright to me, but we'll have the restaurant to ourselves, mark my words.'

He could not have been more wrong. By eleven, they had four bookings, by twelve, fifteen, and by the end of the session, Jamie had served over fifty Sunday lunches. Diana, Laura and Bridget never sat down to lunch. Giles served wine in between eating his own meal and Charlie was quite literally left holding the baby. He and Francis had a pleasant lunch together, even if Charlie's lack of experience meant that most of Francis's meal ended up on the floor.

'High chairs,' Laura announced, when everyone had gone.

'Oh surely not,' said Giles, 'we don't want to turn this place into a nursery.'

'High chairs for Sundays,' said Laura. 'There must have been at least twelve children here today. I agree it's not something we should encourage during the week, but at weekends we must welcome families – a half-price meal for children and high chairs for babies.'

'I could argue with you,' said Giles, 'but on the other hand I have to admit that everything else you have suggested so far has worked like a charm. Your track record suggests to me that I am in no position to disagree . . . on anything.' He bent forward and kissed her on the cheek.

Laura had the grace to blush. 'It's far too early to say we've made it,' she said, but even to her ears the words did not carry any real conviction.

By the time they had all cleared up, it was nearly six. As the restaurant did not open on Sunday evening, the hours ahead suddenly seemed flat to Laura. There had been such a build-up to the opening. Diana sensed her mood. 'Why don't you and Charlie come over to my flat and join Giles and I for dinner? It'll give you a break from this place – if you hang around upstairs you'll get moody.'

'Francis . . .,' Laura began.

'You go,' said Bridget, 'I'll look after Francis, no sweat.'

In the end they went out to dinner, convincing themselves

that it was good market research. They chose a pleasant little French restaurant in the Old Brompton Road, but it was not a patch on Gooseberries they decided. They all drank a great deal of wine. Giles and Diana sat very close together, their arms draped around one another, sexual excitement running high. It left Charlie and Laura feeling slightly stranded, the odd couple out. Charlie became uncharacteristically vocal on the subject. 'For Christ's sake, you two, will you either stop pawing each other or go to bed, you're driving me nuts.'

Giles and Diana paused in their self-absorption and stared at him in surprise. 'Sorry, old boy,' said Giles, 'but I bet Laura doesn't mind.'

'Laura does, Laura's fed up with it, too, aren't you?' Charlie demanded. Laura nodded her agreement.

'In that case,' said Giles, leaping to his feet and taking Diana's hand, 'I'm going to take this gorgeous creature back to her flat where I can continue to show my appreciation without criticism. I'll have the decency to pay the bill on the way out.'

Charlie ran a hand through his long, untidy hair and smiled shyly at Laura, 'Sorry about my outburst, only Giles makes me mad, sometimes.'

'Perhaps you're just jealous,' Laura suggested.

'No, I'm not, I like Di, I think she's great but she's not my type.'

'Any more than Giles is mine,' Laura said.

Charlie smiled, his lop-sided grin. 'What is your type?'

Laura sighed. 'I don't know, I don't think I have one. The first love of my life, David, was very different from my husband.' Her expression threatened to become gloomy.

'Laura, since Giles and Diana are safely ensconced in Diana's flat, why don't you come back to mine and I'll make some coffee? You're not a bit tired and neither am I. If we go our separate ways this early we'll both feel thoroughly miserable.'

'I suppose I could ring Bridget and say I'm going to be a little later than I thought,' said Laura.

'Do that,' said Charlie, 'Greenwich has missed you.'

From the moment Laura climbed into Charlie's car, there

seemed to be an unspoken agreement between them, yet he did not touch her until the coffee pot was empty and the fire they had lit had almost died away. When he did reach for her, he was hesitant – first, he stroked the hair back from her face, then he leaned forward and kissed her gently on the lips. It felt strange to Laura but he smelt good – of varnish, paint and wood, the materials of his trade. She slipped her arms round his neck and kissed him in return, pressing her body to his. He held her awkwardly, as though she was fragile porcelain, and at that moment it was the last thing she wanted.

'Shall we?' Charlie murmured, 'I don't want to rush you.'

Laura hesitated for a moment. She did not want to be a party to the decision. She wanted it made for her. Although she tried to chase away the memory, her last, passionate love-making with Francis came back to her. She had thought of it many times during the long lonely nights since. To defy the memory, as much as for any other reason, she stood up and held out her hand. 'You're not rushing me, Charlie,' she whispered.

They undressed separately in the bedroom – awkwardly turning away from one another. To her horror, Laura found she was neatly folding her clothes. There was no atmosphere of urgency or excitement, the whole situation was clinical and devoid of any real warmth.

Laura climbed into bed first, Charlie followed and to her surprise turned out the bedside light, plunging the room into complete darkness. His caresses were tentative. She shivered from the cold, which he clearly misinterpreted as passion, for he groaned and pulled her close to him. 'I've dreamt of this moment for so long,' he whispered. 'I just can't believe it – that you're really here beside me, like this.' His voice shook with sincerity, he sounded close to tears and his obvious depth of feeling forced Laura out of the apathy which threatened to engulf her.

She made herself respond to him, doing everything she could to excite him. He seemed clumsy and unsure, whether from inexperience or inhibited by his feelings, Laura had no way of knowing. At last she guided him into her and held him tightly as he came with a shout of triumph, while she squirmed beneath him, uttering what she hoped sounded like little cries of appreciation.

'Was it alright?' Charlie asked anxiously.

'Lovely,' Laura murmured into the darkness.

He grunted contentedly, and in seconds, his even breathing told Laura he was asleep.

Laura lay staring up into the darkness, holding close this man who was really no more than a stranger to her at that moment. Her mind was blank, her body felt like lead – it surprised her therefore to find her face was wet with tears.

The dead feeling persisted on the taxi ride home. Wearily, she let herself into the restaurant and having checked that both Francis and Bridget were fast asleep, she wandered lethargically into her own room. She did not bother to wash or clean her teeth, nor brush the long, tangled hair that would be impossible in the morning. She let her clothes fall where she stepped out of them and at last crept under the cold duvet. That her feelings for Charlie were more of friendship than physical attraction she, of course, had always known, but he was a very attractive man, attractive by her standards, by any standards. He clearly adored her and she knew she was very lucky to have a man such as Charlie care for her so much – yet she felt she had so little to offer him. He was, of course, the first man to have touched her since Francis, the first man to have made love to her in a year and a half. Obviously there were adjustments to be made, yet she knew whatever Charlie did or said, he would not reach the core of her, spiritually or physically. What followed this thought was the sudden realization that if Charlie could not, then perhaps no man ever would – certainly not while the mystery of Francis's disappearance remained unresolved. She had conceived and borne his child, which in turn meant she was irrevocably linked to Francis while his fate remained uncertain. If she knew herself to be a widow, if she knew her son was fatherless, then perhaps she could consider forming a new relationship with a man who could be a husband to her and a father to her baby. But until she knew for certain that Francis was dead, she was trapped in a prison that he himself had made for her.

THE MIDDLE:
London, December 1970

CHAPTER FOURTEEN

Charlie Robins was already angry before he reached Laura's new house. Its location irritated him – why Putney instead of Greenwich? Certainly Putney was nearer to Gooseberries and the proposed new restaurant in the Kings Road, but Laura did not work in the restaurant in the evenings any more. Why then did she have to live particularly near them? She had also reverted to type, he thought, as he banged the brass knocker on the dark burgundy front door. This little mews house was altogether too smart, too stylish, too upper class, so very feminine . . . so obviously excluding a man. In that scruffy little flat in Greenwich, they had shared so much in common – it seemed a very long time ago now.

Standing, waiting in the cold, Charlie noticed suddenly that he had forgotten to change in his hurry to get to her. His shoes were scuffed, he was wearing his working jacket and his old cords were worn and none too clean. He wanted to dismiss his appearance as unimportant but it was Christmas Eve, he was taking her out to dinner and he knew he should have made an effort. The door opened and Bridget stood before him. Nearly eighteen now, she was in serious danger of turning into a beauty, despite her aggressively masculine dress and short, cropped hair. 'Oh it's you,' she said, 'come in. She's still working, of course. I told her to stop but she wouldn't take any bleeding notice.'

'Shit!' said Charlie. 'Since she won't spend Christmas Day with me, you'd think she'd at least be ready when I come to take her out to dinner.'

'Don't take it out on me, it's your relationship and your problem. Why not come and see Fram while you're waiting. He's just come out of the bath and if you didn't know better, you'd think he was a real little angel.'

Charlie's face softened. 'This I have to see!'

Francis Melhuish was now eighteen months old, and at fourteen months he had announced his name was Fram. Why, no one knew, but it had stuck and now he was never called anything else. The baby good looks had persisted. He had become a sturdy toddler whose high spirits kept Bridget and Laura on their feet from dawn until dusk, but his persistent good humour and quick intelligence ensured he got away with murder.

They found Fram sitting stark naked on the rocking horse Charlie had given him. He was clutching Marty the cat and rocking the horse backwards and forwards furiously. 'Fram, Fram,' said Charlie. 'Poor cat, let it go or it'll scratch you.'

Bridget laughed and shook her head. 'That cat never scratches Fram. I've got marks all over me body just to show you how vicious it is, but it never touches the baby. Funny, ain't it?'

Charlie scooped the squirming little body off the horse. 'Charlie, Charlie!' Fram chorused.

'Now, let's put on your pyjamas and I'll read you a bedtime story, if you're good,' Charlie said.

'Now, now,' Fram said.

'When your pyjamas are on.'

They stared solemnly into each other's eyes. Charlie, with his thick thatch of dark hair and his beetle brows, forced his expression into a fierce scowl. Fram was not impressed – he giggled – but none the less did as he was asked.

Half an hour later, after a heavy session of Beatrix Potter, Charlie left Fram to Bridget's ministrations and headed downstairs to the drawing room. Laura sat at her desk in the bay window. She was studying some paperwork, her head bent, a little frown of concentration creasing her forehead. She was more beautiful than ever, her long, dark hair – now the subject of a hairdresser's weekly attention – shone and fell in ordered curls to just below her shoulders – the wild, unruly look gone for ever. She was wearing a cream silk shirt and a short, navy corduroy skirt. The skirt had ridden up well above her knees, showing slender legs, encased in matching navy tights. Charlie paused in the doorway – the sight of her always drained him of his anger and frustration. OK, so their relationship was not as permanent or as solid as he would like, but he was the man in her life, the only man in her life, and he felt appropriately grateful to have been awarded such a privilege. 'Laura?'

She looked up at him, squinting slightly as she adjusted her vision. 'Charlie, hello.' Her voice was warm but her mind was preoccupied and she made no attempt to stand up and greet him.

'It's nearly eight,' he said. 'Fram has just been put to bed and it's time we were off.'

'Off?' Laura looked at him questioningly.

'I'm taking you out to dinner, remember?'

'Oh, yes. I tell you what, Charlie, why don't we eat here? I could dig something out of the freezer.'

'No,' Charlie said sharply, 'I'm taking you somewhere special, it's all arranged. It's Christmas Eve, Laura, for heaven's sake – leave that bloody work alone for once.'

'I'm sorry.' Laura shut the file. 'I've just been trying to work through the final figures on Kings Road. That high rent does make a hell of a difference. I hope we're doing the right thing.'

'Drink?' said Charlie, walking over to Laura's drinks cabinet, with as much of a proprietorial air as he dared.

'Yes, why not. It's Christmas Eve, as you say. Where are you going tomorrow, Charlie?'

'Haven't thought.'

'But you must have, everyone has plans for Christmas Day.'

'I had hoped to spend it with you and Fram, as you know, but since you're going to your parents, I've rather lost interest in the whole thing.'

'Oh Charlie, don't be so silly.'

He handed Laura a dry sherry and collapsed into a chair, clutching a large whisky. He took a gulp, enjoying the burning sensation it caused as it slid down his throat. 'Don't concern yourself about me,' he said, with heavy sarcasm, 'there must be plenty of us neglected other halves left in London, I can promise you.'

Laura ignored the barb. 'Why don't you spend the day with Bridget?' she said.

'Bridget! Why?'

'Because she's going to be on her own, too. I invited her to my parents, of course, but she wouldn't come. She says they're too posh. She's got no family she wants to see, and not many friends – it worries me, but she swears she'll be alright here on her own.'

Fleetingly, Charlie noted Bridget's invitation to Marlow, accompanied as it was by the 'of course'. He had been the recipient of no such invitation.

'I don't think that's a very good idea; Bridget and I have nothing in common.'

'No one is suggesting you have,' Laura said, patiently. 'I'm not asking you to take her out on a heavy date. Just spend the day together – here if you like. You needn't be in fear of your virtue, either, because she hates men, doesn't trust them at all.' Laura smiled. 'Who can blame her?'

'What's that supposed to mean?' said Charlie.

'Oh for heaven's sake, Charlie, it's just a joke. Bridget has a special reason for having a pretty low opinion of men, that's all. Anyway, suit yourself, it was only a suggestion.'

'Well, it's not a very good one.' His expression was sulky, he had not eaten all day and the whisky was starting to take effect. He felt aggrieved and suddenly picking a fight seemed an attractive proposition. 'Why is it, Laura, that I always feel that you're doing me some sort of favour?'

Laura was concentrating on tidying her desk. 'I don't know what you mean, Charlie,' she said, wearily.

'I think you do,' said Charlie. 'I don't just mean when we're in bed, though heavens above, you make me feel obligated for that – no, it's all the time. For example, I feel you're doing me a favour by letting me take you out to dinner tonight. If I telephone you, it's as though you are forcing yourself to make time for me, between your business appointments, and again, I get the impression I'm supposed to feel truly grateful. Laura, I'm just a simple flesh and blood human being who happens to love you very much for my sins. I've asked you to marry me but you won't, so why don't you give me up? Shall I tell you why – I suspect it's because I'm useful to have around. Don't you see it's a half-life for both of us. I want to make a home for you, and for Fram. I love that boy quite as much as if he was my own son.'

'I know,' said Laura, quietly.

'So, where's the problem? We have the same friends, we are interested in one another's work, we enjoy doing the same things. Some people might say that was a recipe for one hell of a marriage.'

'You forget, I'm still married,' said Laura.

'In name,' said Charlie, 'but not in fact.'

'I've done nothing about ending the marriage, because for all I know Francis may still be alive.'

'You and he have nothing left in common now, even if he were to appear.'

'We have Fram,' said Laura.

Charlie felt a chill run through him. 'So you think that if Francis knew he had a child, he might come back to you?'

Laura turned away, walked to the mantelpiece and began fiddling with the ornaments that cluttered its surface. Her shoulders visibly drooped as if she were carrying some heavy burden. 'No,' she said, after a silence, 'no, I'm not saying that. If he came back to England, he'd have to go to prison – that's a heavy price to pay for seeing your son. In any case, I don't even know if he wanted children, we never really discussed it.'

'Didn't discuss it in two years of marriage?'

'It was a strange marriage.'

'It must have been,' said Charlie. 'So, if you're not hanging around waiting for him to come back, what are you doing?'

'Please, Charlie. It's been a long week, don't let's start all this now.'

'It's always been a long week, you've always got too much work to do. I'm tired of the excuses, it's time you thought about someone else instead of yourself. You've changed, Laura. Making money, being a success, surrounding yourself with all this junk – who needs it? People are all that matter, relationships should take priority over commerce. I sometimes think you care more about your business than you do about your son.'

'That's not fair,' said Laura. Her dark blue eyes flashed dangerously and she suddenly looked very Greek.

'I wasn't aiming at being fair – just seeking the truth.' He glanced at his watch. 'Look it's getting late. The table's booked for 8.30. Let's go out to dinner and we'll talk some more.'

'No,' said Laura. She met Charlie's eyes steadily. 'I don't want to go out with you tonight, Charlie, not when you're in this mood.'

Charlie stared at her. 'I just don't believe it! I've booked us into the Savoy Grill – champagne, flowers, a special table.'

Laura visibly blanched. 'It's not going to be much fun though, is it, if we spend the evening arguing like this? Promise me, Charlie, you won't talk about our future and then I'd love to come, of course.'

'I'm sorry,' Charlie said, 'that's a promise I can't make. What are we supposed to talk about – the weather? We have a relationship, Laura. Now and again I'm actually allowed to make love to you, I play with your son, I listen to your troubles, and your well-being and happiness are of deep concern to me. You can't simply turn me on and off like a light bulb. I *want* to talk about our future and I want to talk about it tonight.'

'You're behaving like a child,' Laura said, 'I want this, I want that. Well, I don't want to talk about it, Charlie. I'd love to spend an evening with you, a pleasant evening, an evening which isn't going to involve endless recriminations.' She softened a little and smiled. 'It's Christmas, Charlie, Christmas Eve, a time to be lighthearted, happy – a time for children. Here, look, I've been putting together Fram's stocking. Would you like to see what I've got?'

'Don't humour me, Laura. If you're not prepared to pay me the courtesy of discussing our future, then frankly, I can see very little point in our having dinner together.'

'As you wish,' said Laura. The light went out of her eyes.

'You're so cold.' Charlie walked to the door. 'I just don't know what's wrong with you. Something deep inside you must have died, or perhaps it was never alive. I've left Fram's present in the hall – wish him a Happy Christmas.' He turned and closed the sitting room door quietly behind him.

Laura stared at the closed door. 'And Happy Christmas to you, Charlie,' she whispered. Moments later she heard the front door slam and let out a sigh. It was as though a weight had fallen from her – she felt relaxed, lighthearted almost. Their relationship and Charlie's demanding love exhausted her, suffocated her. She knew she had behaved irresponsibly but yet another endless discussion as to why she wouldn't marry him was the last thing she could cope with after such a heavy week.

Bridget appeared at the door. 'Not going out then? Where's Charlie?'

'He left in a huff. Here, come and have a drink, you look tired.'

'Don't mind if I do. That Fram, he wears me out.'

'Is he asleep?' said Laura.

Bridget nodded, smiling. 'Went out like a light. He can't wait for the morning.'

'Damn,' said Laura, 'I wanted to say goodnight to him and try to tell him about the Christmas story. I think he's old enough to appreciate hearing some of it now.'

'I've told him a bit about it – the baby and stuff.'

'Did you?' Laura handed Bridget a gin and tonic. 'You're an odd person you know, Bridget, a very strange mixture.'

'Thanks a bunch. Well, cheers, Happy Christmas.' They sat, as was their custom, on chairs set either side of the fire. 'That Charlie's not right for you,' Bridget said conversationally, after a few moments silence.

'I know,' said Laura, quietly.

'Then I think you ought to tell him so.'

'You think I'm treating him badly?'

'No. Men can look after themselves, and in any case, he likes playing the martyr.'

'Do you know, I think you're right,' said Laura. 'He's also very much the lame duck in his relationship with Giles. Giles is the clever one who earns his keep by sitting in the wine bar all day, while poor old Charlie does all the work. It's exactly the same as his relationship with me. I know he really does care about me, but he can't accept that my feelings don't match his. Normally, in those circumstances, he should have been long gone and found himself a nice girl who appreciates him. Somehow, though, Charlie almost revels in the situation. And then there's his politics – he strongly disapproves of the way in which I live, so how could we ever make a life together without one of us changing dramatically?'

'Still, he's got his good points,' said Bridget. 'He loves our Fram and Fram is mad about him.'

'Yes, and do you know, I think that's what binds me to Charlie really,' said Laura. 'But for Charlie, we wouldn't have Fram and I'd have probably died, too.'

'How come?' said Bridget. It was then that Laura told Bridget about the night of Fram's birth. It was a subject they had never discussed before for Laura preferred not to think about it. Christmas Eve, though, somehow seemed the right time for telling the story.

'Bloody Hell!' said Bridget, when Laura had finished, 'I can see why you stick with old Charlie – fancy the thought of there being no Fram.'

The two women sat in companionable silence for some long time after that, contemplating the idea of life without the baby they both cared about so much. As so often happened, Bridget's uncompromising remark was almost too accurate. Charlie had played a fundamental part in the drama that had given Fram life, and to walk away from him in the circumstances was just not that simple.

By the time Laura entered Fram's bedroom on Christmas morning, he had already discovered his stocking. As is the perverse way of small children, he had unwrapped each present, hurled the contents out of his cot and was playing happily with the packaging. 'Happy Christmas, darling.' Fram gurgled and held out his arms to her. 'Let's sort out your nappy and then we'll have a nice Christmas breakfast with Bridget.'

Their Christmas presents were already packed to take to Meadows Reach, but over a leisurely breakfast, Laura let Fram open Charlie's present. It was in a vast box and Bridget and Laura were quite as excited as Fram, as he pulled at the wrapping. They were not disappointed – it was a horse on wheels – almost a replica of the rocking horse, only much smaller and exquisitely carved, with a real horsehair mane and a little leather saddle and bridle. Fram squealed with delight and having been placed in the saddle, he began pushing himself round and round the kitchen.

'It's wonderful,' said Laura, 'I wonder where on earth he found it.'

'He carved it himself,' Bridget said.

'Did he?'

Bridget nodded. 'He's been working on it for weeks. Brilliant, ain't it?'

Laura felt a familiar stab of guilt. Charlie had planned it all carefully – a celebration dinner on Christmas Eve, followed no doubt by a night spent together. It would have meant him sitting here at breakfast now, watching Fram's face as he opened his present. She had denied him all of it – all the pleasure – and created havoc with all his plans. She stood up abruptly. 'I'd better get dressed or we'll be late. Are you sure you won't come, Bridget?' Bridget shook her head.

There was no way of parting Fram from his horse and the car was well and truly loaded by the time they set off for Marlow. It was an easy drive, with virtually no traffic, and Laura's pleasure was heightened by the accompaniment of carols on the car radio and Fram's happy chuckles in the background. As she left London behind, her worries began slipping away. She was looking forward to Christmas at home again. Now she had established the restaurants in her own right, much of the animosity had left her relationship with her father. He was proud of her now, she knew. She did not want success on his grand scale but she had proved that she could make it in the world without his help.

The long driveway down to Meadows Reach, with its border of poplars to which the frost still clung, reminded Laura so much of the Christmases of her childhood and it was good to be bringing Fram back.

Katrine opened the door, at the sound of the car. 'Darlings, darlings,' she said, taking Fram from Laura's arms. 'Happy Christmas, poppet – you're so big! Come in, come in. Bernard!' she called, 'open the champagne, quickly, Laura's here.' She gave a stage wink. 'And there's someone else here you won't be expecting.'

As always, when someone innocently made a remark such as this, Laura's heart lurched. As far as the world was concerned, Francis Melhuish was dead, but never a day passed without Laura wondering whether she would turn a street corner and come face-to-face with him, meet him at a party, or that he would simply arrive on her doorstep. 'Who?' she asked, anxiously.

'Go in and see.'

William Campling stood with his back to the fire. Laura had seen him briefly at the restaurant opening and Fram's christening, but they had been virtually estranged since the telephone call when William had told Laura that Fram would be his heir. He had aged, Laura noticed. There was a frailness about him that had not been there before. 'Laura, my dear.' He stepped forward and kissed her on the cheek. 'How are you? No, I don't need to ask that, you look wonderful.'

'It's lovely to see you,' Laura said, genuinely.

Bernard came forward and kissed his daughter. 'I can see the surprise on your face, Laura. You're just like your mother, you can never hide your feelings. It's true though, against all the odds, William and I have become . . . well, what shall we say, William, we've reconciled our differences?'

William Campling smiled, 'Something like that.'

Certainly there was a great deal more to it than that, Laura realized as the day wore on. The two men had become great friends, incongruous though it seemed. Bernard, the son of a Manchester mill-owner, and William Campling, with an aristocratic history that stretched back to Doomsday and beyond. Bernard was steeped in commerce while William had spent a lifetime trying to make his estate pay, without success.

'When did those two become so friendly?' Laura asked her mother, later. They were in the bathroom, both more than a little damp from their attempts to bath Fram, whose Christmas excitement had reached fever pitch.

'It was Fram who brought them together.' Katrine picked the struggling, slippery little body out of the bath and plonked him firmly on her knee. 'See, scamp, you are good for something.'

'How? Why?' Laura asked.

'When he was just a few days old, just after we'd all seen you in hospital. William wrote to Bernard and told him that he was making Fram his heir. Apparently he'd had a long talk with Anthony, who has no interest in running the estate. That is why William is with us this Christmas – Anthony and Lavinia are living almost permanently in Sydney now so we're his only family. Anthony does something very important with Australian commodities – these men and their businesses, it's another world. Anyway, he makes a lot of money and really can't imagine ever wanting to spend much time in England.' Katrine shrugged her shoulders. 'Funny man.'

'But he'll inherit the title presumably?' said Laura.

'Oh yes, but apparently he's waived any claim to pass it or the estate on to his children, if after all, he should have any.'

'Lucky Fram,' said Laura.

'Yes,' said Katrine. 'Anyway, your father and William have been plotting ever since to secure Fram's future, and the future of Campling Hall – it's very run down apparently. Don't you dare let them know I've told you all this, promise – I think Pop wants to tell you himself.'

'Promise,' said Laura.

'Good girl, you know you're much easier to talk to these days and you seem much more settled. Your restaurants have helped I'm sure – you have done well, and as for this . . .,' Katrine executed a neat rugger tackle in order to powder Fram's bottom, '. . . well no woman could ask for a more adorable baby than this.'

'Don't say that in front of him, he's spoilt enough,' said Laura, laughing.

Christmas Night was a very relaxed affair. On Boxing Day they attended the meet of the Old Berkely Hunt, followed by drinks in Henley, and then a delicious lunch prepared by Laura and washed down by quantities of claret. Over coffee, Laura suddenly realized that Katrine had removed Fram and that William had made a tactful exit, muttering that he needed some fresh air. She found herself alone with her father, for the first time in a long time. Whether it was the surfeit of wine or the warmth of the log fire in front of which they sat, she did not know, but she felt more relaxed with him than she had done since she was a small child. 'We've been left alone for a chat, I presume,' she said, smiling at him over her coffee cup.

'Something like that. Your mother's idea, of course.'

'Naturally,' said Laura. 'You want to talk about Fram?'

Bernard looked surprised, 'No, no not about Fram – about you.'

'Me!'

Bernard nodded. 'It can't have escaped your notice, love, that I'm not getting any younger.'

'Pop, you look the picture of health. You're not telling me that Bernard Beecham could ever feel the strain of the passing of the years.'

Bernard smiled faintly at Laura's quip. 'As a matter of fact, love, I am.'

'You're not ill, are you Pop?' Laura put down her cup and sat forward in her seat, suddenly alert.

'No, no. I just feel, I suppose, a general slowing down and it's made me think about the future.'

'Go on,' said Laura.

'About you and Francis – I know perhaps I behaved tactlessly when he disappeared. I hated that bugger, and what he did to you by disappearing was the final straw. It's a natural instinct – you must feel it now with Fram – you want to protect your child from everything hurtful and unpleasant. I just wanted you back here under my roof, where I could see no bastard was ever going to upset you again.'

Laura felt tears prick her eyelids. 'I know, Pop, I understand that now but at the time . . .'

'Yes, yes,' said Bernard impatiently. 'The thing is, Laura, it's been well over two years since Francis disappeared, and I think it's time to consider a divorce.'

'A divorce!' said Laura. 'But we don't even know if he's alive.'

'Exactly, and because of that, you don't even know if you're free to marry again. You're a young woman, you must go through the motions of divorce. There's no problem legally – you've been officially abandoned for over two years. You can sue him for desertion and since he's not going to counterclaim, the divorce will go through like a dose of salts.'

'You've obviously looked into this quite thoroughly,' Laura said.

Bernard nodded. 'You have your son and you have your business, it's time you found yourself a good man. I'd like to see you settled happily, before I die.'

'Pop,' said Laura warningly, 'you know I can't stand the settling down with a decent chap lecture.'

'I know, I know, but seriously, Laura . . .'

'And another thing, divorcing somebody who's probably dead seems, well, rather callous, doesn't it?'

'No, it does not,' Bernard almost shouted. 'Hell, no, I'm sorry, love, I wanted this to be a calm discussion, but there can be nothing more callous than walking out on your wife. You're going around with this young chap at the moment – Charlie – I don't know if he's husband material and I wouldn't presume to interfere these days, but while you're technically still married to Francis, I'm sure it must influence the way you think about men, men like Charlie.'

Laura stared at him. 'Yes, I think you're right, I do still feel committed and I think Fram's existence encourages the feeling.'

'Very probably,' said Bernard. 'So, whilst in itself the divorce may not seem important at the moment, it may help you look more towards the future than the past. That's all I'm saying.'

'Thanks, Pop,' said Laura.

'The other thing I wanted to talk to you about is money.'

'Oh, no,' said Laura, 'we always argue about money.'

'Not this time,' Bernard smiled, and surprisingly for such an undemonstrative man, he reached out and took her hand. 'I'm very lucky you know, Laura. There are a great many rich men whose family look on them as no more than a meal ticket. In your case, not only have you made your own life on your own terms very successfully, but trying to persuade you to take anything from me is extraordinarily hard work. I like that, I'm proud of it.' For once Laura was speechless, and Bernard hurried on. 'I've left the major shareholding of Beecham Stores to your cousin, Andrew. He's virtually running the company now and I've been gradually shifting the shareholding over to him year-by-year, to be as tax effective as possible. I intend leaving you 5 per cent of the company.

You've demonstrated considerable commercial prowess – 5 per cent is not enough to interfere with Andrew's progress but it will give you an interest in the company and a large enough income to ensure your comfort. What you do with you 5 per cent, of course, is up to you, but I'd like to think you'll pass it on to your children. I don't mind admitting it's important for me to feel that my direct line still has a continuing involvement in Beecham Stores.'

'I don't like you talking in this way, Pop.'

'Listen Laura and don't interrupt.'

Laura smiled, feeling suddenly about six again. 'Sorry, go on,' she said, with due contrition.

'I've left your mother this house, of course, and a considerable amount of money in trust, which will be administered by our solicitor – as you know, she hates money and everything to do with it, so it seems the best answer.' He smiled fondly. 'Which brings us to you and Fram. On your mother's death, you will obviously inherit her money and this house. I've set up a trust fund for your future children, should you have any, the income from which you can draw. Everything else, however, I have left to Fram. It makes him an extremely wealthy little boy – there are several million involved.'

'A very lucky little boy,' said Laura, 'particularly bearing in mind he's also inheriting the Campling estate, I understand.'

'Yes,' said Bernard, 'and that's one of the reasons for leaving him so much. William and I have studied the long term future of Campling Hall. It is an estate of enormous historical importance, and I want Fram to have enough money to maintain and preserve it for future generations. I cannot think of a better way for my accumulated wealth to be spent – can you?'

'You're both putting an awful lot of faith in Fram.'

'He's my grandson, your son – he won't let us down,' Bernard said gruffly. It was clearly the end of the conversation.

On the day after Boxing Day, Laura and Fram had to return to London. The Kings Road restaurant was opening on New

Year's Eve, with hopefully, a blaze of publicity and a party into the small hours. Knowing the difficulties of finding anyone to work in England between Christmas and the New Year, Laura and Diana had organized everything they could in advance of Christmas. There still seemed a great deal to do, however.

Laura's talk with her father had affected her deeply, she realized, driving back to London. She felt drawn into the family net again, and the sense of belonging which she had formerly shunned now seemed attractive, desirable even. She supposed it was because she felt more confident and secure in herself, but, in turn, this growing confidence made her realize the impossibility of a future with Charlie. Two days away from London had given her the time she needed to look honestly at her feelings for him. Divorce, as Bernard suggested, probably was a good idea, but she knew being free legally, as well as morally, would make no difference to what she felt for Charlie. However painful, she resolved to terminate the relationship as soon as possible – for both their sakes.

As it happened, events moved faster than she could have anticipated. She and Fram arrived back at her house to find Giles, Diana and Bridget sitting round the fire drinking champagne. Laura looked at them in mock disapproval. 'Do you two ever do anything else but drink champagne?'

'We most certainly do,' said Giles, 'and when you're older, I'll tell you all about it.'

'It's very nice to see you, but what are you doing here?'

'We rang to tell you our news,' said Diana, 'and then discovered poor old Bridget was here all alone, so we decided to hold our party at your house for Bridget's benefit.'

'Party, what party?'

'Our engagement party,' said Giles, looking almost coy.

Laura let out a screech. 'You're getting married! Oh, I'm so pleased, I really am – you're made for each other.' It was true – in the months that Diana and Giles had worked together on Gooseberries, they had grown visibly closer. Both private people, with their own secrets to hide, a mutual interest in work provided the bridge between what had been a casual affair and what had grown to become a lasting love. The catalyst had been Giles revealing his true identity to Diana one night. The suave, witty sophisticate disappeared before her eyes as he told her about the misery of his childhood. She recognized what it had cost him to tell her and she was his from that moment.

There followed a great deal of hugging and kissing, a glass was found for Laura and another bottle opened. 'I'm so thrilled for you both, though I have to admit I never thought anyone would succeed in making an honest man of him, Di.'

'Nor me,' she answered, with feeling.

'Who said anything about being honest?' said Giles.

'So when's the wedding to be?'

'Soon, very soon. Now we've made the decision, there's no point in hanging around. Neither of us have any family to worry about so we thought if you and Charlie would act as witnesses, we'll have a thrash for everyone at the restaurant afterwards. If we make it a lunchtime, mid-week, then we should just be able to put the place back together before the evening.'

'Practical as ever,' said Laura. She frowned. 'What about Charlie, have you told him yet?'

'Yes,' said Giles, 'actually he was the first to know, he and Bridget. He's on his way over now.'

'Oh,' said Laura.

Only Diana noticed her crestfallen expression. 'What is it, darling? Have you and he got problems?'

'Sort of.'

'Would you rather he didn't come? We might be able to stop him.'

'No, no, of course not,' said Laura, but she sounded far from convinced.

Charlie seemed strangely elated when he arrived, which was a relief. The champagne flowed, while Laura and Bridget made a chilli and put Fram to bed. It was not until Laura finally returned from the kitchen with supper, that she realized in her absence, Charlie had become very drunk. 'Hello, gorgeous,' he called from the sofa. 'Come and sit beside me and tell me when *we're* getting married.'

'Don't be silly, Charlie, here's your supper.'

'Who wants food at a time like this. We need to make plans. I tell you what, why don't we have a double wedding?'

Laura was speechless, Giles and Diana looked uncomfortable. It was Bridget who came to the rescue. 'Come on, you silly old sod, move up and make room for me. Look have some chilli and bread. I reckon you could do with something to mop you up, you're pissed out of your mind.'

The distraction of food was only momentary. Charlie helped himself and then began again. 'Well, what do you think?' he challenged. 'After all, a double wedding would be double the celebration, for the same price. We don't have to spend our honeymoons together, after all.'

'Charlie, please,' said Laura.

'Charlie, please, Charlie please,' Charlie mimicked. 'What I want from you is a straight *yes* or *no*. I've lost count of the times I've asked you to marry me. I want you to tell me now in front of everyone so I have witnesses.'

'Charlie, you're spoiling Giles's and Di's evening,' Laura said.

'Yes, give it a rest, Charlie,' said Giles.

'I will have an answer and I will have it now.' Charlie stood up, stumbling slightly. 'Will you or will you not marry me, Laura?'

There was an embarrassed, awkward pause. 'No, Charlie,' said Laura. 'I'm very flattered that you should ask me, but no, I won't marry you.'

'Bitch!' Charlie exploded. 'Then what have all these months been about, you two-faced cow.'

'Charlie, stop that!' Giles, too, stood up. 'You've had far too much to drink, I'll take you home.'

'You leave me alone, I've had enough of you as well. You're all self-obsessed, capitalist idiots. God, to think the world is run by people like you. Your priorities are crazy, you're sick – sick with self-indulgence – your champagne, your parties, the clothes you wear. Shit. Do you know the only person who cares a fig about me around here is little Fram?' At the mention of Fram's name, Charlie's features seemed to dissolve and tears began coursing down his face.

'Oh Charlie, don't get upset.' Laura made to put an arm around him.

'Leave me alone, don't touch me. I want nothing more to do with you – any of you. I'll be out of the flat in the morning, Giles, and then you can find out what it's really like to run a business. It won't do you any harm to be out of bed before ten o'clock, serving bloody customers all day, driving vans through London traffic jams, picking up gear. Just try being your own dogsbody for a while, you'll find it quite illuminating. And as for you . . .' he turned to Laura, 'don't ever do this to a man again. OK, maybe you're punishing me for what your husband did to you, but it's not fair to take your vengeance on the whole bloody gender. You're a cold, heartless bitch, and you never intended to marry me, did you? I was useful to have around, to provide you with a screw when you felt in the mood. Well, sod you, Laura, and sod you all.' He turned and flung himself out of the door.

'Charlie, don't be a fool!' Giles dashed across the room and put a restraining hand on Charlie's arm. 'You can't drive – not in this state.'

'Shove off, Giles.'

'No, I'm not letting you leave this house. You'll kill yourself or worse still, you'll kill somebody else.'

'I'm leaving, I said I'm leaving.' Giles was taller than Charlie but Charlie's strength was phenomenal – hardened by his years on the farm, and followed by his time spent heaving around heavy pieces of furniture. When Giles continued to bar his way, Charlie gave no warning of his intentions. He simply brought back his fist and slammed it into Giles's jaw. They all heard the crack, then Diana screamed and Giles's knees buckled as he fell to the floor.

'He meant what he said, he's already gone,' Giles said, thickly. He was sitting up in the hospital bed, looking reasonably cheerful. He had a spectacular black eye where he had caught the edge of a table as he fell and his broken jaw had been wired up, making speech difficult and painful.

'Darling, please don't talk,' Diana took his hands, 'let me explain to Laura. I went round to the flat this morning to collect some pyjamas and so on for Giles. Charlie's room had been more or less cleared – though it's still a terrible mess – and he's left his flat keys on the hall table. There's no note, but he told Wendy in the wine bar that he wouldn't be back. Honestly, you would have thought he'd have at least asked how Giles was – he could be dead for all Charlie knows.'

'I don't think Charlie knows what he's doing at the moment,' said Laura. 'It's as though he has become another person and it has to be my fault.'

'Don't start flaying yourself, darling,' said Diana. 'I'm just so glad you're out of the relationship. I never would have thought Charlie could be so violent.'

'He used to be . . .' Giles began.

'Don't speak,' the girls chorused.

'What I think Giles is trying to say is that Charlie used to be heavily into fairly violent demonstrations in his youth,' Laura said. Giles nodded his agreement.

'I knew he was very left wing, but I had no idea he was involved to that degree,' said Diana.

'Oh yes,' said Laura. 'In fact, I think his beliefs were behind most of our problems. When I had nothing, a no hoper, I was his sort of person, but since Gooseberries, in his view, I've been sliding steadily downhill. Do you know, the first time Charlie took a real interest in me was the day I had no food – that has to be significant.'

'No food, darling, what do you mean?'

'It was when I was about five months pregnant. I had run through my savings, I couldn't get a job and I literally had no money to buy anything to eat. It only lasted a day, but I've never been so frightened in my life. Charlie called round because my rent was overdue, and when I told him I had no money, he marched me straight down to the Social Security people who, of course, immediately bailed me out. Crazy, but I'd never thought of asking for help. Anyway, Charlie took me shopping to buy groceries and then insisted on my having lunch at the wine bar. He seemed to like my vulnerability, and quite honestly I think he's always resented my recovery. Poor old thing, he obviously likes lame ducks.'

'It's more a question of his not liking success,' said Giles, wincing with pain.

'Darling, will you please be quiet.' Diana leant forward and kissed Giles's cheek. 'Well, rightly or wrongly, Laura, I've always thought Charlie rather peculiar and definitely not for you.'

The combination of no Charlie, Giles ill and a new restaurant opening in three days proved quite a challenge for Laura and Diana, and certainly did not give Laura much time for introspection. As soon as Giles was discharged from hospital, they moved him into Laura's house so that he could be subjected to Bridget's ministrations. 'He's going to be a lot more trouble than Fram,' Bridget grumbled.

'No, he isn't,' said Diana, 'provided you treat him in exactly the same way.'

'I am house-trained,' Giles protested.

'Be quiet, darling, you know you mustn't speak. What I mean, Bridget, is that they can eat the same food and they need about the same amount of rest, and when they're both awake, they can entertain each other to give you a break.'

'I'm ill, it's not fair to leave me alone with Fram. He's too rough with me when I'm well, how could you be so heartless.'

'You wouldn't swop jobs, Diana, would you?' Bridget begged.

'I can't,' said Diana, 'but if they prove too much of a handful, just send for Laura and I and we'll smack their bottoms.'

'Promise,' said Giles, looking considerably more cheerful.

The New Year's Eve opening party for the Kings Road restaurant was a howling success. Both Laura and Diana had been secretly anxious about having neither Charlie nor Giles to help them, but they need not have worried. They had fretted about the wisdom of opening on New Year's Eve, unsure whether it was a good night for attracting publicity, with so much other competition around. They need not have worried – journalists flocked to enjoy an evening out at Gooseberries because now they had a track record of success.

After midnight, an area of the floor was cleared for dancing. Jamie was called in from the kitchen to open the dancing with a Scottish reel, which he did most proficiently, somehow managing to look the part despite his chef's uniform. They had trained in a new chef to take over South Kensington, feeling that Jamie was needed at Kings Road in order to see the new location properly launched.

'Thanks, boss,' he said to Laura, with a grin, as she handed him a pint of beer and a whisky chaser when he had finished dancing. 'Hell, this is a great party, and it'll keep going all night at this rate.'

'Happy New Year, Jamie,' said Laura, 'and thanks for everything – we couldn't have done it without you.'

'Without you, lassie, it would never have happened at all. Bless your cotton socks and here's to the next half a dozen restaurants.' They clinked glasses and as they did so, Diana called out from the back of the restaurant. 'Laura, telephone.'

'Telephone! Oh no, who is it, Bridget?'

'No, I don't think so, it sounds like your mother.'

'Oh hell,' said Laura, 'I should have rung them earlier.' She took the phone. 'Hi, Mummy, Happy New Year. I'm sorry I didn't ring before but it's been absolute bedlam here – the place is full to bursting.' There was a silence. 'Mummy, are you there?'

'Oh Laura.' It was her mother's voice but it came out in a strangled sob.

'Mummy, what is it, what's happened?'

'Laura, it's your father, he's – he's had a heart attack. We were at the Jasons' New Year's Eve party.' She was crying so hard it was difficult to understand her, particularly above the noise in the restaurant.

'Did you . . . did you say a heart attack?' Laura shouted. 'A heart attack, Mummy?'

'Yes.'

'Oh God,' said Laura. 'Have you got him to hospital? Which hospital is he at, I'll come right away?'

'There's no rush, darling,' Katrine said, her voice suddenly steady and very clear. 'He's already dead.'

CHAPTER FIFTEEN

It was a difficult decision, and he really did not know what to do for the best. On the one hand, David Lawson recognized that he was probably one of the last people Laura wanted to see at such a moment. They had parted bitterly in London two years before, but even ignoring that, it was his relationship with Laura which had caused the initial difficulties between herself and her father. Reading between the lines they had never really been close since. In addition, if he was honest, David could not remember Bernard Beecham with anything but dislike, and on that basis alone, attending his funeral seemed wrong. Yet however illogical, he felt for Laura's sake he should be there. For all their differences, David knew, perhaps better than most, how much her father had meant to Laura. Their fights had only been caused by the fact that they were so alike. A missing husband, a child, a business – she had coped with so much over the last two years, he wondered if she could stand this as well. With Serena being in the States on business, there was no awkwardness there. Somehow he could not have taken his wife to the funeral, a fact he might have had some difficulty explaining to her.

In the end, he left the decision until the morning of the funeral. He woke to an icy day, with a high wind, snow flurries and a leaden grey sky. Suddenly, it seemed very simple. He did not stop to consider whether Laura had other friends to help her through the ordeal. He just knew he had to be there – not leave her to cope alone.

The funeral took place at Hambledon church, the church Bernard had always favoured for his worshipping. It was not large and when David arrived it was crammed to bursting. The porchway was crowded with photographers, he even spotted a newsreel camera, and once inside, he discovered there was standing room only. Peering through the crowd, he could just see the figures of Laura and Katrine in the front pew. Laura, in black, looked more diminutive than ever.

The service began, familiar words glided across David's consciousness – 'Alpha and Omega . . . man born of woman has but a short time to live . . .' They sang the 23rd psalm and David, watching Laura's shoulders, thought he detected them shaking slightly but she held her head high. The church service ended but he did not follow the other mourners to the grave side – 'dust to dust, ashes to ashes' – he hated that part. Instead, he limped over to the lych-gate and stood looking up and down the village street. The wind was bitter, the sky heavy and turning a dirty yellow, indicating that snow was on the way. He hunched his duffle coat around him, wondering now why he had come after all. It was foolish of him to have imagined he could do anything for Laura. Those days were long gone. The wind tore at his coat and he turned, intending to quietly leave the churchyard, but as he did so he saw Laura and Katrine walking towards him down the path. There was no escape. Beside them walked an elderly man whom David instantly recognized as Lord Campling. Despite his age, the likeness to his son was startling – the slightly beaky nose and high cheekbones. David hurriedly stood aside. The women, their heads bent against the wind were almost past him when Laura saw him. 'David, how very kind of you to come.'

'Hello Laura, I'm so sorry.'

For a moment the entourage halted. 'Please come back to Meadows Reach,' Laura said, 'please.' Her dark blue eyes were full of tears, her face, although pale, was as exquisite as ever. At that moment he would have done anything in the world for her.

'Of course,' he said.

Meadow Reach was quite as opulent as David had remembered, yet already it seemed strangely bleak without the presence of Bernard Beecham. David accepted a glass of sherry and mingled with the large crowd which was accumulating in the drawing room and conservatory. Who were they all? He recognized some local faces but there were so many strangers – staff and business colleagues, he supposed. The strain on Laura and Katrine must be intolerable, he thought. All these people must be the last thing they needed, yet Bernard Beecham was too important a man to have left life quietly.

For half an hour or so, David wandered about talking to the odd person he knew, and then he decided it was time to lay claim to Laura. He could not find her anywhere and with some trepidation, he approached Katrine. She was sitting in the conservatory with a woman who was an older and less-good-looking version of herself – a sister, he presumed. 'Lady Beecham, I'm so sorry about your husband.'

Katrine eyed him up and down. 'David, David Lawson. I can't have seen you in ten years?'

'Something like that. I probably shouldn't be here really but somehow I felt . . .' Normally he had no difficulty in expressing himself, but his voice trailed away.

'You are a good friend of Laura's and you wanted to offer her some support, yes?'

'Yes, exactly,' he said.

'That was kind of you. I don't know where she is, as a matter of fact. I've been worried about her. Have you seen her?'

'No, I was coming to ask you the same question.'

'Try my little grandson's room. Up the stairs, second door on the left. He should be waking about now – I expect that's where she is.'

'Thank you,' said David, 'thank you very much.'

'I'm glad you're here, David,' said Katrine, 'Laura needs support at the moment, more than I do.'

David laboured up the long flight of stairs and knocked quietly on the door. There was no reply. He eased the door open quietly, fearing to wake the child. Laura was sitting on a little nursing chair at the end of the cot. Tears were streaming down her face, but she made no sound, nor did she turn her head. David came in and shut the door behind him. He offered no greeting. Acting instinctively, he walked up to the chair, lifted Laura to her feet and wrapped her in his arms. Her tears splashed all over his neck, her arms went round his waist and they stood thus for several minutes, during which time David realized he had never felt closer to anyone in his whole life, yet they had not spoken a single word.

It was Laura who at last broke the silence. 'David, your poor suit, it's drenched, I'm so sorry.'

David reached in his pocket and pulled out a handkerchief. 'Here, have a good blow and a mop up.'

She did as he suggested. 'I just can't stand it,' she said. 'All those people – all wandering around in my father's house, drinking his drink, laughing and chatting. I'm sure most of them have completely forgotten why they're here.'

'I know, I felt exactly the same.'

Laura smiled at him. 'Yes, you would.'

'Mum, Mum, Mum, Mum.' Fram was sitting up in his cot, his arms outstretched.

'Oh darling, we woke you.' Laura went to the cot and lifted the baby in her arms. 'Come and meet David, he's a very good friend of mine.'

David studied the child. Again the Campling look had come through strongly but there was something different about Fram. There was a warmth in the sunny smile and the eyes were not Francis's, they were Laura's – deep, deep blue and very large. 'I know absolutely nothing about babies,' said David, 'but this one seems very special.'

'He has his moments,' said Laura. 'Sit and talk to me while I change his nappy, if you can bear the smell. How are you, David? Tell me about your life.'

'I'm fine.' David sat down in the nursing chair. 'Business is booming, not on a grand scale but I'm making satisfactory progress none the less, and I still enjoy my work.'

'And marriage?' Laura said, concentrating on the task of keeping Fram on the changing mat.

'Marriage is fine, too. Serena, my wife, is in America at the moment. She's into computers and very high-powered. I don't understand a word she says half the time. She has some very influential clients in the States so she's there quite a lot.'

'You can't enjoy the separations,' Laura suggested.

David considered the question and answered it as truthfully as he could. 'Ours is a fairly relaxed marriage. I don't mean by that we're unfaithful to each other, I mean we don't have a very *domestic* relationship. We decided to live together within the framework of marriage but we still make our own plans independently and when time allows, we meet.'

It sounded rather bleak, Laura thought, but decided not to say so. There was a pause.

'And you,' David asked, 'any plans for re-marrying?'

'No,' Laura replied, 'after all, technically, I'm still married.' The well-remembered tension in her voice made David wish he had not spoken. 'There we go, there's a nice clean boy,' Laura said. 'Now I suppose we'd better find you something smart to wear to meet all those people. Hold him a moment, could you, David?' She plonked Fram in David's arms and much to David's surprise the baby settled happily. He was flattered by his unexpected success.

Laura began searching through a suitcase on the floor, when there was a knock on the door. 'Come in,' she called.

Lord Campling peered round the door, eyed David curiously and then addressed Laura. 'I'm sorry to interrupt but there's a phone call for you, my dear – it's Diana apparently – she's your partner, isn't she?'

'Oh hell, yes, sorry, thank you William. I wonder what on earth she wants.' Laura looked flustered. 'Could you possibly tell her I'll ring her back as soon as I have Fram dressed.

'I've already tried that, my dear, but with no success, I'm afraid. She says it's urgent.'

'But how can it be that urgent? It's my father's funeral, for God's sake. Surely she can manage without me for this one day. I just don't know how she can be so thoughtless.' Laura ran an agitated hand through her hair, a gesture David well remembered.

'Shall I go and speak to her?' he suggested.

'No, no it's alright. I know I'm being silly. Could you just hold on to Fram for a moment.'

With Laura gone, the two men were forced into conversation. Hampered by Fram and with no free hand to click his iron into position, David had no alternative but to remain seated.

'I'm sorry I can't get up, sir. My name's David Lawson – I was in the same year and house at school as your son, Francis.'

'Were you now, and clearly you know my daughter-in-law, too.' There was no warmth in his voice.

'Yes, I've known Laura for many years.'

'Have you . . . I see.' Clearly William Campling viewed him as some kind of threat, and David wondered why.

There was an awkward pause. 'You must be very proud of your grandson, sir.'

'Yes, he's a fine boy.' Another pause. This is very hard work, David thought, I hope Laura isn't too long.

In the hall, the babble of voices made it difficult to hear.

'Darling, are you alright, how was the funeral?' Laura's anger faded. It was good to hear Diana's familiar voice.

'Actually it was ghastly,' Laura said.

'I bet it was, poor you.' Laura suddenly realized that Diana sounded nervous as if she was trying to steel herself into saying something – something unpleasant.

'Di, what is it, William said it was urgent. Is something wrong?'

'Well, yes, I'm afraid there is.'

'What *is* it – the house, the restaurants, Bridget? . . . for Heaven's sake, Di, don't keep me in suspense.'

'Oh Laura, I'm so sorry, this is such an awful way to tell you, and at such a dreadful time, too, only . . . Laura it's Charlie – I'm afraid there's been an accident, and he's – he's dead.'

The combination of the background noise, and Diana's reluctance to give Laura any details, meant it was some time before Laura grasped the facts. When she did, they appalled her. The previous evening, Charlie had apparently called at her house and had been let in by Bridget. He had been very drunk and his unbalanced state had frightened Bridget considerably. She could not get rid of him fast enough, though once he established that neither Laura nor Fram were in, he had left without protest. Where he went from there was anyone's guess. However it seemed likely to have been on a pub crawl with old friends, for he was next seen at an abortive attempt at worker occupation of Elite Engineering, a firm in Hackney. The battle between police and workers was particularly brutal, and at its height, Charlie was accidentally mown down by a police car. He died instantly.

'I had to telephone you,' Diana said. 'I just couldn't see any alternative. I have Bridget here with me because she's in such a state, and the trouble is neither of us knew when exactly you and Fram are coming back to London. I could have waited, but as you can imagine, Charlie's death has made the headlines everwhere – it's on the news, all over the *Standard* . . . I just couldn't risk you seeing the story unprepared.' Diana's voice shook with nerves.

'Poor Charlie,' was all Laura could manage for a while. Then she said. 'I – I bet he was still drunk, that's why he fell in front of the car. He's so strong, he'd never have been shoved around normally. Oh Di, what have I done? I can't bear it, it's happening all over again . . .' Laura threw down the phone and ran up the stairs into the bathroom, where she was violently sick. Then she threw herself on to the floor and sobbed. She was still there when David found her.

'Is her car an automatic?' David asked. Katrine nodded. 'Good, then I'll drive her and Fram back to London in it and catch a train home.'

'There's no need for that, I'll take her back to London and my chauffeur can deliver the car tomorrow,' William Campling said.

'No,' said Katrine with unexpected force. 'If she must go back to London, and I understand how she feels, then she's best with David.'

David sighed with relief. He had already promised Laura he would stay with her, but for a moment it had looked as though her family would intervene. He smiled gratefully at Katrine. 'Will you be alright without her?'

'Don't give me another thought, David, just look after Laura for me, will you?'

David collected Laura's car keys and walked round to the garage. A gleaming Rolls Bentley was parked next to an Alfa Romeo and beside them, Laura's little Renault stood out in odd contrast to her parents' cars. For some reason, the sight of it pleased David. He climbed into the driver's seat. Everything in the car was neat and ordered. A portable tape recorder and a pad and paper lay on the passenger seat –

clearly Laura worked as she drove. The back was mostly taken up with a baby seat, beside which was a carefully arranged box of toys. Always efficient, always organized, she had changed very little after all. Perhaps, therefore, it was not so surprising that he knew with unshakeable conviction that he was the only person who could help her now. It was as though there had been no intervening years. The difficulty of their last meeting, the bitterness at their parting, melted as though it had never existed. All David's concentration was aimed now at helping her through this appalling double blow. He hated the idea of her being involved with this man who was some sort of communist agitator, but this was no moment to consider his own feelings.

As he drove her car round the drive to the front door, memories he had tried to suppress came flooding back – memories of their time together, Laura the child, Laura the teenager . . . He knew, at that moment, with shattering conviction, that with no other woman would he ever share the warmth, the companionship and the joy he had shared with Laura. Since they had parted, he had only been half alive and the half that had died, Serena had never been able to reawaken. The discovery of these feelings did not just surprise him. It terrified him.

CHAPTER SIXTEEN

David and Laura talked very little on their journey to London. For one thing, it was snowing hard, icy and almost dark so that the weather conditions needed all David's concentration. For another, Fram was awake and restless, clearly upset by his mother's grief and there was nothing they could say of any meaning which was suitable for a child's ears.

Laura had become curiously passive. When they reached the house, she allowed David to unload the car, carry Fram into the sitting room, light the fire and put on the kettle. 'Now what shall I do?' he asked.

'I suppose we'd better put Fram to bed.' Katrine had fed the baby before they had left for London, so together – David carrying a now calmer Fram – they went up to his nursery, bathed and put him to bed. For David, sharing this nightly routine with Laura and her son, was an experience he found deeply moving. For Laura, Charlie's rocking horse dominating Fram's room, made her want to run from the house screaming.

With Fram in bed, Laura felt a little better – there was no longer any need to keep up appearances for the sake of the child. By mutual agreement, they abandoned the kettle in favour of a bottle of wine and sat together on the floor in front of the fire. David let her talk. She told him everything about her relationship with Charlie, everything that is, she knew herself. It was clear she had never loved him, and David hated himself for the relief he felt when he realized this was true. The poor man was dead – couldn't he at least share a little of Laura's love with a dead man, who had clearly loved her so much? Apparently not.

'You can't blame yourself, Laura, you just can't,' he said. 'From what you tell me, Charlie's political beliefs were very much a part of him. These violent demonstrations are terrible for everyone concerned, but he was no novice, he knew the score, and the risks involved. So, maybe he was drunk, in which case he should have had more sense than to get involved.'

'No one's sensible when they're drunk, and he was drunk because of me,' Laura said, wearily.

Their conversation continued in the same vein until they were both exhausted. David made some toast, which Laura would not even try to eat, and he opened another bottle of wine.

'I shouldn't be allowed anywhere near a man – look what I do to them.' Laura's voice was thick with tears – she had been crying continuously while David was in the kitchen. 'Francis disappeared, Charlie . . . oh, David.'

'We had some good times,' David said, quietly. Their eyes held, the only sounds in the room were the shifting of the logs and the ticking of the clock.

'I wonder,' said Laura, 'I wonder what would have happened to all of our lives if I had not been successful in that interview for *Opinions*. Funny to think of it – just one single thing, like being successful in acquiring a new job, changes lives – yours, mine, Serena's, Francis's, little Fram, who would never have existed, and Charlie, who would still be alive.' Her voice ended in a sob.

'If Charlie had not come to grief over this particular incident then there would have been another occasion. From what you tell me, poor old Charlie was not very much in love with life?'

'Can you really believe that?' Laura asked.

'I think so,' said David. He was standing by the mantelpiece, and he shifted his weight as he spoke – the strain of walking and standing all day was starting to tell.

'Sit down,' said Laura gently, 'your leg's hurting, isn't it?'

It was the natural way she spoke about his leg that reminded David, yet again, of just how close they had been. He spent a great deal of his working life, these days, dealing with strangers or people he did not know well, and he was used to the fact that they always treated his disability as if it did not exist. To Laura it was just a part of him, like the nose on his face and so she could speak of it without embarrassment. He did as she suggested, sitting down in the chair by her so that she could lean against his knee. 'Only a little,' he said, 'it's been a long day, hasn't it?'

'Let's talk about you, David,' Laura said suddenly. 'Tell me, are you ambitious – do you want to make a million like Pop?'

David shrugged. 'No, I don't think so. I'm not yet thirty – well not until my next birthday – but I think I'm already getting rather complacent. I have a good income, I have a nice house and as a result, I seem to have lost my drive, my enthusiasm. I don't quite know why. I think perhaps . . .' he hesitated.

'Perhaps what?' Laura asked.

He wanted desperately to be honest. 'I'm very fond of Serena, of course, but I think it would help if we had children. If we had a growing family, I'd have more to work for. In a way I live the life of a bachelor who just happens to be married to his permanent girlfriend.'

'Doesn't she want children?' Laura asked.

'No, I don't think so. When I discuss it, she always says let's talk about it in a year or two. She's fearfully ambitious and right to be so, she's a very clever girl, but it's difficult to see how she could ever fit motherhood round her work.'

'That's sad,' said Laura, 'and you're so good with Fram.'

They talked then about Bernard – starting with an attempt to analyse what had motivated his enormous success, and finishing with Laura tearfully telling David just how much she would miss the man she had spent most of her adult life running away from.

'I've got to stop this crying,' she said at last, 'it must be driving you mad. I'll go and make up the bed in Bridget's room and let you get some sleep.'

David put a hand lightly on Laura's shoulder. He was terrrified of doing the wrong thing. 'Are you sure you don't mind me staying? It's too late to catch a train now but I could easily book into a hotel.'

'If you wouldn't mind, I'd like you to stay, I just don't want to be alone tonight.'

'Of course not.'

They changed the sheets together, made some coffee and then returned to the fire. They were both exhausted but neither wanted to part from the other and there seemed no other way to be together.

'It's strange,' said Laura. 'The last time I spoke to Pop, we talked briefly of Charlie. Pop wanted me to divorce Francis so that I could start taking a more positive attitude towards men.'

'He wanted you to marry Charlie?' David was appalled.

'Not necessarily Charlie, but someone.'

David stood up abruptly, and walked over to the curtained window.' He was right, of course, you should marry again, it's just that . . .' His back was towards Laura so that she could not see his face.

'Just that what?' she asked.

'Nothing, forget it.' He turned round but did not return to the fire. Instead he began wandering restlessly around the room.

'How can I forget it with you pacing about like this, David. Tell me what you were going to say – please.'

'Alright, alright,' David stopped pacing and glared at Laura. She could see the tension in him and it shocked her. 'This is neither the time nor the place, but as you insist . . . I just can't . . . I can't stand the idea of there being someone else, someone new in your life. I know I'm being irrational, I know I'm married now and I know a woman of your age must have another chance at happiness.' Laura looked horrified but David could not stop now he had started – the flood gates were wide open. 'I couldn't bear it when I heard you'd married Francis. He's always been such a bastard that man, ever since he was a child. I know I shouldn't speak ill of the dead – presumed dead – but I hated him. The idea of him touching you, making love to you and knowing all the time that ultimately, he would hurt you and let you down, I used to think it would drive me insane. Of course, never in my wildest imaginings did I think he would disappear as he did, but when it happened, I was such a fool. I reacted emotionally, you see, and thought I only had to come to you and you'd fall into my arms again. As we know only too well, that didn't happen, so I decided I would just get on with my life and hope you would be happy again one day. But today, I realized there's never been anyone but you, never has, never can, and when I think someone else might hurt you, I just can't bear it . . .' he turned away, rested his hands on the mantelpiece and hung his head.

His heaving shoulders told Laura he was crying. She stood up. She saw that where his hands gripped the shelf, his knuckles were white with tension. She did not stop to think, she just reached out and put her hands over his. They relaxed their grip at her touch, she pulled them away, turned him round to face her and took him in her arms, holding him close, soothingly, gently as one would a hurt child.

David was first to be aware of the change in the nature of their embrace. He could feel himself reacting to her closeness, but there was nothing he could do to pull away. Gently, he lifted her chin and kissed her, and the moment their lips met, the fuse was lit. All his longing, all his frustrations were released with a single kiss. His lips seemed on fire, he wanted to devour her, to crush her to him, to never let her go.

In seconds they were tearing the clothes from each other's bodies, insensible to reason, to any conscious thought save the need to be one. On the carpet before the fire, he took her with such a force that all she could do was lie there and hold him until he was spent.

'I'm sorry, darling, I'm sorry, did I hurt you? I just couldn't stop. I couldn't wait . . .'

'I know, it's alright. I love you, David. I wanted you just as much.'

A little later they went upstairs into Bridget's room. Laura did not need to say that her room was not possible, that Charlie's ghost lingered there, David knew. On the narrow single bed, with aching tenderness he began to kiss her body, every part known and loved. She had forgotten how well he understood her. Soon she was groaning, begging him to stop, and when at last he entered her again, bringing her to a shuddering, gasping climax, she could think of nothing, no one – not her father, nor Charlie, nor even her son – no one but the man in her arms.

Attuned to the early morning requirements of a baby, it was Laura who woke first. In the adjoining room she could hear Fram bouncing up and down in his cot. He was cheerful at the moment but would start grizzling soon and for Fram, a bad start to the day tended to affect his mood for the rest of it. David lay on his side facing her and fast asleep. Carefully she eased herself out of bed, her whole concentration centred on not waking him. At that moment she did not dare stop to consider the consequences of what had happened. She slipped on a dressing gown, crept out of the room and went to do battle with Fram.

She went through the motions of washing, changing and conversing with her young son, carried him into the kitchen, put him in his high chair and began making his breakfast. Her only concession to allowing herself to consider David's presence was to make two mugs of coffee, rather than one. Coffee made, she left Fram massaging banana into his hair and carried the mugs into Bridget's bedroom. David's eyes snapped open the moment she entered. He did not attempt to move, he just lay smiling at her. She kicked the door shut behind her and leant against it, more for support than anything. His eyes were watching her now, his expression intimate, full of love and longing, demanding, she knew, that she should forget everything – Fram, the coffee, his marriage, Charlie, work . . . and throw herself into his arms. 'Good morning,' he said, gently. 'Tell me, did I imagine what happened last night, was I dreaming or was it all true?'

Laura did not return his smile. 'It was all true,' she said. 'God help us, but it was all true.'

David struggled into a sitting position, the sheet fell away exposing his chest and his powerful shoulders. His physical strength and beauty, combined with the knowledge Laura had of how he had acquired such a physique, brought sudden tears to her eyes. She turned her head away. He patted the bed. 'Darling, come and sit down. I did a lot of thinking last night, when you were asleep, and things are going to be fine.'

She put his coffee on the bedside table and then retreated like a frightened rabbit to sit perched on the end of the dressing-table stool. 'How can you possibly say that?'

'It's very simple really,' said David, confidently, 'I love you, you love me. We should never have parted all those years ago but we did. Perhaps it was not such a bad thing. We've both done a lot of growing up since, seen the rough and smooth of life. I want to make a home for you, Laura, anywhere you like. If it has to be London, fair enough. I'm ready to give up my business this time. I'll sell it off and start something else. Who knows, perhaps I can help you with developing Gooseberries. And as for Fram – alright, so he's not my child, but how could anyone resist him. He's great. Maybe, maybe one day we'll have children of our own, but I can promise you they'll get no more of my love and attention than Fram.'

Laura put down her coffee cup unsteadily. 'David, haven't you overlooked one small point – you're married, remember?'

'No, of course I haven't overlooked it but I think, strangely enough, Serena will understand.'

'Oh, come on,' said Laura, 'you're planning to walk out on your wife for another woman and you expect her to understand. What are you hoping, that she'll be our bridesmaid?'

'Don't be flip, Laura,' David said.

'Well, are you surprised if I am? Good God, think about it for a moment, David. How long have you been married, a year, eighteen months?'

'Just over two years,' said David. For a moment the painful meeting with Laura, which had precipitated his decision to marry Serena, came back into his mind with perfect clarity. Unlike on that occasion, he must not blow this, he thought, he must not lose her now.

'Big deal, two years,' said Laura. 'Do you think that represents an adequate amount of time to spend on making a marriage work?'

'It was the wrong marriage, Laura. I married Serena for all the wrong reasons – to get even with you, I suppose, to prove that I could live without you. Well, if ever I had any doubts – either of us had any doubts – surely last night proved we have to be together.'

'That was sex,' said Laura.

'That was *love*,' said David. They stared at each other in

silence, the intimacy of the night before suddenly seeming a million miles away. How could they have been so close and were now suddenly, inexplicably, so far apart, David thought desperately.

'David, let me make something clear. I appear to have already fouled up two men's lives and I'm just not prepared to be the one to break up your marriage. It's simply not morally right to take away another woman's husband.'

'Oh, don't be so pompous, Laura. It's *my* marriage and *my* wife and I think you should leave it up to me to decide what's morally right or wrong. Serena's first love has always been her work. I want family life – children, a companion, someone with whom I can share my life, rather than talk to long distance. Serena wants none of those things. If we're talking moralities, she has no right to stop me having the things that she herself is not prepared to give.'

'Now who's being pompous,' said Laura. 'You knew what Serena was like when you married her, or if you didn't, you certainly should have done. You accepted her for what she was. OK, so you made a mistake, so you found out that the kind of life you share with her is not what you wanted. Well, tough, David, you can't just opt out of your obligations because life doesn't quite come up to scratch.' She knew how much her words were hurting him, but she dare not think about it.

'If you did not exist, Laura,' said David, 'it is true I would stay married and faithful to Serena for the rest of my life, *but you do exist*. I have always loved you and I always will, nothing and no one in the world can change that. I've given up too easily in the past, but I'm not giving up this time.'

'David, I want you to get up, get dressed and leave this house now,' said Laura. 'I want you to remember last night as something which happened because we were both emotionally upset by my father's funeral and Charlie's death. It was, if you like, a night spent together for old times' sake, something enjoyable but not something which should start changing the fabric of our lives. It was sex, David, nothing more, just good sex.'

David stared at her in silence, trying to come to terms with the words she had spoken. 'Is that really how you saw last night?' he asked at last, his voice barely above a whisper.

'Yes,' said Laura, without hesitation.

'Are you saying you don't love me?'

'I'm saying I'm very fond of you, but that one night of infidelity is no reason to leave your wife.'

David's face showed no emotion. He threw back the bedclothes and swung his good leg out of bed, pulling the paralysed one after it. He tried to stand and hop over to where his clothes lay but in his emotional state, he could not get his balance. 'Shit, God dammit,' he shouted, 'pass my bloody leg iron, would you? Christ, you'd think at a moment like this, at least I'd be able to walk out of your life with some sort of dignity.'

Laura, trembling, stood up and passed him his leg iron. His vulnerability almost broke her resolve – she dare not stay. Turning, she ran out of the room, into the kitchen and slammed the door behind her. Fram had been busy while she was away. Having applied liberal quantities of banana to just about everywhere, he had poured orange juice into his cereal bowl and then tipped the whole lot into his high-chair tray. He was now playing mud pies with startling success. Fram, the floor, indeed amazingly far-flung corners of the kitchen, were all covered in goo. 'Oh Fram,' said Laura and burst into tears. While Fram was impressed that his wickedness should have caused so much emotion, the smile of delight faded and he, too, began to wail. The bellow from his healthy young lungs completely drowned his mother's wracking sobs, so that when, moments later, David Lawson limped out of their lives, all he heard from the other side of the closed kitchen door were the typical sounds of a family breakfast – something which he knew now he would never experience.

CHAPTER SEVENTEEN

'We've been here before, haven't we?' said Chris Berry. He and Eleanor were sitting in their garden room. It was getting late and Chris had drunk a great deal too much brandy, which always made him aggressive.

Eleanor was worried about his drinking but even tentative suggestions that he was overdoing it caused his anger to flare out of control, and these days she was just too tired to cope. 'Been where before?' she asked.

'Don't be dense, Eleanor – you know perfectly well what I mean. Why is she here again, that's what I want to know, and why does she always choose us to have her emotional crises all over?'

'I don't exactly know,' said Eleanor. 'I've been wondering the same thing myself, but I do have a theory.'

'Go on then,' said Chris, wearily, 'let's have it.'

'Well . . .' said Eleanor, 'when life becomes too difficult for Laura to cope with, I think she has to go back to the point where everything started to go wrong – to the core of her disquiet, the cancer in her life, if you like.'

'Oh charming, and so you're saying that's what we represent?'

'In a way, yes. You see we were the first people to see Laura after Francis disappeared. We are the only people, outside her parents and Lord Campling, who were a part of that drama. She tries to put it behind her, to go out and face the world, but when she stumbles and falls, she is drawn back, like a magnet I suppose, to the beginning again.'

'Bloody medics can always explain everything away. Don't you think she just enjoys coming here for free booze and food, and an endlessly sympathetic ear?'

'You used to be such a nice man,' Eleanor said. Her voice was sad, not critical. She was simply making an observation, but it was clearly the wrong thing to say.

'I was? Has it ever occurred to you that I may have changed for a reason.'

'We've both changed, of course,' said Eleanor, 'but you used to be so kind, there was so much love and compassion in you, and humour, too. Where's it all gone, Chris?'

'Drained out of me by mortgages and children, I expect.'

'A lot of people would envy you your family life. We have a lovely home and two nice children who are happy and healthy.' Eleanor could hear the resentment in her own voice.

'We also have the biggest bloody mortgage I've ever heard of, and those happy, healthy children never give me a moment's peace. All we have to look forward to is years of school fees, clothes, orthodontistry, new bicycles, first cars . . .'

'Enough,' said Eleanor standing up, 'I've had enough, Chris. If you're not happy with us, why don't you go off and find yourself the sort of sterile lifestyle which doesn't interfere with your much-coveted peace. I'm sure, if you try, you can create a little world where you can concentrate exclusively on pleasing yourself, where other people's feelings are of absolutely no importance. There are hundreds of people doing it all over Oxford – academics, writers, musicians – why not join them? The only difference is they have a legitimate excuse for their isolation while you're nothing but a second-rate publisher, going nowhere, who's so self-absorbed that you're rapidly becoming a second-rate human being as well.'

Left alone after her outburst, Chris attacked the brandy bottle with renewed enthusiasm. There was plenty he could say to the bitch in response to her allegations – like how dreary she had become, how the demands of her job and her two sons always left her too tired for anything – sex, entertaining, a meal out . . . he wondered suddenly whether Eleanor could have found out about his affair with Maeve O'Neal, but then dismissed the thought. It was just not possible.

He had met Maeve at a publishing bash several months before. The evening was boring him rigid and he was taking solace in the whisky bottle when he noticed one of the girls working for the caterers. She had the bright red hair, startling blue eyes and pale skin that belong exclusively to the southern

Irish. He had asked her name. 'Maeve O'Neal, but what's it to you, mister?' she had answered, in a soft Irish brogue, with a bright smile to match.

'I don't know, yet,' he had answered truthfully. Later, over dinner, he discovered she was a postgraduate, studying English literature, with the hopes, ultimately, of becoming a writer. He knew part of his attraction for her was the fact he was a publisher, because he moved in publishing circles and knew the kind of people who interested her. However, he also flattered himself that it was not as simple as that. They were brilliant in bed together, better than he and Eleanor had ever been. She was so young, so inventive, so, well, yes – wanton – not at all the good Catholic girl who, he frequently teased her, she should be. It was tempting to go to her now, just to get up, walk out of the house and go straight to Maeve. He thought of her room, of the wild clutter of books and the king-sized bed on which she worked and they made love. Who could blame him, he thought, after what Eleanor had just said, yet he knew it would be a mistake. Up until now, he and Maeve had been very discreet. He did not feel ready to tackle the affair out in the open – for one thing, he did not know what Maeve wanted from him, and he was also frightened of losing his children.

He stood up and wandered into the sitting room, restless, unhappy and, despite the brandy and the hour, very far from sleep. A heap of Laura's clutter was piled together on the dining-room table. That bloody woman – things were always worse when she was around. He could not understand what Eleanor saw in her. He stared at the collection with some annoyance – some notebooks, a pile of Fram's Lego, cigarettes and a lighter. When and why had she started to smoke? It was bad enough putting up with a smoky atmosphere in the office all day, but to come home to it as well was too much. What did she scribble all day in these notebooks, anyway? He picked up one and flicked through it, barely bothering to glance at what was there. Then his eye caught the illustrations in the margin and he began turning over the pages more slowly. Finally, he sat down at the dining room table, his personal problems completely forgotten, his thoughts totally absorbed in what he had discovered.

Chris was waiting for Laura when she came down to breakfast the following morning. 'Those recipe books of yours, Laura, what made you start illustrating them?'

Laura and Eleanor were doling out cereal to the children. Laura glanced up at Chris apprehensively and was shocked at what she saw. His eyes were red-rimmed from brandy and lack of sleep, he hadn't shaved and his manner was, as always, hostile. 'Oh, I don't know, to cheer up Jamie after a heavy night, I suppose.'

'Jamie?'

'He's our chef, but I dream up most of our new dishes – it's one of my main contributions to the business. I always try them out at home first before passing them on to Jamie and something nearly always goes wrong – some ghastly domestic drama – so I simply draw pictures of myself getting more and more frazzled in the margin.' Laura smiled. 'Jamie likes them, he says they're the best part of the recipes. It's just a bit of fun.'

'Fun . . .,' Chris said, slowly. Food, fun – yes, that was it. 'Laura, how would you feel if I took your notebooks in to one of our editors today?'

Laura looked at him in astonishment. Whatever reason Chris had for asking her about her recipes, she had assumed it was the prelude to him ridiculing her. She knew it had been a mistake to come back to the Berrys. Chris still resented her and Eleanor seemed so preoccupied and miserable.

It had been a panic reaction. Within a few hours of David leaving, the police had been knocking on her door to ask about Charlie. She, of course, could tell them virtually nothing about his political activities, but the interview had been harrowing, and after they had left she knew she had to get out of London again – fast. Diana, Bridget and a rapidly improving Giles said they could cope with the restaurants, she could not bear the thought of Meadows Reach without her father, and so the Berrys had seemed the obvious place to come at the time. Now she regretted it.

She forced herself to concentrate on what Chris was saying. 'Your recipes are unusual but judging by the ingredients, fairly cheap, right?' Laura nodded. 'That's good but they wouldn't stand up on their own without those manic little illustrations which really pull the whole thing altogether. It's a new approach to cooking – fun rather than drudgery – most cookery books talk down to women, yours would sympathize.'

He had Eleanor's attention now. 'I didn't realize you were so appreciative of the housewife's plight.'

There was a bitterness in her voice, which made Laura wince, but for once Chris did not rise to the bait. 'These days there is a lot of money to be made from recipe books, provided one can think up a new angle. You've got one and it would be very cheap to produce.'

'Hang on a moment,' said Laura. 'Let me get this straight. You're suggesting we turn my recipes into a book?'

'Why not? Just think what it would do for the publicity of the restaurants – PR on a plate, and you'd be making money, too. It could be big, very big. These illustrations, they're truly international, they're every woman, any woman . . . the world over.'

'Can I have a look?' said Eleanor, curiously.

'Yes, I'll fetch one,' Chris was back in a moment.

Cereal forgotten, Eleanor sat down at the kitchen table. 'These are good, Laura, very good – he could be right, you know.'

'It's very nice to know that you think *I*'m right about something, even if I am a second-rate publisher.' Chris could not resist the jibe.

Laura looked from one to the other, not understanding what was going on, but recognizing the aggression. 'Look, Chris,' she said, trying to diffuse the atmosphere, 'it's awfully kind of you to take an interest but I'm sure you have more than enough to do without concerning yourself with my scribbling. I was thinking of going home today actually. It's been very kind of you to have me but . . .'

'Go home, you can't go home now, not until I've discussed this with my colleagues. It's a bit of luck actually – we have our editorial meetings on a Thursday. Can you be around at lunchtime – you did mention something about going to see your mother today?'

'No, I've decided against it,' said Laura. 'As I said, I was really planning to go back to London.'

'Couldn't you stay with us for one more night?' The sudden change in Chris flabbergasted both women.

Laura glanced at Eleanor. 'Is that alright?'

'Of course it's alright,' said Eleanor.

'Good,' said Chris, 'I'll show the notebooks around first thing this morning and then perhaps, if it sparks off any interest, we can meet for lunch.'

Laura spent the morning trying not to think about what Chris had said. This new Chris, the one she recognized as much from Eleanor's troubled eyes, as from his own erratic behaviour, did not inspire confidence. Besides which, she had no time to write a book . . . yet writing *was* her first love. The restaurant trade, although exhilarating, was also very draining. It was physically wearing, mentally taxing and a surprisingly emotional business. As she wandered around Eleanor's house, helping with the chores, seeing to the needs of the children, she found herself beginning to fantasize about how the book should be presented. She tried to fight off her thoughts but they persisted, and it was a relief to think of something besides her father, poor Charlie and the expression on David's face when she had told him they had no future together.

There were three telephone calls during the morning. The first was a girlfriend of Eleanor's who wanted to dump her children on Eleanor the following day. The second call was from a house-painter, touting for business. On both occasions Laura tried to ignore her disappointment. The third call was from Chris. 'The Elizabeth Restaurant, one o'clock. Borrow Eleanor's car,' he said, 'can't stop, I'm in a meeting.'

'At least tell me what happened, Chris – give me some idea of what to expect,' Laura persisted.

'Let's say that at the Elizabeth you will hear something which will be to your advantage.'

The man sitting beside Chris in the Elizabeth looked absurdly like Winnie the Pooh. The centre of his head was entirely bald, and on either side sprang two eccentric tufts of hair, like ears, to complete the picture. His girth was certainly of Pooh proportions, his face open, friendly and kind. At any moment Laura expected him to ask her whether she had brought along a pot of honey.

Chris jumped up at the sight of Laura. 'Laura, meet Gerald Seaton, he's head of our non-fiction.'

Winnie the Pooh stood up, stuck out a paw, pumped Laura's hand enthusiastically and smiled a sweet smile. It was obvious that they liked one another immediately. In Gerald, Laura saw someone upon whom she could rely, something certain in an uncertain world. Gerald saw an exquisitely pretty young woman, who looked little more than a child with her wild hair and vivid colouring, and who had him wishing fervently that he was twenty-five years younger.

Wine was ordered, and they talked while they waited for it to arrive, about the weather, the merits of the Elizabeth Restaurant, indeed anything but the subject that had brought them out to lunch. In the end Laura could stand it no more. She looked directly at Gerald. 'So what did you think of my notebooks, Mr Seaton?'

'I thought they were quite wonderful, my dear.'

'Wonderful,' Laura queried, 'but not commercial?'

'Wonderful and highly commercial. Indeed, extraordinarily commercial.'

Laura felt the blood rush to her face. 'Do you . . . do you mean it?'

'Of course, my dear, I never flatter.'

'It's true,' said Chris, 'he can be an absolute bastard when he doesn't like something.'

'Thank you, Christopher, that will do.' Gerald turned his small bright eyes to Laura. 'There is one snag. If we were to turn your jottings into a book, I would want to publish in time for next Christmas.'

'What does that mean exactly?' Laura asked.

'Well, it's a simple enough book to produce – in fact that's part of its charm. I thought perhaps we could present it rather like a child's exercise book, with just a second colour to brighten it, and containing about fifty recipes.'

'I like the idea,' said Laura, truthfully.

'There,' said Gerald, 'it must be right. Let me see, if we

could have a manuscript with us by the beginning of June, then we could probably publish mid to late October.'

'June?' said Laura. 'There's a lot of work to be done – all the illustrating as well as working out the recipes themselves.'

'I know,' said Gerald. 'I'm well aware of what I'm asking. The alternative is to wait a year and do it the following Christmas, but the sooner we can launch these books of yours the better. It's a startlingly original idea and I wouldn't like anyone else to pip us to the post.'

'Books . . .' said Laura, '. . . you mean, you think there could be more than one?'

'I'm, sure of it. If we can start with your basic restaurant recipes, we can then move into other areas. I don't know what exactly – you're the expert – but, say, fish, pastry, picnics, children's parties.'

'Yes,' said Laura, feeling a stir of excitement, 'yes, we could.'

'How long, honestly, do you think you need?' Chris asked. 'Of course I've explained to Gerald about your restaurant interests, but what I haven't mentioned to him is that you have a two-year-old son.'

'And a mother's help,' said Laura. She considered the question. 'Fram isn't the problem, as long as I have Bridget around – the restaurants are the real commitment. I wonder, I wonder . . . if Di would cover for me for a few months.' She looked at Gerald, 'I could do with a break as a matter of fact, it's been rather a difficult period.'

'Di, I assume, is your partner,' Gerald said. Laura nodded. 'Well, my dear, I'd have thought it would be very much in her own interests to cover for you. If your book does well, and I see no reason why it should not, it will make your restaurants.'

'Yes, I'd thought of that,' said Laura.

'Well, ponder on it, my dear,' said Gerald.

'I don't need to,' Laura said suddenly. 'I'll do it . . . by June.'

'But we haven't even discussed money.' Gerald was amused.

'I never do,' said Laura, 'I can't bear it. You must talk to my agent.'

'Oh God,' said Gerald to Chris, in mock horror, 'you didn't tell me she had an agent. Now I suppose we'll have to pay this wretched young woman a decent advance.'

'Agent or no agent, I would have expected that,' said Laura, firmly. She was learning fast, Chris thought. Gerald preferred his authors cheeky – the more difficult they were, the more of a challenge they presented, the more interest he took in their future.

'£10,000!' Laura stared across the desk at Harry Sutherland. Pride gave him a hectic flush which in turn made him look more sleek than usual. He smiled roguishly. 'Not bad, eh?'

'Not bad, it's a monstrous amount of money for an advance,' said Laura. 'Are you sure you've got the noughts right?'

'Quite sure. Mind you I've let them have all rights. They think it can be an international seller. For all this money, they're not simply thinking UK market – it's America they're after.'

'I just don't believe it,' said Laura.

'Believe it or not, the first instalment is on its way. So, I've done my bit, now it's up to you to come up with the goods. How are you going to manage it?'

'Well,' Laura admitted, 'it's taking some organizing. I want to stay in London until after Fram's second birthday, which is on March the 19th. Also, that will give my partners time to get married and have a honeymoon. They want to go to the Caribbean, and they deserve a break.'

'Good grief, what wonderful lives you people lead,' said Harry, 'so exotic.'

'Not me,' said Laura. 'Anyway, in a nutshell, around the 20th of March, Fram and I and my mother's help, Bridget, need to get out of London and find somewhere quiet where I can work. If I stay in London, I won't be able to leave the restaurants alone. The question is, where do I go?'

'No problem there,' said Harry. 'A friend of mine has a cottage which he rarely uses at Port Navas in Cornwall. I send all my erring authors down there, when they've fallen behind on a deadline. It's a fantastic place to work, right on the

Helford River, with very presentable hostelries all round you – you'll love it.'

'You're making this sound like an order,' said Laura.

'It is,' said Harry. 'Shall I arrange it?'

'Why not? I had vaguely thought of going back to my parents' home. My mother's in Greece at the moment visiting relatives, so we would be alone. However, I think I might feel spooked so soon after my father's death.'

'It's not a good idea,' said Harry. 'You want to go somewhere which makes no demands on you. Leave it to Harry.'

Laura got up to go. 'You know, Harry, I can't resist saying this. Three years ago, I suggested to you that I wrote a recipe book and you threw the idea out of court. All you were interested in was my sensationalizing my husband's disappearance. It would be churlish of me, I suppose, to say now "I told you so . . .".'

'It would be churlish,' Harry agreed, 'because I don't withdraw a word of what I said. I told you then that you had to be someone before you could write such a book and now you're the proprietor of two restaurants, which puts you in the position of being an authority on the subject. Besides which, the presentation is so novel, and how was I to know that you had some strange power over Gerald Seaton. Up to now I've always found him a difficult old bugger to deal with, but where you were concerned, he couldn't have been more accommodating.'

'It's my fatal charm,' Laura suggested.

'Evidently,' said Harry.

The cottage at Port Navas was everything Harry had promised – and more. Laura, Fram and Bridget arrived just after seven o'clock one cold, wet Monday evening in late March. Laura had been in considerable doubt about the whole project when it came to saying goodbye to her home, her business and London for two months, and by the time she had driven the seven hours it took to reach the cottage, she knew she had made a mistake. Bridget was deeply suspicious of anywhere outside London and the thought of both countryside and the sea frankly frightened her. She had not admitted as much to

Laura, but she had never seen the sea in her life and she saw no reason to start now – London was where she belonged. On the journey, she was morose and monosyllabic, and had made it clear to Laura that if it were not for Fram, she would not be a party to such a hare-brained scheme. Fram's contribution was not inconsiderable. In fairness, it was not an ideal journey for a small child, and to prove the point, he threw several tantrums, was sick and wore poor Bridget to a frazzle with his restlessness.

Yet when at last they stepped from the car, a strange calm overtook all three of them. They gazed the length of the mysterious little creek, at the water inky black, at the trees above their heads crowding in, protectively rather than menacingly so. It felt warmer, the Cornish air soft and friendly on their upturned faces.

Laura took a deep breath and, taking the key Harry had given her, unlocked the front door. It was a gem in every way – a perfect country cottage, complete with an old Cornish range and a loft ladder to the bedrooms. 'If you can't write there, you'll write nowhere,' Harry had assured her, and she could instantly see why. As promised, Mrs Trethaway, from the village, had been in to light the range and leave some basic stores. The beds were made, fresh flowers were everywhere and the cottage felt warm and dry. It was perfect.

Despite the strange bed, Laura woke late the following morning. Sun was streaming in at the window and she lay for a while watching the light making patterns on the beams, thinking of David. It was the kind of place he would love, with the water and boats on his doorstep. She turned her head and gazed at the empty pillow beside her. The thought that she would never see him beside her again filled her with such a sense of loss that she squeezed her eyes tight shut in an attempt to blot out the pain that rushed to greet her. I'll never love another man, never, she thought. How could I have let him go? And yet how could she not? She had brought nothing but misery to the men in her life. To break up David's marriage would be the final horror, and make her burden of guilt unbearable.

In an effort to escape her thoughts, Laura jumped out of

bed, seized her dressing gown and walked over to the window. She was in time to see Fram and Bridget walking up the track beside the creek, towards the cottage. Clearly they had been exploring for some time for, even at this distance, Laura could see they were both pink-cheeked from the wind. They were laughing, walking hand-in-hand and just for a moment, Laura felt a stab of jealousy. She had not been much company for Fram recently. She knew the state of melancholy she had been fighting was best kept away from the child, and she had therefore allowed running the restaurants in Giles's and Diana's absence to totally absorb her. Now, however, she had to come to terms with life again. She had responsibilities – a child, a career, a home of her own to maintain, and these practical considerations were helping her, she knew. Watching the laughing child now skipping ahead of Bridget up the path, she made up her mind that it was not just work to which she would dedicate herself during this three months in Cornwall. She would take the time to be with her son, to get to know him again, for in some respects he seemed almost to have become a stranger. She tightened the belt on her dressing gown and climbed, gingerly, down the ladder to greet them at the front door.

Their days in Cornwall followed a pattern which took no account of weekends, changes in the weather or anyone's state of health or temper. There was a great deal of work to be done on the book, and so every morning, from half-past eight through until lunchtime, Laura worked alone in her room. Then she would come downstairs and often she, Fram and Bridget, would have lunch at the Port Navas Yacht Club. It saved cocking and it was good to get out and meet other people. After lunch each day, Laura took charge of Fram, leaving Bridget free to do as she wished. Sometimes, in the early evenings, they would meet up at one of the pubs on the Helford River and chat to the locals, Fram perched on a bar stool, very much the centre of attention. There were no tourists yet, just one or two obsessive sailors, and in the wonderfully relaxed atmosphere, all three of them blossomed. Fram looked better than he had done in all his short life.

Bridget, too, put on some much needed weight and became visibly more relaxed by the day. Laura, enjoying the contrast between hard work and the holiday atmosphere of the afternoon, daily found her unhappiness easier to bear. Meanwhile, the manuscript piled up in the corner of her bedroom in a most satisfactory manner.

They had no telephone in the cottage but at his request, after a few weeks work, Laura rang Harry and assured him that everything was going well. 'I told you the cottage would work its magic,' Harry said.

'The trouble is,' said Laura, 'I never want to leave it.'

'It's not the real world down there, you know that.'

'Maybe not,' said Laura, 'but you can keep the rat race.'

Diana wrote regularly, sending a note of the weekly takings from both restaurants and keeping Laura abreast of any changes in staff or menu. The business was apparently doing well, but it held no reality for Laura. It seemed a million miles away, in another life, in another time and certainly absolutely nothing to do with her.

As Bridget grew healthier she also became more attractive and was soon much sought after by the local Cornish boys. She would have none of it, however. Laura took her to task about it one evening. 'Bridget, you can't go on like this. There's no harm in spending an evening with a boy now and again. They're nice lads down here, they won't do you any harm.'

'Will you stop lecturing me,' Bridget said, her eyes blazing. 'I do me job, don't I? I look after your little Fram, run your errands, keep the place clean, but what I do with my private life is my business, not yours.'

'I'm only talking like this because I'm so fond of you,' Laura protested. 'If I didn't like you so much, Bridget, I wouldn't be concerned.'

'Whether you like me or not is up to you, but it gives you no right to start telling me how to run my life.'

Laura still did not give up. 'What happened with your father was dreadful, terrible and I appreciate I find it difficult to grasp the effect it must have had on you. But you're such a pretty girl, Bridget, you have your whole life ahead of you and you're wonderful with children. Somehow you must overcome your fear of men – it would be a tragedy if you didn't marry one day.'

'You're a fine one to talk,' said Bridget. 'What about you then, why didn't you marry Charlie, poor bugger. Let's face it, if you had, he'd still be alive wouldn't he, and little Fram would have a father.'

It was a dreadful thing to say and Bridget regretted it the moment she spoke. 'I didn't love Charlie enough to marry him, but you're right, I'm not in a position to lecture anyone about men.' Laura turned away so that Bridget could not see her face. As usual, Bridget had put into words what no one else dared to say.

Realizing the damage she had done, Bridget's voice softened. 'The thing is, Laura, you're in exactly the same state as me. We got hurt in different ways, but the result is the same – it's put us off men. I'm sorry for what I said about Charlie, but you brought it on yourself – so just cut out the criticism, OK?' It was their only quarrel in two months.

All too quickly, June came round. Laura finished the manuscript a week earlier than she had planned and so their last week in Port Navas, the three of them spent together exploring the Helford River in a little boat they hired. It was a perfect week – the tourists had begun arriving but the school holidays had not yet started, so they were still fairly thin on the ground. Their three months together had cemented their relationship. It had also healed wounds and provided peace of mind. In their different ways, neither Bridget nor Laura wanted to go home, yet they felt unable to voice this sentiment to one another. Duty called and they knew they had no alternative but to respond.

When the morning of their departure came, they were slow and clumsy in their efforts to pack up. Several of the locals with whom they had made friends, came to wave goodbye, only adding to the poignancy of their departure. They bumped Laura's car down the track, out on to the Constantine road. As they climbed out of Port Navas, there was a gap in the hedge and far below them they could see the Helford River, winding its way like a bright ribbon through the soft Cornish countryside. Laura stopped the car for a moment. 'We'll be back,' she said, gently.

'Promise,' Bridget said, in a hoarse little voice. It was the first time that Laura had ever seen her cry.

CHAPTER EIGHTEEN

Being back in London was far more difficult than Bridget and Laura had imagined. In truth, taking up the reins of their old lifestyle appalled them in different ways. For Bridget, the sudden introduction to rural life had been love at first sight. City-bred and street-wise, too much open space frightened her, but on the banks of the Helford River, where the trees folded down into the water, she had found a tranquillity of spirit which she did not know was possible and which she had certainly never expected. For Laura, it was the sudden contrast in her working life she found most difficult to cope with. In Cornwall she had worked hard but to her own timetable and at her own pace. It was rewarding work, too. Back in London Diana and Giles only needed her when they wanted time off, and what particularly grated was the routine and set hours, after three months of pleasing herself. Only Fram seemed to enjoy the return to London, for in the early days of September he began playschool. A naturally gregarious child, who had spent little time with other children in his short life, he revelled in playschool – in fact he had to be dragged away screaming at the end of each session, such was his enthusiasm.

Once again, Laura found herself uncertain about the future. Gerald Seaton was very pleased with the manuscript, and apart from a few minor alterations, all Laura could do was sit and wait for the book to be published. No longer fulfilled by the restaurants, she was aware of a restlessness which troubled her night and day. She was ready for a change, yet recognized she owed it to Fram to stabilize their lives.

Giles and Di, while making every effort to include her, were very much in love and very committed to the business. Whilst Gooseberries had been Laura's brain child, she was the first to admit that without Giles and Di she would never have got the project off the ground. Now they seemed to revel in the hurly-burly of restaurant life, which she was rapidly beginning to loathe.

To compensate for leaving Cornwall, Laura began taking weekend trips away, always including Bridget and Fram. In mid-September, on a beautiful sunny autumn morning, she took Fram and Bridget back to Meadows Reach to see her mother. It was a weekend which heralded yet another change that was to rock Laura's shaky hold on security.

Katrine looked well, having returned from Athens just a week before. When Fram was in bed and Bridget tactfully excused herself for the night, mother and daughter sat on in the dining room, drinking the ouzo Katrine had brought back with her.

'How long are you planning to stay, darling?' Katrine asked.

'Oh, just for the weekend, Mummy.'

'And then back up to London with no more breaks in Cornwall?'

'I don't know yet,' said Laura. 'If the first book sells then I'll be asked to write more.' She told her mother then about how much she had loved Cornwall and how unsatisfactory her London life now seemed.

'Well,' said Katrine, 'you were brought up in the country, my darling, it's not surprising.' She hesitated. 'Have you ever thought of coming back here to Meadows Reach? You and I – we have always been good friends and now your father is . . . is no longer here with us, I don't think we would quarrel, do you?'

'No, of course not,' said Laura. 'But . . . it's been quite a struggle, as you know, to make an independent life for Fram and myself since Francis disappeared, and I think I need to hold on to that independence. It would be all too easy to come back home to mother, but I think it would be wrong. I have a business, my own house and perhaps a new writing career. To come home would be a retrograde step, I feel.' And too near David Lawson, she thought.

'I understand, darling, it's what I expected you to say, but I had to check.'

'Check?' said Laura.

Katrine hesitated and refilled their glasses. 'I've been

thinking, darling, that perhaps I might return to Athens. It's not so far away,' she hurried on, 'and heaven knows, we're not short of money. You and Fram can come and see me as often as you like. In fact you'll probably see me more than you do when I'm here. We can take holidays together in the summer, my sister has that villa on Corfu you know, and . . .'

'What are you saying, Mummy, are you saying you're leaving England altogether?' Katrine nodded. Laura stared at her appalled. 'You mean you're leaving Meadows Reach for good?'

Again Katrine nodded. 'It is such a big house for one woman, I'm lost in it, and without Bernard . . . well, to be honest, Laura, he always loved this place, it was a status thing for him, it demonstrated how successful he had been, but for me it was more of a museum than a home. Now I'm on my own, well . . .'

'But you can't,' Laura burst out, 'you simply can't.'

Katrine stared at her daughter's anguished face. 'Why can't I, Laura?'

'Because, because our whole lives are tied up in this place, because you made your life here with Pop. It seems . . .'

'Unfaithful to his memory?' Katrine asked.

Laura nodded, tears suddenly coming into her eyes. 'Yes, something like that, I suppose.'

'Laura, darling,' Katrine said, 'I need a fresh start – what you seem to have forgotten is that I am twenty-two years younger than your father. I'm only fifty-three now, I can't just give up on life.'

Her words struck home. Laura knew in an instant she was being unfair to her mother, but still she felt a burning resentment.

'I come from a long-living family,' Katrine continued. She smiled. 'It's a terrible thought but I could be around for another thirty years. England is not my home, Greece is my home. My mother is there, my mother's brother, my sisters, my nephews, my nieces . . .'

'But not your daughter and grandson,' Laura said, dully.

'No, not my daughter and grandson. Laura,' she laid a hand on Laura's arm, 'you and Fram are the most important people in my life and you will always be, but although I've tried to help you over the years, you've always shunned it. Think about how often you've actually come to see Pop and me since you grew up – three, four times a year, at the very most. Why should I sit around in a country which is not my own, in a great house I don't like, waiting for my daughter to remember I exist and grace me with a visit?'

'You make me sound like a monster,' Laura said.

'Do I? I don't mean to,' said Katrine. 'Don't think for a moment I blame you for what's happened in the past. Your father, bless him, was not an easy man, and then you had to face that terrible thing with Francis while you were so young – then having to bring up a baby without a father, and then Charlie . . . You've done marvellously well, but your need for independence has not helped to develop a close mother and daughter relationship. I find it difficult to talk to you, I mean *properly* talk to you. For example, we could not share the grief we both felt at the death of your father. Every time I tried to talk, you turned away. At home, Mama and my sisters, we all cried together, shared our emotions – within, oh, twenty-four hours of being with them, I was better.'

'What if I said Fram and I need you now.'

'I'd think you were being selfish,' said Katrine bluntly. 'Laura, you are only twenty-five, the best years of your life are still ahead of you. You must make the most you can of them. For me, the best years of my life are over. I adored your father, you know that, but he is dead and there is no point in looking back, except to the happy memories of the times we shared together. From those memories, I will always draw strength, but I am, how do you say, stuck in this body of mine for heaven knows how much longer, and I must find a way of leading a fulfilled, and as far as possible, happy life. I am sorry, Laura, but I'm going home.'

'Which is something I now can never do again,' said Laura, tears suddenly spurting out of her eyes. 'You do realize don't you, that your returning to your home deprives me of mine.' She stood up and ran from the room, knocking over a chair clumsily as she went, blinded by her own tears.

Katrine sat on with the ouzo. She had been dreading telling

Laura of her decision but she had not envisaged it would be this bad. 'Oh Bernard,' she whispered, 'what have I done?' Yet instinctively she knew that Bernard would have applauded her decision. They had always shared their feelings and he, better than anyone, had known how much she missed Greece, her family, the weather, the life so casual and spontaneous, compared with the formalities of English society. She suspected, too, that Bernard had anticipated this decision. Initially she had been surprised that she, rather than Laura, had been left Meadows Reach, for many times she and Bernard had discussed how much Laura loved her family home. Now, however, she thought she understood, for it gave her a last trump card to play in her bid to gain her daughter's understanding.

Over breakfast the following morning, confronted with a pale and silent Laura, Katrine played her card for all its worth. 'You ran out on me last night, Laura, when I was halfway through what I was trying to tell you.'

'I thought you'd finished. When – when are you planning to leave England?'

'Almost immediately, I thought,' said Katrine. 'I hate being in this house without Bernard, it gives me the creeps. I thought perhaps the end of next week.'

Laura stared at her. Bridget had taken Fram for a walk, sensing that something was wrong between mother and daughter. 'So this is the last time we'll ever be together at Meadows Reach?'

'Not unless that's what you choose,' said Katrine.

'What do you mean?' Laura asked.

'It means that I'm giving Meadows Reach to you.'

Laura's face flushed. 'To me, but I thought . . .'

'I'm sure I'm doing what your father expected me to do. Meadows Reach is yours, to do with as you wish. I have already asked for the deeds to be transferred into your name. If you wish to sell it, that's up to you. If you wish to keep it as your home, or one of your homes, as I very much hope you will do, then that's your decision too.'

'But how can Meadows Reach be a home for Fram and me with neither you nor Pop here? You and he are Meadows Reach – without you, it's just a big, rather showy house.'

'Exactly,' said Katrine, 'that's what I've been trying to tell you. *People* make a home and without you and your father, Meadows Reach is just a shell.'

Ten days after Laura's return to London, she received a registered parcel containing all the documentation relating to Meadows Reach – the deeds, insurance policies – it was all there including two sets of house keys. 'It's yours, my darling,' Katrine wrote. 'Try and be happy. It is not good that you are so sad, so young. I know your father would have liked to think of you and Fram at Meadows Reach. Make his dreams come true, if you can. If not, take time to have some dreams of your own.'

Laura threw the envelope and its contents in the bottom of a filing cabinet. However, the thought of Meadows Reach standing alone and forlorn haunted her. At night she dreamed of it, wandering ceaselessly through the rooms night after night, until her restlessness woke her. For the first time since his death, she dreamed, too, of her father, and in the end she gave way to the pressure of her own emotions and made the pilgrimage – this time alone with Fram.

She arrived at the house one cold, dull Wednesday in the first week of October. The central heating had been turned off and the house was freezing. She turned it on immediately and lit a fire in the sitting room but Fram could feel her tension, and, having the beginnings of a nasty cold, was fractious and difficult. She had intended to stay for several days, to try and make a decision about the house's future, but by mid-afternoon she knew she could not bear to stay the night. Instead, she called on Mrs Jenkins who lived down the lane and who had been the family retainer for many years. 'I'm going to shut up the house for the time being,' she informed Mrs Jenkins, 'while I decide what should be done with it. Would you take on the job of caretaker?'

If Mrs Jenkins disapproved, she said nothing. They struck a deal on wages and Mrs Jenkins agreed to cover the best of the furniture with dust sheets, keep the central heating on low, check the house daily, organize for the gardens to be kept neat and await further instructions. 'It's a sad time for you,' she ventured, but at the sight of Laura's expressionless face, she said no more.

Late the same afternoon Laura carefully locked the front door, heaved Fram into the car and drove off down the drive. She did not look in the mirror, she did not dare. She felt a traitor, as though she was betraying her father and everything he stood for, but the decision was made. Two days later *The Gooseberries Guide to Foolproof Cooking* hit the book-stalls and nothing was ever quite the same again.

'But why "Gooseberries", Miss Beecham, it's rather a strange name, isn't it?'

Laura told the story of the gooseberry bush with as much sparkle as she could muster, which was not easy since the interviewer appeared not even slightly interested. Indeed, she was beginning to wonder why Yorkshire Television had even asked to interview her about the book.

'Oh, I see,' he said, following her explanation, 'rather an obscure link, isn't it?' Laura hated him. 'And tell me, Miss Beecham, isn't it – how shall we say – somewhat insulting to call your potential reader a "fool"?'

'I'm not calling the reader a fool,' Laura said, hotly, 'I'm simply saying that my recipe book is a foolproof guide.'

'I'd have thought that was much the same thing.'

Laura glared at him. His thick panstick makeup was starting to run and although the lights were hot, they were not that hot. She did not envy the man his job, clearly it was extremely nerve-wracking and suddenly she felt her anger drain away. 'Look,' she said, 'this book is intended to take some of the myths out of cooking. We all have to eat, so at some stage in our life, most of us have to cook. There's such a lot of unnecessary cant talked about cooking. Most books are so purist – cooking should be fun, relaxing, rather than a chore. My book simply shows people how to save time, save money and produce a range of delicious dishes with the minimum of hassle. All those plushy recipe books with great big colour photographs showing impossibly exotic dishes, are alright for the few people who have the time to make a science out of cooking, but for most of us I think they are positively off-putting. Remember, all my recipes have been well tried and tested in my restaurants. These are a selection of our most popular dishes, and what I am demonstrating is just how easy they are to prepare.'

'Well thank you, Miss Beecham, it sounds most interesting.' The interviewer looked relieved, the allotted time was up, and Laura had finished at precisely the right moment. 'Laura Beecham's book is published this week, it's called . . .'

Laura hurriedly vacated her chair for the next interviewee and walked off the set, her whole body drooping with fatigue. All the way up the motorway to Leeds, she had been fantasizing about a hot bath and an early night and now her goal was in sight. She had not expected an author promotion tour to be so exhausting, but at least there was no late-night radio interview tonight. She was walking towards the studio exit when a tall, thick-set figure stepped into her path. 'Miss Beecham, I have to congratulate you. I think you handled that little creep just great.'

Laura looked up and found herself staring into an amused pair of pale blue eyes. He was a handsome man with a deeply tanned skin, which contrasted sharply with his shock of white hair. An intriguing face, familiar, very familiar – Laura frowned, trying to place him. 'Thank you very much,' she said. 'I thought for a moment I was going to fall out with him, which would have been stupid. It's just that these tours are so exhausting one does tend to lose one's sense of humour.'

'I should say. Hey, I tell you what, why don't you let me take you out for a meal to restore your spirits?' The suddenness of the invitation for a moment completely silenced Laura, and the man pressed home his advantage. 'Look, no one can have a good time in Leeds on their own. OK, so I'm acting a little fresh, but I'm a white knight really, and you look like you could use a little company. Pardon me, I'm assuming you are alone, are you?'

'Yes, as a matter of fact, I am,' said Laura, 'but what I really want to do is to go back to my hotel and have an early night. I have to be in Bradford tomorrow morning at nine.'

'Bradford . . . that's no problem, if you leave at eight you'll have a whole heap of time. Come on Miss Beecham, what do you say?'

'Silence, please,' said a voice behind them.

'Oh hell, we'll be in trouble in a moment. Come on let's get out of here.' He took her arm and shepherded her through the studio door into the corridor outside. 'Would it help at all if I introduced myself?' he said. 'My name's Max Morgan.'

'Max Morgan, of course.' Laura recognized him now. 'Laura Melhuish,' she said, holding out her hand to take his.

'Melhuish, but I thought your name was Beecham?'

'*Was* Beecham,' Laura corrected. 'I used to be a journalist before I married. Beecham is my maiden name and I thought it was sensible to stick with it when it came to putting a name to this book.'

Max looked decidedly crestfallen. 'Married – now that's strange, I didn't put you down as married.'

Laura grinned at him. 'Well since you're going to play the white knight, whether I'm married or not really couldn't matter less.'

'Touché,' said Max, laughing. 'OK, *Mrs* Melhuish, will you have dinner with me?'

Sitting in Max's vast American car as they hurtled through the dark, wet streets of Leeds, Laura tried to piece together what she could remember of Max Morgan. She knew he was Canadian, that he was a chat show host, mostly in the States, but also she remembered he had presented several series in England. Surreptitiously she glanced at him as he drove. He really was extraordinarily good-looking in a solid way, with his angular face and firm, square jaw. He exuded power and confidence – he is the sort of man who is always in control, she thought. In fact, it was oddly restful being with him, although they had only just met, because he was so very much in charge. She wondered at his age. The white hair, in contrast to his relatively unlined face and firm figure, made it difficult to judge, but she guessed him to be somewhere between forty and fifty.

Max took her to a little French bistro somewhere in the north of the city. Clearly the patron knew him, and they were given a quiet, corner table.

'Do you spend much time in Leeds?' Laura asked, when the meal was ordered.

Max shook his head. 'No, I'd never been here in my life until three weeks ago. I'm doing a short series for Yorkshire

TV, interviewing notable northern personalities. It's all in aid of the media effort to try and prove to the world that the UK doesn't stop at, where is it – Watford?'

Laura laughed. 'Something like that. I'm afraid I'm no more familiar with the north of England than you are. For me, it's always been the place one travels through on the way to Scotland. I hadn't realized how vast it is or how beautiful.'

'You know, you British are a crazy bunch. You live on this tiny little island and none of you go any further than your own backyard. Now in North America, we think nothing of travelling a couple of hundred miles for a party and most self-respecting Americans can do the whole of the UK in a couple of weeks.'

'You're Canadian, aren't you?' Laura asked.

'Yes, I am. Now Canada is a beautiful country. Have you been there?'

Laura shook her head. 'No, I'm not very well travelled.'

'Shame. What does your husband do?'

Laura hesitated. Normally, when asked the question, she simply said she was a widow, but for some reason, she felt she wanted to tell Max the truth. 'It's a difficult question to answer,' she said. 'He disappeared three and a half years ago.'

'Disappeared?' Laura nodded and taking a deep breath told Max the whole story.

They seemed to have so much to say to each other. Courses were delivered and collected, wine was drunk, but Laura was not conscious of any of it. She was captivated by Max, by his vibrant personality and easy humour. He seemed to have been everywhere, done everything and his evident enthusiasm for living was a positive inspiration. 'You know, you make me feel very old,' Laura said, at one point.

'Old! That's rich coming from you,' said Max. 'Let me guess, you're twenty-two, twenty-three?'

'Twenty-five,' said Laura, 'but sometimes I feel a great deal older.'

'Ah, that's because you've had it tough. Still, it's no bad thing. Youth is an awful burden, you know – the sooner you can get shot of it, the better.'

'That's a novel approach,' said Laura.

'Well, hell, it's true. I've had more fun since I turned forty than I ever had in the first forty years of my life. I'll be fifty next birthday and I'm positively looking forward to it. Fifty is a great age.'

'For a man, yes,' said Laura, 'but not for a woman.'

'Why, because women are not so sexually attractive at that age?' Max asked.

'Yes, I suppose so,' Laura said.

'That's crazy. Provided you go on looking at each day as a positive challenge, it doesn't matter how old you get – there's so much that's new and fulfilling – it's just a question of adjustment.'

'I suppose you're right,' said Laura. 'I've not always found it easy to adjust though, particularly in the last few years.'

'That I can understand,' said Max, 'and to be honest, I still miss my wife dreadfully.'

'Your wife? You're married?' It was a question Laura had been wanting to ask for some time.

'I *was*,' said Max, 'in fact I was married for twenty years to the same woman, but the last seven years of her life were fairly hellish . . . she had Parkinsons.'

'Oh, I'm so sorry,' said Laura.

'Well, there's no need to feel sorry for me but it was rough on Pamela, it took her a long, painful time to die and there was so little one could do to help. I have to admit, that during the period she was ill, we drifted apart. It was impossible not to. I was working all over the world and I'm a man like any other, I had the odd affair. Not that she minded – in fact quite the reverse – she encouraged me to do so. Would you believe her only gripe with me was that I wouldn't divorce her and marry someone else. I just couldn't do that.'

'She must have been very special,' said Laura, 'to be that unselfish.'

'You're so right – it was kids, you see, that worried her,' said Max. 'She'd never been a strong person and long before Parkinsons was diagnosed, we already knew we couldn't have children – or rather Pamela couldn't. She wanted me to have some kids before it was too late.'

'Do you mind not having children?' Laura asked.

'I guess I do. I don't think men mind about these things as much as women but I would love a son.'

'Not a daughter?' Laura asked.

'Son, daughter, whatever, but I guess every man wants a son.'

'Yes, I suppose they do.' His words instantly made Laura think of Francis and Fram. Fram, the son he did not know he had, if he still lived.

'Hey,' said Max, gently, 'you've switched off. What are you thinking about – you suddenly looked very sad?'

'I was just thinking about my husband and Fram, my son. Francis didn't know I was pregnant – well, neither of us did – when he disappeared.'

'That's sad,' said Max, 'that's real sad. I guess we're both what you might call "children of storm".'

Laura smiled into his eyes. 'Yes, I suppose you could say that.'

The radio interview in Bradford, the following morning, took no longer than ten minutes. From there Laura went to the *Bradford Telegraph and Argus*, where she was interviewed by a reporter with whom she then had lunch. She was booked into the Queens Hotel in Bradford for the night, but with no more interviews to do that day, she felt restless and did not relish the idea of spending so long on her own in a strange city. Dinner the night before with Max had disturbed her in a way she could not explain, least of all to herself. Her nerves jangled dangerously and the old uncertainty about her future loomed large in her mind. She was also missing Fram, badly. The following day she had a slot on the Breakfast Show for Radio Piccadilly in Manchester and on a sudden impulse, she cancelled her booking at the Queens, rang ahead to the Piccadilly Hotel and made a reservation. The drive would do her good, she decided.

The drive across the Pennines did help. The traffic on the M62 was heavy but the view across the moors calmed her. By the time she checked into her hotel she felt more relaxed – an early dinner in the restaurant, a bath and some late-night television viewing should sort me out, Laura told herself as she took the lift to her room.

She had barely unpacked and certainly neither washed nor changed, when the telephone rang, its shrill note making her jump in the silent bedroom. She lifted the receiver. 'Laura. Hi, it's me, Max.'

'Max!' she said. 'Thank you so much for last night, I did enjoy it.' Then a thought struck her. 'Good grief, how did you know I was here?'

'A little detective work,' Max said. 'I rang the Queens Hotel to speak to you and they told me you'd checked out. I knew you were due in Manchester tomorrow so I guessed you'd gone straight there.'

'Well, it's very kind of you to telephone,' said Laura. They had arranged during the previous evening to meet once Laura was back in London.

'I'm not just telephoning,' said Max, 'I'm expecting you to get your act together because I'm taking you out to dinner in – let me see – about fifteen minutes' time.'

'Where are you, for heaven's sake?'

'Downstairs in the lobby, of course,' said Max, laughing at her surprise.

'You're impossible, Max. I thought you were supposed to be in London today?'

'I was in London today,' said Max. 'I went to London, did my business and luckily telephoned you from there before leaving to go north again. It meant I could take the M6, which must have saved me a couple of hours at least.'

'You are crazy,' said Laura, 'you must be exhausted.'

'Not at all. I'm just very excited at the thought of seeing you again. So, as they say in my part of the world – *get your ass down here, Mrs Melhuish.*'

Dinner the second evening was even more of a success. Max and Laura talked and laughed their way into the early hours of the morning without either being aware of the passage of time. Laura found herself more relaxed, more light-hearted, more at ease than she could ever remember being, certainly since Francis's disappearance. Max seemed to fill so many roles – he was a charming, attractive man, and his charisma and confidence, together with his age, reminded Laura in many ways of her father. Towards the end of the evening their conversation became more serious. 'Laura,' Max said, 'what exactly are you doing with your life? Are you hanging around hoping that one day this husband of yours will show?'

'I don't know,' Laura answered truthfully. 'When I try to make some kind of decision about the future, I always manage to drum up an excuse for doing nothing at all.'

'Are you divorced or what?' Laura shook her head. 'Well surely that's the right course of action,' said Max. 'At least it will set you free. I mean look, Laura, if the guy walked out on you that long ago, whether he's alive or dead, there's no way he's coming back. At least divorce will give you a sense of freedom.'

Laura looked at him strangely. 'You know, that's just what my father suggested.'

'Well then, you take your old man's advice – it has to be the right thing to do.'

'I think I probably would have done something about it by now,' said Laura, 'but my father died shortly after we talked it through, and somehow without him, I've never taken the initiative.' She knew this was not really the reason. Freedom from Francis would mean she could hurt someone else, like Charlie, like David . . . it was safer for her to be married.

They talked then about Bernard. 'Wow! So Bernard Beecham was your father, I've always admired that guy,' said Max. 'I interviewed him once, you know, when he was on business in Toronto. He certainly made me work hard.'

'Did you,' said Laura, 'did you really, Max?'

'Yeh – he was one hell of a guy, we got on famously, had dinner afterwards. Strange, isn't it, that I should be sitting here now with his daughter.'

The conversation drifted on to other things, but later that night in bed, Laura thought again about what Max had said. The link with her father somehow seemed very important – it gave Max some sort of credence in her eyes and confirmed the things she already suspected about him – that he could be trusted and relied upon. When they had parted that evening Max had kissed her gently on her cheek and assured her that they had a lot of good times ahead of them – together. Laura suddenly knew that he was right.

CHAPTER NINETEEN

'You know something,' said Max, 'I've been thinking about Gooseberries – in fact I've been doing some research, strictly without your permission, of course.'

Laura and Max were sitting in front of a blazing log fire in Laura's house. It was New Year's Day and they had known each other for two and a half months. They were easy with one another, close friends, but Max had made no move to develop the relationship beyond friendship, for which Laura was truly grateful. At that moment, she was half asleep. They had been up all night, first at the restaurants and then at Giles and Diana's flat, where they had put the world to rights over bottles of champagne.

'And what conclusions have you come to?' Laura asked sleepily.

'You could really make something of those restaurants. You could have them all over England, North America, too – Jesus, the whole sodding world come to that.'

Laura heaved herself into a sitting position from where she had been lying in front of the fire. She eyed Max sceptically. 'Max, are you drunk or something?'

'I'm not drunk, baby, I'm sober as a judge. Now you listen to what Uncle Max has to say – it makes sense, it really does.'

'It can't make sense,' said Laura. 'I do have *some* capital – a little – but only just enough to open another two restaurants in Central London, which we're planning to do this year in any event. I suppose I could sell my Beecham Stores shares but I know Pop didn't want me to do that, and yes, there is Meadows Reach, but I can't seem to make a decision about that.'

'You don't need capital,' Max said.

'I do need capital,' said Laura, 'that's one thing I have learnt from my father. He expanded slowly, carefully. When you're on a winning streak it's all too easy to go mad, go on and on, borrowing more money, running before you can walk. In no time at all you're in an over-trading position and then bang – it's all up in smoke.'

'And I'm not suggesting you borrow the money either. I'm suggesting you use other peoples'.'

'How do you mean, rob a bank?'

'Come on baby, concentrate, this is serious.' Laura forced her tired mind to function. When Max was enthusiastic about something, not only was he very dynamic, he also had the persistence of a terrier. There was no way he would give up until she had listened to what he had to say. 'Franchising,' Max said, triumphantly, 'we sell Gooseberries franchise operations – initially to the American market because Americans understand franchising. You guys, here in the UK, just don't want to know . . . yet, but it's only a matter of time.'

'I don't know what you're talking about,' said Laura. 'I know I'm being dense but you'll have to explain it very slowly and carefully, remembering to take account of my delicate state.'

'OK,' said Max, 'you have this wonderful concept, right? You have these two quaint little restaurants.'

'Don't be patronizing,' said Laura.

'Will you button it a moment while I tell you.'

'Sorry,' said Laura.

'You have these two quaint little restaurants called Gooseberries. They have a unique menu, right? And the decor is the same – all that stripped pine and white-washed walls, dead simple, very distinctive, and the Staffordshire crockery – again different – your very own style. That in itself might be enough to sell the idea, but in addition, you have a bestselling book. They tell me it's selling millions in North America.'

'Thousands, I think,' said Laura, gently.

'OK, OK, but it *will be* millions and it's called 'Gooseberries' too, that's important. So what do you do, you sell Gooseberries franchises.' Laura looked blank, and Max sighed. 'You say to a guy,' he explained patiently, 'a guy, named Joe, who wants to open a restaurant – "what are you doing, Fella?" He says he is going to open a restaurant called

Joe's Place. You say to him – "No, Joe's Place will take too long to get established, you should open your restaurant and call it 'Gooseberries'. You have to pay us a fee and a regular cut of the profits but this is how you make out with the decor, Joe, this is the crockery, this is the food you serve, here are the recipes. We'll offer you national advertising and your restaurant will be mentioned in our recipe books." Jesus, you could offer bulk-buying facilities for all his equipment – knives, forks, plates and ultimately food and drink as well. You could have your own label, wine even.'

'You don't think it would be a bit odd to sell a fermented grape juice called "Gooseberries"?' Laura suggested.

'Will you stop taking the piss,' Max said. 'This is for real.'

He seemed genuinely agitated and as it was rare to see Max in a serious mood, Laura did her best to comply. 'OK,' she said, 'I hear what you say, but it sounds like a great big con to me. Why should Gooseberries do any better than Joe's Place?'

'Because it's an international name,' Max said, exasperated.

'But it's not, Max. I do seem to have a bestselling book on my hands, but as you say, otherwise, we just have two quaint little restaurants in SW3.'

'But you could have two thousand quaint little restaurants –an international chain. Now, I don't need to tell you about the advantages of international chains – you're Bernard Beecham's daughter, remember?'

'But I don't have Bernard Beecham's talents,' Laura protested.

'I disagree,' said Max, 'or you wouldn't have got this far. Still, I'm not going to argue about that – I'm telling you what you can do. Far from it being a con, you'd be actually helping poor old Joe, because he's sure as hell going to have a rough ride trying to establish his restaurant without you.'

'Max, I hear what you say,' said Laura, 'but I'm more suited to writing than big business. My publishers are desperate for me to follow up this first book's success with a second book as quickly as possible. It's what I enjoy doing most – I really can't see that this franchise business is my style.'

'But you wouldn't have to be involved, Laura, not in the

day-to-day running, anyway. All you have to do is grant licences and take the money.'

'The other thing my father taught me is that making money is never easy. It's hard work – always. There has to be a catch in this somewhere, Max.'

Max collapsed onto the sofa. 'Would you do me a favour, Laura, would you at least think about it?'

'I'll think about it,' she promised, 'but first I have to work out how and where I'm going to write this book.'

'When does the publisher want it?'

'May, June at the latest – they want to catch Christmas again. Last year, Fram and Bridget and I went down to Cornwall, but my agent says the cottage is already booked this year for one of his other crisis-ridden authors. It's a damn nuisance, we had been relying on that place.'

'There's a better place to go than Cornwall,' Max said. 'Better because the climate is good, the location is beautiful but isolated, and best of all, it's free.'

'It sounds wonderful,' said Laura. 'Where have you in mind?'

'Vancouver Island. I have a cabin there. Well, it started out as a cabin but it's a proper house now – four bedrooms, hot water, central heating, and it's right in the middle of the forest, miles from anywhere. Let's you and I and Fram and Bridget go there for a few months. As you know, I only have three or four more weeks' work in the UK, so we could be there by mid-February. You'll come won't you, Laura?'

'Absolutely not,' said Laura. 'It's an impossible idea.'

The Air Canada flight crew were brilliant with Fram. The plane was half empty so they had plenty of time to spend with him. He strutted up and down the aircraft aisles, a steward's peaked cap at a jaunty angle on his head, and proved to be a great hit with the other passengers. The fact that when he was not leaping round the plane, he was flat out asleep, made the ten-hour flight far less tiring than Bridget and Laura had anticipated. It gave Laura time, perhaps too much time, to become highly introspective about her decision. It had surprised everyone and although nobody had been outwardly critical, Laura gained the impression that none of her friends approved of the idea of her spending three months with Max on Vancouver Island. Everyone, of course, assumed they were already having an affair, and since it was none of their business, Laura had not bothered to deny it. Only William Campling had been openly critical. 'You won't be settling out there for good will you Laura?' he asked when Laura and Fram stayed the weekend with him before leaving the country.

He looked far from well and Laura was quick to reassure him. 'William, it's a three-month trip, I promise. I'm going to write a book. It's just like last year, only we're going to Vancouver Island instead of Cornwall. A change of scene will do us good – it's very kind of Max.'

'Can't stand the fellow,' William said, grumpily.

Giles and Diana's worries were easier to assuage. 'What about the new restaurants, Laura? We have to make some decisions.'

'Well then, make them,' said Laura. 'Goodness knows, you don't need me.'

'I think you're rather under-estimating your contribution,' said Giles. 'You've always been the prime mover in this business and now suddenly you're disappearing to Canada and telling us to get on with it. I've got my other commitments you know, it's putting an awful lot on Di's shoulders – I really do think you're being rather selfish.'

'Selfish!' Laura burst out. 'That first book of mine really put us on the map. We wouldn't be able to even talk about expansion without the publicity it's given us. A second book in the same vein is going to make us a household name.'

'She's right, darling, you're not being very fair,' said Diana.

'I suppose not,' said Giles. He grinned at Laura. 'Ignore me, I'm just jealous as hell. Antiques seem rather tame when compared with international publishing.'

They decided on two locations for the new restaurants – one in High Holborn, essentially to pick up the lunchtime business trade, and another in Highgate, which they recognized as being something of a gamble.

'You will be here to do the publicity, won't you,' said

Diana, 'particularly where Highgate's concerned. I'd be too terrified to open without you.'

'Three months is all I'll be away,' said Laura, 'three months is what I said and three months is what I mean.'

And I do mean it, Laura thought to herself, as the sinking feeling in her stomach told her they were dropping height ready for the final approach to Vancouver Airport. Yet she, too, had to admit a degree of unease. Max was a tried and tested friend now, always caring and considerate. He had travelled ahead of them by two days to prepare the cabin and he was wild with excitement at the prospect of their staying in his home. No, it was not that she did not trust Max but somehow she knew that once she moved into his world, their relationship would change. She was not in love with him, she was sure of that, but she found him quite irresistible. His exuberance and enthusiasm were inspiring and goodness knows what he might talk her into doing, away from the restraints of home. And then there were his motives – surely it was not everyone's idea of fun, offering a temporary home to a woman who was not his mistress and who was going to spend large parts of every day shut away on her own; to an East End waif who mistrusted him, who thought going abroad was like going to hell; and a raucous baby, who was not even his. Max Morgan had to have a reason for making such an offer. All Laura could not determine was what that reason could be.

Max was there to meet them at Vancouver Airport. He put them in a taxi and whisked them across the city to a much smaller airport – little more than an airstrip. Jet-lagged and exhausted, the three of them stood around helplessly while Max loaded their baggage into a six-seater aircraft, then he helped them into their seats and climbed confidently into the cockpit.

'*You're* not going to fly us?' Bridget said, appalled.

'I certainly am,' said Max, 'now fasten your seat belts.'

'I'm not flying in this,' said Bridget, 'I didn't want to go in the other plane but at least it was big. I can't stand this – I'm getting out.'

'Don't be ridiculous, Bridget,' said Laura, wearily. 'How long does the flight take, Max?'

'Fifteen minutes, if that,' said Max. 'Bridget, it's safer than driving a car – there's a hell of a lot less traffic up there.'

'I'll be sick,' said Bridget.

'Then here's a paperbag to be sick in,' said Max, uncompromisingly.

Once airborne, however, everyone was too fascinated to feel sick. Fram rapidly recovered his spirits and began pointing out boats far below them. As they neared the coast of Vancouver Island they saw row after row of great logs stacked in the water, awaiting shipment. The sun was shining, the island a mass of green, contrasting with the deep blue of the sea. 'It's beautiful,' said Laura.

'I told you,' said Max, triumphantly.

In a haze of fatigue, Laura, Bridget and Fram sat in the back of Max's vast station wagon as he drove out of Cassidy Airport. 'Lie back and rest awhile,' he said. 'I live on the other side of Chemainus. It'll take us about half an hour or so and the country isn't very pretty round here. You just wait though, you just wait.'

They did as he asked and woke to the sound of him hooting his car horn. They had turned on to a grassy track and Max was waiting impatiently for some goats to cross in front of the car. Either side of them, trees crowded the track which was little more than a wide path. 'Where are we?' Laura asked.

'Almost home – this is one of the old trails.'

'Trails?' said Laura.

'Red Indian trails. You have to realize civilization, as we know it, is new to Vancouver Island. A hundred years ago, no white man had ever set foot here.'

'I'm not surprised,' murmured Bridget, 'it looks bloody unfriendly to me.'

'Bridget,' said Laura, warningly, 'just watch your manners. You didn't have to come, remember?'

'Yes, I did,' said Bridget, 'someone has to look after you and Fram – you're bloody hopeless at looking after yourselves.' To the casual observer, Bridget's words would have sounded angry and resentful but Laura knew they covered the warmth of real affection – for no one else would Bridget have left England.

They bumped along the track for what seemed like miles and then suddenly, ahead of them, the trees parted revealing a wide glade – perhaps as much as half a mile in width. There, in isolated splendour in the midst of it all, was a large log cabin. It was perfect in every way. It had a high pitched roof and a balcony completely surrounding the house. A great pile of logs stood by the front door, chickens scratched around the step. Here and there the odd animal grazed – a couple of goats, a cow, two or three sheep, and at the sound of the car there was manic barking as two huge black labradors bounded out of the front door to greet their master.

For a moment they were all too stunned to speak, for the evening sun was glinting on the windows of the house, turning the wood golden and highlighting the greenery all around them. 'This has to be paradise,' Laura said quietly.

'It is, baby. Come, I'll show you.'

The promise offered by the exterior of the cabin more than fulfilled itself inside. It was the height of simplicity with its wooden walls and ceilings, but it was a bright and cheerful place. There were rag rugs on the floor in a riot of colours, red woollen curtains at the windows, and a huge kitchen range in which a fire burned brightly. The walls were hung with drying herbs, old copper pots and some exquisite watercolours of what were obviously local scenes. Everything had a gleaming and polished look – it was almost too good to be true.

Bridget followed Laura, carrying the sleeping Fram and staring around her open mouthed. 'Shit!' was all she could manage to say to express her feelings.

'It's beautiful. Max, I had no idea it would be like this,' said Laura, turning to him.

He smiled like a child, with open pleasure. 'It's a very simple life. We just have this room where we eat and do the cooking, and the room next door which is much the same but with a load of easy chairs which are all quite shabby I'm afraid. There are three bedrooms upstairs, one for each of us. He glanced at Bridget, 'and I've put the campbed for Fram in your room, Bridget, is that OK?'

Bridget let out a rueful sigh. 'Yes I suppose so, me and Fram are used to bunking up.'

Laura looked at her, apologetically. 'Is that OK, only I have to do my work somewhere?'

'We put a desk in what I thought would be your room,' said Max. 'It has a great view over the forest, in fact it's the best room in the house.'

'*We*,' said Bridget, 'you keep saying *we*! Does someone else live here, too?'

Max smiled. 'Yes, Buck, I haven't told you about him yet.'

'Buck! Who's Buck?' asked Laura.

'I guess you'd call him the Bridget in my life. He'll be in directly.' Max glanced at his watch. 'He's probably rounding up his precious ducks. He does a roaring trade in duck eggs in these parts, but we have so many foxes round here, he has to shut them in at night.'

The bedrooms proved every bit as inviting as the kitchen below. In Laura's room there was an open fire and a stack of logs just waiting for a match. As Max had promised, the view was spectacular. She had not realized that they had been travelling slowly uphill on the trail, but from her bedroom window, she saw the forest fall away below her, only to rise again perhaps twenty miles away, climbing the lowlands of a mountain until it gave way to the snowline. As with downstairs, the furniture was simple – a large bed, a chest of drawers, a cupboard, the same rag rugs and bright curtains. Without any doubt, Laura knew this was a place where she could work, and work well.

Fram was too tired to eat so they put him to bed. Laura grinned at Bridget, 'God knows what time he'll wake up but bring him into me when he does and I'll find him something to eat. You look really tired.'

'Have you taken a look in the mirror yourself,' Bridget said, 'you look ghastly and anyway you're supposed to be working, Fram's my job, writing's yours.'

'I won't be doing anything for a couple of days,' said Laura, 'I have to find my bearings first.'

'Lucky little sod, that Fram, isn't he? Us women fighting over who should have the pleasure of a sleepless night,' said Bridget, sagely.

A delicious smell greeted the two women as they came down

the stairs a few moments later. Max was standing waiting for them, warming his back against the range, and a slim, young man was laying the table for supper. In the gentle lighting, all they could see was his shiny, straight black hair falling over his face as he concentrated on the task, but when he raised his face at the sound of their tread, they saw immediately that he was of Red Indian descent. He was very striking – his eyes grey and deep-set, his nose hawk-like, his cheekbones high in an otherwise narrow face. He didn't smile but he studied them calmly.

'This is Buck, who I was telling you about. Buck, this is Laura and Bridget. Fram you won't meet until tomorrow, I guess.' Buck came forward and shook hands solemnly but uttered not a word. Both Laura and Bridget felt his scrutiny as he shook their hands.

'Are you responsible for that delicious smell, Buck?' Laura asked. He nodded.

'It's rabbit stew,' said Max. Bridget wrinkled her nose in distaste. 'No, it's really good, Bridget,' he said, 'in fact it's Buck's speciality.'

'Well, if it's that good,' said Laura, 'perhaps I could include it in my next book. What do you say, Buck?' Buck shrugged his shoulders.

'Come and sit down,' said Max. 'I've opened a bottle of wine, we'll feed you like kings and then the best thing you can do is hit the sack.'

Buck solemnly spooned out bowls of steaming stew and placed on the table a dish of potatoes. Then he returned the casserole to the stove and sat down in a rocking chair that was half in shadow, so that he was barely visible.

'Aren't you going to join us, Buck?' Laura asked. The boy attracted her. He could not be much more than eighteen or nineteen but the dignity in his face and his bearing somehow made it distasteful to her that he should wait on them and then not join them at the table.'

'I've already eaten, thank you,' he said, speaking for the first time. His voice was very low but fine and clear. Laura glanced at Max. 'Won't he even join us in a glass of wine?'

'Buck doesn't drink,' Max said, 'but why not fetch a glass of juice, Buck, and come and join us.'

'OK.' The boy fetched his drink and sat down carefully, next to Bridget.

'So what do you people do around here all day?' said Laura. 'We don't want to interfere with your routine.'

'Well,' said Max, 'since I've been over here, something's come up. I checked into the TV studios as usual, and they want me to cover a documentary right away. It's very dull, – the rise of commerce in Vancouver, but it's money and exposure.'

'When do you start?' said Laura.

'Not until next Monday and they don't reckon it will take more than eight or nine weeks. I can commute daily from the island.'

'Isn't that a chore for you?' said Laura. 'Wouldn't you be better staying in Vancouver?'

'Absolutely not,' said Max. 'For one thing I want to see something of you guys, and in any event, I don't have to work long hours. It'll be over every day by four. I've already chartered a plane for the period and hired a pilot. I don't like flying when I'm tired.'

'And what about you, Buck, what do you do?' Laura tried to draw him into the conversation.

'I look after you,' said Buck, 'cook meals, clean up, that sort of thing.'

'That's very good of you,' said Laura.

'It's my job.'

'What do you do when Max isn't here?'

'He looks after the place for me,' said Max.

'I have the animals,' said Buck, 'they need much looking after, and the garden, too. We buy no vegetables, I grow them all.' There was pride in his voice. 'I also paint,' he added.

'Do you?' said Laura. 'What sort of painting?'

'These paintings on the wall. They're good, aren't they?' Max said.

'Really!' said Laura looking at Buck. 'You did these?' Buck nodded. 'They're exquisite, they were the first thing I noticed when I came into the room.' The boy flushed with pleasure. 'Have you ever tried to sell any,' Laura said, 'or even just exhibit them?'

Buck shook his head. 'No, I do them for myself, not for anyone else.'

'I've tried all that stuff, Laura,' said Max, 'you can argue with him until you're worn out. His paintings are his business, his creation, he doesn't want to sell them – crazy, isn't it?'

Laura looked at Buck. 'Well, no I don't think it is crazy. I can understand it. These paintings must take a long time, they're so intricate. I'm not surprised you don't want to part with them after the time they must have taken to paint, Buck. You certainly are a man of many talents, this stew is great. You're very spoilt, Max. How long have you had Buck to look after you?'

'Nine years,' said Max.

'Nine . . . years!' Laura looked from Max to Buck. 'But you could have been no more than a little boy. How on earth did you stumble across each other?' They both looked uncomfortable. 'It's a long story, too long to tell you on your first evening. We'll get round to it.' The tone of Max's voice did not bear argument.

It was three o'clock in the morning when Fram woke and began screaming his head off because it felt like breakfast time but it was pitch dark and he didn't know where he was. Bridget scooped up the little boy and hurriedly carried him downstairs, before he woke the rest of the household. A dim light still shone in the kitchen and she saw Buck sitting in the rocking chair, a rag rug on his knee, on which he was obviously working. The range glowed brightly. 'Sorry to disturb you,' Bridget said, awkwardly, 'only the baby's hungry. Is there anything he could eat – bread, fruit or something?'

'I have it ready for you,' said Buck, 'it's in the larder, I'll fetch it.' He returned with a neat tray containing yoghurt, bread and butter and some fruit.

Fram sat on Bridget's knee and began tucking in, eyeing Buck, as he worked silently on the rug. 'What man?' Fram demanded, after a while.

'His name is Buck. He lives here with Max,' said Bridget. She smiled slightly at Buck. 'Don't you ever sleep?'

'Oh yes,' he said, grinning back, 'but mostly in the winter. Spring's almost here and there's a lot to do.'

'Where do you sleep?' said Bridget, then regretted the question and concentrated hard on feeding Fram.

'I have my own cabin round at the back of the house. It's small but I like to have a place of my own.'

'Have you really been here since you were a boy?'

'Since I was nine. I ran away from my folks.'

'Me, too,' said Bridget, instantly wondering what had prompted her to make such a remark.

'You OK now?' Buck asked. Bridget nodded. 'Nice baby,' he said.

'Yes, he's great.' Bridget gave Fram a hug and he answered her with a wide smile, displaying a mouthful of yoghurt.

'Nice lady too, your boss.'

'Yes, she is,' said Bridget.

'Different from the others. I guess old Max might be serious this time.'

'The others? Have there been a lot of other women?' Bridget asked curiously.

Buck nodded. 'It's why he bought this place. His wife got sick so he bought the cabin to have somewhere to bring his ladies. It went on for seven years, until Mrs Morgan died. Then he decided to make this his permanent home, so we built on a bit.'

'You don't sound as though you approve.'

'Not my place to approve or not approve,' said Buck. 'She was kind though, Mrs Morgan. I only met her once when he brought her here for a holiday, but she had more going for her than the rest of his ladies put together – until perhaps this one, this Laura.'

'Well, I don't know anything about his relationship with Laura,' said Bridget. 'I don't think it's serious, but then if it's not serious, why are we all here?'

'Who knows?' said Buck, 'but I guess you might as well enjoy it now you are.'

And enjoy it they did. Within a few days, the four of them had shaken down and were surprisingly compatible. Laura slipped into much the same routine as in Cornwall, working during the morning and then taking charge of Fram so that Bridget could be free in the afternoon. Where before Bridget had explored the Helford River, now she helped Buck with his garden and his animals, with chopping wood – indeed anything but the cooking. No one was allowed to interfere with that.

By early March the weather was warm and sunny, with a temperature equivalent to an English June. They grew brown and healthy with the outdoor life and Max said he saw a difference in them every evening when he returned home. At weekends they all joined Buck in his country pursuits and although occasionally Max invited some neighbours round for a meal, they remained largely insular, cut off from the world except for Buck's weekly shopping trips into Chemainus. It suited them all extremely well.

CHAPTER TWENTY

The bed was narrow but since both of them were slight, there was plenty of room. They lay on it together, carefully not touching, sharing the one pillow and lying on their backs, blowing smoke rings into the air.

'You're a crazy kid, do you know that?' Buck said.

'I'm bloody not,' Bridget replied.

'You are so.' Buck raised himself on one elbow and looked down at her. Her tiny elfin face had filled out, not too much, just the right amount. Her eyes still looked too big for her face, her hair still stood on end and she had lost none of her individuality. She just looked well and healthy and to Buck very desirable. 'You are so,' he repeated, 'and I tell you why, because you're just like me.'

'I'm not like you,' said Bridget. 'I'm far more sensible.' She smiled as she spoke.

'We are the same, just the same,' Buck insisted. 'We work hard, we don't let anyone give us shit, we're tough, survivors and . . . and, hell, I'm going to kiss you.'

Before Bridget could even think of moving, his mouth swooped down on to hers. She felt a sense of rising panic followed by stark terror. She fought him like a cat, scratching and kicking until he stopped, breathing heavily as much from shock as passion. 'Don't you ever do that again.' She sat up in bed, her eyes blazing. She looked about ready to kill him.

Buck sat up too. 'What's wrong, you don't like me, is that it?'

The anger in her died at the expression of hurt in his eyes. She knew little of his background, even after all these weeks, but she knew there was an essential loneliness about him. It was likely, she realized suddenly, that she had just destroyed the first bridge he had attempted to forge with another human being in a long time. 'I'm sorry, I just can't stand all that stuff, Buck.'

'Sex?' Buck asked.

Bridget nodded and then, surprising them both, she put her head in her hands and began to sob. 'Sorry, sorry,' she murmured.

'Don't be sorry.' Buck pulled a handkerchief from his pocket. 'Here.' She took the handkerchief and rubbed at her eyes fiercely. 'Can you tell me about it?' he asked.

'Tell you about what?' Bridget turned her face away.

'Something happened to you, something bad. It has to be that. Come on, you must tell me.'

And so, for only the second time in her life, Bridget spoke of her father's abuse, but with Buck she was far more specific than she had been with Laura. He listened in silence to her halting explanation and when she had finished, he took her hand, which now she gave him without resistance. 'I thought it was just me who had it tough, kid,' he said, gently.

'Why did *you* run away from your family?'

'My old man drank. We lived on a reserve, on the edge of the Rockies. It hurt his pride, there was no work. Tourists came and gawped at us like we were caged animals. Me and the other kids, we'd known no different but my father had. Anyway, he drank to forget and when he drank he used to beat us up, I mean real bad. One night he drank more than usual, got angrier than usual. By then he was half out of his head anyway, booze had got to his brains and . . . and he killed my mother, and then he set about my little sister and killed her, too.'

'Oh my God,' said Bridget. 'What about you?'

'I'd been out playing football. I came back in, there was blood everywhere. My father was sitting in a chair, he looked like he'd just seen hell itself . . . his eyes. Oh God . . .' Buck's face was ashen at the memory. 'In his hand he still held the knife he had used on them. He was slow – booze, the exertion, the shock. I wrestled him for the knife and when I got it from him I stuck it straight in his heart. It felt good, Bridget, real good.'

'Buck!' Bridget stared at him. 'How old were you?'

'Eight.'

'What did you do – Christ – what the hell did you do?'

'I came out of the shack, went to a neighbour's, stole some gasoline and spread it all over our home – inside and out. Then I set light to it. Everybody was in such a hurry to put out the fire, nobody noticed me slip away. I don't know what everyone thought – I don't know whether they think I died in that fire or not, but I don't imagine anyone guessed I murdered my father. There can't have been much left, it was an inferno.'

'So then what did you do?' The story shocked Bridget to the core.

'Survived – just. I wanted to run away as far as I could and I ended up in Vancouver.'

'And then what happened?'

'I picked the pocket of this old guy, duffed him up a bit I guess, and the cops chased me. I got down to the harbour and jumped this boat that was just pulling out. I hid under a pile of sails until we were well clear of shore.' He looked at Bridget. 'The boat belonged to Max Morgan and he was on his way to the island. He had just bought the cabin and he had his wife with him. It was she who spotted me first and she persuaded Max to let me stay awhile. It's why I never liked him cheating on her.'

'So you've stayed ever since?'

'Yeah,' said Buck. 'No one has ever checked up on me. One or two nosey people have asked about me – Max says I'm the orphan son of his former gardener, but do you know something, I've never told him . . .'

'Told him what?' Bridget asked.

'About my . . . family, about what I did. I told him my parents were killed in a fire but until now, I've never told anyone the truth. It feels good – telling you.' Suddenly he looked very young.'

'Poor Buck,' Bridget whispered, and without hesitation or fear she slipped her arms round his neck and pulled his face down to hers.

They knew nothing, either of them, about making love. Buck was not a virgin – there had been the odd girl on his trips into town, but these episodes had been purely physical and left him feeling curiously empty. The horrifying couplings with her father had done nothing to equip Bridget for the welter of emotions that now seemed to be engulfing them.

They kissed deeply, trembling in each other's arms. 'Do you want me to stop?' Buck asked.

Bridget shook her head.

'Only I guess there's something I ought to tell you – I've, well, only done this with prostitutes before so I probably won't be much good . . .'

Bridget moved away a little and stared up into his face. In a single sentence he had healed her. In being so totally honest with her, she suddenly trusted him completely. 'We'll work it out,' she whispered.

And they did. The afternoon slipped into evening as they discovered each other's bodies and their own, wondering at the desperate pleasure they could bring to one another – shy at first, but with growing confidence, until at last they came together in a shattering climax which left them sobbing for joy in each other's arms.

The evening sun, slanting through the curtains of Buck's cabin, finally woke Bridget. She looked at the clock on the bedside table, it was after 8.30. She sat up abruptly and then looked at Buck. He lay sleeping on his side, facing her. In sleep the wariness left his face. He looked more relaxed and happier than she had ever seen him. The knowledge that she was responsible for this thrilled her. With a terrifying certainty, Bridget realized that she loved him and would always love him. She was no longer a free spirit, the independent street urchin. She had given her heart, her mind and her body to this man and she would never be free again.

He must have sensed her watching him for his eyelids fluttered open and he smiled at her. 'You look kind of sad and serious.'

Bridget tried to make light of it. 'I've just seen the time, they'll be wondering where the hell we are.'

'No, you weren't thinking of that,' said Buck, 'you were worrying about what was going to happen to us now.'

'That too,' Bridget admitted.

'Come here.' Like a hurt child running to its mother's

arms, Bridget snuggled back into Buck's embrace. They both let out a deep sigh of contentment. 'Will you stay here with me, when Laura returns to England?' Buck said, gently.

'No,' said Bridget. 'I owe her a lot and I love Fram, I can't just walk out on them.'

'Not even for me?'

'Not for anyone.' She hesitated. 'Why don't you come to England? It seems you're not all that struck on Max.'

'He's been good to me,' said Buck, 'in his way, but it's true, I feel no particular loyalty towards him – I've worked hard for what he's given me.'

'Then why don't you come back to England with us?'

'Because I love this place, I can't leave it.'

'It is . . . very special,' said Bridget, 'even I can see that, but it's just a place, Buck.'

'Until now, until you, there's been no one in my life . . . since my family died. This place has been everything to me – a mother, a father, a friend. I know all the animals in the forest, I know every blade of grass. I love my ducks and geese and, yes, my vegetables too. To separate me from this place would be like pulling up a plant by the roots. I'd wither and die, I really would, Bridget.'

'Perhaps you're just afraid to go out and face the world again?' Bridget suggested.

'Perhaps, but whatever the reason, I can't leave, not yet.'

'And I can't leave Laura either, not until she can find a replacement for me. I suppose we'll just have to hope Max and Laura marry.'

'Yes,' said Buck, 'that would help. I guess we'll just have to wait and see.'

Laura came downstairs flushed from her exertion of getting Fram to bed. Max handed her a glass of wine and they went outside and sat on the verandah in the last of the sunshine. 'I swear that boy grows every day,' said Laura. 'It does suit him here, it suits us all. You've been so kind, Max.'

Max smiled at her. 'Kindness doesn't come into it, it's a pleasure.'

'You know it's Fram's birthday next week,' Laura said.

'Really! Which day?'

'March the 19th.'

'Wow! What is he, three?'

'Yes,' said Laura, 'I can't believe it, the time's just flashed by.'

'We must have a birthday party. I could fix for a bunch of kids to come over.'

'No, no,' said Laura, 'let's just have a tea party together, if you can get back from work in time.'

'You bet I'll be back from work in time. I've never grown out of birthday cake and jelly.

'It's strange,' said Laura, 'but I can't ever imagine you being a child.'

'That's because I haven't been one for a very, very long time,' said Max, sagely.

'No, it's not that, it's just that you're always so very much in charge. I can't imagine a time when, well, someone else was running the show.'

'Is that a criticism?' said Max. 'Do I boss you around too much?'

'No,' Laura answered truthfully, 'I like it, I find it very restful, after fighting all my own battles for so long.'

'How did the book go today?'

'Well,' said Laura, 'very well. I did some checking up and I think I shall have it finished by the end of April.'

'And I should just about have wrapped up my show by then, too. We could have a few weeks off together before going back to England.'

'Well, a week anyway,' said Laura, 'that would be great, though heaven knows, what I'm doing now can hardly be called work with Buck doing all the cooking and Bridget looking after Fram. Where are they, incidentally?'

'Can't you guess?' said Max. Laura shook her head. 'In the sack, I should think.' Laura frowned. 'You mean . . .'

Max laughed. 'You're such an innocent, baby. Haven't you noticed the way they've been looking at each other?'

'I don't think you're right,' said Laura, 'Bridget really doesn't care for boys.'

'Maybe not until now, but I guess her attitude has changed. You wait, you'll see I'm right.'

Fram's birthday party was a big success and the weeks that followed slipped by. Laura, too, realized that the relationship between Buck and Bridget was very serious and visibly deepening. Responsibility for Bridget weighed heavily upon her, and she was in two minds whether to encourage the relationship or try and protect Bridget in some way. Buck was clearly so important to her. If things went right between them, it would heal the scars of the past. If things went wrong, it would leave Bridget irrevocably damaged. The same, of course, could be said of Buck, Laura realized. His haunted eyes told her that whatever his past, it had been no less tragic than Bridget's. Two hurt, young people reaching out to one another and trying to give life another chance. It was both touching and terrifying, but when Laura tried, tentatively, to raise the subject with Bridget there was no way the girl would confide in her. It was private.

During the first week in May, Max completed his documentary and Laura her book. They were lazy, sunny days which they all spent largely outside, having barbecues and picnics and taking it in turns to spend time with Fram. Bridget and Buck were quite open about their relationship now, walking round hand-in-hand. Laura found herself watching them, remembering those early days with David.

'There's something quite unique about being very young and very in love,' Laura said, one evening to Max, watching Bridget and Buck as they wandered off into the forest, arms around each other.

'One can be in love at any age,' Max said, gently.

There was something in his voice that made Laura uneasy. She knew she was taking him hopelessly for granted, accepting his friendship and hospitality as though it was her right, yet offering nothing in return. He was so easy to be with, so jokey and casual. Life was one long party – there simply was no need to face up to life's harsher realities when you were with Max. Live for today was his rule for life. Yet now he was looking at her in a new way and she could feel tension between them. Sometime, she supposed it was inevitable that this moment would come, but she knew, as yet, she was not ready for it. She tried hurriedly to change the course of their conversation. 'I hope those two don't hurt each other.'

'Forget those two – what about us, Laura?'

'W-what about us, Max?' Laura said.

'We've known each other for eight months, right?' Laura nodded. 'And for three of those months we've lived together but in separate bedrooms.' Laura nodded – her safe, secure friend seemed to be disappearing before her eyes. 'I've been patient for an impatient man. I know you've been hurt in ways you've never really told me, and I know the difficulties you still feel about Francis . . . but it's time to move on, Laura, and I want you to marry me.'

'I'm married,' Laura said, in a hoarse little voice.

'We can get you unmarried, baby.'

'But I'm not sure it's the right thing to do. My independence has been hard won, Max. I'm not sure it's sensible to give it up.'

'Who's talking about sensible – sod your independence. You need me, you know you need me. Imagine life without me now, you'd be lonely as hell. You can't turn me down, not after all these months.'

'Love, Max, you haven't mentioned love.'

'I love you, of course I love you,' he said. 'Otherwise why the hell would I be asking you to marry me? Look, we can have a great life together.'

'I love it here, Max, but I – feel I belong in England . . .,' Laura began.

'So what's the problem? My job takes me all over the world. We'll have a home in England and a home in Vancouver. There's a possibility I may have some work in New York later in the year, but we could get an apartment there, too. Let's face it, between us, we're not short of cash.'

'What about Fram and schooling?'

'Good God, he's only three, we'll cope with that.'

'And children, do you want children?'

Max smiled. 'It's up to you. Yes, of course I'd love some children, lots of brothers and sisters for Fram. He should have some, he's very spoilt.'

'Is he?' said Laura.

'Inevitably, doted on by two women.'

Laura thought she caught an edge to his voice and was quick to leap to the defence of her son. 'He has no father, don't forget that.'

'He does now,' said Max, 'if you'll let me be one.' There was a silence between them, emphasized by the stillness of the forest around them. The whole world seemed to be waiting for her decision. 'Life is for living,' Max said, softly. 'It's far better to regret the things you've done than the things you haven't. Laura, we'll make a great team, we'll be happy together – trust me.'

'I do trust you,' said Laura.

'Then come here.' He held out his arms to her and she shifted along the little wooden bench until he could draw her to him. He kissed her, gently. His mouth, warm, firm on hers felt good, comforting and secure. Max stood up and taking her hand lifted her until she stood beside him. The moon was riding high in the sky and its light was shining full on to Max's face. He really is incredibly attractive, Laura thought. 'Come on,' he said, 'there's a full moon, it's a night for love. Let me show you what an old man can do to make you happy.'

As with everything else that Max tackled, he gave himself one hundred per cent. He was a skilled lover, very confident but also generous in his desire to please.

Yet to respond to him seemed wrong. In the dark recesses of her mind, Laura tried to cling to memories of Francis, of Charlie . . . of David, but no thoughts would come. It was as though Max blew away all her past as he entered her, relentlessly thrusting into her with his big, powerful body until some disembodied voice, which she did not at first recognize as her own, cried out in pleasure.

It continued all night, they slept little – Max's energy was prodigious. Each time she was on the very brink of sleep, Max would reawaken her desire and they would begin again. It was as if he wanted to imprint himself upon her and eradicate her past. And by morning it was hard to remember the time before Max Morgan was her lover.

As soon as they got up, things moved very fast – too fast for Laura, but she was caught up in the whirlwind. At breakfast Max announced their engagement to Bridget and Buck, who looked not entirely surprised. 'I guess that might make life a little easier for you two, eh?' said Max.

Buck flushed slightly. 'It might,' he said, non-committally.

After breakfast, leaving Fram with Bridget, Max bundled Laura into the car, drove to Cassidy Airport and took the plane to Vancouver. Within an hour of landing in Vancouver, Laura had an exquisite sapphire engagement ring on the third finger of her left hand and was sitting in the offices of Max's solicitor, Michael Sacks.

'Of course,' said Michael, 'divorce proceedings will have to be started in England, but we have close colleagues over there. In fact our senior partner is also a partner in the firm, Butterworth James in Gray's Inn Road. They're very good and there's no reason why they shouldn't start work right away, if I brief them.'

'I do have a solicitor,' Laura said, 'he's handled all my family's affairs for years.'

'Yes, yes,' said Max, 'but if we go to him, we'll have to wait until we get back to the UK to brief him. If Michael takes some of the details now, he can get things moving right away. That so, Mike?'

Michael Sacks nodded, 'Yes, I can.'

'So how long will it take from start to finish?' Max persisted.

'Well, from what you've told me, there are going to be no complications and no contesting – three months at the outside.'

'Three months,' said Max, 'great. That means we can be married in August, Laura.'

'Yes I suppose so,' said Laura, still somewhat shell-shocked.

'OK,' said Michael, 'so I'd better take down these details.'

Laura was feeling decidedly punch-drunk by the time they left Michael Sacks' office. 'Now we're going to drink champagne,' said Max. Clearly there was no way he was going to slacken the pace even after the night they had just spent. 'There's someone I want you to meet, baby. I'll call him from the restaurant.' Max took Laura to an exotic-looking French restaurant called Edouards, ordered champagne, made his telephone call and came back looking pleased with himself.

'So who am I going to meet?' said Laura. She was still staring at her engagement ring, trying to come to terms with what was happening.

'My brother, Tom.'

'Your brother! You've never mentioned to me that you had a brother.'

'Well, you never asked,' said Max, cheerfully. 'He's my little brother, nine years younger than me, though he looks ten years older but that's because he's in a dead-end job. He needs livening up, Laura, and you're the person to do it.'

'I am,' said Laura, 'why, how?'

'Wait and see,' said Max.

Tom Morgan was not at all like Max to look at. He was head and shoulders shorter, with dark, receding hair, warm, brown eyes and was really very slight when compared with Max's bulk. However, he had a clever face and a quieter manner than his brother which Laura found rather restful besides Max. Tom was effusive in his congratulations. 'I'm so pleased,' he said, and he sounded genuine, 'knocked out in fact. This guy needs steadying and you look just the person.'

'That makes me sound terribly dull,' said Laura.

'Not at all,' said Tom, 'in fact if all English girls look like you, I'm emigrating.'

'They don't,' said Max, 'besides which we need you here in Canada.'

'You do?'

'Yeh,' said Max. 'Tell Tom about Gooseberries, Laura.'

Laura looked surprised. 'OK, if you like, I can always hold forth about my pet subject.' In a few moments she told him how she had developed the restaurants and the book.

'Oh, I know the book,' said Tom. 'So you're Laura Beecham. I must say, lady, you certainly have some bestseller on your hands there.'

'So it appears,' said Laura.

'And this brings us to the point,' said Max. 'What you don't know about Tom yet, Laura, is that he works for

McDonalds. He's a trouble-shooter, he travels round the various McDonald operations sorting out messes. Right, Tom?'

'Something like that,' said Tom, wearily.

'And you know what McDonalds are, Laura?'

'Well, yes, they're a burger restaurant aren't they?' said Laura.

'Yeh, they're a burger restaurant but they are also a franchise operation. Look Tom,' said Max, 'what do you say to the chances of franchising Gooseberries in North America? It's quite unique – all we'd need is a pilot restaurant here in Vancouver – one which we ourselves would own.'

'It's a good idea in theory but you need considerable capital,' said Tom.

'I guess Laura and I could put up fifty–fifty, couldn't we Laura?'

Laura nodded. 'Yes, I suppose so.'

'Obviously, in addition to the restaurant we would need capital to properly market the franchise concept. What would that cost?' said Max.

'A hundred thousand dollars minimum,' said Tom.

'Jesus, that much?'

'I've earned more than that in US royalties on the first book,' Laura said, suddenly. 'I received a statement last week and I was going to talk to you about it, actually, Max. I don't know what on earth to do with the money.'

'Well, here's your answer.'

'Do you really think it would work?' said Laura, feeling the sudden stirrings of excitement.

'I think it could,' said Tom, 'but if you want me involved, I mustn't jeopardize my job – there's the wife and kids to support, remember.'

'Of course we want you involved – we want you to run it, Tom. What say we go into business fifty–fifty,' said Max, 'Laura and I have 50 per cent and you have 50 per cent. We will put up the capital, you put up the work. What's your salary at the moment?'

'Fifteen,' said Tom.

'Supposing you draw a salary of fifteen for the first year,

after which we simply work on a profit share. What do *you* think, Laura?'

'It sounds alright,' said Laura.

'Well, Jesus, then, you guys, let's do it.'

It was after five before they left the restaurant but Gooseberries Franchise Operation was born. By then, they were all wild with excitement and Laura and Max talked of nothing else on the plane home.

'Max, you are amazing,' said Laura, in bed later that night. 'You certainly do have a way of making things happen.'

'And that's the way it's going to be from now on, baby. You and me are going places, and we'll love it. Do you believe me?'

'I believe you,' said Laura, with only the smallest twinge of disquiet.

CHAPTER TWENTY-ONE

Maeve O'Neal heard the key in the front door as she vigorously stirred the pot of bolognese. 'In here, darling,' she called. When there was no answering call, she took the pan off the stove and walked through into the hall. Chris Berry stood there, very pale, still in his duffle coat with a muffler wound round his neck. In his hand he held a suitcase. 'What's wrong, darling?' said Maeve, warmly. 'You look a bit odd, and what's the suitcase for?'

Chris let the suitcase drop to the floor with a thud. 'I've done it, Maeve.'

'Done what? Hey, take off your coat, come into the kitchen and I'll open a bottle.'

'No, listen damn you. *I've done it*, I've left Eleanor.'

'Left Eleanor!' Maeve stared at him. 'Why?'

'Why? The girl asks why?' Chris tore at his coat, dragged it off himself and threw it to the floor. 'Because it was now or never. Where did you say that drink was?'

'I'll fix it right away,' said Maeve. 'Do come into the kitchen, darling, you look perished.'

He followed her distractedly. 'There was a board meeting today, at work. I think I mentioned to you that the Managing Director's been due for retirement for some time.'

'What's that got to do with Eleanor?' Maeve asked.

'Listen, will you.'

'Sorry,' said Maeve. She poured out a hefty whisky, considered it, then doubled it in size and added just a splash of water. 'Here you are, darling.'

He accepted it gratefully, took a great gulp and visibly relaxed. 'The old man announced his retirement today, and his successor. He's appointed Gerald Seaton in his place and in Gerald's place . . .' he paused dramatically, '. . . he's appointed me. That means I'm head of department for non-fiction, I have a place on the board and a massive increase in salary – nearly double.'

'Congratulations,' said Maeve.

'Is that it,' said Chris, 'is that all you're going to say?'

'Well, yes,' said Maeve, genuinely puzzled.

'Don't you see the implications? All this extra income means I can afford to divorce Eleanor now.'

'You're going to divorce her?'

'Maeve, will you stop being so dense.'

'I'm sorry.'

'Look, my future in the company is secure now and amazingly enough it's all because of Laura Beecham. The success of Gooseberries has quite literally trebled our profits in the last couple of years and, of course, it was me who introduced Laura to the company and Gerald who signed her up. Strange really, just that chance meeting in Rhodes.'

'What chance meeting?' Maeve said. 'I can't keep up with you this evening, Chris.'

'Oh it doesn't matter. I must tell you about Laura sometime. Anyway, darling, the point is, I'm free. Will you marry me?'

'No,' said Maeve.

'What do you mean, no?'

'I love you very much, Chris, but I certainly don't want marriage.'

'But why ever not? We have a wonderful time together. We enjoy the same things, we laugh at the same jokes. We're great in bed, aren't we?'

'Yes, of course we are,' said Maeve, 'but I don't want marriage, or kids or domesticity. I like us just the way we are.'

'Oh great – well I don't. Just imagine what it's like to have to go home every night and think up excuses for being late and see the reproachful look in Eleanor's eyes. How would you like that?'

'I don't know – it's never happened to me,' said Maeve, 'but it's your choice – either you're faithful to your wife or if you're not, you have to accept the consequences.'

'You've suddenly turned into a hard little bitch.'

'I'm not being hard, Chris, but don't you think you should have asked me if I wanted to marry you, before walking out on Eleanor? You'll always be a very special person to me but you can't simply move out of Eleanor's life and into mine. If you want to leave your wife, fair enough, that's up to you, but I want absolutely nothing to do with it.'

'Are you saying you don't want to see me any more?'

'No, I'm not but don't think you can move in here. It's not what I want, Chris.'

Chris slammed down his glass, spilling whisky as he did so. 'Bloody amazing, isn't it? I walk out on my wife, abandon my kids for you and you won't even give me a bed for the night, when you're the whole reason I've done it.'

'I'm really sorry, Chris, but we should have discussed it first.'

'I just assumed . . . I'm an old-fashioned guy who happens to believe that when you sleep with a person, month in, month out, year in, year out, it's because you love them and would like to be with them all the time.'

'I do love you but, no, I don't want to be with you all the time,' said Maeve.

'Alright, that's it then, I'm going.'

'Stay for supper first,' said Maeve.

'Not likely, it would choke me.' Chris turned, almost ran out into the hall, picked up his suitcase, threw on his coat and opened the door.

'Chris, don't go like this,' said Maeve. She went to put a hand on his shoulder.

'Don't touch me, I don't want to be infected with your . . . your callousness.' He barged through the door, slamming it behind him and stumbled down the steps to the street. It was only then he realized that for the first time in his life, he had nowhere to go.

On the same cold, November evening in which the Berrys' life fell apart, Laura was sitting in the first-floor drawing room of the newly acquired house in Harley Street. She loved the house with its tall, elegant rooms, yet she still hankered for the little mews in some ways. She was lying back on the sofa, talking to Max long distance. 'How's New York, darling?'

'Jesus, it's cold,' said Max. 'How's it with you?'

'OK. Just typical England in November weather – damp, dank, dull and windy.'

'Are you OK, you sound kind of depressed?'

'No, I'm fine,' said Laura. 'I'll just be glad when this baby's born. The doctor assures me I don't have two in here but honestly you'd think I had a football team. I wasn't nearly this big with Fram.'

'You weren't well when Fram was born – now you're fat and happy.'

'You can say that again. Any news of Tom?'

'Yes, he's going great shakes, he signed up another couple last week.'

'What does that make, seventeen?'

'Eighteen,' said Max.

'Not bad in as many months,' said Laura, thoughtfully. 'Darling, I'm missing you so much – you will be back in time for the baby, won't you?'

'I'll be there on the dot.'

'Promise.'

'I promise. Love you, baby.'

'Love you too, Max.'

She had barely put down the receiver when Bridget popped her head round the door. She was very quiet and miserable these days. They had holidayed briefly on Vancouver Island during the summer, but it had not given Buck and Bridget very long together. Laura felt horribly guilty. She knew that because another baby was due, Bridget would not leave her, feeling the upheaval for Fram would be too much at such a time. Undoubtedly, her true place was with Buck, yet nothing Laura could say would persuade the girl to stay on in Vancouver Island. 'Perhaps when the baby's a few months old,' was the extent to which Bridget was prepared to commit herself.

'Diana's here to see you,' Bridget said. 'Do you feel up to it, you look dead tired to me?'

'Yes, I'm up to it, it'll be great to see her.'

'Don't fuss, Bridget, of course she wants to see me,' said Diana, striding into the room. 'I'm a veritable tonic, aren't I, darling?' She kissed Laura on the cheek. Success and marriage had done wonders for Diana. She was now a truly beautiful woman – stunningly good-looking and expensively dressed.

'Gosh, you make me feel a frump, sitting here in this ruddy tent,' said Laura. 'Help yourself to a drink.'

'You too, darling?'

'No thanks, I'm off the juice with this one – blood pressure.'

'Poor old you, you're having a rotten time, aren't you?'

'Better than last time round,' Laura reminded her. For a moment, they both thought of Charlie, and recognizing it, Diana raised her glass in a silent toast.

The two friends were back to their old relationship, but on Laura's return from Vancouver Island the previous year, freshly engaged to Max, they had nearly fallen out irrevocably. Both Giles and Diana had been appalled that Laura had committed herself to a fifty-fifty deal with Tom Morgan to franchise Gooseberries. 'We don't know anything about the man,' Giles had said.

'He's Max's brother, surely that's enough.'

'Why? We don't know anything about Max except for glimpses of him on the box.'

'Steady Giles,' said Diana, 'Laura is going to marry him.'

'OK, that's fine, but we're not.'

The battle had raged for some weeks. Giles felt that what had taken place in Vancouver was tantamount to sharp practice since Laura had not been free to act alone on behalf of their partnership. To ease the situation Laura suggested she split her 50 per cent with Giles and Diana. Max thought it a ridiculous proposal since it was Laura's international success with the book which had made franchising the restaurants possible. In the end, Giles and Diana had taken 10 per cent each in the new franchise company, Laura and Max 15 per cent each, and Tom 50 per cent, and Max and Laura had provided the capital. Even so, it had never really been a successful compromise. When Max came back from the States full of excitement to report on the latest development, the invariable reaction from Giles and Diana was lukewarm, suspicious even, regardless of the achievement.

Laura tested the water now. 'That was Max on the phone. Tom has just signed up the eighteenth franchise restaurant. We're going to make a lot of money this year.'

'Bully for Tom, he makes it sound so easy. I don't know, I must be losing my grip, but I just can't find a manager worth her salt these days, let alone a franchise operator. I'm having trouble with the girl in Oxford, and with Cambridge and Bath opening in a couple of weeks, I don't know whether I'm coming or going.'

'Now if they were franchise operations . . .' Laura began, grinning.

'Shut up,' said Diana. 'We've agreed, no franchising in this country – for the time being, at any rate.'

'I give in – look, would it help if I went to Oxford for you?'

'What, in your condition?'

'There's nothing wrong with my condition,' said Laura, 'I'm still a month away from having the baby. I can stay the night with the Berrys and make two days of it, and see my publishers at the same time. What do you want done?'

'I've lined up a couple of possible replacements. I'd like you to interview them and if either of them is any good, sack the current manager and put in a new girl.'

'Alright,' said Laura, 'I'll go tomorrow, if Eleanor can have me.'

The day was a long one but it went well and by the end of it, Laura had survived the gruesome task of firing the incompetent manager and replaced her with a very likeable young woman who could start immediately. By the time she reached the Berrys' house she was exhausted, but she completely forgot her own tiredness at the sight of Eleanor – her eyes were red and puffy, her face chalk-white. 'Good God, Eleanor, what on earth's happened?'

'Is it *that* obvious something's wrong?' Eleanor said, wearily.

'It certainly is,' said Laura.

'Wait a moment while I shoo the boys into the garden.' There was a scramble for wellingtons and anoraks and when her sons were safely outside the back door, she turned to Laura. 'Chris has left me,' she said, and burst into tears.

By the time Laura left for London the following morning, she felt utterly drained. She had sat up most of the night with Eleanor, sifting through the ruins of her friend's life. She had offered to go and see Chris or Maeve, but as Eleanor had said, there was no point. Whatever happened, she would not have Chris back, even for the boys' sake. It was a very sad business and Laura couldn't help but feel guilty, knowing that her success with *Gooseberries Foolproof Guides* had contributed to Chris's decision. 'Better he went than we continued leading this half-life,' Eleanor had said, but she couldn't meet Laura's eye as she said it.

Max arrived back in London two days later than he had originally promised, but still two days before the baby's anticipated arrival on December the 20th. Because of the birth being so close to Christmas, Laura and Bridget had everything ready for the festive season, with all the presents wrapped and even Fram's stocking filled. Somehow though, when Max arrived he threw the whole household into chaos as usual. Fram was wild with excitement to see his step-father. They were not close but no child could resist Max, particularly when he arrived with armfuls of presents, many of which he was too impatient not to give people immediately. For Fram, he had brought a real Red Indian outfit, for Bridget an exquisite little pearl choker and earrings, and for Laura, not one, but three beautiful full-length kaftans – one for evening wear, two for day wear – perfect for covering up her large bulge.

Laura had accepted, long ago, that marriage to Max was not going to be an ordinary affair and that it was no good hoping for a nine-to-five husband, or even a full-time husband. When he was away, she missed him sorely but when he was with them she had to admit, privately, that he was exhausting and that probably she needed the regular breaks from him which his work necessitated.

On the day the baby was due, Laura went for a check-up. James Hodgson, her gynaecologist, was adamant that all was well. 'We'll let this little one cook a bit longer,' he said. 'If nothing's happened by the end of Christmas, I'll induce it, promise.'

On Christmas Eve, Giles and Diana came round for supper and it was the easiest meeting the four of them had ever had. In fact so relaxed was the atmosphere that when Laura grew sleepy, she felt confident enough to leave Max alone with Giles and Diana and go off to bed. On the way to her bedroom she stopped at Fram's room and hung the stocking on the end of his bed. She sat down beside him for a little while, watching him as he slept. As every day went by he grew more like Francis in looks but his temperament was as sunny and placid as ever. She had worried about his reaction to the new baby but so far he had shown nothing but enthusiasm. She kissed his smooth brow and went to bed.

Her waters broke at 12.35 that night. Max went into a complete panic but Bridget, who was woken by Max thundering up and down the corridor, immediately took charge. She called James Hodgson, who in turn arranged for an ambulance to take Laura to the Westminster Hospital. By the time she and Max reached the hospital, her contractions were coming every two minutes.

'You don't mind, baby, that I won't be there when it's actually born?' Max asked anxiously.

'Of course I don't,' said Laura, 'we've been through all that.' She grimaced with pain.

'It's just that I'm sure I'd be sick – in fact I think I'm going to be sick now,' said Max. His reaction amused Laura. Normally so competent, the baby's birth terrified him.

'Oh dear,' said the nurse with a grin, 'I see we have trouble here, Mrs Morgan, your husband's clearly going to be a difficult patient.'

Holly Katrine Morgan was born at three minutes past four on Christmas morning. When James Hodgson handed her to Laura, she saw in her baby daughter the replica of herself – dark, tiny, with fierce blue eyes. She was wailing loudly, too.'Not very much wrong with that one,' said James Hodgson, 'but I reckon she's going to be a handful at sixteen.' Laura laughed.

The baby was taken away, weighed and washed and then mother and daughter were wheeled back to their room. They all were waiting for her – Max, Bridget, Fram – Fram holding his baby sister for the first time, while still rubbing the sleep from his eyes, very proud and in charge; a tearful phone call to Katrine, who promised to be over from Athens the following day; and then, at last, peace, nothing but her and Holly, alone.

Laura heaved herself up in bed and looked at her sleeping daughter, then gently she lifted her out of the cot and cradled her to her breast. Fram would always be special, extra special because of the circumstances of his birth, but this baby, too, was special in a different way – born in the security of a good marriage. Laura relaxed back on the pillows and thought about her life – a crazy but happy marriage, two healthy children, two delightful and contrasting homes, a highly successful career . . . she was so lucky. For a moment her thoughts turned to Eleanor and she thought of what life had done to them both. Five years ago, Eleanor seemed to have everything while Laura's life was in tatters. Now the roles were reversed – it was strange, frightening. The baby stirred slightly in sleep, and as Laura watched her, the fear left her and in its place contentment grew and blossomed. She returned Holly to the cot, lay back in the pillows and drifted off into a dreamless sleep.

CHAPTER TWENTY-TWO

'A hole in the heart! You're telling me my daughter has a hole in her heart?' Max was pacing backwards and forwards across the room. Laura sat in bed like a collapsed doll. 'Jesus, just what does this mean?'

Laura turned huge, hopeless eyes towards Simon Littleton who looked from one parent to the other. Of all the many facets to his job, telling the parents was invariably the most difficult and distressing. 'Your daughter has a fairly large hole in her heart. Years ago, such a hole would have been inoperable, but these days the kind of surgery Holly needs is available. However . . .'

'However!' yelled Max, 'What do you mean, *however*?'

'Max, please be quiet. Mr Littleton, what do you mean?'

'There is an added complication. Little Holly has a faulty valve as well. It will be necessary to graft a piece of tissue on to her heart. Altogether, I'm afraid, it's going to mean fairly major open heart surgery.'

'And what are the chances of success?' said Max.

'Moderate,' replied Simon Littleton.

'Moderate! What the hell does moderate mean? You bloody medics make me sick.'

'Mr Morgan,' Simon Littleton's voice was icy, 'you're not helping anyone by shouting. I'm very sorry about your daughter and you can be assured we'll do everything in our power to help her lead a normal, healthy life. Right now, however, your wife needs you to be calm, your daughter needs you to be calm and I need to show you exactly the extent of Holly's problems.' Taking a piece of paper from the pad Laura had been intending to use for thank-you letters for all the flowers that festooned the room, he drew a series of diagrams, at the end of which Max and Laura were left in no doubt that their daughter was very sick indeed.

'How long before she can have the operation?' Laura asked.

'Well, that's the problem,' said Simon Littleton, 'she needs to be as strong as possible. Either one of these two operations have been successfully undertaken on babies of just a few weeks old, but not both. We would like Holly to be at least a year old, more if possible.'

'A year,' said Laura, 'but will she survive that long?'

'That's the crucial question. Obviously she's going to have to be very carefully monitored, she's going to need drugs and she's going to need to be near expert help. The Brompton Hospital, here in London, is probably the best in the world for this sort of thing, but it is a balancing act – we must operate neither too soon nor too late.'

'Does that mean we must stay in London?' said Laura.

'No, not necessarily, depending on Holly's progress, but most certainly in this country. I think it important to make that very clear, bearing in mind Mr Morgan's profession. Holly must be within a few hours' reach of us at all times, and within minutes in the first month or so of her life.'

'I understand,' said Laura. Max remained silent. 'Will she need to stay in hospital long?' Laura asked.

'She shouldn't do.' Simon Littleton smiled reassuringly. The worst was over now, the mother at least was starting to think positively. He frequently marvelled at the recuperative powers of the human mind, particularly when it came to a mother fighting for the life of her child. 'We need to run a few tests on her but then there's no reason why she shouldn't go home with you in a week or ten days, just like any other baby. Thereafter, unless there are any hiccups, we'll need to see her weekly, for the time being.'

After he had gone, Laura and Max sat silently in the little room. Laura expected Max to come to her, to put his arms round her and comfort her, but he made no attempt to do so. She waited for words of reassurance – none came. 'It's going to be a sod of a year, isn't it?' was all he could manage, at last.

'Yes,' said Laura, 'but we must fight for her, Max. I'm sure with all the love and care we have to offer, we can pull her through this.'

'All the love and care in the world isn't going to replace a damaged heart,' Max said.

'But it can prepare her for the ordeal of her operation, build her strength and spirits.'

'If she lives that long,' said Max. His voice was angry and cold and at his words, Laura burst into tears. 'I'm sorry, baby,' he said, standing up but making no attempt to come to her. 'It's just a hell of a shock.'

'It's come as a shock to me, too,' said Laura, between tears, 'but we have to face it together.'

Max stopped his pacing. 'How can we face it together, when I'm going to be three thousand miles away.'

Laura stared at him. 'But you'll cancel the rest of your New York show, won't you?'

'Cancel it, how can I cancel it? I've signed a contract, I'm there for another three months, Laura, and there's no way round it – you know that, we discussed it a long time ago.'

'I knew that when we were expecting to have a healthy baby, but with Holly so ill . . .'

'Laura, there is nothing I can do to change it, I have to earn the bread, remember?'

'We need never work again, Max. We have enough money between us to see ourselves and our children through the rest of our lives, if it's managed carefully.'

'Oh great! So I'm supposed to sit around on my ass while you play the little rich girl.'

His words stung Laura for it was the one thing she had striven all her life to avoid. 'No, you're not,' she said, 'but we've just been told our baby might be going to die and that has to be the most important consideration at the moment.'

'We're all going to die, sooner or later,' said Max.

'Do you think that kind of cheap remark helps?' Laura was crying hard again.

'I don't know,' said Max, 'I don't know what I think.'

'But you do think it's alright for you to walk out on us, just when we need you most.'

'I have no alternative,' said Max.

'Yes, you do,' said Laura, 'you're just too bloody selfish.'

'Sod it,' said Max, 'I need some air. I can't take any more of this.'

The relationship between Laura and Max did not improve over the next few days. For Laura the whole situation was so disorientating. To her, her daughter looked in perfect health. She was a slightly larger baby than Fram had been and her darker skin made her look less frail and vulnerable than he had done. She suckled well, slept well and seemed as placid as, if not more so than, Fram. Only two things were different, which Simon Littleton had warned her about – sometimes Holly seemed a little clammy, almost sweaty and the extremities of her body, her fingers and toes, were always ice-cold. Without Max's support and love, Laura felt very isolated in her grief and terror for Holly's future. The fact that this child might not be with her for ever heightened her maternal instincts, so that she could hardly bear to have the baby out of her sight. Max, by contrast, seemed to lose interest in his daughter from the moment he knew she was so ill. When he came to visit, although he made an effort to be kind and showered them both with presents, he made no attempt to hold or even touch Holly and his decision to return to New York remained unshakeable. Indeed, Laura and Holly came out of hospital ten days after the birth, and just twenty-four hours later, Max left for New York.

Surprisingly quickly after his departure, life took on a sense of normality. Holly continued to be a good baby, although she did sometimes have frantic and prolonged bouts of crying for no apparent reason. On enquiring about this, to her distress Laura was informed it was probably pain, and painkillers were administered which did seem to help. However, apart from these occasional spells, the weekly trips to the hospital and the revolting medicine Laura was forced to give the baby, the normal routines of new-born life slipped smoothly into gear.

Bridget was wonderful – totally absorbed in her care of the baby, while still having time for Fram, who was suffering a little from jealousy. As best she could, Laura explained to him that his sister was not well, feeling it was better to prepare him in some way for the possibility that she might not live.

Max telephoned frequently, and, distanced as they were, Laura found it possible to regain some of their old camaraderie, to the extent that when friends attempted to be critical about his return to the States, she leapt to his defence. Indeed, when in March he announced he was returning to England she genuinely believed that they could pick up the threads of their marriage again. Holly had turned into a beautiful baby, with big blue eyes and a mass of dark curls. The family did not meet Max at the airport for fear of tiring Holly and when he arrived he was obviously struck by the change in his daughter. Certainly the plump little arms and legs, waving in the air as she lay gurgling on a mat, were reassuringly lively. Max was full of his show and its success and he had news of Vancouver Island, too, where he had managed to escape for a few days' holiday.

At the mention of Chemainus, Bridget questioned him forlornly about Buck, and for the first time since Holly's birth, Laura realized that in her preoccupation with her baby, she had completely forgotten Bridget's predicament. Later that night, when Bridget and the children were in bed, she talked to Max about it. 'Max, do you think Buck is missing Bridget as much as Bridget is obviously missing him?'

'I should say so,' said Max. 'It's hard to tell, he's a funny kid. We've never been able to talk much, but he did ask about her a lot.'

'Now you're home,' said Laura, 'I think it's only fair that I should let Bridget go. I think if I presented her with a one-way ticket to Vancouver, knowing that we have your support now, she'd jump at it.'

Max looked uneasy. 'It's not as simple as that, baby,' he said.

'How do you mean?'

He got up, threw a log on the fire and then came and sat beside her on the sofa, taking her hand. 'I've been offered a six-month chat show in L A. It will be syndicated all over the States – they promised me that – probably here in Britain, too. It's a wonderful opportunity, something I've always wanted, always worked for.'

Laura felt her heart hit her boots. 'When would this . . . be?' she asked.

'It's due to start in a couple of weeks.'

'A couple of weeks! Then . . .' she looked at him, incredulously, '. . . then you've already signed the contract, Max.'

'Yes, I have.'

'Without telling me!'

'They sprang it on me real fast. They wanted a deal there and then, or not at all. I couldn't talk to you about it on the telephone.'

'You could have flown over. If you had time to go to Vancouver Island, you had time to fly back here and discuss it with me.'

'You make decisions about your career without discussing them with me,' said Max, defensively.

'Not if they involved me living somewhere other than with my family.'

'I've always spent the major part of my life in North America, you know that.'

'Yes, but you know I have no alternative but to live in London for the next year, or longer for all we know.' They stared at each other, there seemed to be a great gulf opening up between them.

'I'm sorry, Laura, but when it comes to decisions about my career, I have to make them alone. I've worked too hard, too long, to get to this point. I simply can't throw it up.'

'*Won't*, you mean,' said Laura.

Max spent the night on the sofa while Laura tossed and turned alone in their bed. She simply could not believe that he had taken the decision without her – it seemed incomprehensible to her. In the morning, when he came upstairs to the bedroom – early so as not to arouse the suspicion of Bridget and the children – she was calm, though her eyelids were heavy from weeping. 'Six months,' she said, 'that brings us to September. I have no alternative but to agree to it because you've signed the contract, but can I have your word that whatever happens, you'll be back in England for Holly's operation? It's not likely to happen until the contract is over, she's making good progress. However, if it was earlier than planned, you'd have to drop everything and come.'

'Of course, baby,' said Max, smiling. He came and sat on

the bed and slipped his arms round her. She remained rigid within them. 'Come on, don't be mad at me. We've got two whole weeks together now so let's make the most of them.' He was gentle and loving now he had his own way but somewhere deep within Laura, something very fundamental had happened to her feelings towards him. He was no longer her prop, the man on whom she could always rely. He had let her down and she knew she could never quite forgive him.

In June, two things happened. On Holly's routine visit to the Brompton, she was proclaimed to be in good health and Simon Littleton suggested that a short holiday in the country might do everyone some good. Fram was starting school in September and Laura was anxious for him to have some sea air. Then, two days later, Gerald Seaton telephoned and suggested it was time she wrote another book. The thought of Cornwall suddenly appealed to Laura and Harry confirmed that the cottage was free. Laura had been totally unable to persuade Bridget to go to Buck. 'When Holly's operation's over, then I'll go,' she'd said. Laura remembered how much Bridget had loved Cornwall – it was small recompense for being parted from the man she loved but it was something. Within a matter of two weeks it was organized. Diana and Giles, in any event, had been running the restaurants since Holly's birth and were happy to continue to do so. With a brand new contract in her pocket and a two-month leasing agreement for the cottage, they were all set to go.

On their first evening back in Port Navas, Bridget and Laura sat over the remains of the little coal fire for a long time. 'A lot has happened to us in a couple of years, Bridget,' Laura said. Bridget nodded. 'I just feel so sorry for what you're suffering on my behalf.'

Bridget shrugged her shoulders. 'Just imagine where I'd be now if you hadn't taken me in,' she said. It was the nearest she had ever got to saying thank you.

Fram, of course, had no memory of his previous trip to Cornwall, so he fell in love with it all over again. The weather was perfect and Holly, in nothing more than a nappy and T-shirt, was soon as brown as a berry. With two small children and Holly needing special care, Laura had no intention of attempting to finish the book she was writing. She worked on it for two or three hours every morning but for the most part, she concentrated on giving everyone a good time. The days slipped by – one into the other – trips on the river, sunny days on one of the many beaches, long cosy evenings in front of the fire in the cottage. On this holiday, neither Bridget nor Laura had any inclination to go out in the evenings, but after one particularly beautiful golden day, they were reluctant to go home. They had spent most of the day at the Bar Beach and were walking back to the Ferryboat Inn, where they had parked their car when Laura suddenly said, 'Why don't we stop at the Ferryboat and have an early supper? It would do us good, we're behaving like a couple of old spinsters and Holly had a good sleep this afternoon.'

'Yes, please, yes, please,' said Fram. 'Can I play on the fruit machine?'

'I expect so,' said Laura. 'What do you say, Bridget?'

'Good idea, might brighten us up a bit, as you say.'

When they reached the Inn, Laura sent Bridget and Fram inside to bag a table. 'I'll just take Holly down to the sea and wash her toes,' she said, 'she's covered in sand.'

Laura pushed Holly's buggy across the sand, to the edge of the sea. Holly was in a happy, gurgling mood and Laura made a great play of washing her plump little toes and drying carefully between each one. 'This little piggy went to market, this little piggy stayed at home.' Holly shrieked with delight.

Something made Laura look up – a premonition perhaps. Forgetting the baby she stood up and stared. Down the beach a figure was walking towards them – small, squarely built. With the sun shining directly in Laura's eyes, he would not normally have been recognizable, but it was his walk that left her in no doubt – the one straight leg dragging its way through the sand. Holly, suddenly abandoned, began whimpering. Laura picked up the baby in her towel and, as if drawn by some force over which she had no control, she walked towards the figure. They stopped feet from one another. 'Hello, Laura,' he said.

'Hello yourself,' said Laura, unable to fight the surge of joy she felt at looking once more into the eyes of David Lawson.

CHAPTER TWENTY-THREE

'Is this yours?' David said, smiling at the baby and putting out a tentative finger, which Holly immediately grasped.

'Yes, her name's Holly and she has a hole in the heart,' Laura blurted out. She never mentioned Holly's problems on a day-to-day basis and certainly she had never used such a description to introduce her before. Shock at seeing David had her behaving like an idiot.

His face showed instant concern. 'Oh, I'm so sorry, Laura. Is it operable?'

'They say so, but the problem is complicated by the fact that she has a faulty heart valve as well. If she can just hold on until she's around a year old, they reckon she has a good chance.'

'It must be a terrible time for you and . . . your husband,' David said. 'I must say, you're looking very well, but the strain must be awful.'

This is extraordinary, Laura thought – they could stand on the sand, picking up the threads like old friends. It was as if their last bitter parting had never happened.

'I didn't know this part of the world was one of your haunts,' said Laura.

'It's not, normally,' said David. 'There's a young lad here at the Ferryboat who is setting up a hire-boat business and luckily selected one of my designs. He ordered half a dozen, with the option on four more, and because of the size of the order, I thought I should come down and commission them personally. Look, they're over there.' Sure enough, a row of David's boats were lined up on swinging moorings and, fleetingly, Laura wondered why she had not noticed them that morning – the style was unmistakable. 'So you're going back home pretty soon?' she asked.

'Tomorrow morning, crack of dawn.' Laura felt an odd mixture of relief and regret. 'And you?' said David.

'I'm here for a couple of months, with Fram, Bridget and little Holly – we still have nearly four weeks to go.'

'But not your husband?'

David did not mention Max by name, but Laura assumed he must have read the press coverage of their wedding. She made as light of the situation as she could. 'He's committed to a chat show in Los Angeles. It's a wonderful opportunity for him, but I can't leave the country because of Holly.'

'That must make things even more difficult for you,' said David. The warmth of his sympathy sent a warm glow through Laura. She could not help but contrast his immediate understanding to Max's apparent indifference. 'Where are you staying?' David asked. He was proving an instant hit with Holly, who was stretching out her arms to him. 'May I take her?' he asked. 'Though heaven knows I've no practice. The first and last baby I held was Fram.' The circumstances of that meeting silenced them both for a moment, while David privately cursed himself for his tactlessness.

'She's rather sandy and wet, but if you're sure you don't mind,' said Laura, at last. 'We're staying at Port Navas, in a cottage. I'm suppposed to be working on a book but I'm spending more time with the children. Actually we're about to have some supper here tonight.'

'And I'm staying here. Shall we join forces?'

'If you can cope with two noisy children and a love-sick Bridget.'

'I think I can handle that,' said David, grinning at Holly.

The sight of David holding her child so tenderly brought sudden tears to Laura's eyes. 'I'll just fetch the buggy,' she said, turning away hurriedly, her emotions in turmoil. Nothing had changed. With a sinking heart, she knew marriage to Max had not even dented her feelings for David – they were as alive and vibrant as ever, intoxicating, dangerous and to be suppressed at all costs.

The five of them had a very happy supper. It was still warm enough to eat outside so that Bridget and Laura could be quite relaxed about the mess the children made. David plied both women with ferocious quantities of wine and even managed to raise a smile or two from Bridget.

By the time supper was finished, the children were starting to become tired and tetchy and it was evident that they would have to leave. 'Let me run you back to the cottage,' David said.

'Good Lord, no,' said Laura, 'I have the car here.'

'What about all the wine you've drunk?'

'What about all the wine *you've* drunk,' she said, laughing. 'Seriously, David, I'm fine – I know the roads well round here and I'll take it very slowly.'

Bridget had gone ahead and was strapping the children into their car seats. 'Always so independent,' David said. 'Nothing changes.'

They lingered for a moment. 'It's the only way to be, isn't it?' Laura said.

'Sometimes it's good to have a shoulder to lean on.'

Laura nodded. She felt dangerously near to tears again. The meeting had been so unexpected, so brief and now they were to part and might not meet again for years – for ever. She pushed the thought to the back of her mind. 'I hope you have a good trip back to Oxfordshire,' she said.

David took both her hands in his. 'No banalities, Laura. It's been wonderful to see you but I hate to think of you coping alone with Holly's problem. I want you to promise me two things. Firstly, as soon as anything definite happens to Holly, in other words, when she has the operation, will you let me know? She's a sweet child and I really do want to know how things go with her.' Laura nodded. 'And secondly, whilst I know you have plenty of friends, if you hit any sort of crisis in the next few months, anything – Holly or whatever – and you need a helping hand while your husband's away, please get in touch with me. We made the mistake of letting our feelings run away with us before, but I promise it will never happen again. Think of me as a friend, a good friend who probably knows you better than most, and on whom you can utterly rely.'

A tear slid down Laura's cheek but she made no attempt to brush it away. 'Thank you, David.' She put a hand on his shoulder and leaning forward kissed him quickly on the lips. Then she turned and ran to the car. 'Wave goodbye to David,' she instructed the children and slipping the car into gear, she drove up the hill. She did not dare look back.

They had been back in London for just two weeks when Bridget and Laura noticed a change in Holly. Outwardly she looked well. Her skin was still golden brown from the sun but she became tired and irritable very easily and for most of the day was very listless. Her tiny body was nearly always clammy and under the suntan Laura detected a pallor that had not been there before. She telephoned Simon Littleton, who agreed to see her immediately, which in itself terrified her.

'You're going to have to keep her very quiet for the next few months,' he said, having examined Holly carefully. 'You just have to buy her as much time as possible, but I'm going to give you an emergency number and take you through the procedures you need to know in case anything should go wrong.'

'What do you mean . . . go wrong?' said Laura.

'In case she has a heart attack.'

'May she?' Laura said.

'It's possible.'

'Then can't we do the operation now?'

'There are a number of problems. I want her to be as old as possible, and also it is a question of fitting her in. The Brompton attracts heart patients from all over the world. I think in view of her condition I will now actively put her on the waiting list, which I hadn't done before, but it's going to be a few months before she can have surgery, unless, of course, there's an emergency.'

'You mean my daughter may die because foreign babies are being given precedence?' The months of strain were starting to tell.

'No, of course not,' said Simon Littleton. 'As I said to you before, it's a balancing act – trying to choose the right moment to operate on Holly to give her the maximum chance.' Recognizing Laura's stress, he took a long time explaining the procedures she should adopt and as soon as Laura got home she went through them with Bridget. When they had finished and bathed and put the children to bed, they sat on either side of the kitchen table and stared at one another.

'It's alright, love, she's going to make it. She's a tough little number, that one,' Bridget said.

'Oh Bridget, I hope you're right,' said Laura and putting her head in her hands, she began to sob.

Bridget went in search of the brandy bottle and returned with two hefty measures. Laura sipped hers distractedly. 'That rotten bastard should be with you at a time like this,' Bridget suddenly burst out, her words heavy with contempt.

Laura, shocked at her venom, raised her tear-stained face and stared at her. 'You mean . . . Max?'

'Of course I mean Max.'

'But, Bridget, he has his work.'

'Sod his work. His kid's fighting for her life and you're at breaking point. There's only one place that man should be and that's right here. Shit, I could wring his sodding neck.'

'Oh Bridget, I wouldn't let anybody else in the world but you say that, but I have to admit, it's how I feel. It's as though the moment he knew there was something wrong with Holly, he lost interest, disowned her, almost.'

'I think it's simpler than that,' said Bridget, 'I think he's just a selfish bastard, a spoilt brat who can't stand anyone else having centre stage. It's sick.'

'I don't know about sick, but it is all such a mess,' said Laura. 'Max over there when he should be here, you here when you should be over there . . .'

'Don't start that again,' said Bridget.

Laura blew her nose and, rallying a little, raised her brandy glass. 'You know something, Bridget,' she said, 'we're a pretty good team, you and I.'

They clinked glasses. 'The best,' said Bridget.

By the end of July, Holly no longer had the strength to sit up unless she was propped with cushions. All the natural progress that an eight-month-old baby should be making, in terms of crawling and learning to stand had been completely halted. What was more distressing was that she was clearly in considerable pain. After a particularly sleepless night, when it seemed she would never stop crying again, Laura put herself and Holly in a taxi which took them straight to Simon Littleton's consulting rooms without an appointment. Once there,

Laura informed the receptionist that she would sit in the waiting room with Holly screaming her head off, until he saw them. Within minutes, the receptionist ushered mother and daughter in to see him and one look at them both had him reaching for the telephone, and calling the Brompton Hospital.

The operation was fixed for Monday week, the first week in August. Simon explained a little of the operation. 'The surgeon works with a team,' he said. 'There is only one man in the world that can handle Holly's operation – it's just lucky he happens to be British. It is open heart surgery and, of course, it's micro-surgery. The team open her up and then the great man comes and does his special bit, and then the rest of the team stitch her up again. During the period he is actually working on her heart, the heart's function will be taken over by a machine. She will have a scar from the base of her throat down to about two inches above her tummy button, but bearing in mind her size, by the time she's eighteen the scar will have shunk to next to nothing – if it's even visible at all.'

'If she reaches eighteen,' Laura said.

Simon stood up, walked round the desk and sat down beside Laura and Holly, who had now become quiet, too exhausted to cry any more. He looked down at the baby. 'Laura, may I call you Laura?' Laura nodded. 'You have to believe that your daughter is going to live to be at least a hundred or neither you nor she will have the strength to go through with this operation. Holly has a good chance of survival but the next few weeks are going to be rough, and if you don't have faith in her, then frankly, my dear, she doesn't stand a chance.'

Laura met the steady gaze of Simon Littleton. He was a strange-looking man with a high-domed, totally bald, head and a long, thin, pointed nose. Whilst his eyes were filled with compassion, there was a presence about the man which commanded both awe and respect. 'I have faith,' said Laura, and as she said the words she knew they were true.

'Good girl. Now you're not alone in all this – the surgeon operates on six or seven babies during the period from about nine o'clock in the morning until two in the afternoon. All you mums and dads will be together, going through the same thing. The babies will be moved out of the operating theatre into Intensive Care, where they're likely to remain for two or three days. After that, it's the children's ward for perhaps another week, ten days, depending on Holly's progress. There will be a period of a year, perhaps two years, on drugs, and then bingo, she'll be giving that young brother of hers a run for his money. 'Now,' he got up briskly, 'you'll be getting hold of your husband immediately, I presume. He will be able to be here for the operation, I trust?'

'Yes, of course,' said Laura, 'he promised he would be.'

'Good. I want Holly in at two o'clock on Saturday afternoon, so they can run all the necessary tests on Saturday and Sunday. There's a lot of preliminary work to do.'

A sudden fear gripped Laura at the thought of the tiny body being cut open. 'Does she really have to have this operation?'

'Well, it's your decision, of course. If you don't wish to proceed then she need not, naturally.'

'And if she didn't, what would happen to her?'

'I think it's doubtful, looking at her now, that she would ever learn to walk, she hasn't enough strength. Therefore, she would spend her life in a wheelchair which, in turn, would mean her muscles would never develop properly and she would be virtually helpless. As to a prognosis on her life expectancy, it's hard to tell. She's quite a character but I would be surprised if she'd make it to the teenage years, certainly not beyond fourteen.' His words were terrifyingly uncompromising.

'Then I don't have any choice, do I?' said Laura.

'Not really,' Simon replied, quietly.

'What do you mean?' Laura's voice was verging on hysteria.

'Baby, I'm saying I can't make it. I'm truly sorry but I can't walk out in the middle of the series.'

'But you promised, you said you'd be here for the operation, you know you did, Max. It's been bad enough your not being here in the last few months – she's so ill now – but you have to come home for the operation, you just have to. I can't cope with this on my own, I really can't.'

'Sure you can, baby – you've got Bridget.'

'Bridget is not my husband, Bridget is not Holly's father.'

'I'm sorry, Laura. I just can't get to you at the moment.'

All thought of pride was gone, Laura was desperate. 'Please, please, Max – a deal is a deal, you promised.'

'Yes, and the doctor fella said he didn't want to operate on Holly until she was one. My contract finishes in September. Jesus Christ, Laura, I thought that allowed plenty of time, plenty of slack in case he wanted to operate earlier. How was I to know the kid was going to deteriorate so fast – I'm not a doctor?'

'The kid, the kid!' Laura screamed. 'We're talking about your daughter.'

'Mummy, Mummy, don't shout.' Fram came running into the room.

'Shush, Fram, Mummy's talking to Daddy.'

'Don't shout, I'm frightened,' he said. He put his arms round Laura's neck, pressed his face to hers and began to cry. The last few months had been hard on Fram, she knew. The rising tension was starting to affect both him and Bridget, who in many ways was still little more than a child herself.

Everyone needed her yet she had no one. She took a grip on herself for Fram's sake. 'So are you saying, Max, that although I have given you a week's notice to sort things out, you're not going to be here for Holly's operation?'

'I can't be, Laura. You know the show goes out Sunday nights and it's live. With the time difference and the time it will take me to cross the Atlantic, I couldn't make it until Tuesday. On Wednesday, we start rehearsing again for Sunday's show – it's a very full-time job.'

'If you don't come back Max, if you don't somehow fix it, then I'd rather you never come back again.' Her voice was icy calm now.

'Oh come on, Laura, that's hardly fair.'

'Fair or not, I mean what I'm saying.' With that, she put down the phone and taking Fram on her lap, drew him to her. 'I'm sorry Mummy shouted, darling. It's just a very worrying time now, you do understand?' He snuggled close to her and for a few moments they sat perfectly still, drawing comfort from one another.

'As I was frightened just now,' Fram said, after a while, 'do you think I could have an ice-cream to make me feel better?' If only all our problems could be solved that easily, Laura thought.

Strangely enough, once Laura realized that Max was not going to be there for the operation, she found what seemed to be a whole new cache of hidden resources. For Holly's sake, she had to cope, would cope, and it was no good leaning on Bridget for support – she had more than a full-time job keeping Fram calm and happy.

On the Saturday Holly was due to go into hospital, the four of them had a party lunch together. Bridget organized jelly and balloons and a special 'good-luck' cake in the shape of a horseshoe. Holly was more cheerful than she had been in several days. She sat in her high chair, banging out rhythms with her spoon, a paper hat sitting drunkenly on her head. Just for a second, Laura allowed herself to think that this might be the last time her children ever sat together at a table. Then she remembered Simon's words and pushed the thought away.

The Brompton Hospital was like something out of Dickens – long, gloomy corridors, exposed pipework, flaking paint – it was impossible to believe that the most advanced heart surgery in the world took place in these decaying surroundings. There were five babies due for surgery on Monday. The parents were shown an accommodation unit, where they could make tea and coffee, watch television, and those who did not live in London could stay the night. Everyone else's husband was there except Laura's, but strangely, it didn't worry her. They were a team – the parents – instantly welded together by communal agony. It was not possible to feel an outsider. They were an army going into battle – the price of defeat, the lives of their children.

On Monday morning Laura packed a small bag, kissed a still-sleeping Fram, hugged Bridget and left the house at 6.30. When she arrived at the hospital, she was told Holly had spent a peaceful night and was already drowsy from the pre-med. She was the second baby to be operated upon. Laura waited by her cot until, in a sudden flurry of activity, she had just time to kiss her daughter before the trolley took her away.

Then, as she had been instructed, she went to the flat, where one-by-one the other parents joined her. There was a forced cheerfulness in the room, husbands cracked jokes. The hours ticked by. At half-past eleven one of the husbands mysteriously disappeared and returned with two litres of wine and a pile of plastic cups. 'Not enough to get silly on, just enough to keep our spirits up,' he said. He was right – it helped. Someone offered Laura a cigarette and she smoked for the first time in several years. More coffee was made, and then the parents of the first baby to have been operated on were called – half an hour later, it was Laura's turn.

The child lying on the bed bore virtually no resemblance to Holly. She was wired up in every conceivable way – her nose flattened by a plaster, from which a tube protruded. She lay like a discarded rag doll, and for Laura, the sight would have been appalling but for one single factor. 'She's pink,' Laura said, looking at the nurse in amazement, 'she's pink! I'd never realized . . .'

The nurse smiled and pressed her hand. 'Yes, it's the first thing everyone says.'

'Was . . . was the operation a success?'

'The doctor will come and see you later but certainly, she looks good, doesn't she?'

Several hours later, the surgeon confirmed that the operation, as far as he could tell, had been a success. They had repaired the valve with a piece of tissue taken from a rat, which horrified Laura. 'There is the possibility of rejection, of course, we have that to face,' he said, but as much as any medical man could be, he sounded cautiously optimistic. Clutching at this thread of comfort, Laura rang Bridget and her mother, and asked Bridget to ring Max with the news. Bridget sullenly agreed.

From then on, there was very little the parents could do but wait. A holiday atmosphere developed, until at four o'clock in the afternoon, one of the babies – a little girl called Gemma – died suddenly. It brought home to everyone the tightrope they were all walking and from then on, the parents hovered round their babies' cots, too frightened to leave them for a moment.

For two days and nights Laura kept vigil, either sleeping on a sofa in the flat or sitting by Holly's bedside, and it was not until the second day that it began to dawn on her that Holly was not responding like the other babies. One of the children had already left Intensive Care, the others were awake, some even smiling and tubes were being removed thick and fast. Holly, however, just lay there. Now and again her eyelids flickered but otherwise, she moved not a muscle. The doctors were evasive, saying that children's recovery rate varied enormously. Laura began to doubt these platitudes and in her desperation, rang Simon Littleton. 'I'll come over and find out what's going on,' he promised.

At four o'clock on Thursday afternoon, when Laura had enjoyed no more than about four hours' sleep in sixty, she was called into a little side room just off the Intensive Care Unit. There were four men present – the surgeon and the anaesthetist, both of whom she recognized, a third man was introduced as a senior paediatrician and Simon Littleton. 'We've been having a conference about your Holly,' the surgeon said, 'you're right in assuming she's not responding as she should, but we're not sure why. I don't want you to become too alarmed, Mrs Morgan, but it is possible there's been some sort of brain damage.'

It was the one thing that Laura had never considered. In her mind, the options had been that Holly was either going to live or die – the concept of a half-life as being a part of the nightmare simply had not occurred to her. 'Oh, no.' The days of strain, the exhaustion caught up with her in an instant. She burst into tears and began sobbing.

Simon put an arm round her. 'Only could be, Laura, only could be. Mr James, here, the anaesthetist, is going to try some drugs on Holly which should, perhaps, give us some indication as to what's happening. Now come on, remember what you promised me.'

'I'll try,' said Laura.

The four men trooped into the unit where Holly lay. She was as before, unmoving and there was so much instrumentation around her that Laura could not even reach out to touch her, never mind hold her. Someone drew up a chair for her. 'Now,' said Mr James, 'watch this monitoring board here. See all these lights? These are Holly's various bodily functions – her breathing, her heart, the blood circulation . . . this one here is the heart. Now I'm going to try one or two drugs and see what effect they have on stimulating Holly's system. Watch the board.'

The room was suddenly full of people. Several nurses had apparently abandoned their posts to watch. It seemed to Laura as though she and Holly were players on a stage and this was the audience. If only she could touch her, pick up the tiny hand . . . Mr James inserted the first injection. Nothing happened for a moment and then all the monitoring systems began to dip violently. Agony clutched at Laura. Mr James barked some unintelligible order, another injection was brought. Again it was plunged into the tiny hand and the lights rocketed down still further. 'She's going, she's going,' said Laura. 'Let me hold her, please let me hold her.' She leapt to her feet.

'Sit down,' Mr James roared at her. He seized yet another needle and pressed home the injection. The lights stopped plunging and suddenly, miraculously, they began to rise.

Laura dragged her eyes away from the monitor to look at her daughter's face. The eyelids flickered, opened, and in a tiny whispered voice, she began to cry.

'Holly, darling, it's alright, Mummy's here.'

The surgeon stepped forward. 'Let's get these bloody machines out of the way,' he said. Carefully he removed the various wires from Holly's body. As soon as she could, she turned her head and stared at her mother. Tears continued to trickle down her face but she made no sound now. Gently the surgeon picked up the tiny body and handed it to Laura. 'Keep her as flat as possible,' he said.

The moment Laura took Holly in her arms, a great sigh of relief came from both mother and daughter. A ghost of a smile crossed Holly's face. 'You're going to be better soon, darling,' Laura whispered, fighting for speech through her tears.

'Mum,' Holly managed, before her eyelids shut in the beginning of sleep.

Laura looked up at the surgeon, full of fear, but he was smiling. 'This diagnosis is subject to confirmation, Mrs Morgan,' he said, gently. 'Sometimes medical science is too clever by half. I'm fairly certain that what Holly has been suffering from is shock, and rather than all this machinery we've been linking her up to, the only equipment Holly really needs is the oldest in the world.'

'What's that?' Laura whispered.

'Her mother's arms,' the surgeon replied.

CHAPTER TWENTY-FOUR

The afternoon that Holly was moved out of Intensive Care into the children's ward, she and Laura received their first visitors. Katrine had flown from Athens, Diana and Giles arrived with armfuls of flowers but the most important visitors of all were Bridget and Fram. 'I wasn't sure whether to bring him,' Bridget said, 'but he was mad keen to come.'

Fram ran up to the cot. 'She's a lovely colour,' he said, and everyone laughed with relief. It was true, she already looked a very different child, though she was restless and obviously still in pain.

Flowers arrived from William Campling, Harry Sutherland, from Laura's publishers, from Eleanor, Tom Morgan and the staff of Gooseberries but there was no word from Max. At last the excitement began to die down and everyone left – Bridget and Fram were the last to go. 'You look like shit,' said Bridget, conversationally.

'You know something, Bridget, you always have the knack of making someone feel very special,' said Laura.

'Cut the crap, why don't you go home with Fram and I'll stay on here with Holly overnight – she won't mind my being here instead of you.'

Laura shook her head. 'No, it's been so awful, Bridget, I just can't leave her yet.'

'But she's on the mend and out of Intensive Care.'

'Yes, but we very nearly lost her.'

Bridget stared at Laura. 'When? How?'

Laura glanced at Fram who had wandered over to the corner where the toys were kept, and slowly, hesitantly told Bridget of the drama with the monitoring machine.

'It must have been . . .' Bridget shook her head, 'I can't find the words, you must have wanted to scream the place down.'

'I can't really believe it happened now,' said Laura, 'it's like a sort of awful nightmare.'

'I understand how you're feeling, I really do, but wouldn't you be able to help Holly if you had a rest? You need to get out of this place for a bit and recharge the batteries – for both your sakes.'

Laura shook her head. 'I'm alright, honestly, I'd much rather you went home and gave Fram a good time.'

'He's missing you,' said Bridget.

'I'm missing him, missing you all, but it won't be long now.'

Almost immediately after Bridget left, Laura began to regret her decision. Holly was fretful and difficult. She was running a slight temperature and whatever Laura tried to do, she could not make her comfortable. The other children who had been operated on at the same time as Holly all had their parents with them, but in their case, there were two parents involved so that they could take it in turns to have a sleep. Laura knew that such was her fatigue, she was not doing Holly justice, and when finally a nurse took pity on her and sent her off to bed, she was too tired to argue.

In the morning, pale and wan, she sat by Holly's bedside again. The baby seemed more at ease this morning and the temperature had gone. It seemed to Laura that she had always been in the hospital – she could remember no other time. She was a total wreck – her hair needed washing, her clothes were creased, she had long since abandoned any attempt at makeup. She was sitting in a chair, by the cot, holding Holly's hand, trying to stay awake to recite a nursery rhyme when Bridget found her. 'Hi, Laura, I've brought someone to cheer you up.'

Laura looked up, through tired eyes, to see David Lawson standing before her. 'Hello, old thing, how's it going?'

'David!' She looked from David to Bridget. 'How did you . . . what are you doing here?'

'Bridget telephoned me last night, after a bit of detective work. She reckoned I was needed to help cheer you up.'

'Bridget, you shouldn't have . . .' Laura began.

'I had me orders,' said Bridget. 'When you went off to the

bog that time we met down in Cornwall, David told me to get in touch with him if you needed anything. I reckon you need something.'

'Like what?' said Laura.

'A booze up with David. Fram's spending the day with his pal, Oliver, and I'm going to look after Holly while you go out and have a bloody good lunch. Then David's going to take you home and you're going to have a sleep, and a bath, and then if you must, you can come back here again. I'd rather you left me here until tomorrow though.'

Laura smiled, it all sounded too good to be true. 'Do I have any choice?'

'None at all,' said David. 'Shall we go?'

He took her to an Italian restaurant just across the road from the Brompton and only a few doors from the first Gooseberries restaurant. 'There's a much better restaurant than this up the road,' Laura said.

'I'm well aware of that, but I'm not letting you in there or you'll get involved in work.'

'I don't feel as if I can ever get involved in anything again,' said Laura. 'It's as though I've fought some immense battle . . .'

'But you have,' said David. 'Bridget told me all about it, about how Holly nearly died. Come on, let's order some food and a bottle of wine and then I'm taking you home to bed.'

Over lunch David talked Laura through the ordeal, and as she unburdened her anxieties, she began to feel better. 'Her poor little throat, it's so sore from where they shoved tubes down her. All she's able to manage is yoghurt.'

'Children are so quick to heal. You'll be amazed – two weeks from now, even a week from now, she will be a different child.'

'And I still don't really know if the operation's been a success. They keep saying they're pleased with her progress but what does that mean?'

'Why don't you speak to the specialist who has been dealing with Holly's case – I'm sure he will explain to you how things are going. Surgeons tend to be rather too grand to be able to spend the necessary time explaining what they're up to.'

'That's a good idea,' Laura said.

'What's his name?'

'Simon Littleton, his various numbers are in the address book at home. I'll ring him from there.'

'No you won't,' said David firmly. 'Leave it to me, I will call him and ask if he can pop round to the hospital tomorrow to see you.

'Would you really do that?'

'Of course. Now there's no point in giving you a cup of coffee because it might wake you up; I'm taking you home.'

The house was strangely quiet without the children and Bridget. 'Do you want a bath before you go to bed?'

'I don't think so,' said Laura.

'Right, you pop upstairs and get into bed and I'll make a cup of tea and bring it up to you. Then I'll sit downstairs while you sleep so you know if there's any sort of crisis or any problem, I'll hear the phone.'

'David, you're being so kind.'

'Shut up and go upstairs,' he smiled at her and limped into the kitchen.

She watched his retreating back, conscious of a great feeling of relief at having someone else take charge. Then she climbed the stairs, wearily. At Holly's door she paused and went inside. The cot had been remade with fresh sheets, ready for her return. Her favourite toys were lined up and Bridget had brought back some of the cards from the hospital and pinned them up on the wall. The possibility that Holly might be going to get better suddenly took on a reality, and armed with this belief, Laura walked into her bedroom, undressed, climbed into bed and before David even arrived with the tea, she was asleep.

When she woke the curtains were drawn and the room was in virtual darkness. Rolling over, she saw the clock by her bedside table had stopped. She wondered what time it was, but only idly. David would let her know if there were any problems. She was almost at the point of drifting off to sleep again when she noticed a dark shape sitting in the chair by the window. So what was David doing up here? He had promised to always keep a safe distance in future – was this safe –

probably yes, in her state. She began to drift again but her eyes strayed back to the figure who seemed to be hunched forward, apparently asleep too. If David was asleep then perhaps he had not heard the phone. Laura sat bolt upright in bed and stared at the figure. It was not David, it was too big. She leaned over and snapped on the bedroom light. The figure straightened up with a jerk. It was Max. 'Oh, you're awake,' he said, 'good.'

'Max! When did you arrive?'

'About an hour ago. Who the hell was that guy downstairs? Lawson, David Lawson – he says he's a friend of yours. What the bloody hell was he doing here when you were in bed?'

Laura stared at Max, unable to believe that this was his first greeting. 'David is a friend of mine, I've known him a very long time, and as to what he was doing here, he was doing the job you should have been doing – helping me get through this.'

'Oh he was, was he? Well, anyway, I sent him packing.'

'I hope you thanked him.'

'Thanked him for what? He was sitting in my drawing room, drinking my booze, talking on my telephone.'

'I suspect he was trying to telephone the specialist for me.'

'Oh yes, he left a message to say Simon Littleton will be at the hospital tomorrow about eleven o'clock. How are you feeling, baby?' He came and sat on the edge of the bed and leant forward to kiss her.

'Don't touch me,' Laura almost shouted at him. 'How can you turn up when it's all over, cross-question me about a friend who's been helping me and not even ask how your daughter is.'

'I know how my daughter is, your chum David told me. It seems she's making a fine recovery.'

'She nearly died, Max.'

'I heard that, too,' said Max, 'It must have been awful. Look, why don't you get up and I'll take you out to dinner.'

'Don't you want to go and see Holly?'

'I'll see her in the morning, with you. I've checked with Bridget, she's happy to stay the night and she's fixed for Fram to stay over with his chum – Oliver, is it, so the night is ours.'

'What are you suggesting we do,' said Laura,' 'go out and celebrate?'

'Why not?' said Max.

'Celebrate that the crisis is over when you weren't here to be any part of it?' Laura said.

'No,' Max replied, evenly, 'but I am here now. I've recorded next Sunday's show and therefore I have a week's leave.'

'I don't know why you bothered to come,' said Laura.

'Because I love you and the children.'

'But not enough,' said Laura.

'Look, will you stop trying to make me feel guilty – I'm doing the best I can. I'm sorry if I let you down, but there really was nothing I could do. I felt dreadful about it, believe me, but I can't seem to do anything right these days. I thought our marriage was going to be such fun, too.'

The wistful tone to his voice softened Laura a little. 'Max, you're not a child, you're supposed to be a fully responsible adult. I want our marriage to be fun as well, but neither of us knew we were going to have a baby with a heart defect. It's been a tough year and we're not out of the wood yet, but it would have been a great deal less tough if I'd had your support.'

'You've had as much of my support as I can give, Laura. You know the kind of guy I am, you knew me well enough before we married. This domestic stuff is just not my scene, unlike, apparently, that little guy, David. What's with his leg, anyway?'

'He had an accident when he was a child – it's left him partially paralysed.'

'Paralysed – I can't stand sickness,' said Max.

'That,' Laura replied, 'is patently obvious.'

CHAPTER TWENTY-FIVE

'We are now commencing our descent to Vancouver. The weather there is perfect, sunshine all the way, folks.'

Bridget hugged Holly closer to her, more to comfort herself than the child. It was three years since she had fallen in love with Buck and two since she had seen him – two years in which they had communicated not at all. Buck could neither read nor write, and whilst Bridget could do a little of both, there was little point in writing if her letter had to be read by a third party. If she had known it would be two years before she saw him again, would she have left Vancouver Island, Bridget wondered. In the time since she and Buck had been apart, this child, sitting so healthy and confident on her lap, had been born, nearly died and survived – a little life of high drama now well established. It served to emphasize the length of time they had been apart. Perhaps Buck had married someone else. Max had not mentioned him at all on his last visit at Christmas, but then the tension between Laura and Max had been riding so high, she had not felt she could mention her own problems. The wheels jolted on to the tarmac and Laura, sitting beside her, turned and smiled, reaching out to squeeze her hand. So she knew . . . Bridget thought, she had not forgotten.

Only Max was there to meet them at the airport. He was in a buoyant mood. He swept Laura into an embrace, then Bridget and finally picked up the children, carrying one on either hip as they squealed with delight. Laura seemed genuinely pleased to see him, Bridget noted. They were through customs in a trice, then across the city by taxi and into the little plane to take them to Cassidy. Max talked all the while, exclusively about his work – there was no mention of Buck at all. Perhaps he has gone, Bridget thought with a rising panic. She glanced up and was aware of Laura's eyes on her.

'How's Buck?' Laura asked Max, not taking her eyes from Bridget's.

'Oh he's fine, fine. He's waiting for us at home.'

He's not going to be at Cassidy Airport, was all Bridget could think. If he really wanted to see me, surely he would have come to the airport.

The short flight, followed by the bumpy ride in Max's old station wagon seemed to go on for ever, but at last they were on the trail and then turning into the clearing to where the log cabin was standing just as before.

'Look Holly, look, here we are,' Fram shouted. 'Where's Buck, I want to see Buck. Give me Holly, Mummy, I'll go and show her to Buck.' As the car stopped, Fram was out and seizing his little sister from his mother's lap, staggered with her the short distance to the steps. Buck must have been watching for them, for the door opened and he was beside Fram in a moment, picking up both children with ease and grace, and grinning from ear to ear.

He has grown better looking than ever, Bridget thought – there must be hundreds of girls after him. Buck lowered the children to the ground and taking one small hand in each of his, began walking at Holly's pace towards the car. Laura jumped out and went to him, followed by Max but Bridget found she could not move. Laura was saying something to Buck but she could not hear what it was through the glass of the car. Suddenly Buck dropped the hands of the children and started towards her. His gesture released her – she was out of the car in seconds, standing on trembling legs.

'Bridget . . .,' Buck began to run, opening his arms as he did so and she, quick as lightning, sped towards him and threw herself into his arms. As they closed around her, she knew, without any doubt, that nothing had changed.

That evening, when the children were in bed, both exhausted from the journey, Laura tapped on Bridget's door. 'Buck's heavily involved in the kitchen and Max is chopping wood – let's go for a walk.'

'I don't know how you've got the strength,' said Bridget.

'Just a short one, I want to talk.'

They left the clearing and started down one of the many

paths through the forest. It was a beautiful evening, the sun glinting through the trees. 'Vancouver Island in May has to be one of the most beautiful places in the world,' said Laura. Bridget nodded silently. They reached a fallen tree and Laura sat down on it. 'Bridget, if he hasn't asked you already, Buck's going to ask you to marry him, isn't he?'

'He hasn't yet,' said Bridget.

'But he will, we both know that. We've been friends a long time, you and I,' Bridget nodded, 'and been through a lot together, one way and another.'

'Yes,' Bridget mumbled.

'When you walked into the restaurant that day, you had no one in the world, did you?'

'No,' Bridget said.

'Now you have me and Fram and Holly, and you'll always be a part of our family, whatever happens to us all. You've made friends, too – the restaurant staff, Jamie, Di and Giles. They are important to you because, again, they represent something you didn't have before – a sense of belonging.' Bridget, perched on the edge of the tree looked down at her feet and said nothing. 'But none of us can take the place of a companion for life,' Laura said, quietly. 'You and Buck belong together, you know that, and you must never, never be parted again. He loves this place and you, and you love him, so you must make your lives together here.'

Bridget looked up at her with tortured eyes. 'I do love them kids so much,' she said.

'I know, but close as you are to them, there is no substitute for children of your own, Bridget. Buck is a good man, you've been through terrible times, both of you. You owe it to yourselves and each other to make one another happy.'

'I'm dead scared, Laura, that's the truth.'

'I know,' said Laura.

'You're right, you are my family now and you're going to be so far away. Might you . . . is there any chance of your settling here or in New York if Max continues to work over here?'

'I think it's time Max came to England for a while, don't you?' said Laura, quietly. 'Fram's very happy at school and

Holly's still going to need regular check-ups for a couple of years.'

'Yes, I suppose so,' said Bridget, 'but what will you do without me to help you?'

'It will be difficult and sad,' said Laura, 'but infinitely less sad than you sacrificing your happiness for us. None of us could bear that – neither me, nor the children when they are old enough to understand.'

'Anyway,' said Bridget defiantly, 'he probably won't even ask me.'

He did ask her that very night. 'You can't leave me again,' he said, simply, 'the baby's OK now and it's their life, Bridget. I think they're more than Max Morgan deserves but Laura has to make her own way – she didn't have to marry the guy.'

'Do you think he'll go back to England with them?' Bridget said.

'I guess not, but you're not answering my question – marry me, Bridget, make your life here, with me. You have to, I can't live without you any more.'

They were lying on the bed in Buck's cabin. They had not made love yet, their emotions were too raw and exposed, they just held each other close. 'I love you,' Bridget whispered.

'Then marry me, please, please,' Buck begged.

Bridget looked up at his proud features, softened now by longing. She smoothed the hair back from his face. He was trembling, tears glistened at the corner of his eyes. She was causing all this pain. 'I won't leave you again, Buck, I promise,' she whispered.

The wedding, Laura said afterwards, was quite the most beautiful ceremony she had ever attended. It took place in the little chapel in Chemainus. Bridget discarded her usual jeans and shirt for a simple white cotton dress and a garland of wild flowers in her hair. Buck opted for a new white shirt and trousers. They were a startlingly beautiful couple, with Fram and Holly proudly attending as page and bridesmaid. There was no question of a honeymoon, they wanted to stay at the cabin, to be with the family until they returned to England. Max had installed a big double bed in Buck's cabin and Laura presented them with their first ever bank account, with a deposit of $20,000. 'We can't accept this,' said Buck, 'we can get by on my salary.'

'You can and must accept it,' said Laura. 'I have plenty of money. Bridget will tell you that. Neither of you will receive anything from your parents – just look on me as representing what your parents would have done for you, if they could.'

Both Buck and Bridget knew it was a poor excuse, for their parents would have done nothing for them at all, but they accepted the money at last, aware that it gave them more security than either of them had known in their lives.

The weeks rolled by – sunny, relaxed – and on the surface, Laura and Max seemed closer than they had been in a long time, but in the privacy of their bedroom a battle raged. For reasons she could not begin to explain, Laura could not bear him to touch her.

'God dammit, Laura, what the hell's wrong with you?' Max shouted one night, when once again Laura turned away from him and said that she was too tired.

'I don't know,' she answered truthfully, 'I just feel I . . . I can't.'

'Won't.' Max snapped on the light. 'Things have never been right between us since the baby was born,' he said.

'Yes, I agree,' said Laura, 'but it's not a physical problem.'

'What the hell is it then?'

'I don't know.'

'You just don't want to make love to me, right?'

'Yes,' said Laura.

'Do I revolt you, is that it?'

'No, no of course not.'

'Then what? Is this your idea of revenge because I wasn't around for Holly's operation?'

'Not consciously,' said Laura.

'Shit, what the hell does that mean – subconsciously, then?'

'I don't know, I just don't know,' said Laura. 'Please don't shout, you'll wake the children.'

Things did not improve as the weeks passed, and their plight was somehow all the more painful in the face of Bridget and Buck's ecstatic happiness. One day Max suggested that he and Laura should go into Victoria for lunch, leaving the children with Bridget. It was a beautiful day and she would rather have picnicked in the forest, but Laura sensed that they were reaching crisis point and needed to talk away from the family.

They spoke very little on the way, but once seated in the restaurant, Max wasted no time. 'Laura, I want to talk to you about us and our future, both as you see it and I see it.' Laura nodded. 'I take it that you still want me to live in England . . .'

'Yes, I do,' said Laura, 'I'm committed to England because of Fram's schooling and Holly's check-ups.'

'Bullshit,' said Max. 'You can live anywhere in the world. We can find a consultant who can be properly briefed to watch over Holly, and in any event, you've only got to look at the kid to see she's making wonderful progress.'

'Things can go wrong,' said Laura, but she knew Max spoke the truth. There had been no hint of rejection, the hole had healed and the repaired valve was working strongly and well.

'And as for Fram's schooling, that's a joke. He's six years old – if he was thirteen, I'd agree it would be a major consideration, but at six he can be educated anywhere. The truth, is, Laura, you just don't want to live in North America, do you?'

'I suppose that's true,' said Laura, reluctantly.

'OK, baby. Now this is the bottom line. I've been offered a three-year contract in Washington – three years, mind you, they're that confident. It's another chat show, but a political one, aimed at cutting through the crap these senators and their like hand out. It is a very important show – it will put me on a par with your Robin Day, only in a far bigger way because there'll be a far bigger audience.'

'Have you signed yet?' said Laura.

'No, of course not.'

'I don't know why you say "of course", you normally do before discussing it with me.'

'Well this time I haven't, this time I'm trying to do it right, so don't knock it, Laura.'

'I'm sorry,' said Laura, genuinely.

'If I sign the contract, I'm due to start work in September

and because of the length of period involved, I need to set up an apartment and get organized. The thing is, Laura, I'd like you and the children to be with me. There are plenty of good schools in Washington – international schools – and there'd be no problem with doctors. I think a fresh start might be just what we need.'

'Why can't you work in England, Max?' Laura said, 'Heavens, you were working in England the first time we met.'

'Yes, but that was because I hadn't made it. In those days I was taking any kind of work I could get. Now I'm big news in the US, I really am, Laura.'

'I know that by the fact we're always being stopped in the street, but don't you think your family need more of your time and attention than we've had to date.'

'Yes, I do, which is why I'm suggesting you come to Washington. Look, let me put it another way,' said Max, 'our relationship isn't so great at the moment, is it?' Laura shook her head. 'So . . . you can't take everything away from a guy, Laura. You don't want to make love to me. Right now, you just seem to see me as a sexless friend, and then, in addition, you're asking me to give up the career chance of a lifetime. If I do that, Laura, I'll have no balls left.'

The point he was making was not lost on Laura. 'Yes, I can see that,' she said, quietly.

'So, will you at least think about Washington? Hell, it's only for three years, you'll love it, I promise you, and so will the kids.'

'I don't know why you want us with you really,' said Laura. 'As you say, I'm not much of a wife at present and the children drive you crazy most of the time.'

'I want you because I'm proud of you.'

Laura wondered about Max's last remark on the way home to Chemainus. What was he really seeking – a respectable family life, to back up his new-found status and image? It was an unworthy thought and she tried to push it to the back of her mind, but somehow the suspicion seemed firmly lodged. It was not his family he really wanted but the image they projected. The decision would have to be faced in the next few days, she knew that. It was not fair to Max to keep him waiting around and besides which, if they were to make the move there were so many plans and arrangements to be made. Something would have to be done with the house in London, they would have to find an apartment in Washington. Laura felt tired at the thought. Then there was Gooseberries . . .

Laura's mind was reeling by the time they reached the cabin but as they drove into the glade, Bridget came running out of the front door and all thoughts of the future were banished by a sudden terror for the present. She leapt from the car. 'Has something happened to one of the children – Holly?'

'No, no, the children are fine,' said Bridget, 'but we've just had a telegram from Anthony Melhuish – Lord Campling died this morning.'

'Oh dear, I'm so sorry,' said Laura, 'he's been so much on my conscience of late . . . I should have taken Fram to see him, before we came away.' Max joined them and slipped an arm round Laura's shoulders.

'The thing is,' said Bridget, 'Anthony is wondering if you and Fram could go back for the funeral. He says he knows it's a lot to ask, in the middle of a family holiday, but well . . .,' Bridget's tone became suitably reverent, 'since Fram is the old man's heir, Anthony felt he should be there.'

CHAPTER TWENTY-SIX

It was good to have her son to herself, Laura decided as she and Fram sat side-by-side on the plane to Heathrow. It was good but because of the circumstances, she was terribly aware of how little effort she had made to forge a link between William Campling and his grandson – indeed, because of the circumstances of his father's disappearance, she rarely talked of the Camplings to Fram. That he was to inherit his grandfather's lands, home and one day his title, came, of course, as no surprise to Laura, but she realized it came as a considerable surprise to Fram. At six he was able to grasp, or begin to grasp, the implications and importance of what had happened. 'So will I really be Lord Campling one day, Mummy?' he asked for the third time.

'Yes, Fram, you will, unless Anthony has any children, but he's not expected to and Grandfather has given you his house because he, too, believes you will be Lord Campling one day when you're grown up.'

'I won't have to live there all on my own without you and Holly, will I?'

Laura laughed and hugged him. 'No, of course not. You won't have to live there at all for some time, or ever, if you don't want to, but Grandfather very much hoped that one day you would, when you get married and have children of your own.'

Fram nodded. 'Has Campling Hall been given to me because my proper Daddy is dead?' he asked, suddenly.

All through his babyhood, whenever the question of his father arose, Laura had tried to explain Francis's disappearance. Usually Fram became bored with the explanation, but now, she realized suddenly, his grandfather's death had kindled an interest which she must try to deal with honestly and openly. 'We don't know if Daddy is dead or not,' she answered, 'but we think so.'

'Tell me about the boat and what happened again,' Fram said. She began the story which she had told him many times before – an edited version, of course, which left out their argument and the interest of the Fraud Squad.

'It's a pity you went to sleep really,' Fram said, when Laura had finished. It was an innocent, childish remark, with no hint of criticism, but instantly it rekindled in Laura the sense of guilt which was never far below the surface so far as Francis was concerned.

'Yes, darling, I agree,' she said, heavily.

Back at the house in Harley Street, they rang Anthony Melhuish who suggested that after a night's sleep, they came straight to Campling Hall. It transpired that William Campling had died of a massive coronary, which he would barely have been aware of before it killed him. That at least brought Laura some comfort. She then rang Max and it was agreed that Bridget and Holly should travel back to England with him at the end of the week – the idea being that Bridget should collect her things and immediately return to Vancouver, leaving Max and Laura to settle their future. That decided, Laura put her own troubles firmly out of her mind in order to concentrate on the Camplings.

Anthony and Lavinia Melhuish, now Lord and Lady Campling, seemed genuinely pleased to see Laura and Fram. Their old-world English courtesy and the elegant formal living at Campling Hall, came in such stark contrast to the cabin in Vancouver, that Laura and Fram felt fairly disorientated. None the less, they were made welcome and there was no hint that his father's will had in any way upset Anthony. On the first evening, when Fram was in bed, they sat discussing it. 'I don't know whether Father ever explained it to you Laura, but it's not Lavinia who can't have children, it's me,' said Anthony. 'So even if poor old Lavinia fell under a bus and I remarried, which heaven forbid . . .,' he gave his wife a warm smile, '. . . it wouldn't make any difference to Fram ultimately inheriting the title. All you have to ensure, Laura, is that young Fram grows up with a healthy regard for the opposite sex, so that he marries and produces plenty of Campling heirs.'

'I'm sure that can be arranged,' said Laura, smiling.

'The problem we do have, however, is that there is no money. By the time death duties are paid, Fram will have the estate but no money with which to run it.'

'But that's no problem,' said Laura, 'I had no idea you were unaware of the plot your father and my father hatched up years ago. Through my father's will, Fram has all the money he needs to maintain the estate, and the trust fund is so arranged that it can be dipped into at any time for the purposes of maintaining the estate, before Fram comes of age and has control of the funds himself.'

Anthony leaned back in his chair and let out a sigh. 'Wonderful – what a relief. I wonder why Father never told me about it.'

'I am sure he meant to tell you about it in due course,' said Laura. 'Although he was frail, he was in good health generally, and I imagine he thought he had a good few years left to finalize his affairs. I never discussed it with him either. I only knew about the agreement Fram's grandfathers hatched between them because my own father told me the details. I suspect William may have found the whole situation faintly embarrassing. At the time Francis and I married he was very against the match, as you know. My father misinterpreted William's disapproval – assuming that he would have preferred his son to marry someone, well, more of your class.'

'That wasn't the case at all . . .' Anthony protested.

'We all know that now, but at the time it was the only explanation Francis could offer for his father's attitude.'

'Francis! I shouldn't speak ill of him in the circumstances Laura, but by God, he was a bastard.'

Laura was taken aback by the vehemence of Anthony's tone. 'Yes . . . well, anyway, once William had explained that he was simply against his son marrying *anyone*, our fathers became great friends – the common link being Fram and his future. Your father wanted to preserve Campling Hall while my father did not want the fortune he was leaving his grandson to spoil him or be squandered recklessly. Linking the money to Campling Hall ensures this. It's a good scheme.'

'Then we must do everything we can to fulfil our fathers'

hopes for the future,' said Anthony. 'Tell me about this trust? Does Fram inherit control of it at twenty-one?' Laura nodded, 'and in the meantime, who are the trustees?'

'My mother, myself and your family solicitor. A mix of both families, in other words.'

'And I am custodian of Campling Hall until Fram is twenty-one. What say you we form a subsidiary trust of which you, I and say, Fram, at eighteen are the trustees – the purpose being to supervise the maintenance of the estate in the meantime.'

'It's a good idea,' said Laura, 'and very much along the lines our fathers were thinking, I imagine.'

'Good. I can't imagine the lawyers will have any problems arranging it, provided the trustees of your father's main trust are happy. Incidentally, if you and your family would like to move into Campling Hall, you know you're more than welcome. Lavinia and I won't be needing it.'

Laura shook her head. 'Thanks, but no, we're already spoilt for choice – I have my old family home under dust sheets in Marlow, we have the house in Vancouver Island, our London home, and my husband wants us to live in Washington for a few years.'

'Good lord, so will you be moving to the States for a while?'

Laura shook her head. 'I honestly don't know. To be frank, Anthony, I don't really want to, and in view of Fram's inheritance, I feel somehow he should stay in this country and learn to love this place as your father did.'

'I know that's what my father would have wished,' said Anthony, 'but I appreciate your problem – it's your marriage and your life, Laura. You must do what you think best.'

It was an emotional few days – the burial of William Campling in the family vault, the return of the rest of the family to London, and then Bridget's departure, resulting in cascades of children's tears and a sudden desperate desire, on Laura's part, to beg her not to go.

'Just telephone me, if you need me,' Bridget said, 'and I'll come running – promise me.'

'On one condition,' said Laura, 'that you'll do the same.'

'You've got yourself a deal,' said Bridget, giving a poor

imitation of her urchin grin. The two women embraced and Laura cried all the way back from Heathrow.

The children were understandably difficult to settle that night and it was after eight by the time Laura came downstairs and set about the task of cooking dinner for Max. 'This country is so inefficient,' Max said, 'in the U S, when you're too tired to cook, you just send out for it.'

'I'm not too tired to cook,' said Laura. 'Just pour me a drink and give me some space, would you Max? It's been a gruelling few days, one way and another.'

He poured them both a glass of wine and sat down at the kitchen table, watching her as she worked. 'We have to talk about it, Laura.'

'I can't,' said Laura, 'not tonight.'

'OK, but when? There are so many decisions to be made. I'm going to have to fly out to Washington next week, one way or the other.'

'You've signed the contract then,' Laura said, dinner suddenly forgotten.

'Yes, Michael sorted it out for me in double-quick time while you and Fram were on your way over here.'

'I see . . . so there's no room for compromise,' Laura said. 'If we want a married life together with the children, I have to go to you, not the other way around. I thought we were going to make a joint decision – now I'm being presented with an ultimatum. You've done it again, Max.'

'I had to,' said Max, 'they were hassling for an answer, God dammit, I don't think I'm being unreasonable.'

'Things have changed for Fram, you know,' said Laura. She was suddenly galvanized into action again, and began flipping the chops in the grill pan.

'OK, he's one hell of a privileged little guy, but I don't see what difference that makes.'

'If he's going to inherit one of the oldest titles in England, he ought to have an English education.'

'Don't start that again,' said Max, 'we've been through it all. I'm not arguing with you, but he doesn't need an English education at six, nor seven, eight nor even nine. There's time, Laura – the time it takes for this contract to run.'

'You've never been so anxious for me to join you before,' Laura said, suspiciously.

'That's because I've never had a stable job before,' Max said. 'It's been a six-month contract here, six weeks there, three months somewhere else – this is three years, this makes it worthwhile putting down roots.'

'Can you at least give me a couple more days to think about it?' Laura said, after a pause.

'Alright, until Friday, but no longer.'

Without Bridget, Laura suddenly found how restrictive life could be with two small children. It was the following afternoon before she had made arrangements for Fram to go to Oliver's, and for the baby-minder who had helped them occasionally in the past, Mrs Everett, to come and look after Holly. Max, needless to say, was too busy to help – the children were exclusively her responsibility. Eventually, just after three, Laura dropped into Fulham Road, to the offices of Gooseberries, which were now based in the old flat, above the first restaurant, where she and Fram had once lived. Diana looked pleased to see her but a little tired. The two women embraced warmly. 'How are things?' said Laura.

'Great, just great!' said Diana, 'you'll be proud of me – I'm really getting results. Bath is making money, Cambridge is making money, Oxford's absolutely raking it in, and although Bristol's only been open a month, it's already breaking even. As for London . . . it's going mad, even Highgate.'

'You are super, and I do feel guilty,' said Laura.

'No need to, darling, I'm loving every minute of it, at least I am at the moment.'

'What's that supposed to mean?' said Laura.

'I've got a lot to tell you, but tell me about you first. I'm sorry to hear about William Campling.'

'Yes, it was sad.'

'I gather Fram's copped the lot.'

'What a charming way you put things, Di. As a matter of fact he has, but it was not unexpected.'

'Goodness, a right little Lord Fauntleroy, we've got then, haven't we?'

'Heaven forbid,' said Laura, laughing. 'Oh, it is good to see you, Di. Tell me all the gossip.'

'Ummmm, let me think,' said Diana. 'Ah, here's one which will be close to your heart – David Lawson's getting divorced.'

Laura turned away from Diana so her friend would not see the flush she felt creeping into her face. 'Good heavens, why on earth is he doing that? Has he found someone else?' She tried to keep her voice casual.

'Not as far as I know, though my spies are a little vague on the subject. I think basically that he and Serena have just drifted apart. She's wedded to her wretched computers, he to his boats and there's no children to hold them together. Sad though – poor David doesn't have much luck with women.'

'Meaning?'

'Meaning nothing, darling, I'm not having a crack at you. Well, yes, I suppose I am really, but honestly, you shouldn't have let that one get away.'

'Perhaps not,' said Laura. She was longing to ask more but pride forbade her. 'Alright, so that's dealt with my old flame, what else?'

'Well . . .' Diana hesitated, 'I don't quite know how you're going to feel about this.' She tried to look serious but a huge grin began spreading across her face. 'I'm pregnant!'

'Oh Di, you're not! That's marvellous, wonderful. Let me give you a hug. When is it due, is Giles pleased, can I be a godmother?'

'Hang on,' said Diana, laughing. 'Yes Giles is pleased, yes, most certainly, you can be a godmother, and it's due in six months' time.'

'Six months – and you haven't even the smallest bump yet.'

'That's because of my great height, darling – it's just little shortarses, like you, who show off these babies.'

'Thanks a lot,' said Laura. 'So let me see, the baby's due in December, no January.'

'That's right, mid-January, they reckon.'

Laura was still grinning. 'Well, I must say, that's the best news I've heard in weeks.' Suddenly she sobered. 'Oh, my God, the business!'

'I wondered when you'd come round to thinking about that,' said Diana.

'Do you want to work after the baby's born?'

Diana shook her head. 'No, not for a few years, anyway. I'm coming to motherhood rather late and since I had such a rotten childhood myself, I'm going to make damned sure this little brat has a hundred per cent of my time and attention.'

'Quite right, too.'

'But it is a fact, darling, that Giles can't handle the restaurants, the wine bar and the antiques single-handed. We'll have to start looking around for someone.'

Laura stared at her for a long time. Everything suddenly seemed very simple. 'We don't have to do that, Di. I'll take over.'

Laura did not wait until Friday to tell Max of her decision. She took him out to dinner that night, having persuaded Mrs Everett to stay on, and told him as carefully and tactfully as she could. Diana's baby had created the catalyst which made her decision possible. Of course she knew an outsider could be brought in to help Giles, but she did not even suggest this to Max as an option. Max took the news surprisingly well. He said he understood the position perfectly and no, Laura was not to feel guilty about it. In fact, after all the brash, bombastic bullying of previous days, it was almost as though he was as relieved as Laura that she had made her choice.

When they got home that night, for the first time in some months, they made love. Max was gentle and unusually sensitive. Whether he was trying to impress upon Laura what she would be missing or whether he was trying to change her mind, Laura could not tell. Afterwards, they lay in silence for a while, very far from sleep. 'I can come back to England for ten days or so, every three or four months,' Max said. 'And then in the summer, you can bring the children out to Vancouver as usual, and I should be able to grab some decent time off then. They'll probably cut the show during the holiday period, anyway.'

'Yes, of course,' said Laura, anxious to reassure, to heal the wounds they had inflicted upon one another before they parted. It was futile though, for whatever they said or did, once Max left for Washington, an irrevocable decision had been made. It was a turning point, Laura realized, as she lay awake long after Max's even breathing told her he was asleep. There was no escaping the truth. The fact they had faced together that evening was the certain knowledge that their lifestyles were incompatible, and if neither of them were prepared to compromise, then their marriage was little more than sham.

THE BEGINNING OF THE END:
London, Christmas 1979

CHAPTER TWENTY-SEVEN

'I can reach, I can, I can!' Holly danced around the Christmas tree on tiptoe.

'No, you can't, stupid, give it to me.' Quite apart from the four years that separated Holly and Fram in age, Fram clearly had inherited the Campling height and was tall for his ten years, while Holly, at six, was the image of her mother, small and slender. Fram grabbed the coloured ball from Holly and held it above his head.

'Give it back, Fram. I'm doing it, Mummy said I could do it.'

'If you try to do it, you'll knock all the decorations off the bottom of the tree. Anyway, why should you do it all by yourself? It's only fair that we should do it together.'

'Give it back, give it back,' Holly shouted.

'No.'

'It's not just Christmas, it's my birthday as well – that's why Mummy said I could do the tree.'

'Will you be quiet,' Laura burst out. She was sitting at her desk in the bay window of their drawing room. 'I've had more than enough of you two today. If there's any more nonsense like this, there'll be no tree at all – I'd rather have it taken down and chopped up for firewood than have to listen to you arguing.'

Both children turned hurt, surprised faces towards Laura, united for a moment in condemnation of their mother's attitude.

'You wouldn't, would you, Mummy?' Holly said, in a small voice.

'No, of course she wouldn't, brainless,' said Fram, 'she's just in a bad mood.'

'And enough of your cheek, young man,' said Laura. 'How am I supposed to work with you bickering all the time.'

'You're always working,' said Holly. 'It's not fair – we should be allowed to make a noise sometimes.'

It was not an unreasonable criticism, Laura knew. Exasperated, more with herself than with the children, she threw down her pen and stood up, pressing small, delicate fingers into her aching temples.

'Are you going to stop work?' Fram said, hopefully.

'Yes, darling, I am. I'm sorry I shouted at you both just now, it's not fair. You're quite right, Holly, if you can't make a noise on Christmas Eve, when can you? I just don't like it when you quarrel. Come on, let's all do the tree together.'

They spent a happy half-hour decorating the tree and they had just finished when Scotty came to collect Holly for her bath. Scotty had been with the family for four years now, taking over Bridget's role and, Laura had to admit, running the household with considerably more efficiency than Bridget had ever done. Scotty was in her late fifties. Her real name was Florrie MacDougall, but long ago the children had named her Scotty, for obvious reasons. She was a spinster, born and brought up in Edinburgh, and had qualified many years before as a Norland nanny. She was a little too proper for Laura's liking, but she had a good sense of humour, particularly after a couple of whiskies, and she worked like a Trojan. 'Come on, wee miss, if we don't get you to bed soon, Father Christmas won't come.' She took Holly firmly by the hand and Holly did not argue – one didn't with Scotty.

'Yes, it's time you went up, love,' Laura said.

'Daddy *will* be coming tomorrow, won't he?' Holly turned anxious eyes towards Laura.

'Yes. His plane gets in mid-morning. He'll be here in time for Christmas lunch – promise.'

'I wish he could have come tonight so that he could see what Father Christmas brought me in my stocking.'

'Never mind, you can show him when it's all opened.' The logic seemed to satisfy Holly and she trotted off in Scotty's wake.

'You know, Ma, it really is time you told her the truth about Father Christmas,' Fram said. 'She's getting far too old for all that stuff.'

Laura smiled at such a commendable show of sophistication. 'You're probably right, Fram,' she said, 'but one more Christmas won't hurt, will it?'

'S'pose not,' Fram said. He was standing by the fire, hands in his pockets. 'It's just a bit of a bore, having to keep up the story.'

He really is an extraordinary child, Laura thought, watching him. His brooding, handsome face was mature beyond its years and sometimes she almost felt as though she was the child and he the parent. He seemed in such a hurry to grow up and his thirst for knowledge was insatiable. He was at prep school now, boarding at the Dragon in Oxford, and there were few doubts that he would be awarded a scholarship to Eton, his father's old school. Exceptionally bright, incredibly good-looking, popular with his peers, kind to his sister – except very occasionally – Laura sometimes felt he was almost too good to be true. And what had happened to the years – they had slipped away. She remembered the plump little baby, brown as a berry, that first year in Cornwall. Could this possibly be the same person – this tall, elegant young man, who looked nearer fifteen than ten. 'I do love you, darling,' Laura said, on impulse.

Fram scowled. 'Oh don't start all that sloppy stuff, Ma.'

She grinned. 'OK, but you're not too big to give your mother a Christmas hug, are you?' He smiled and shook his head and she went to him and put her arms around him. Then she drew away and studied his face. 'I'm very proud of you, you know, and I think, perhaps, I don't say it often enough. Holly's right, I don't spend enough time with either of you – particularly you being away at school so much. A New Year's resolution for 1980 – things are going to be very different round here, promise.'

'It's OK really,' said Fram. 'Holly fusses.'

'Holly is right to fuss. Now, what are you going to do? Are you staying up for dinner with me or is it to be supper in front of the TV with Holly?'

Fram looked at her anxiously. 'There's a Bond film on tonight, Ma, would you mind?'

'Of course I wouldn't mind, it's your holiday. I'll come up

and join you later.' She watched him leave the room and then went to the trolley and poured herself a drink. She was not proud of her sense of relief, but she was glad of a little time on her own. She threw another log on the fire and stretched out on the sofa, immediately comforted by the warmth and the drink in her hand.

It had been a tough few years – not tough by most people's standards, with plenty of money in the bank and no serious problems with either child – but she had needed all her wits about her to cope with the business. Diana who, as a matter of course, always overdid everything, was now a mother of three in four years. She adored motherhood and, clearly, there was no way she was coming back into the business. Giles revelled in his family life, too, and, of course, he had his antiques business. Laura, therefore, had taken up the role of full-time managing director of Gooseberries (UK) Ltd. She also travelled to North America two or three times a year to keep an eye on Gooseberries' expansion there, and then there were the books. It was a lot for one person to cope with, but an added responsibility was the fact that to all intents and purposes, she was also a single parent. Sometimes Laura felt that she was intolerably stretched in all directions.

Laura and Max were still married – at least, technically. He always came home for Christmas and each summer they spent in Vancouver Island. However, even when they were in Vancouver, Max was hardly a full-time parent – in truth, the family made the journey more to see Bridget, than Max. His first couple of years in Washington had been very successful but then the ratings had dropped on the show and it had closed early. Since then he had done shows for whatever network would take him, which had him travelling all over North America in a seemingly insatiable need to achieve constant success and recognition for his own peace of mind. Certainly money was not the spur – quite apart from Laura's wealth, Max, in his own right, had to be very comfortable – his earnings were still high and his interest in Gooseberries' North American franchise ensured he need never work again, if he so wished. Something drove him – it was hard to tell what – but whatever it was, it was far stronger than the pull of his family and far more important to him than his marriage. Laura had long ago accepted the situation. When friends such as Di and Eleanor questioned her monastic state, she simply made the point that she was too tired for a hectic emotional life anyway. No, her life was not easy, but it was reasonably stable – at least she had thought it was, until she had met her agent, Harry Sutherland for lunch that day. It was his revelation, she knew, that had caused her to shout at the children.

Laura had turned down Gerald Seaton's suggestion that they should have a big PR gathering to celebrate the one millionth UK sale of the original Gooseberries book. Instead, Laura had opted for a quiet Christmas Eve lunch with Harry to talk about the future. Increasingly she was aware that she was not fulfilling her children's needs and what she wanted to do was to find a first-class person to take over as managing director of Gooseberries (UK) Ltd and revert again to her first love, writing. The question she needed to ask Harry was what the future held for Gooseberries books.

'Inexhaustible,' Harry assured her. 'The market in the States, particularly, is vast. As you know, your restaurants have a considerable cult following and the books have sold well, but, of course, you've never really written precisely for the American market.'

'No, I haven't, that's true,' said Laura.

'You should take yourself out there for a few months and study the scene. A couple of hard-hitting Gooseberries books aimed directly at the US palate would mean I could retire in the next two or three years.'

Laura had laughed. 'You're never going to retire, Harry.'

'Oh, I don't know. Thanks to you, I can nearly afford it and I would like to spend a bit of time with the Missus before one of us drops off our perch.'

'You have a good marriage, don't you Harry?' Laura said.

'Not bad, though it's taken me three goes to get it right. She moans about my drinking, quite rightly, but as I said to her, I'm not unfaithful to her like I was to the others so what more can she ask? In truth, Laura, she's a wonderful woman, putting up with my wicked ways, and I want to pay her back somehow. God knows why, but what the crazy lady seems to like best is having me around.'

'Then I'd better start writing on a full-time basis, hadn't I?' said Laura, smiling.

'That's about the size of it.' Harry raised his champagne glass. 'Anyway, here's to the millionth copy. No small achievement, my dear – well done.'

Their meal was served and when the waiter had withdrawn, Harry said, in a tentative manner, unusual for him. 'On the subject of marriage, Laura, how's yours?'

Laura normally side-stepped the issue with most people, but not with Harry. 'Pretty non-existent, I suppose,' she admitted. 'When he's here, Max is charming to me and the children but it's more like receiving a visit from a favourite uncle than a husband and father. He has literally nothing to do with our lives on a day-to-day basis.'

'It's very sad,' Harry said. 'And how's his career going?'

'I don't think terribly well,' said Laura. 'You know what he's like – he's so ebullient – he tells you everything's wonderful whether it is or it isn't, but reading between the lines, I don't think he's quite the flavour of the month that he was.' Harry said nothing and Laura looked at him shrewdly for a moment. 'You've heard something, haven't you, and you're wondering whether to tell me about it. I'm right, aren't I?'

Harry took a sip of his wine. 'I wish you weren't so damned astute, my dear. It's nothing, nothing much.'

'Don't be ridiculous, Harry, you wouldn't have even considered raising the subject, if it was nothing much.'

'Well, as you know, I was out in New York a few weeks ago, tying up the American rights of Gooseberries 4.' Laura nodded. 'I had dinner, one evening, with an old chum of mine, Bill Reynolds, he runs a small TV studio just outside LA and you know how these media people all know one another. Anyway, he reckons . . . well, he reckons it's Max's social life which is really affecting his career.'

'His social life?' said Laura.

'Well, he knocks around with a fairly wild crowd.'

'You mean women?'

'Yes – women, booze, that sort of thing. Apparently, all

this high life makes him pretty difficult to work with, and unreliable, too.'

'Is there a specific girl?' Laura asked.

Harry hesitated. 'Should I be telling you this?'

'Definitely.'

'Well there's a young T V presenter, in L A – you know he's doing this show there now?'

'Yes, of course,' said Laura.

'Her name is Angie Duncan and it seems this Angie's a bit of a swinger.'

'I see.' Laura said nothing for a moment as she absorbed what Harry had told her.

'I've upset you,' said Harry, 'I'm sorry. It's a hell of a stupid subject to raise, particularly today when we should be celebrating.'

'No, it's alright, honestly,' said Laura. 'I mean, I knew he couldn't be faithful to me, not bearing in mind how little we see of one another. Women seem to be able to lead celibate lives without too much fuss, but I know it's not a practical proposition for the average man, especially a man like Max. I'm just surprised that your chum believes Max's social life is affecting his work – he's always been such a professional.'

'That's exactly why I mentioned it,' said Harry. 'The last thing I want to do is pass on idle gossip for the sake of it, or stir up trouble between you and Max. It's just that it sounded so out of character, I wondered what was happening to the guy.'

'He's home tomorrow for a few days, I'll talk to him,' Laura said.

Harry hesitated for a moment and then pressed on. 'It's no life for you, Laura,' he said. 'You're a very attractive woman and you also happpen to be a terrifically nice person. You've had your share of hardship, too – more than most of us in many ways. Surely you recognize you deserve something better than an occasional marriage with a man who is not even being faithful to you?'

'Don't start the well-worn lecture, Harry,' said Laura. 'I know you don't like Max, most of my friends don't either, but he is Holly's father and he is my husband, and because of that, I'm happy to go along with things the way they are for the time being. There's been too much disruption and change in our lives. OK, so it's not ideal, but it works after a fashion.'

'It's a bloody shame and a simply appalling waste,' Harry said, heatedly.

Now, lying back on the sofa, Laura thought back over the conversation. It did upset her, she found, knowing that Max had a regular woman in his life. Perhaps it's just hurt pride, she thought, but whatever the truth might be behind her emotions, Laura resolved to try once again to straighten out things between herself and Max over Christmas and New Year.

Max arrived three hours late for Christmas lunch the following day. Laura was furious, yet when he strode through the door with armfuls of parcels, full of good cheer and apparently genuine pleasure at seeing them all, she forgave him. They had a riotous afternoon and evening, playing silly games with the children. Scotty got hideously drunk and needed very little persuading to do a highland fling, before passing out on the sofa for the rest of the day.

On Boxing Day, Katrine arrived from Athens and they partied all over again, going out to friends in the evening. There was an endless round of drinks and dinner parties and suddenly New Year's Eve was upon them. It was not until January the 2nd that Laura finally managed to arrange for the children to be packed off to friends for the day so that she and Max could spend a little time alone. Katrine had returned home and Laura gave Scotty the day off, so they could have the house entirely to themselves. She managed to persuade Max not to go out to the pub to meet friends, lit a fire in the drawing room, sat him in front of it, poured him a drink and then said, 'Let's talk.'

Max smiled. 'Sure thing, baby. What do you want to talk about?'

'Us, you, me.'

'Everything's great with me,' said Max. 'I'm permanent in Los Angeles now. The show's going well there and I like the place. I like the warmth and the sunshine, I just don't know how people cope without it.'

'You mean, how people live in England?'

'That's right. L A is great, Laura. The kids will love it, all that sun and beaches and crazy lifestyle. And as for the people . . .' he shook his head, grinning roguishly.

'When you say *the kids* . . .?' said Laura.

'Well, I thought perhaps next summer you and the kids might like to come out to L A rather than Vancouver Island. 'In fact,' Max said, casually, 'I'm going to sell Vancouver Island in the Spring.'

'You're what?' said Laura.

'Well, it's the best time of year to put it on the market, when the forest is starting to come alive.'

'Max, you *can't* sell it.'

Max's affable expression changed to one of irritation. 'Why not? Who says I can't?'

'I say you can't. It's Buck's whole life and Bridget's too, now.'

'Look, those two have had a pretty easy ride, haven't they? They get a salary for doing piss all and a beautiful home to live in. Fact is, though, I can't go on playing Father Christmas for ever – it's time they stood on their own two feet.'

'But your home is beautiful because of what Buck's put in to it – you know that's true, Max. Besides, the children adore it, it's a home from home for all of us.'

'I'm sorry, Laura, but the decision's made. I simply can't afford to have two homes – it doesn't make any sense.'

'Are you short of money, Max?' Laura asked.

'As a matter of fact I am fairly tight.'

'But you can't be – what about all the money you make from Gooseberries?'

'Laura, you really have very little idea about the cost of living in the U S. I can't begin to tell you how damn rich you have to be to live in any comfort in L A.'

Somewhere at the back of Laura's mind, alarm bells started ringing. She had played a scene like this once before, long ago, on a yacht moored off a Greek island. Then it had ended in tragedy. 'I'll buy it.' She reacted instinctively, desperate to offer help where once before she had refused it.

'I don't want charity from you.' Max stood up, angrily.

'It's not charity, Max, but if you need to sell the house for financial reasons, I would like to buy it – not for your sake, not for mine, nor even for the children's, but for Bridget.'

'You're crazy – you've done more than enough for that kid.'

'That's for me to decide. I don't know how I'd have coped in those early years without her. Let me buy Vancouver and give it to Buck and Bridget.'

'You are crazy,' Max said, but Laura could see he was weakening.

'Look, I'll sit down and write you out a cheque now. You tell me the asking price and I'll pay it – that way you'll save on agent's fees.'

Max stared at her. 'OK – I don't mind admitting, Laura, it would be a help. I'm afraid I can't give you the deeds right now, though, they're with Michael Sacks in Vancouver. However, I swear I won't cash the cheque until they're on their way to you.'

'Max, we're married,' Laura said. 'What are you saying, that I shouldn't trust you?'

'No, no of course not, baby – sorry.' Max smiled warmly. They agreed a price and Laura wrote out a cheque. Max accepted it, humbly. 'Thanks a lot,' he said, avoiding her eyes.

'Max, are you in some kind of trouble?' Laura asked.

'Shit, no, what makes you think so?'

Laura shrugged her shoulders. 'I don't know, I suppose I never thought for a moment you'd ever consider selling Vancouver Island – it seems so very much a part of you.'

'Things change, times change, people change,' Max said. 'One has to move on, Laura – on and up.'

'Does one?'

Max nodded. 'It's no good looking over your shoulder – it's now that's important – do you remember me telling you that when we first met? Jesus, we could all be blown to hell tomorrow or fall under a bus. Today is all that counts.'

'I don't see it like that,' said Laura, 'particularly where children are concerned. You have to think ahead and build for the future – their future.'

'Don't start lecturing me about the children again, baby. Hell, I've been a better father than your first husband.'

Laura stood up abruptly and walked over to the window. 'That's rather below the belt, Max.'

'Is it? I do my best, you know. I come over here as often as I can and try and pick up the threads. Fact is though, the choice we should split was yours.'

'No it wasn't, it was *yours*,' said Laura, 'you refused to live in England.'

'And you refused to live in America,' said Max. 'It is traditional, you know, for families to live where the man can get work. You're a very tough lady, Laura – independent, gutsy, I like that, but you're also strong-willed and selfish. Things have to be done your way or not at all. Well, I'm sorry but I'm not prepared for that, not when it comes to my career. Hell, you bitch away at me about what a lousy father I am – how often do you ask yourself what kind of mother you make? You insist on living 6000 miles away from your children's father, and from what Scotty tells me, the poor kids hardly see you because you're always working.'

'What's Scotty being saying?' Laura turned to face him, angrily.

'Nothing disloyal, before you start having a go at the poor old girl. She thinks the sun shines out of your television set, but she does worry about you and she worries about the children.'

'You should just try being a single parent and running a business as well,' said Laura. 'It's very easy to sit in judgement, it's not so easy putting it into practice.'

'Then why don't you let me help,' said Max. 'Come and live in LA, you'd love it. It would do you good, make you unwind a little.'

'Don't be stupid, I can't disrupt the children's schooling, particularly Fram's.'

'OK, forget it. I would like to see the kids this summer, though. As you're obviously not keen on LA yourself, why don't you send them out to me on their own and then I can see for myself just how difficult your job really is?' He was issuing a challenge, throwing down the gauntlet, Laura thought. He's not really interested in the children, he just wants to score points.

'You couldn't possibly look after them on your own,' she said, 'you're never at home, at least I can never reach you on the phone.'

'I can get Bridget to come and help me,' Max said. 'If you're giving her a house, it's not going to space her out to spend a few weeks looking after Holly and Fram.'

'We'll see,' said Laura.

'Why don't we ask them tonight and see what *they* say, rather than have you make all the decisions for them.'

'Oh, can we go, Mummy, please?' Holly said, that evening. 'And Daddy, can we go to Disneyland, can we?'

'Of course you can, honey,' Max said.

'Will we be allowed to fly on our own?' Fram wanted to know.

'Kids a lot younger than you do it all the time,' said Max. 'Mummy hands you over to a stewardess at Heathrow, she looks after you on the flight and I pick you up at the other end. It's no problem.'

'How do you feel about it, darling?' Laura turned to Fram, hoping for support.

'Well . . .,' Fram hesitated, aware he was being controversial. 'I'd really like to see the film studios and all that sort of thing. It does interest me.' Laura knew her thoughts were illogical, but she felt Fram was being disloyal and it was all she could do to stop herself from saying so.

'He wants to see the film stars,' Holly said. 'Do you know, he's got pictures of girls with no clothes on in his study at school – yuk.'

Max looked amused. 'Have you, Fram?'

Fram was embarrassed. 'Well, just a few, we all do.'

'Good on you, boy. Well we can certainly show you some fairly luscious stuff. There you go, Laura, they're mad to come. What do you say?'

'Well,' said Laura, reluctantly, 'provided Bridget is free then what do you say to spending the month of August with your father?'

'Great,' said Fram.

'Lovely, lovely,' yelled Holly.

The decision was made. In the years that were to follow, Laura would again and again see that moment in tableau form – Fram, Holly, Max, grouped round the sitting-room fire, looking to her eagerly, waiting for her to say the words that would change their lives, each and every one, irrevocably and for ever.

CHAPTER TWENTY-EIGHT

Eleanor Berry came with Laura to the airport to see the children off to Los Angeles, in the last week of July, that year. They both agreed it was Laura who was going to need the moral support – the children were far too excited to be even slightly apprehensive. Laura had just about come to terms with Fram's absences at boarding school, but she and Holly had never been apart before. As she admitted to Eleanor on the telephone the day before they were due to leave, when you had nearly lost a child and watched it fighting for life, it left you with an added vulnerability. 'Do you think she's too young to be going off on her own, Eleanor?' Laura asked anxiously.

'Come off it, Laura, she's not going on her own. She's going with her brother and when she arrives in Los Angeles, she's going to be staying with her father and looked after by Bridget. Statistically, she's probably a lot safer doing that than crossing Baker Street with you every morning, on her way to school.'

None the less, it was an emotional parting for Laura, although she managed not to let her feelings show. She spent too much money on both children in the Heathrow Sky Shop, pressed extra dollars into their hands they did not need and made them swear that they would ring her the moment they arrived at their father's house. They barely listened – instead they regaled Eleanor with full details of all the places Max had promised to take them.

Apart from a flying visit at Easter, they had not seen Max since the Christmas holiday. They had kept in touch by phone, of course, but with even less frequency than before. It was this that made her uneasy, Laura knew – her husband had become a virtual stranger to her – was she right to be handing her children over to him? At the departure desk she had a moment's doubt. She spoke directly to Fram, her eyes dark with anxiety. 'Are you positive you want to go, darling, because we can easily cancel it if you're not sure?'

'Of course I want to, Ma,' he said, with an open easy grin, 'and don't worry about Holly, I'll take good care of her.'

'I know you will, darling.' Laura kissed them both, smiled gratefully at the air stewardess who was taking them aboard and then turned quickly away so that they would not see her tears.

'Come on, old girl,' said Eleanor, 'I think what you need is a large gin.'

Over drinks round the pool of the Sheraton Skyline Hotel, Laura insisted they talked of Eleanor's problems. 'I'm so glad you're coming down to stay for a few days,' Eleanor said. 'I think I'm going nuts, I really do. I know Chris doesn't want us back because otherwise he'd say so – he is such a straightforward person – and yet, sometimes when he looks at me . . . Oh hell, Laura, I have to be imagining things. After all, it's what women on their own are supposed to do, isn't it – fantasize about men.'

'Not usually about their ex-husbands,' Laura said, gently.

Since the day Chris Berry had walked out on his wife, Eleanor had not seriously considered another man. She had tried, but Chris had been her first and only love and though she had met men kinder and better-looking – and there were a surprising number available in and around Oxford as the divorce rate soared – she had never been even slightly tempted to become involved. Chris's affair with Maeve had ended apparently with his leaving home – something Eleanor could not understand. Initially he had lived in a bed-sit, ridiculously only a few streets away from his family. Then, after six months, he had managed to rent a cottage in Stonesfield. From the very beginning of their separation, Chris and Eleanor had agreed that he should have the boys every Sunday. For the first few years, he had collected them at 9.30 and returned them at 5.30. Recently, though, he had started staying for lunch with Eleanor and then taking the boys out in the afternoon – more recently still, he had started suggesting that the four of them went out in the afternoon.

'Of course,' said Eleanor, 'it's far better for the boys to see us together and that's probably what he's thinking, too. Yet somehow, Laura, I can't help feeling he's lonely and God knows, I am. Bearing in mind we share two children, it all seems so stupid, and yet . . .'

Laura looked at her friend and sighed. 'Are you actually divorced?'

Eleanor nodded. 'Yes, I sued him for divorce in the angry days, though looking back on it now, God knows why – I haven't exactly done anything with my freedom. Let's have some more drinks, or we're both going to end up in tears.' Eleanor concentrated on summoning a waiter and while she did so, Laura watched her. The years away from Chris had done her good in some respects. Five years ago she had let herself go, staggering tiredly from home to work in old tweed skirts and shapeless Shetland sweaters. Three years ago, she had been promoted to senior registrar at the John Radcliffe hospital and she had used the increase in salary to good effect. Her hair, which had been showing signs of grey, was now fashionably streaked, and in the soft green cotton skirt and shirt she wore now, she looked confident, well-groomed and yes, sexy. She had a light tan which suited her and made her green eyes sparkle and she smiled more readily these days. By contrast, Laura felt pale and washed out. Yes, she thought, if Eleanor wants her husband back, without doubt, she can get him.

The two women journeyed to Oxford that afternoon to a big welcome from the boys – Laura had not seen them for some months. They all had supper together, then the boys went to bed and Eleanor sat watching Laura pace the room until eventually the expected telephone call came through.

'Mummy, Mummy!' It was Holly's voice.

'Darling. How are you, are you alright? How's Fram?'

'We're fine, super fine. We had a great flight.'

'Did you sleep?'

'Of course not,' Holly said, clearly horrified at the idea. 'We had orange juice and a super lunch and there was a film, and we had blankets to keep us warm and the stewardess was very kind, and, you'll never guess what?'

'What?' said Laura.

'The pilot let Fram watch him driving the plane.'

'Did you go and see too?' Laura asked.

'No, I thought I might be sick. Here's Fram.'

'I'm going to be an airline pilot,' Fram said, firmly.

'No doubts?' Laura said, laughing.

'Absolutely not,' said Fram.

'How are you both, are you alright?'

'A bit tired,' he said, 'but OK. Max has a super house.' Fram had taken to calling Max by his Christian name recently, though as a little boy he had always called him Daddy. It was another pointer towards his growing maturity.

'How is Max?' Laura asked.

'He's fine, very brown, and Bridget's fine, too. It's lovely to see her.'

'You'll write me the odd letter, won't you?' said Laura.

'Yes, of course Ma, don't fuss. Here's Bridget.'

Laura talked to Bridget and Max in turn. They all sounded very competent, very in control and all very happy to be together. Fleetingly, Laura regretted not being there too, but this month on her own was going to be used ultimately for her children's benefit. She was going to spend the time finding someone to take over the running of Gooseberries. It was a decision she had made months ago but only now had taken steps to implement it.

'How are they, alright?' Eleanor asked as Laura put down the phone.

'Yes, fine – everybody seems absolutely fine. They had a good flight, apparently.'

'What did I tell you,' said Eleanor. 'Feel a bit better now?'

'Much.' Laura smiled at Eleanor. 'You are a good friend.'

'Not all that brilliant, I suspect, but I do try,' said Eleanor. 'Like some coffee?'

'Love some.' Laura watched as Eleanor walked through to the kitchen, wondering whether this was the right moment to say what was on her mind. To hell with it, she thought, no moment is ideal. 'Eleanor,' she followed her through into the kitchen, 'how would you feel about my having a word with Chris?'

Eleanor looked up from filling the kettle. 'Had a word with Chris about what?'

'About you, about your relationship – just to see how the land lies.'

'I wouldn't have thought he'd have confided in you, Laura. Oh dear, I don't mean that to sound rude.'

'I know exactly what you mean,' said Laura. 'There was no love lost between Chris and I when you were married, I know that. I also realize I put a considerable strain on you both in those days, always descending on you in a sodden heap when things went wrong. In recent years, though, Chris and I have got on very well. I think we respect each other and work together extremely successfully. We see one another quite a lot, actually.'

'I had no idea,' Eleanor said. There was an edge to her voice.

'Oh, come on, Eleanor!' Laura said, grinning, 'I'm not Chris's type any more than he's mine, you know that better than anyone.'

'Yes, yes, I'm sorry,' said Eleanor, 'but surely, if you get on as well as you say, you must have spoken about me and our marriage already?'

'No,' said Laura. 'When Chris got his promotion and became my editor in Gerald's place, we made a pact that we would never talk about his private life, nor mine either, come to that. I felt – no, in fairness, we both felt – it would be disloyal to you to do so, and we've always stuck to the bargain. The nearest we ever get to talking about things outside work is the children – we do discuss their progress a little, but even that's fairly low-key.'

Eleanor looked at Laura warily. 'What would you hope to achieve by talking to Chris about me?'

'Find out how the land lies, without giving him a hint, I promise, of how you feel.' Laura looked at Eleanor candidly. 'I take it you would like to give things another chance, if he was willing?'

'I don't know,' said Eleanor, 'it would depend upon the spirit in which he wanted to try again, but honestly, Laura, I don't think he does.'

'OK, but you don't *know* whether he does,' said Laura, 'and the problem is, you're too proud to make the first move, as, I suspect, is he. The one thing neither of you could take is rejection by the other.'

'That's probably true,' Eleanor admitted.

'Look,' said Laura, 'I've already told Chris I was coming to stay with you for a few days, and while I'm in Oxford, he is arranging for me to be photographed for a book jacket. He's fixing it for the end of the week. Supposing I give Chris a ring tomorrow at work, and suggest we have a lunch to talk about the photographs before the shoot. Quite genuinely, I do have some ideas on the subject – to be honest, I had planned to talk to him on the phone because it'll take no more than a couple of minutes, but he doesn't know that. We'll have lunch and I'll simply open up the subject of you and see what happens. It's not unnatural to speak of you since I'm staying with you.'

'No, Laura, I – I don't think it's a good idea,' Eleanor said.

'Eleanor, tell me truthfully – do you still love him?'

Eleanor turned away hurriedly, but not before Laura saw tears come into her eyes. 'I'm not sure – well yes, I suppose, yes, I do love him, God help me.'

'Then isn't it worth taking a bit of a risk, to find out how he feels – besides which, it isn't a risk, I'll make damn sure he has no idea I've spoken to you on the subject. Please, Eleanor, let me try – for my sake, if not for yours.'

'Your sake, why your sake?'

'Because you've done so much for me over the years,' said Laura, 'and I've done nothing in return except be semi-responsible for the break-up of your marriage.'

'Don't be ridiculous,' said Eleanor, 'how on earth can you make out a case for that?'

'It's simple,' said Laura, 'the success of my books gave Chris his promotion, which in turn gave him sufficient financial elasticity to leave you and attempt to set up a home with Maeve.'

'That's ridiculous,' said Eleanor, 'you might just as well say that the head of PR in Chris's company is responsible because he hired the caterers who employed Maeve.'

'Now you are being obscure,' said Laura. 'Anyway, we can

agree to differ on that. The fact is I do feel guilty, so go on, Eleanor, let me have a crack at it.'

'Alright,' said Eleanor, 'but you won't give him so much as a hint of how I feel, will you?'

'I promise,' said Laura.

It took Laura two days to make an appointment with Chris. Even then he was short of time and suggested a quick snack at Browns, which was far from ideal, as it tended to be noisy and overcrowded. Walking up St Giles towards the restaurant, Laura began to have serious doubts about the wisdom of what she was doing. Yet she knew she had to go through with it now – Eleanor's expression as she had said goodbye that morning had left her no alternative.

Chris was already at a table, with a bottle of wine and two glasses in front of him. He looked pale and strained and yes, unhappy too. His appearance encouraged Laura. As soon as Chris began discussing the book-jacket design, Laura decided truth was the best policy, or rather her version of the truth. 'Sod the book jacket, Chris,' she said. 'I do have a few ideas but nothing we can't iron out with the photographer when we seen him. It was Eleanor I wanted to talk to you about.'

'Eleanor!' Chris stared at Laura. 'I thought we agreed . . .' he began.

'Yes, we did and rightly so, but that was a long time ago, Chris. Things have changed, we've changed. Do you still love her?'

'Good grief, Laura, you don't believe in mincing your words, do you?'

'Well, do you?' Laura bullied.

'I . . . I don't know,' he said. 'She's the mother of my children.'

'OK, then let me ask you an easier question,' said Laura. 'Is there anyone else in your life?'

'No, not at present.'

'When was the last time there was?'

'Laura, please!'

'Come on, I am your highest-earning author – I'll change publishers unless I have the truth. I mean it, Chris.' Her eyes sparkled dangerously.

'It's none of your damn business but there hasn't been anyone serious in over a year. After Maeve, I made a bit of a fool of myself, messing around with girls half my age. I got laid so many times I didn't know whether I was coming or going, so to speak.' He grinned, a little more like his old self. 'Looking back, I can't sort out one from the other now, and I certainly can't remember their names – I guess I was a little crazy at the time.'

'So what do you want now?' Laura asked, 'from women, I mean.'

Chris hesitated, but only briefly. It was a relief to open up his feelings. He had not confided in anyone in a long time. 'I'm not a man who's any good at being on my own. I suppose I want a permanent woman in my life, someone who I can love and respect, a good companion. I'm tired of all this bachelor business, the one-night stands. God I sound so old, don't I?'

'No,' said Laura, evenly, 'but you do sound an awful lot more mature than you did.'

'OK, Methuselah!' The waitress arrived, they ordered and it was Chris who opened up the subject again. 'Do you think she'd have me back?'

'I'm not sure,' Laura said, anxious to stall the direct answer.

'Have you noticed . . .' Chris refilled his glass, '. . . have you noticed, Laura, how damned attractive she's become recently? She was always good-looking but just lately – wow!'

'Yes,' said Laura, 'and she really has to fight off the admirers these days.'

'Does she?' Chris's head jerked up.

'Yes,' said Laura. 'She's one of those women who, as you say, have always been attractive but who are really at their most stunning in middle age. I envy her. I was quite passable at sixteen but I've been going downhill ever since.'

Chris grinned. 'I have to disagree with that statement.'

'Kind of you,' said Laura, smiling. 'Back to Eleanor, though – for example, take yesterday. She came to Heathrow with me to hold my hand while we saw the children off to Los Angeles and afterwards we went for a drink at the Sheraton Skyline.

Honestly, Chris, she was turning heads left, right and centre, and to be frank, I was as jealous as hell.'

'The dirty bastards,' said Chris.

'Oh come on,' said Laura, 'If you don't want her any more, you can hardly begrudge her finding someone who does – and there is certainly no shortage of applicants.'

'Are you trying to tell me she has someone serious in her life?' Chris was on the very edge of his seat now – Laura had not imagined it would be this easy to wind him up.

'No, I don't think so,' she said, 'but take the advice of an old friend, Chris, if you do want Eleanor back you really will have to get your skates on.'

There was silence for some time while their food was served. Chris had ordered spaghetti but it stood cooling while he stared broodily into space. 'Anyway,' he said, after a while, 'I know she wouldn't have me back.'

'She might,' said Laura, 'if she believed you really loved her – few women can resist that.' Unbidden, the image of David Lawson came into Laura's mind. She had written to him to thank him for his help at the time of Holly's operation. Holly was now seven years old and they had not met since. She forced her mind to concentrate on what Chris was saying. There was enough unhappiness in the world – she had to help this couple overcome theirs . . . somehow.

'He telephoned me at work,' Eleanor said, as she burst through the door of the house that evening.

'Great,' said Laura. 'What did he say?'

'He said that he'd had lunch with you today and gathered you were staying with me. Since that meant I had a ready-made baby-sitter, he thought it would be a good opportunity to have dinner together, to discuss Eddie's schooling.'

Laura grinned. 'What did you say?'

'I said I'd have to ask you, as I didn't know what your plans were.'

'Oh Eleanor!'

'Well, I didn't want to seem too keen, did I?' She looked positively girlish.

Please God let them start telling each other the truth, Laura thought. 'Well ring him back right now, then send the boys off to friends for the night, and I'll check into a hotel so you have the house to yourselves.'

Eleanor blushed like a sixteen-year-old. 'Oh don't be ridiculous, Laura. The evening won't end like that. If you don't mind keeping an eye on the boys . . .'

'Sorry, I can't,' said Laura, firmly. 'I have other plans of my own – I'm afraid you'll just have to find someone to have the boys. I'll be staying at the Randolph. Tell Chris, I'll see him at the photographer's studio at 11.30 tomorrow.'

'Laura . . .,' Eleanor began.

'Just do it, Eleanor. Take the gamble – you have in the palm of your hand the happiness of the three people you care most about in the world. Don't blow it.'

Eleanor took an age getting ready that evening. She and Chris had agreed to meet at the Trout at Godstow at 8.00, but she was so apprehensive that Laura was terrified she would cancel at the last minute. Finally Laura got her as far as the front door. 'Wish me luck,' she said.

Laura kissed her. 'Remember, Eleanor, what an utterly useless emotion pride is,' she said. 'It's cost me my happiness many times. If you want him and he wants you, don't let anything or anyone stand in the way. Forget the past, just think of the future.'

Laura shut the door after checking that Eleanor had driven off in the right direction. There was nothing more she could do. It was so easy to preach to other people about their lives, yet what a mess she had made of her own. Here was she playing Cupid, when her own emotional life was a desert – except, of course, for the children. The children – one by a man who could be alive or dead, the other by a man who was a husband in name only. She cut off her morbid thoughts firmly, and hurried upstairs to pack a case.

The Trout at Godstow was quieter than usual for a summer's evening, but it was still too busy for Chris. He had arrived half an hour early, resisted the temptation to have a drink in order to keep a clear head and was very nervous indeed by the time he saw Eleanor walk through the doorway of the pub.

'Supposing I collect a bottle of wine and some glasses and we wander across the bridge to the abbey as it's such a warm night?' he said. 'We can come back for dinner, of course, but at least we can have a drink away from all these bloody tourists.' His voice was too loud. Several people turned round, and they both winced with embarrassment.

'Suits me,' said Eleanor.

One way and another, Chris took some time getting served. He made a fuss about the wine not being chilled enough, and another bottle had to be found, during which time, Eleanor sat quietly watching him. He was rude to the barman, intolerably impatient, clearly very nervous and when it came to paying, he had forgotten his wallet and Eleanor had to lend him the money. By the end of this little interlude, Eleanor had fallen irrevocably and hopelessly in love with him again.

They walked in silence over the bridge and turned down by the banks of the Thames to the old ruined abbey where, six centuries earlier, a group of monks had conceived a notion for learning that was to become Oxford University. They perched on a piece of ruined masonry in the evening sunlight and Chris poured the wine. He raised his glass to Eleanor, and for the first time, met her eye. She looked particularly lovely, and he felt sick to the stomach with fear. Where to start? How to start? What to say? Was it too late? His mind reeled, tangled, recoiled. He drank the complete glass and then looked at Eleanor again. There was warmth and understanding in her eyes, he was sure of it. A caring, a concern that he had not seen anyone show towards him for a very long time. He felt tears prick the back of his eyes, and to his horror, before he could control them, they started between his lashes and began running down his cheeks. He gulped a sob, tried to brush them away, but it was hopeless. Eleanor said nothing. She simply took the glass from him, wrapped her arms around him, and held him against her chest, rocking him gently, as she would his sons.

When at last he had control of himself, he drew away a little. 'I love you,' he said.

'I love you, too,' said Eleanor.

He stumbled over the words. 'C-can I come home?'

'Yes, of course,' she replied.

'Now?'

'Yes, now.'

'There should be more to say,' he said, 'more explanations. You should ask questions, you have a right.'

'There's nothing more to say,' Eleanor said, 'it's over, all the sadness. Everything begins from this moment. If we look back, we're finished. The only way to go is forwards.'

'Together,' Chris whispered, in the moment before he kissed her.

The studio seemed to be a mass of quite unnecessary people for one single shot, Laura thought, with mild irritation. She hated having her photograph taken at the best of times, and an audience was the final straw. There was the photographer, the photographer's assistant, a makeup artist, three representatives from the publisher, including Chris, an advertising executive and two girls from the publisher's PR department. Chris was also accompanied by Eleanor, who had taken the day off to be with him. Their happiness was radiant, startling in its intensity . . . and catching. Laura basked in reflected glory, feeling that for the first time in months, perhaps years, she had actually achieved something.

The photo session got under way – it went well and was quickly completed. When it was over, Chris, in a moment of wild extravagance, appeared with half a dozen bottles of champagne, the formal excuse being that it was the correct way to launch Laura's new book. In reality Laura knew differently. Before the shoot, Chris and Eleanor had confided to her that they were getting remarried as soon as possible. She raised her glass to them in silent toast, and they smiled at her in a way that made her heart melt.

The party was breaking up, the set dismantled and people were starting to drift off to their respective offices or the pub, when Laura saw the familiar burly figure of Harry coming through the door of the studio. 'Typical!' she called out to him. 'Trust you to arrive when the work's finished, but there's still some champagne left. Would you like . . .?' her voice trailed off.

Harry looked dreadful. He was white to the point where his skin was almost green and his eyes were red-ringed. He stood before her shaking and quite literally ringing his hands, his comfortable bulk hunched and misshapen. 'Laura,' he said, and as he spoke her name, he started to cry.

'Harry, for God's sake, what's happened, what's wrong with you?'

At her words, Chris strode across the studio and took Harry's arm. 'Harry, old chum, what on earth have you been up to?'

Harry roughly shook himself free of Chris. 'Laura, oh God.' His face crumpled again but he seemed oblivious to his tears. He walked up to her and grabbed her shoulders. 'Laura, you have to prepare yourself for some terrible, terrible news.'

Terror flooded Laura's face. Chris and Eleanor saw it and instinctively reached for each other. 'The children,' Laura said.

'Yes,' said Harry.

'Holly . . . her heart?'

'No, Fram.'

'Fram! He's hurt himself. What's happened, an accident, is he ill?'

The tears dried suddenly on Harry's face and his trembling stopped. He held tight to Laura's shoulders and when he spoke his voice was steady. 'Fram's dead, Laura. It's the worst thing in the world for anyone to have to tell you, but it's true, you have to understand what I'm saying – your son is dead.'

CHAPTER TWENTY-NINE

Chris and Eleanor Berry stood watching, as a British Airways stewardess hurried the tiny, shrunken figure of Laura towards passport control. The moment their friend was out of sight, they turned to one another, almost falling into each other's arms and clinging tight, afraid to let go. The noise and excitement of the airport remorselessly echoed around them but they were oblivious to it. At last, they drew apart and Chris, taking Eleanor's hand, led her back to their car. They drove in stunned silence to Oxford and without discussion sat in the car outside their children's school until it was time for them to be collected – they urgently needed the reassurance of seeing their sons. They took them home, told them that their father was back with them for good, and after a celebration supper of burgers and chips, packed them off to bed.

They were moving by instinct, both seeming to know what was required by the other to bring some modicum of comfort – the need to touch and feel well-remembered things, to hold tight to everything that was dear to them both. It was a chilly night for August and Chris lit the fire in the sitting room, while Eleanor made coffee. They sat on the floor together, very close. 'I was thinking,' Eleanor said, at last, 'that when we met Laura, you know, that first time in the taverna, Fram actually existed.' She smiled slightly. 'He was not even a tadpole then, just a fertilized egg travelling towards its resting place in the womb, but the beginnings of a human being, none the less. Funny that, we knew Francis Melhuish all his life, from within a few hours of his conception.'

'How will she cope?' Chris said. 'How does one cope with the death of a child?'

Eleanor studied him in silence for a moment. He seemed to have aged during the day. The boy with whom she had fallen in love so many years ago, had gone for ever. Sitting before her was a sad, tired, middle-aged man. 'I come across the situation a fair amount in my work, of course. When I say a "fair amount", it seems to happen often because the death of a child always leaves an indelible mark.' She hesitated. 'I think the thing one needs to recognize is that normal, loving parents never will get over it, and until they can accept that, they can't come to terms with the burden of their loss.'

'We never talked enough about your work,' Chris said, suddenly. 'You're the one who has always had to deal with life head on and meet the challenge of coping with all the really important issues, while I . . ., well, I've just messed about, flogging a few books. I think that may have been one of the problems, deep down. I felt inadequate. You're much brighter than me, at the time you were earning a lot more money than me and doing a job far more important than mine. I think I wanted to get back at you in some way – not very noble but probably true.'

'I've thought about that, too,' Eleanor said, honestly. 'On the one hand, at the time, I felt you should have made more of an effort to understand what I was doing and make more allowances for the pressure. Sometimes I would come back from work having, say, just watched someone die on the operating table, only to have you grizzle at me because supper wasn't ready. The fact is, you'd had a hard day, too, and you needed your supper, and if you hadn't had the misfortune of being married to a doctor, your wife would have seen to it that supper *was* on the table. Yes, my work is important, but that doesn't make me better than you. And another thing – just because I'm dealing with life and death and pain every day, it shouldn't make me intolerant to the importance of life's little niggles.'

'Are we going to make it?' Chris said.

'You bet your life,' said Eleanor, 'we owe it to Fram.'

'To Fram?'

'He was young, rich, titled, privileged, good-looking and super intelligent . . . but what does all that amount to when compared with a life painfully cut short? He never knew what it was to be a man, to be loved and love as a man, to attain independence, to have a family of his own and enjoy the fruits of a long life. We have those things within our grasp, Chris, and we must not waste them when the fates have decreed that we should live and Fram should die.'

Chris raised his coffee mug. 'To Fram,' he whispered.

'To Fram,' Eleanor echoed.

They clinked mugs, sipped their coffee and began to relax a little. As they did so, the extraordinary and terrible emotions of the last twenty-four hours seemed set to choke them, until, at last, in silent despair, they let the tears run down their cheeks. Once again, Laura's life had touched theirs and they could feel the effects already at work.

Laura boarded the jumbo just before take-off, and was immediately greeted by an airways doctor, who had been waiting to receive her. He showed her to her first-class seat and sat down beside her. 'It's a long flight, Mrs Morgan. We know all about the circumstances – Harry Sutherland sent me. Would you like a shot of something to help you sleep?'

Laura stared at him. 'No, I have to be clear-headed. My daughter, you see, my daughter . . .'

'It's alright, don't try to explain,' the doctor said. 'I could give you something that would help you sleep now, but would have you alert and better able to cope at the other end.'

Laura shook her head. The concept of obliterating the pain seemed like a direct insult to Fram. 'No,' she said, firmly. 'No, I'm quite alright, thank you, I just want to be left alone.'

'If you're sure,' the doctor said, uncertainly.

'Quite sure,' Laura said.

Minutes later the plane took off and soon a stewardess brought Laura a complementary glass of champagne. 'A meal will be along directly,' she said.

'Nothing to eat, thank you,' said Laura.

The stewardess looked at her sympathetically, clearly the cabin staff, too, knew what had happened. 'Is there anything I can get you at all?' she asked, gently.

Laura shook her head. 'I think I'm best left alone, if you wouldn't mind.'

Largely, they did as she asked. As the hours ticked by, they brought her blankets and the occasional coffee, but essentially they left her to herself . . . and her thoughts.

Fram, her first-born. Now it seemed to her that she had always known he was a child doomed, born of tragedy. No wonder he had been in such a hurry to grow up. Had he known, instinctively, that time was short? There were the men she had loved – her father, David, Francis, Charlie, Max . . . and then her mother and Holly – Holly a child of her own image – they were two of a kind. But standing apart from them all was Fram, and suddenly, with perfect and terrifying clarity, Laura knew why – because she had loved Fram more than she had loved any other single human being . . . yet she had never told him so, and now it was too late.

At Los Angeles airport, Harry Sutherland had worked hard to ensure that everything ran smoothly for Laura. She was escorted off the plane ahead of the other passengers, and hurried through passport control and immigration with the minimum of fuss. There was no baggage to collect, and when she reached the airport terminal, a British Airways stewardess took her to a side exit, to avoid the press, she explained, and handed her over to a small, dapper man with gold teeth and an impressive suntan. 'The name's Bill, Ma'am, I'm a pal of Harry's. He asked me to collect you and take you to your husband's home. I have a limousine outside.' He hesitated. 'I'm real sorry, I know all about why you're here.'

'Thank you,' Laura managed. She followed the little man outside to a waiting car. It was driven by a black chauffeur in an expensive-looking maroon uniform, who put an arm around her protectively and eased her through the crowd, which seemed to be waiting for her. Light bulbs flashed, making her jump and the heat hit her like a wall. She was dressed in the same woollen dress she had worn for the photo session, so long ago now. It clung to her damp body agonizingly, but it didn't seem to matter – nothing mattered. 'What time of day is it?' she asked Bill, as the car gathered speed, heading for the perimeter of the airport.

'Seven o'clock in the morning, Ma'am. Unfortunately it means we've caught prime time – it'll be a slow journey.'

'How long will it take?' Laura asked.

'An hour.'

'An hour!' For some reason she had imagined Max's house would only be ten minutes from the airport. The thought of waiting another hour before being reunited with Holly was too much. She felt tears well up behind her eyes and her throat constrict, yet she forced control upon herself. If she started to cry now, she knew she would never stop and for Holly, she had to be strong. After the initial appalling shock and disbelief, it had been her first and principal instinct – to get to her daughter fast.

They had travelled for some distance in silence when Bill spoke. 'I think I'd better let you know, Ma'am, that we've worked out a plan – your little housekeeper and I – for getting into the house without having to face the press. Those bastards are knee deep outside your husband's house.'

'Press?' said Laura. 'There were pressmen at the airport, too, weren't there?'

'Yeh, I'm afraid the news will be all over the world by now.'

With a sinking heart, Laura thought immediately of her mother – would anyone have thought to ring Katrine, so that she did not read of her grandson's death in the paper? 'But why the publicity?' she said to Bill. 'Why should one little boy's . . .,' she stumbled over the unfamiliar word, '. . . death cause all this interest?'

'Because of the circumstances, and because of who you are. Max Morgan's an international figure and then your son . . . I understand he was an English lord.'

'He did not live long enough to inherit the title,' Laura managed to say.

'No matter, he was going to, and that's what makes a good story. Sorry, but that's how those guys work. And then, Ma'am, if you don't mind my saying so, you're pretty well-known, too. You write books, I understand, and then there's Gooseberries, everyone knows Gooseberries.'

'You . . . mentioned circumstances?' Laura said.

Bill shifted uneasily in the seat beside Laura and leaning forward, closed the glass panel that separated them from the driver. 'Harry told me I must warn you about this and I've been sitting here trying to find the words. Your husband, Mrs Morgan, has been arrested.'

'Arrested!' said Laura. 'For what?'

'Apparently, your husband was giving a party to welcome the children, and there were a lot of drugs being passed around. When the police arrived following your boy's accident, they rounded up a whole bunch of people, including your husband. Most have been released, but your husband has been detained.'

Laura forced herself to ask the question. 'I – I don't really know anything about my son's accident, other than that I understand he broke his neck, diving into a swimming pool – at least, that's what they told me in England, and then I caught the first flight over here. I just don't understand how he could have done such a thing, he's . . . he was such a good swimmer, and although he was only eleven, he could dive very well.'

Bill took a deep breath. 'He'd been drinking, Mrs Morgan. It's the reason your husband is still in police custody. There were some pretty wild people at the party and they encouraged your children to try some very potent wine cup. Then your husband suggested the boy show off his diving prowess. He missed his footing, taking off from the top board, and hit the stone edge of the pool.'

Laura shut her eyes tight, to try and avoid the image of Fram hurtling towards the side of the pool. 'Could you stop a moment. I – I think I'm going to be sick,' she said. The driver stopped just in time for Laura to jump out of the car. She went on retching long after there was nothing left in her stomach, her whole body seemed torn apart. When at last she had finished, Bill helped her back into the car and gave her his handkerchief. Tears were streaming down her face but she was not crying as such – it was as though one-by-one her life juices were draining from her. 'I'm sorry, I'm so sorry,' she said.

'Don't be silly, Ma'am, you're doing real well. I don't know how a person copes with a thing like this.' They drove on. 'Only about ten minutes now,' he said.

'Let me get this straight.' Laura mopped her face with the handkerchief, the perspiration and the tears mixing together so that in seconds Bill's handkerchief was drenched. He produced another – it was one of the few things he had thought of providing in the long bleak hours during which he had waited for Laura's flight. 'Let me get this straight,' she repeated, 'you're saying that my husband let my son get drunk and then dive into the pool, and that the reason he did such a terrible thing was because he and some of his friends were on drugs?'

'I guess so,' said Bill hesitantly. Having the facts spelt out like that enhanced the horror of the situation, yet the lady was right, she needed to understand what had gone on. Christ, she had guts. 'I think it was coke they were on, not heroin or anything stronger,' he said, desperate to provide her with some crumb of comfort.

'And who told you all this. It could be some story the press or police have dreamed up?' The round blue eyes were steely.

'No, I don't think so,' said Bill. 'Your housekeeper, Bridget, told me.'

Laura shut her eyes to try and stop the world spinning, but it spun all the more. She opened them hurriedly. 'So then, it's true,' she whispered.

'Yes. It was Harry who reckoned that I should try and find out exactly what had happened so I could tell you about it in advance of your arriving at the house. He suggested Bridget was the only person to trust, since there's some pretty wild stories flying around. Is that right – she seems a nice kid, and boy, is she in a state over this.'

'Yes – thank you, Bill,' said Laura, looking at the little man properly for the first time, 'this can't have been easy for you and I'm very, very grateful. In fact, I'll never forget it – what you and Harry have done to help.'

'That's OK, Ma'am, I just wish it hadn't been necessary. Here we go now, we're turning into Rainbow Boulevard – your husband's house is just up here on the left. Oh hell, you must know that, sorry.'

'No, I don't know it,' said Laura, 'I've never been here before.'

Bill glanced at her strangely, and then opened the glass panel. 'Right, Tommy, turn left here before the house, that's it. Now you see where the fence is down – yeh, yeh, that's it, drive through there and then straight across the lawn. Keep your foot down, Tommy, just like I told you.'

'This is the back of your husband's neighbours' house,' Harry explained. 'We have their permission to drive across their lawn to avoid you having to face the press again – I guess it's what good neighbours are for.'

They bumped along a track and then, as Bill had indicated, took off across a piece of lawn towards a stone wall. The lawn was perfect, and it pained Laura to feel the tyres biting into its flawless surface. Then she forgot everything for there was a door in the wall, and as they neared it, it flew open and Bridget came running out.

The sight of the familiar little figure was the trigger to Laura's self-control. The car had barely stopped before she was out and running the short distance into Bridget's arms, tears streaming down her face, her body wracked with sobs. The two women clung together for a moment, blindly seeking comfort in each other's arms and then there was a single strangled cry – 'Mummy!' – and Holly, too, hurtled through the door. They scooped her up into their arms and the three of them clung together, swept along on a tide of grief that had them shaking, convulsing and far too frightened to let go of one another.

Bill stood watching them, tears pouring down his own face now. He searched for a handkerchief, then realizing that there were none left, he wiped his tears away on the back of his sleeve, turning to apologize to the driver for his weakness.

The driver was out of the car and leaning against the door, tears, too, sliding down his shiny mahogany face. The two men stared at one another in silence for a moment. 'Life is a shit sometimes, ain't it, mister?' the chauffeur said.

Bill nodded. 'Come on, let's get out of here. We've done all we can, though, Christ, it's piss all in the circumstances.'

Laura carried Holly into the house, preceded by Bridget, who took them straight upstairs to the bedroom she had prepared for Laura's arrival. 'Harry said you'd come without any clothes,' said Bridget, 'So I went out to a store and bought you jeans, a couple of T-shirts and some sandals. They're there, I'd expect you'd like to change. Shall I take Holly downstairs while you have a shower?'

'No,' mother and daughter said in unison.

Bridget looked carefully at Laura. 'Shall I leave you two alone for a bit?'

'Yes, please,' said Laura. When Bridget had gone, Laura sat down on the bed and gently eased Holly out of her arms. She saw that Bridget had also left her a towelling robe. 'Let me just put on that robe, Holly. I'm really hot and sticky and I was sick on the way here, so I probably don't smell very nice.'

'You do smell nice, you smell of Mummy,' Holly said, watching Laura anxiously with her big, round blue eyes, red-ringed now. Laura peeled off the sodden dress and slipped on the robe. Holly's eyes never left her mother – she was too frightened to let her out of her sight. 'The police have taken Daddy to prison,' Holly said.

'I don't expect he's in prison, he's probably just down at the police station,' Laura said, in an effort to bring some form of comfort.

'Buck says he deserves to be in prison, I heard him saying so to Bridget this morning.'

'What do *you* think?' said Laura. She came and sat down on the bed again and pulled Holly on to her lap. She knew, instinctively, that the one thing she must get Holly to do was to talk – it was the only way to help her.

'I don't know,' said Holly. 'Angie says not, Angie said he's being made a . . .,' she hesitated, '. . . a scapegoat, is that right?'

'That's the right word,' said Laura. 'Who's Angie?'

'Oh she's a friend of Daddy's. She works with Daddy in his office, but they're real friendly.'

'*Really* friendly,' said Laura, 'you're starting to sound American.'

'That's what Fram says . . .,' Holly began and then stopped. At the mention of her brother's name, she began to cry.

Laura felt her own control ebbing away and had to force herself to concentrate. 'Are you going to tell me about the party?' she asked gently.

Holly nodded and she wiped her tears away with her fist. 'It started out as really good fun,' she said. 'There were lots of famous people, film stars and stuff. Daddy had the place decked out so it looked really smart – streamers and balloons – and everyone who came wore these amazing clothes and there was a band and a bar and all the food you could ever want in the world. Fram said . . .' Holly hesitated, 'Fram said it was all silly but *I* thought it was really great. Fram said he thought the people were all horrid, but I didn't at first because they were nice to me.'

'Go on,' said Laura.

'The barman made this stuff, he called it a punch and it was pink with lots of fruit. Daddy said we should have a glass and that it would cheer up Fram. We did have a glass and it tasted nice, so Daddy said we could have some more. I had three glasses.'

'How many did Fram have?'

'Oh, hundreds,' said Holly.

'Hundreds?'

'Well, an awful lot. He started getting really silly, falling about and giggling, but it stopped him being in a mood – Daddy was right about that.'

'Where was Bridget while all this was going on?' Laura asked.

'Oh she wasn't there. Daddy didn't invite her to the party.'

'How do you mean?' said Laura.

'Well,' Holly looked confused. 'Fram said . . . Fram said that Daddy was a snob because he hadn't asked Bridget and Buck to the party as they were servants. They had to help to get it all ready, though, and Fram said it was really mean. I think that's why he was so cross, before he started drinking the punch.'

Laura forced herself to continue. 'And then what happened?'

Holly, too, hesitated. 'Well, Fram has been doing a lot of fancy diving since he's been here, he's really good at it,

Mummy.' Holly's face started to crumble but she continued with an effort. 'Daddy said why didn't Fram show his friends what he could do. So Fram climbed up on to the diving board. I *told* him not to go because he'd drunk so much punch. Oh, Mummy, he kept falling down the steps, trying to get up to the board and everybody thought it was funny. I was so frightened, but Fram went right to the top board.'

'Holly,' said Laura, 'don't go on if you don't want to.'

'I want to tell you, Mummy. He got up on to the board at last and he nearly fell off straight away. Then he stood up and started waving to everyone and everybody waved back and laughed. He put his hands above his head, I think he was going to do a swallow dive, but then he kind of tumbled off sideways.' She was crying so hard now that her words were indistinct. 'Mummy, he hit his head on the side of the pool and then fell into the water. A friend of Daddy's, some man, jumped in straight away and got him out, but his head was all . . . funny, all on one side and he was very white, kind of. Everybody started to say he was dead and they laid him on a lilo by the pool and then a doctor came.'

'What did you do?' Laura asked.

'I sat and held his hand, I didn't know what else to do.' Laura conjured up the appalling image of seven-year-old Holly sitting by the pool holding the lifeless hand of her brother. It was Holly who filled the silence which followed. 'The doctor came,' she said. 'He was very kind, he was also very cross with everybody except me. He said that there was nothing he could do for Fram and then he picked me up. I was crying a lot and I wanted you, and the doctor shouted at Daddy and everyone that he was calling the police and they should not be in charge of children. Then he took me to my room and talked to me . . . and, told me Fram was really dead. I – I told him about Bridget and you, and then Bridget came, and then they put a needle in my arm and I went to sleep.'

'When did you wake up?' Laura said.

'This morning, very early, and Bridget said that you would be here soon and you were. Mummy, Mummy, poor Fram.' The sobs finally took over and mother and daughter, both exhausted, lay down on the bed together, holding each other tight. 'I feel better now you're here,' Holly said, after a while. 'What's going to happen? What will happen to Fram?'

'We'll go home,' said Laura, 'you and me . . . and Fram, just as soon as I can arrange it.' Holly nodded. 'Have you had any breakfast?' She shook her head. 'OK, I'm going to tuck you up in bed, turn on the TV and fetch you some breakfast. Alright?' Holly nodded, and satisfied it was safe to leave her for a little while, Laura fastened her robe and went downstairs.

Bridget was sitting on the bottom of the stairs, her head in her hands. She jumped up at the sound of Laura's footsteps. 'How is she?' she said.

'Alright. She told me all about it, at least, her version. You'd better tell me yours, Bridget.'

The story Bridget told was, in essence, much the same as Holly's, except there was more background detail. Her grief was so raw, so exposed that it terrified Laura. Bridget and Buck had arrived a week before the children and Max had given them a tiny room in the servants' quarters, next door to the kitchen. He had made it very clear that their duties would be considerable but that they certainly would not be living as part of the family, as they had done on Vancouver Island. 'He's changed,' Bridget said. 'I – I never liked him, I think you know that, but he's very different. I'm afraid I made him angry right away, because I realized that . . . oh, I don't know if I should tell you this, Laura, but what does it matter, nothing matters now . . . he – he's having an affair with this girl, Angie Duncan.'

'Yes, I know,' said Laura.

'Do you?' Bridget looked surprised. 'Well, he kept having her to stay the night and I said he couldn't do that once the children came. He said it was none of my business. I wrote to you about it, I don't know if you got the letter?'

Laura shook her head. 'No, I haven't.'

'Anyway, it worried me, I didn't think it was right.'

'It wasn't,' said Laura. 'Go on.'

'Well, the children arrived and it was lovely to see them. They were very excited, of course, to start with, but all Max wanted to do was dress them up and take them to grown-up parties, like they were dolls. Neither of them liked Angie, especially Fram who I think guessed what was going on. They soon got fed up with it. They spent most of the time with Buck and me, which Max didn't like but couldn't stop. Anyway, he said he was going to have this party, in honour of the children, but he asked no other kids along – just his showbiz cronies. By then, the other thing I'd discovered was that Max was seriously into coke. He snorts the stuff morning, noon and night. God knows how he's managing today without any. Anyway, the party was all arranged and then Max made it clear that he didn't want Buck and me there – not just at the party – not in the house at all. Buck was really cross. He said we should go home to Vancouver Island but I said we couldn't because of the children. He said we should take the children, too, they'd have a better time – if only I'd agreed . . . Anyway, Buck said we'd better have a day on the beach. I wasn't happy about it, Laura, but I went, shit, I went. How could I have done, how could I have left them?'

'Bridget,' Laura took her hand, 'you mustn't blame yourself, it's not you who's to blame, it's Max and me.'

'But I could see the way things were going, I knew Max was a little crazy. I just thought it was safe to leave them because they were staying in their own home. I wouldn't have let him drive them anywhere – he drinks too much for that and then there's the coke. But in their own home, I didn't see how they could come to any harm. And Fram . . . Fram was so sensible.' Bridget hesitated. 'All the while we were on the beach, I was restless and in the end Buck said we'd better go back because I was such a pain. When we drove up to the house, I saw that all the cars had gone. It was only four o'clock, I knew that couldn't be right and then I saw the police cars . . . and then, oh Laura, I knew.'

'How long after the accident did you arrive?' Laura said.

'About an hour. The doctor was marvellous – we had to sober Holly up before we could give her a shot to knock her out. I hope you think that was the right thing to do but I felt that she needed you around before she tried to cope with the reality of what had happened.'

'You did the right thing, you've done the right thing all through, Bridget, I'm so grateful to you.'

'Grateful to me!' Bridget spat out the words. 'If I'd taken more care, your son would be alive.'

Laura seized Bridget by the shoulders and shook her, roughly. 'There's enough sadness and loss over this, Bridget, without adding unnecessarily to it. Fram's death is not your fault – it is my fault and Max's. Max directly, because he allowed Fram to drink too much and dive into the pool, mine because I've let a failed marriage drift on for years, without taking the time and trouble to see what it was doing to Max.'

Bridget turned away. 'I loved him so much, he was . . . he was like my own child, Laura.' She began to sob again.

'I know, I know,' said Laura. 'It's awful now, but in a few months you will feel better. What you and Buck ought to do is to have some children of your own.'

'We can't,' Bridget wailed.

'Why not?'

'There's something wrong with my ovaries, the doctor says. Your children are my children, Laura.'

Unable to cope with Bridget's grief, Laura left her at the bottom of the stairs and went in search of the kitchen. Buck was there. He held Laura in his arms for several moments but spoke not a word. Then, still in silence, he got together some breakfast for Holly and helped Laura take it upstairs. Holly looked a lot more cheerful and was sitting up in bed, watching cartoons. Laura gave her breakfast and watched over her as she ate it.

'I'm going to have a shower,' said Laura. Holly nodded, barely taking her eyes off the television. Laura showered and put on the jeans and T-shirt Bridget had bought for her. Then she came back and sat on the edge of Holly's bed. 'I've just got to leave the house for a little while to sort out a few things. Bridget will stay with you.'

Holly's preoccupation with the television dissolved. 'Do you have to go out, Mummy?'

'Yes, I do, darling.'

'Can I come with you?' Her insecurity was very evident.

'No, I want you to stay here. I promise you, I won't leave the house again, not after today, and I won't be away for more than a couple of hours now.'

'What are you going to do?' Holly asked.

'Sort out the arrangements for our going home.'

This seemed to satisfy the child. 'Can we go home very, very soon,' she said, 'tomorrow?'

'I don't know about tomorrow,' said Laura, 'but very soon, yes. I'll send Bridget up in a moment. She's very miserable, Holly, so will you try and cheer her up?'

Holly nodded, sagely, obviously taking her responsibility very seriously. 'You won't be long will you, Mummy?' she begged.

Bridget was still sitting on the stairs when Laura left Holly's room. 'Where is he?' Laura asked, quietly.

Bridget did not have to ask who she meant. 'They wanted to take him to the city morgue,' she said, 'but I wouldn't have it and the doctor agreed. He's at the doctor's surgery. Shall I get you a cab? They can collect you round the back again to avoid the press.'

'Yes, please,' said Laura, 'and then would you go and sit with Holly until I get back. She's nervous about my going out. I said I was fixing up travel arrangements.'

'Yes, I won't leave her for a moment.'

'And Bridget, be brave for Holly – keep her cheerful.'

'Yes, I – I'll try.'

Ten minutes later, Laura was in a cab, on the way to see her son.

CHAPTER THIRTY

Timothy Dalton gripped the doorknob and then paused – this was not something he was going to enjoy. Surreptitiously, he peered through the small glass panel, in the top of the door. The woman sitting waiting for him was not at all as he had imagined – she was much younger than he had expected and apparently more composed. He noted the thick dark curls, so different from her son's. The boy, poor lad, had clearly favoured his father. Taking a deep breath, Timothy walked through the door. 'Mrs Morgan?'

'Yes.' The woman stood up. Her voice trembled a little and she was deathly pale. From the age of her son, he guessed she must be over thirty but she certainly did not look it, in fact despite her distressed state, it was still possible to see she was startlingly good-looking.

'I'm Dr Dalton,' he said. They shook hands. 'I don't know whether you've been told yet but I attended your son at the time of the accident.'

'You're English!' Laura said. For some reason it suddenly seemed terribly important that the man who was custodian of her son's body was a fellow countryman.

'Yes, there are a few of us about, even in this sin city.' He smiled, hoping to lighten the mood.

'I'm so glad,' she said, simply. 'Would you take me to see Fram now, please.'

He nodded. She was right, this was no moment for passing the time of day, the sooner the ordeal was over, the better. He led her through to a little ante-room off the surgery. The body lay on a stretcher, covered by a sheet. 'Would you like me to stay or would you rather be alone?' he asked.

Fleetingly, Laura looked at him, as a drowning man must look at a lifebelt just out of reach. Then she lifted her chin. 'Alone.'

'Shall I uncover him for you?'

'Yes, please.'

He drew back the sheet and left the room as quickly and as quietly as possible.

It took Laura several moments to walk to the stretcher. She did not know what to expect and did not dare think about it. When at last she managed to inch her way close enough to see the body, two reactions were instantaneous. She was shocked to see that he was apparently unblemished – clearly the doctor had straightened his neck and there was no sign of the impact of his fall. It could have been Fram sleeping, except that her second shock was the realization that he was no longer there. The body she was looking at was not Fram, it was simply the husk, the container which had once held her son. The knowledge brought her both relief and a terrible sadness. It was at once comforting to know that he was not trapped inside his body in this dingy little room, but wherever he was, he was out of her reach – she had lost him for ever. Tentatively, she reached out a hand and touched his cheek – it was as soft as it had ever been, but it was also cold and stiff. Bolder now, she felt beneath the sheet, and found his hand. Drawing a chair to the side of the stretcher, she sat down and held his cold hand in hers, pressing it to her hot, tear-stained face as if trying to warm it back to life. She sat for some long time, not sobbing, but weeping quietly, staring into his face, to try and remember every detail of it, for she knew she would never see him again.

Eventually, Timothy returned. 'I think it's time you came away now, Mrs Morgan.' He lifted her gently from the chair, took her hand from Fram's and led her through to his consulting room. Only when he had her safely in a chair, did he return and cover the boy's face. In his room again, he poured two cups of coffee and handed one to her.

She took it. 'Thank you,' she murmured, and began sipping it distractedly. He waited for her to speak, sensing it was the right thing to do.

'How much would he have felt – would there have been pain and was he conscious at all before he died?'

The question was so inevitable that Timothy was ready with the answer before she had finished speaking. 'It would be very understandable if you expected me to answer your question with a platitude, whatever the truth. Often, when relatives ask what you have asked, I do stretch the truth to try and relieve their grief. However, in the case of your son, I can promise you he died immediately and painlessly on impact with the wall of the swimming pool. In addition, judging by the amount of alcohol in his blood stream, I think he would have been too drunk to even sense any danger. We all have to die, Mrs Morgan. Your son's death is a terrible tragedy because of his age, but his method of leaving this life has to be envied.'

'Can I believe you?' Laura implored.

'Yes, I swear you can, Mrs Morgan.' Timothy put every ounce of sincerity he could into his words because he knew them to be true. Dealing in half-truths was sometimes easier, he realized. Fram Melhuish had not suffered, he was sure of it, but convincing the boy's mother was another matter. He tried to change the direction of her thinking on to the practicalities.

'Mrs Morgan, do you have anybody in this country who can help you – a relative, a close friend? I gather your husband's in custody at the moment.'

'No,' said Laura, 'not really. My husband has a brother, Tom, but I'm not sure how he will react to all this.'

'Then would you like me to make all the arrangements for you, with regard to your son?' Laura stared at him – she seemed to be barely aware of what he was saying. 'Arrangements do have to be made, Mrs Morgan.'

He could see she was making a strenuous effort to pull herself together. 'Yes, of course they do and it's very kind of you to be so helpful.'

'Do you want your son buried here in America or in England?'

'Oh, in England,' said Laura. 'He – he must be buried on the family estate.'

'Do you want to return to England soon?'

'At the very earliest opportunity,' said Laura.

'Well, I've signed the death certificate. Shall I arrange for you to fly your son's body home in the next few days? You presumably will want to travel with him?'

'Yes,' said Laura, 'and my daughter, Holly, too.'

'Leave it all to me then. I'll organize the paperwork and fix the earliest flight I can. Is there someone in England with whom I can tie up arrangements for meeting you at Heathrow?'

Laura gave him Harry Sutherland's address and telephone number. 'This really is most terribly kind of you,' Laura said, 'everybody is being . . . so kind and helpful.' She stood up, hesitantly. 'I suppose I – I had better go.'

'I think, perhaps, it would be a good idea if I examined you just to make sure you are alright, just routine – blood pressure and one or two things like that. It would be sensible after such a terrible shock.'

Laura shook her head vehemently. 'No, no, I'm alright.'

He let it pass, he could see to argue with her was pointless. 'What about Holly, then – how is Holly today? She coped wonderfully well at the time.'

'She seems to be doing alright,' said Laura, 'but I don't know what sort of reaction she'll have in the long term.'

'Yes, you need to watch her,' said Timothy. 'One thing you should look out for is a possible sense of guilt.'

'Guilt!' Laura stared at him. 'We're the guilty ones – Max and I – there's no one else to blame, least of all, poor little Holly.'

'I know that and you know that, but she may not. I think she feels she should have stopped her brother diving – it's what she said to me several times.'

Laura stared at him. 'She said something like that to me as well, when she told me what happened.'

'I'm just issuing a warning shot,' said Timothy. 'Don't take it too seriously, not at this stage anyway, when you've so much else to think about. However, what you must avoid is that sort of emotion going inwards. I don't think she needs any psychiatric counselling or anything like that, she's too well balanced, but you need to tell her, about twenty times a day, just how wonderful she was and how well she coped. Children are incredibly resilient. So far as her physical well-being is concerned, now you're here, I think it better if I don't see her again because I was so much a part of the accident. However, if you're at all worried about her, just call me and I'll be right over.' He hesitated. 'In fact, it's not Holly I think we have to worry about – it's you who concerns me, Mrs Morgan.'

'What do I matter?' said Laura.

'That's exactly the kind of reaction you must avoid,' Timothy replied. 'Remember, you still have a child, a child who's going to need you.'

'May I go and see him just once more?' Laura said suddenly.

'I don't think it's wise.'

'I didn't say goodbye,' said Laura, 'I won't be a moment, I promise.'

Laura drew back the sheet herself this time. The image of Fram's face blurred before her. She leant forward and kissed him. 'Goodbye, darling,' she murmured and as she carefully covered his face once more, an extraordinary thing happened –the tears dried and the anguish of a moment before was replaced with an icy rage. She turned abruptly to Timothy Dalton, who stood just a few paces behind her. 'Could you call me a cab.'

'Yes, of course. To take you home?'

'No, do you know where my husband is being held? That's where I want to go now.'

'I'll check to see if it's OK for you to visit him,' said the sergeant behind the desk. He sauntered off, chewing gum, his gun holster nonchalantly slung round his hips. Laura hated his casual attitude but then she was hating everything and everyone at that moment. He returned, a few minutes later. 'Come with me, lady, you've got a quarter of an hour.'

'This will only take five minutes,' Laura said.

She was shown into a tiny room, with a barred window high up on the wall. There was a let-down bed, a table and a chair, and on the bed sat Max. He looked terrible – more terrible than Laura would have believed possible. He was unshaven, haggard and clearly having some sort of drugs withdrawal, for he was shaking like a leaf. The sight of his suffering gave her positive pleasure.

'Laura, oh Laura, I'm so sorry,' He stood up, hesitantly and took a step towards her.

'Sit down,' Laura screamed at him. He jumped like a startled rabbit and sank back on to the bed. 'This is the last time you and I are ever going to meet, Max. The moment I get back to England, I'm going to file for divorce. I do not expect it to be contested and I do not expect you to seek any form of custody or access to Holly. You will never see her again either, unless once she is eighteen, she chooses to seek you out. At that age, it will be her decision. You have destroyed one of my children – I will not let you destroy the other. If you try to oppose me, I will break you, Max, if it takes every penny I own.'

'I'm broken already,' he said.

'Good, and I hope it hurts. You murdered Fram just as surely as if you'd stuck a knife in his heart, and as far as I'm concerned, no pain or suffering you feel now can begin to compensate for what you've done.'

'I realize you must feel bitter . . .,' Max began.

'Bitter! You've killed my son – I'm not bitter, I hate you, Max. I could scratch your eyes out with my bare hands, and you only have Holly's existence stopping me doing that right now. You deserve to suffer for the rest of your life and I sincerely hope you do.' She turned, walked to the door and began banging upon it. As she waited for it to be opened, she kept her back towards Max, not daring to move for fear of the consequences of her own rage.

'Laura.' The voice from the bed was pleading. 'Baby, I know I should have behaved more responsibly, but it was just an accident, a terrible, tragic accident. I didn't know he'd been drinking – Bridget was supposed to be looking after the children.'

Lying to her was the final insult. She drummed her fists on the door. 'Get me out of here, get me out of here!' she screamed.

The sergeant came running and flung open the door. 'Did he touch you, did he hurt you, lady, did he so much as lay a finger on you?' The sergeant advanced menacingly towards Max.

'No,' said Laura, suddenly the anger giving way to a terrible weariness. 'It's not me you need to protect – it's him. He's the one in danger.'

Tom Morgan was waiting for Laura when she returned to the house. By this time, the press had discovered the back entrance, and were clamouring all round her as she staggered out of the car. 'Have you seen your husband, Laura, are you going to divorce him? What are your views on drugs? Who will be Lord Campling now?' At the last question, Laura struck out blindly at her persecutors, and only Tom's intervention stopped her trying to claw them to pieces. Only half an hour before, she would have felt just as aggressive towards Max's brother as she did towards Max. However, Tom was nothing like his brother, she was exhausted, and the sight of a familiar face was comforting. 'I'm here to help,' he said, simply, 'put me to work – anything.'

'Have you been to see Max?' she asked.

'No.'

'Are you going to bail him out, or something?'

Tom shook his head. 'He can rot there as far as I'm concerned.'

The sentiment was just what Laura needed to hear to confirm that Tom was still a friend. First, she checked on Holly, who was busy playing card games with an exhausted-looking Bridget. Then, with Tom's help, Laura made the necessary phone calls, firstly to her mother and then to Anthony Campling, Scotty and, lastly, Harry. The calls were easier than she had expected because everybody already knew of Fram's death. Harry had been very thorough and had managed to tell family and friends before the world's press had done the job. Anthony Campling was flying home from Australia that afternoon and told Laura he would make all the arrangements for the funeral at Campling Hall. Harry had been helping Scotty beat off reporters and had already received a call from Timothy Dalton. 'I'll meet you at the airport,' he promised. 'I'll have my car waiting for you and Holly, and a hearse for Fram. The hearse will take Fram straight to Campling Hall and Scotty will be waiting for you at home.'

By six o'clock that evening, everything had been arranged. They would be flying at 2.30, the following afternoon, and for Laura and Holly, it could not be too soon.

'What do you want to do about the business?' Tom asked, when all the arrangements were finalized. He was worried about Laura, she seemed too calm. He had poured her a whisky in the hopes it would relax her but he noticed she had not touched it.

'Business?'

'Gooseberries – the American franchise – you presumably won't want anything to do with Max and me from now on.'

Laura looked at him. 'You, Tom, of course, but Max, no.' Her voice hardened. 'You work it out – you and Max can either buy me out or you and I will buy Max out. I don't care. Do whatever you think best for yourself and the business.'

A little later, Laura went upstairs and sent Bridget off to bed. 'Would you like me to come to England with you?' she said.

'No, it's only going to prolong the agony for you. Make Buck take you home to Vancouver Island as soon as possible and pick up the threads of your life again. Holly and I will be out to see you one day – that's a promise.'

Holly was growing sleepy, although she had been in bed all day. Laura shook out a couple of the sleeping pills Timothy Dalton had given her, gave half to Holly and one and a half to herself. She hated pills, but the following day was going to be a long one. She went through the motions of preparing for bed, then climbed in beside her daughter and took her in her arms. They both cried themselves to sleep that night.

The following day, Tom took them to the airport. Fram's body had gone separately and it had been arranged that Laura and Holly should wait in the VIP lounge until it had been loaded on to the plane, for fear of upsetting Holly.

'Max has been bailed,' Tom said, as they drove.

'When?' Laura asked, sharply.

'A couple of hours ago, by Angie, I guess. The police are having trouble making a charge stick for what happened to Fram, but I guess the publicity will finish him, anyway. God knows what he'll do.'

'You're not asking me to feel sorry for him, are you?' Laura said.

'Shit, Laura, what do you take me for?' said Tom.

At the airport, Tom stayed with them until they boarded. Once on board the plane, Holly became almost normal, chatting to the stewardesses and gazing out of the window. It was only when they were actually taking off, she asked the question Laura had been dreading. 'Will we see Daddy again?'

Laura fended off the question. 'Do you want to?'

'No,' said Holly.

'Why not?' Laura asked.

'Because it was his fault Fram died.' Laura was shocked by the vehemence of her tone.

'Did someone tell you that, Holly?'

'No,' said Holly, 'I figured it out for myself.'

Laura took her hand and squeezed it. '*Worked* it out for myself,' she corrected, trying to direct Holly's thoughts away from the accident, but Holly had not finished. 'Daddy made Fram get drunk and he made him climb up on to the diving board. I don't want to see him again, not ever – I hate him.'

Her words should have been music to Laura's ears, but such strength of feeling did not seem right in a seven-year-old. 'Forever is a long time, Holly. When you're older you'll probably understand that Daddy didn't mean to do what he did.'

'I still won't want to see him again,' Holly said. 'We were having a horrid time anyway, Fram and I, even before . . . before the party.'

'I know, darling, and you needn't see him again, not until you're grown up anyway and not even then, if you don't want to.'

They sat in silence, holding hands, watching Los Angeles fall away below them. Laura, Fram, Holly – the three of them had been through so much together, shared so many adventures . . . yet never, never in her worst nightmares had Laura imagined that their final journey together would be like this.

CHAPTER THIRTY-ONE

The day of Fram's funeral was beautiful, in a way that only an English summer's day can be. The corn was almost ripe on the estate, the air was languid, heavy and full of fragrance – the scent in the rosewalk which led to the family vault almost overpowering. The glorious weather made the day even more difficult to bear. This was Fram's home, the place he would have tended, nurtured and loved through manhood into old age. These were his fruits – fruits which now he would never enjoy, nor indeed would any Campling, for there was no one to follow him.

In deference to Laura and Holly, who had insisted on being at her brother's funeral, only family and very close friends attended. Anthony and Lavinia were there, of course, and Katrine, all the estate workers and of Laura's friends, just Eleanor and Chris, Giles and Diana, and David Lawson.

After the service, Eleanor, Chris and their boys did their best to entertain a distraught Holly while Anthony and Laura walked in the garden. 'What happens now,' Laura said, 'about the estate I mean?' She knew she had to keep talking. To be left to her thoughts, even for a moment, would have her hopelessly out of control.

'I've been looking at the position,' said Anthony, 'it's the one possibility that never occurred to my father. He never thought for a moment that a strong, healthy boy like Fram would fail to outlive me. Fram died intestate which means that his estate automatically goes to his next of kin – in other words his parents, which, of course, means you.'

'I don't want it,' Laura said, 'you have it, Anthony, it's yours by right, I have no right to it, nor Holly either.'

'No,' said Anthony, 'my life's in Australia now, it's what I chose and I'm too old to start again in England. Alright, I appreciate that Campling Hall has belonged to people of my blood for hundreds of years, and, yes, I do have a sense of responsibility towards it. However, sad though it is, Campling Hall is not for Lavinia and I.'

'So what do we do?' said Laura.

'What about the National Trust? I'm sure they'd be delighted to take it on. That way, the place will be preserved and open to the public to enjoy. Its history is incredible and being so close to London, it should bring in the crowds. I also thought . . . I know, it's early days and too soon for you to talk about it, but I thought perhaps some sort of memorial to Fram, linked to a children's charity, might be a good idea. I wish I had known him better, but he struck me as a very caring person. In his name, with the backing of this wonderful old building, we might be able to do a lot of good.'

Laura stopped and turned to Anthony. It hurt her to look at him. He did not have the flamboyant good-looks of Fram, his father or even his grandfather. He was a faded version of them, but the Campling looks were there all the same and impossible to ignore. 'You're a very good man, Anthony,' she said.

'If we're handing out compliments, I think you're a wonderful woman and a damned brave one, too.' He smiled. 'Do you remember the first time we met, that day you turned up here unexpectedly?'

Laura felt a twist in her stomach. 'I was thinking of having an abortion,' she said, in an anguished voice. 'To think he might never have lived . . .'

'I know,' Anthony said, quietly, 'my father told me. God knows, this is not how it should have ended, but you gave him life, Laura, and some very happy years, and the people who knew him are the better for it.'

It had been intended that after the funeral Laura and Holly should stay with the Berrys for a few days, but both of them had a very strong instinct to go home. They knew it would mean fighting their way in and out of the house, past reams of reporters, but being prisoners in their own home, seemed preferable to being in someone else's. The matter was discussed as they all sat around drinking dreary cups of tea, and the sudden change of plan left Laura, Holly and Scotty without transport.

'I'll run the three of you back to London,' David said.

Laura looked at him and smiled and the conversation around them drifted into the background. 'You always seem to run me back to London after funerals,' she said, sudden tears in her eyes.

'You can be certain it won't be like last time,' David said, painfully.

'I know,' Laura said.

It was after seven by the time they arrived back at Harley Street and the press had thinned considerably. David climbed out of the car and announced to those remaining that if anyone so much as spoke to Laura or took a photograph, he would knock their teeth down their throat. No one doubted that he meant it.

Scotty took Holly straight up to bed, David cooked everyone scrambled eggs which Laura could not eat, and then they all went up and said goodnight to Holly.

Holly, Laura could not help noticing, instantly warmed to David. 'Are you a very old friend of Mummy's?'

'Very old indeed,' said David.

'Is that why you've got some white hairs?'

Laura looked at David's hair and noticed the touch of grey for the first time. 'Good grief, David, the passage of time.'

'Yes,' he smiled up at her from his seat on the edge of Holly's bed. 'Do you know something, Holly? Mummy was only a few years older than you the first time I met her.'

'Was she pretty?'

'Very, just like you.'

'Why have you got a funny leg?'

'I had a car accident when I was a baby.'

'Will you ever be able to walk properly?'

David shook his head. 'No.'

'Poor you,' said Holly. She let him kiss her goodnight and clung to Laura only a moment longer than normal. 'It's nice to be home,' she said. Her voice was wistful but there was no sign of tears.

As it happened, David did spend the night with Laura that night, but certainly not as they had spent the night after her father's funeral. Instead, they sat by the fire and talked about every subject under the sun – their childhood, their relationships, their parents, their work, their marriages – in fact they talked of everything except Fram.

'Are you lonely?' Laura asked David.

He shook his head. 'Surprisingly, no. Serena was away so much anyway that I was used to living on my own before our marriage packed up.' He grinned. 'Don't get me wrong, I haven't turned into a monk – there's been the odd girl here and there, to calm my fevered brow.'

Laura smiled at him. 'I bet there has – all my girlfriends have always been a little in love with you.'

'Flattery will get you everywhere,' David said, 'so just for that, I'll make some more coffee.'

The grey light of dawn was starting to filter through the curtains before, finally, they got to the subject they had both been avoiding but which had been central in their thoughts. 'Where do I start without him?' Laura said. 'I don't really want to go on living, you see, David, that's the truth.'

There were no tears now, she was deadly calm and it frightened him more than any show of hysterics would have done. 'Holly,' he said, quietly.

'Holly is the one person who can stop me going out of my mind, I know that, but is it fair to use a seven-year-old as a prop?'

'Do you have any other choice?'

'No, not really,' said Laura. 'You can rage at fate, you can blame yourself, you can blame other people, but when all is said and done, this terrible thing has happened and cannot be reversed – yet somehow I can't accept it. I know we buried my son today – yesterday I suppose now – but I expect him to walk through that door at any moment, David, and I feel that if I try to face the knowledge that he never will, I'll completely fall apart.'

'One day at a time,' David said, 'that's all you can do. Every morning you have to get up and think to yourself, I will get through today somehow. I will try and make my daughter happy and relaxed and as near back to normal as possible. At the end of the day, I will go to bed and that will represent one more day of learning to cope.'

'But I don't want to learn to cope,' Laura said, desperately. 'Do you know what appals me more than anything else, David?' David shook his head. 'The thought that I might get over his death one day, that I might learn to smile, that I might be happy again, that's what I can't take.'

'So what are you going to do,' said David, 'wallow in grief for the rest of your life, making yourself and everybody around you unhappy? Is that going to be your memorial to Fram, two more ruined lives – yours and Holly's? What do you think Fram would have wanted you to do?'

'I don't know, I don't know,' said Laura. 'He was only a child.'

'A child he may have been, but he loved you very much. No one wants to inflict suffering on someone they love. He was your only son, your first-born, and his life was tragically cut short. There is no escape from the appalling pain those facts inflict on you, but to deny yourself the opportunity of one day being able to smile again, is not showing any kind of loyalty or dedication to Fram, it's simply wallowing in self-pity.'

Laura put her head in her hands. 'That's a cruel thing to say.'

David got up and limped over to the sofa to where she sat. He sat down beside her, took her gently in his arms and pressed her head into his shoulder. 'Only real friends can tell the truth,' he whispered into her hair. 'You'll always have the truth from me, Laura, and you always have. Let me help you through this – I can. I'm not flattering myself that I'm the only person who can, but I'm certainly one of the few, because I know you so well.'

'It's not the help I need,' said Laura, 'this is something which has to come from within – I have to work it out for myself.'

'But with a little help from your friends. You must feel very alone at the moment. We haven't discussed it, but I assume your relationship with Max is over?'

Laura drew away, her face flushed, her eyes bright. 'I'll never see or speak to him again. I'm filing for divorce tomorrow.'

'Then you've lost your son and your husband.' David kept an arm round her shoulders. 'Don't take the independence kick too far, Laura, it's always been your failing. I'm around – my business runs smoothly, with or without me, though it's not something I normally care to admit. I have no commitments, no wife and, regretfully, no children. If you want help, advice, a shoulder to cry on, a gin and tonic at the local, a holiday, a weekend in the country . . . look to me. I promised you when Holly was so ill, no strings, and I really, truly mean it. I've learnt my lesson with you, Laura. I love you dearly, but if I am to maintain this friendship which means so much to me, I recognize that we are looking at just that – friendship – and I will never try to change the status again.'

A feeling of warmth flowed through Laura at his words and she relaxed against him. All her life, she realized, she had been seeking somebody upon whom she could rely, who would demand nothing but would be there when she needed them . . . and all these years David had been waiting in the wings. 'I love you, too, David,' she said, 'and what you have said means more to me than I could begin to express. Thank you, and thank you from Holly, too.' She buried her head in his chest and at last began to weep, pouring out her grief to the only person who could give her the comfort she needed.

The days in London immediately after the funeral were difficult for Holly and Laura. Holly was not due back at school for another two weeks, and whilst there were arrangements to be made and papers to be signed, the main activity surrounding Fram's death was over and time began to hang heavy on both of them. Holly did not want to see her friends and neither did Laura want to see hers. They felt it wrong to go out and try to enjoy themselves, yet the house seemed empty and terribly quiet without Fram. With Fram's room, Laura could do nothing. Scotty suggested that she should clear it out but Laura turned on her viciously – Fram's room was to stay exactly as he had left it, and was much visited by Holly and Laura, but always separately. They both found comfort in the room but they never discussed it.

When at last Holly's school term began again, it was a relief to them both, for the responsibility of trying to keep the other happy was removed one stage. Laura had spoken to the headmistress of Holly's school and she was confident that her daughter would receive every care and understanding. Indeed, within two or three days of Holly's return, she seemed very much her old self and began having tea with her school-friends again.

Friends bombarded Laura with invitations but she turned them all down. Giles and Diana were coping manfully with Gooseberries, Diana having hired a temporary nanny. Laura recognized, however, that it was not fair to expect them to go on with this for long and so she telephoned Diana one day and suggested that they went ahead with trying to seek a manager. Within two weeks, a young man called Matthew Fornby had been installed. Giles and Diana conducted the interviews, but Laura did see Matthew before he was appointed and warmed to him immediately. It was a great relief to have Gooseberries taken off her hands, but at the same time, it left her with few responsibilities besides meeting Holly from school each afternoon. Harry suggested that she start work on another book, but her mind was all at sea and prolonged concentration quite impossible. 'I'll just have to drift awhile,' she told Harry.

'Don't leave it too long.'

Tom Morgan wrote from Vancouver and told Laura that, after due consideration, he could not work with Max in the circumstances. Arrangements were therefore made for Tom and Laura to buy Max's share in the business, which Max handed over without any fuss or discussion. Meanwhile, Anthony Campling, back in Australia, had set the wheels in motion for the National Trust to look at Campling Hall. They were wildly enthusiastic about it and wanted urgent discussions with Laura but she could not face it. 'Not yet,' she said, 'in a few month's time perhaps.'

Eleanor came to stay for a few days. Both boys were now at boarding school and Chris was away at a book fair. 'You're doing the right thing,' she told Laura, 'it's what everyone advises but few people actually do. When you've suffered a terrible tragedy like this, or indeed any appalling shock, if you start making violent decisions, they are always the wrong ones. Look on what's happened to you as a deep wound to your emotions. That wound has to be given time to heal before you start putting any strain upon it. You're ticking over, coping with Holly and that's all you should attempt for some while.'

'But for how long?' Laura asked.

'For as long as it takes.'

The days dragged by. Eleanor went home and Laura was left alone. It was a dull, miserable autumn, the weather cold and damp. Harry, in a fit of inspiration, presented Holly with a little Cairn puppy, as an early birthday present. Although the dog was allegedly Holly's, secretly Harry hoped that its needs would interest Laura. Instead, fond though she was of the puppy, it was Scotty who fed and walked it and told Holly of its latest antics when she returned from school each day. Laura just did not have the energy.

The other problem was that Laura had stopped eating. Scotty spent hours every day preparing little delicacies in the hopes of tempting her, but food seemed to revolt her and she was losing pounds week by week. 'She's committing suicide, silly wee thing,' Scotty said to Harry one night. Laura was already in bed and they were sitting over a whisky in the kitchen, talking in hoarse whispers, in case Laura should appear.

'Then something has to be done before Laura becomes seriously ill – it would be the final straw for Holly,' said Harry.

'Like what? It's time you had some ideas,' Scotty said. She liked Harry. He took a healthy interest in the whisky bottle, he could tell a good story and he flirted with her outrageously, which she pretended to hate but clearly adored. There had never been a man in Scotty's life since a young sub-lieutenant, who she had loved passionately and who had died in 1941, in a sea of blazing oil, in mid-Atlantic.

'A holiday,' Harry suggested, 'at Christmas. Somewhere in the sun. Perhaps she and Holly could go to the West Indies or Australia to see Lord Campling. A change of scene might do her good.'

'I don't think she has the energy,' said Scotty.

'We could arrange it for her.'

'You know what she's like, she hates being organized. She's bound to be furious and she wouldn't go – she's very stubborn, that one.'

'Then you and I could go instead, Scotty,' said Harry roguishly. 'I can just see you in your bikini, sitting under a palm tree.'

'Och, what a thought,' said Scotty, 'I look like a scrawny old plucked chicken without my clothes on.' The image seemed all too accurate for Harry to contradict.

Laura recognized her downward spiral for what it was. She wanted to do something about it, for Holly's sake, but was powerless to do so. She no longer felt she deserved to live, and it was not purely because of Fram – her guilt centred round Francis and Max as well. Francis Melhuish had been a deb's delight, a wildly good-looking, much-sought-after bachelor until he had married Laura. Over the two years of their marriage, he had changed into a fraudulent, drunken failure, and that transformation had cost him his life. Max had been a successful international entertainer, with a string of girlfriends and an ego flying high, with a love of life and an ebullience second to none. Now his life was destroyed, his reputation would never recover from the scandal of Fram's death, and he was, in all probability, a drug addict. Two lives in ruins, and then there was Charlie. Poor Charlie – even in Laura's lowest moments, she recognized that his death was in all probability an accident, but without his relationship with Laura, would he, too, be alive? The more Laura looked at her various relationships and her two marriages, the more she became convinced that she brought disaster on everyone who cared about her. Why, she was not sure but she suspected it was because she was too forceful a character. In the case of Max and Charlie, her business success had stood between them, and in the case of both marriages, the fact that she was a Beecham had been an aggravation rather than an advantage. She was a walking disaster area – she had destroyed two husbands, a lover, and above all, her son. Now she was terrified of destroying Holly as well. Maybe the child would be better away from her influence, for the more Laura looked at herself, the more she seemed to be the herald of disaster. Clearly, if her frame of mind had persisted indefinitely, it would ultimately have destroyed her. But one night, something happened, something which once again changed everything and destroyed, for ever, the central core from which the ripples of Laura's self-destruction flowed.

Holly was in bed, asleep. Scotty was out for the evening, at the cinema, with another nanny. Laura had supper on a tray in front of the television and was watching the ten o'clock news, mindlessly – sunk in her own misery. The door bell rang. Normally at such a time of night, she would have been careful about opening it without knowing who was there, but in recent weeks, her ability to concentrate on the most mundane of matters was negligible. She opened the door without a thought, therefore, switched on the porch light and looked up with uninterested eyes at the man standing before her. For a moment nothing registered. Then her eyes widened in horror and disbelief. Was she finally mad . . .

. . . For this was the recurring nightmare that had haunted her for years. The man standing before her was, without doubt, Francis Melhuish – her dead son's father, returned from the dead himself.

CHAPTER THIRTY-TWO

'Laura, I know this must be a terrible shock . . .'

His voice – she had forgotten the sound of his voice, yet immediately, it was distinctive and so terribly familiar. 'Yes . . .' she managed.

'I took an awful risk coming here but I felt I had to, when I heard about our . . . son's death, I thought you might need me.' At the mention of Fram, Laura crumpled. Francis caught her before she fell as the world spun around and tears blinded her. He lifted her frail form easily and carried her into the hall, slamming the front door behind them. On hearing the sound of the television, he followed it into the sitting room. Once there, he laid her down on the sofa and turned it off. He knelt beside her. 'I didn't know what to do – whether I should telephone you first or not. I couldn't risk writing in case someone other than you opened the letter.' Laura's eyes flickered open and she struggled into a half-sitting position. She simply stared at him, her mind rolling away the years to those last few bitter moments on the yacht when she had lost him, she believed, for ever. 'I read about Francis in the press,' he was saying, 'all about the accident. I have to admit that until then, it had never occurred to me that we could have a child. To find out now, only with the news of his death . . .' he shook his head, '. . . I just acted instinctively. I thought I must come and find you, to help you.'

'Help me!' Laura said, suddenly rallying. 'Where were you when he was born? Where were you when he was growing up? If I couldn't have your help during his life, why should I need it at his . . . at his death?'

'I didn't know we had a son,' Francis said. 'If I'd known, of course, I would have come before.'

Laura stared into his face. It was a mirror image of Fram's – this was how Fram would have looked in middle age, had he lived. The thought ground into Laura's heart, she twisted her head this way and that, as if fending off blows.

'Laura, Laura, please, I'm so sorry to cause you such distress.' Francis slipped his arms around her and pulled her clumsily towards him. She did not fight him, she just pressed her damp face against the rough tweed of his jacket, and thought – *this is Fram's father, this is my last link – while he holds me, I'm holding Fram.* Her body shook with shuddering sobs. Francis leant forward and still keeping his arms around her, lifted her up on to his knee.

It was a long time before Laura stopped crying. When at last she was spent, she excused herself and went upstairs. In the privacy of her bedroom, she blew her nose, brushed her hair, and tried, largely unsuccessfully, to repair the ravages of her crying. Then she checked Holly's room, to make sure that her daughter was still asleep – she was.

Francis had poured himself a hefty whisky and was standing by the fire when she came downstairs. He looked completely at home and as relaxed as though the circumstances were normal. His composure angered Laura, but when he looked up and smiled at her, with Fram's smile, the anger vanished. 'What would you like to drink?' he asked.

'There's some wine in the fridge in the kitchen, I'll get it.'

'Stay where you are – where's the kitchen?'

'Second on the left,' said Laura.

He returned with the wine, poured her a glass and handed it to her. 'I am very sorry to have shocked you like this, Laura.'

'I was so sure after all this time that you were dead. Why did you do it, Francis? What happened?' Her voice was anguished.

'Shall we sit down?' he said. They sat together on the sofa and Laura kept on staring at him like a bemused child. 'After that . . . that night, the night of the row, when you went to bed . . .' Francis began, 'I sat up for sometime thinking about the future. As I expect you know, I was very severely in debt.'

'Fraudulently in debt,' Laura said, bitterly.

'Well, that's one side of the story.' As ever, Laura thought, he could not admit his own failings. 'Anyway, I thought it all through and decided the only sensible course of action was to disappear and take my debts with me, to an apparently watery grave.'

'Didn't you think about me, or our marriage?'

'Of course I did,' said Francis, 'that's one of the reasons I decided to go. My being dragged through the courts and possibly imprisoned would have been dreadful for you. You were, and I'm sure still are, an extremely competent woman. I knew you could cope without me, but, of course, I didn't know about the child.'

'So?' said Laura.

'So, I faked my own death – suicide by drowning was what I hoped you would all think. I climbed over the side and swam ashore, being careful to leave my passport and most of our money behind so that everyone would think it wasn't planned. I did have a little money. When I reached the shore, I struggled up the beach and collapsed just out of sight of the sea, behind a rock and slept until morning. I didn't have your athletic prowess, Laura – the swim bloody nearly killed me for real, I can tell you.'

'Then what did you do?' said Laura.

'There was a track leading up from the beach.'

'That family, you stopped at that family!' Laura said, incredulously.

'Good heavens, did you find them, too?' She nodded. 'Yes, well I stopped at them and gave them some money and they gave me some dry clothes and something to eat. I told them to tell no one, but with my dreadful Greek, I wasn't sure that they'd understood.'

'They understood,' said Laura, heavily.

'It was about seven o'clock by the time I got up to the main road. I hitched a lift from a tourist heading back to Rhodes. It was lucky really – he and the family had been on holiday in Lindos for a fortnight and were catching a plane out that morning, so it meant they would not see any local press. They dropped me off at Rhodes. I went straight to the harbour and had just enough money to pay for my passage on a little cargo boat bound for Crete. I'm not particularly proud of this, Laura, but I would imagine that by the time you woke up, I was already some miles away from Rhodes.'

'Why didn't you tell me what you were doing?' Laura said.

'Because it would have put an impossible burden on you. It's why I told nobody – Anthony, my father.' He smiled, that charming Campling smile. 'You're all nice, honest people and you would have found it impossibly difficult to lie to the police – not that the Greek police, at any rate, fared too well out of it, I'm afraid.'

'How do you mean?' said Laura.

'That little police chief, who was put in charge of trying to find me, got bumped off, you know, by his own kind, I think.'

'You're joking!' said Laura.

Francis shook his head. 'You have to remember the political situation at the time. The Colonels were in power in Greece then. Several English people had gone missing in odd circumstances and then the son of an English lord was the final straw. Of course, I had no idea of the implications at the time, but you know how obsessed the Greeks are with politics and these missing tourists considerably undermined the Colonels' regime. Greece's whole economy depends on tourism and certainly I was the most important person to go missing during that period, and the most significant. That poor little policeman was some sort of scapegoat.'

'How awful,' said Laura, conjuring up the long-forgotten face of Andre Koyokopis.

Francis continued after a pause. 'In Crete I found a room in Ayios Nikolaos. It's a charming little port on the north-west coast of the island. It's a big tourist resort now, but then it was just struggling out of obscurity. I began working in a taverna and of course, being English, I managed to attract a lot of tourists. The patron made me a partner and I stayed there about a year. Then I opened my own place and I have three tavernas in the town now and a couple of wine bars – business is booming.'

Laura looked at him sceptically. Exhausted and confused as she was, Francis's well-remembered plausibility was still in evidence. She scrutinized him in silence for a moment. His hair needed cutting. His clothes were clean and he wore them, as usual, with elegance, but they were well worn. 'So you're well pleased with your decision?' she said.

'I miss England, of course, but life is easy in Crete. The climate's wonderful, the people kind.' He averted his gaze. 'I . . . married again, too.'

This was something Laura had not considered. 'Really?' she said, feeling suddenly absurdly hurt.

'Yes, the taverna-owner's daughter.'

'That sounds convenient,' said Laura.

Francis smiled at her. 'Don't be bitchy, darling, it doesn't suit you.'

'Have you any children?' She had to ask the question, though it was agony to do so.

'No,' said Francis. 'I think that's really why hearing I had a son affected me so much. I felt I just had to come back, whatever the risk.'

'You presumably didn't come into the country on your own passport?' Laura said.

'No,' said Francis.

'So what is your name these days?' Her tone was cynical.

'Joseph Clarke.'

'Joseph Clarke.' Laura smiled slightly. 'It doesn't suit you.'

'Maybe not, but it's what I'm used to now. I've been Joseph Clarke for thirteen years.'

Laura stood up a little unsteadily and walked over to the bookshelf. She lifted down a photograph of Fram and took it to his father. 'This was your son,' she said, quietly.

Francis took the photograph frame and stared at it in silence for several moments. Laura, watching him, saw two tears escape from the corner of his eyes and trickle down his cheeks. She could not ever remember seeing Francis cry before. 'Oh Laura,' he said, 'I'm so sorry. Please tell me about him, please tell me all about him.'

Hand-in-hand, Laura and Francis went upstairs to Fram's room. They tiptoed past Holly's and once inside, Laura turned on the light and shut the door. She showed Francis everything –his school photographs, his new squash racquet, never used, his pens and pencils, the desk at which he worked, the books he enjoyed, the old teddy bear he pretended he no longer liked . . . Francis was thirsty for knowledge and for Laura, sitting on Fram's bed, talking about Fram, it was wonderful therapy. She told Francis every detail she could remember, every anecdote.

'Why Fram?' Francis asked, after a while.

Laura shrugged her shoulders. 'He called himself Fram.'

'It's nice.'

'It's different,' she said. 'We never knew him as anything else – extraordinary to think you didn't know that.'

'What did you tell him about me?'

'I told him about the yacht and said I believed you must be dead. It's what I believed myself. I'd assumed you'd fallen overboard, by accident rather than design.'

'You mean you didn't think I might have committed suicide?'

Laura nodded. 'No, despite all your problems, I didn't see you as the type to take his own life.'

'Did Fram miss not having a father?'

'There was Max . . .' Laura managed, in a choked little voice.

'You'd better tell me about him, Francis said. 'Was he really responsible for Fram's death as the papers said?'

Laura talked on, telling Francis of the accident, of her marriage to Max, of Holly and her operation. 'When I hear all this, I feel dreadful,' Francis said, after a while. 'If I had not disappeared, none of this would have happened. Alright, I'd have had a fight on my hands in court, possibly even a few years in prison, but I'd have seen my son grow up, and if you hadn't married Max then Fram wouldn't . . .'

'Stop it,' said Laura. 'Don't you realize thoughts like that run through my mind every minute of every day. Max and I just happened to be in the same television studio fleetingly. We overlapped by no more than half an hour, but because of that, Fram is dead.'

'Laura, you can't and mustn't blame yourself. Blame Max if you like, blame me – God knows, we both let you down, you and Fram, but never blame yourself.'

'How can I help it?' said Laura.

Francis sat down beside her on Fram's bed and took her hands in his – she was crying hard again. 'You're exhausted and shocked and it's all too much for you,' said Francis. 'I'm going to put you to bed.' She didn't argue as he helped her to her feet and led her gently from the room. 'Which is your room?' he whispered. She pointed down the passage. Once inside, he sat her in a chair while he pulled the curtains and drew back the counterpane. Then he helped her out of the chair and lay her down on top of the bed. Tears were still streaming down her face. She put her hands over her eyes, turning her face away from him. 'I'm going to undress you now,' he whispered.

She did not argue with him. He undressed her as if she were a child and then helped her under the duvet. Minutes later, he joined her, and switching out the lights, he took her in his arms and drew her close.

It was extraordinary how familiar his body felt, how easily they could lie together – almost as though they had never been apart. Laura had shared a bed with no one but Holly in a long time, and the sudden comfort of being wrapped in someone's arms was balm to her agony of mind. Within seconds, she drifted off to sleep.

At sometime during that night, Francis made love to her. She woke with a start to him kissing her, his body already taut and trembling beside her. She did not stop him. Her mind simply drifted away. She was in Cornwall again watching Fram the toddler running along the beach . . . To be free of her body was wonderful – she moved around the country to the places she loved, her mind apparently flying at will. Dimly she was aware of somewhere beneath her, two writhing bodies, but they were nothing to do with her. Only when at last Francis, in shuddering climax, called out her name, did her mind seem to jolt back into her body. She was shocked at what had clearly happened between them, but too tired to do anything but lie there as Francis continued to caress her and whisper endearments. Mercifully, sleep took her again.

'I'm supposed to be early at school today because there's a play rehearsal,' Holly nagged, over her bowl of cereal, 'and you're not even dressed yet, Mummy.'

'I will be in a second,' said Laura. 'You finish your cereal and drink your orange juice and I'll just go up and dress. When you've had breakfast, put your satchel in the car and wait for me there.'

'No, I'll come up and get you,' Holly said, 'just to make sure you're really hurrying.'

'I said go straight to the car – now do as you're told.'

'Don't be in such a bad mood,' Holly said.

'I'm not in a bad mood,' Laura said. 'Can't you just do something without an argument for once.' She slammed her way out of the kitchen and instantly regretted it, but could think of no way of withdrawing her angry words. She bounded up the stairs into her bedroom and locked the door behind her.

Francis was still lying in bed. 'Can I get up now? I'd love to see Holly.'

'No you can't,' said Laura, 'and keep your voice down.'

'Why not?'

'Because she's not ready to cope with this sort of complication – she loved her brother very much.' She hurried into the bathroom and threw on some jeans and a sweater.

'What are you doing?' Francis asked.

'I'm getting dresssed so that I can take Holly to school. It's one of the responsibilities of parenthood, you know, taking one's children to school.' Her voice was waspish and she was barely out of the bathroom when the door handle turned.

When she could not open the door, Holly began knocking furiously. 'Why have you locked the door, Mummy? What are you doing?'

'Holly,' Laura screamed, 'I told you to wait for me in the car.' There was the sound of sobbing as Holly ran along the corridor and down the stairs. 'Oh God,' said Laura. She turned her venom on Francis. 'You get up and get dressed but discreetly. Scotty's around – she's our housekeeper – and she must not see you on any account. I'll be back in about a quarter of a hour.'

Holly cried all the way to school. Outside the gate Laura stopped the car. 'Holly, I'm sorry, I didn't mean to shout at you this morning. It's just I didn't have a very good night.'

Holly did not answer, her little face was set and pale. She simply picked up her school bag, climbed out of the car and slammed the door behind her. The expressions on the faces of both mother and daughter were so alike as to be comical at that moment, but all Laura could feel was pain and guilt. She drove home furiously, slammed her way through the front door and found Francis in the kitchen helping himself to toast. The sounds of Scotty hoovering could be heard above them. 'Has she seen you?' Laura said.

Francis shook his head. 'No, not yet.'

'What do you mean, *not yet*? You fool, she'll recognize you. Look, you'd better come with me, we'll have breakfast in a hotel. Go and get in the car, I'll just tell Scotty I'm going out.'

'I don't know what all the fuss is about,' Francis said, as they drove down the road a few minutes later.

'You've seen pictures of your son,' Laura said, exasperated. 'Anyone who knew him well will recognize that you have to be his father. It was madness for you to come here.'

They had breakfast at the Britannia Hotel and all the tenderness and poignancy of the night before had gone. In its place Laura felt only confusion and a mounting irritation with Francis. 'What are your plans?' she asked.

He was tucking into a hearty breakfast while all she could face was coffee. He shrugged his shoulders. 'I don't have any. It was a spontaneous thing, coming over here to see you, I just thought I ought to be around. Obviously I'll have to go back to Crete in a few days but I'd like to see as much of you as possible while I'm here, particularly after last night . . .' He smiled at her, a warm, intimate smile, which made Laura's flesh crawl. How could she have let him use her as he had done last night. It was humiliating and wrong – she must have been out of her mind.

'Don't you feel some sort of guilt about last night – so far as your wife is concerned?'

Francis shrugged his shoulders. 'It was a marriage of convenience.'

'Was?' said Laura.

'Well, still is, I suppose, just.'

Laura looked at him levelly. 'You walked out on me and

your father and brother. You clearly wanted us to believe you were dead. I don't understand why now you've decided to make an appearance and destroy the very thing you wanted to create. What's changed?'

'The cirumstances,' said Francis. 'A son who was born and died, without my even knowing.'

'You know your father is dead?'

'Yes, I read about that in the papers, too, and Anthony is living in Australia, I understand.'

'Yes,' said Laura. 'Obviously he was over in England for Fram's funeral – you've only missed him by a week or so.'

'So what's going to happen to Campling Hall?' Francis asked.

The remark was apparently innocent, and a natural progression in the conversation, but it struck a chord so far as Laura was concerned. Francis appeared uncaring as to the answer, he was busy concentrating on his eggs and bacon, but the seeds of doubt were sown. 'I don't know,' she said, evasively, 'it hasn't been decided yet.'

'I presume, though, that my father had left it to Fram?'

'The papers must have told you that,' said Laura, brusquely, suddenly very anxious to change the subject. 'The most important thing to think about at the moment is what's going to happen to you now you're here.'

'I had hoped I could stay with you,' said Francis.

'That's out of the question because of Holly and Scotty, I've already explained that. I think the best thing is to check into a hotel for a few days.'

'I want to be with you though, Laura and talk to you, to be around when you need me.'

'I'm not sure I do need you, Francis,' Laura said.

He grinned. 'You needed me last night.'

'Last night was different, last night was born of shock and misery. We're back in the real world today.' As she spoke the words Laura realized just how true they were. Francis's reappearance had snapped her out of her inertia. The pain was as sharp, if not sharper than ever, with the constant reminder of Fram sitting opposite her, but she was suddenly alive again. She did not yet recognize it, but the cancerous guilt which she had carried with her since Francis's disappearance was gone for ever. 'We'll find you a hotel to stay in,' Laura said, 'that's the first thing to do, a place somewhere near us.'

'Then can I come round this evening and talk,' said Francis, 'when Holly's in bed?'

'I – I don't know,' said Laura, 'I need time to think.'

'Alright,' said Francis, 'as you wish. And, of course, I do see the problem of Fram and I looking so alike – it was not something that had occurred to me when I was considering the risks of coming to England. I will have to be careful. I'm sure the files will still be open and I'm bound to be arrested immediately if the law gets wind of who I am. The story is still too hot, particularly since Fram's death.'

It was true. Fram's death had resulted in a lot of muck-raking in the press – Francis's disappearance and the fraud charges had been thoroughly chewed over again, during the last month. It pained Laura dreadfully that her son's death should have been linked to the sordid antics of his father, but certainly the story was fresh in everyone's mind and Francis was therefore taking an appalling risk.

Breakfast finished, they were preparing to go when Francis said, casually, 'Laura, I haven't had a chance to go to the bank yet. I'm awfully sorry but could you pay for the breakfast?' Again there were warning bells, but she paid without comment.

An hour later Laura was back in her home, having found Francis a hotel just up the road. Scotty gave her a strange look when she entered but said nothing and Laura suddenly thought of the rumpled bed upstairs and felt herself grow hot with embarrassment. What on earth did Scotty think – that she had picked up some man off the street? There was no way she could think of a satisfactory explanation.

She went through the motions of the morning – opening the post, having a cup of coffee, going upstairs to Holly's room and packing a leotard and a pair of tights for her ballet lesson which she went to straight from school. Her thoughts, she felt, were schizophrenic in the extreme – here was a man who had been her husband, who had fathered her beloved child and who she had allowed to make love to her last night. A man she thought was dead, was now alive. Whatever he had done in the past, it was so long ago now, surely it hardly mattered? In any case, it was only money, and put in the context of what had happened to Fram, nothing seemed all that important. On the other hand, his casual reference to Campling Hall worried her, as did his lack of cash to pay for breakfast and his apparent total disregard concerning his unfaithfulness to his wife. What did he want? It had to be something besides offering her comfort. Did she trust him, she asked herself? No, was the answer, and yet for Fram's sake, Fram . . . Fram.

It took her until half-past eleven to make the telephone call she should have made immediately. She lifted the receiver and dialled David Lawson's number.

CHAPTER THIRTY-THREE

The crowd of people in the lounge bar of the Duke of York in the Old Brompton Road was mercifully thinning by the time David arrived. He looked around in bewilderment for a moment, then saw Laura, grinned and limped over. 'Hello, old thing,' he said, bending to kiss her cheek. 'What are you drinking?'

'You're going to have to be quick, they're closing in a moment,' said Laura.

'I'll get a bottle of wine, then. Have you eaten?'

'I don't want anything.'

'You'll do as you're told.' He returned a few minutes later clutching a bottle of wine and a pile of sandwiches. 'Smoked salmon, they cost me a bloody fortune so if you don't eat some, I'll force-feed you.'

'David, we're not here to talk about my eating habits.'

David almost slammed the food and wine on to the table. 'If you're going to cope with what I suspect you're going to have to cope with, you've got to be up and fighting, Laura. Eat those sandwiches and drink that wine or I won't help you.'

Laura allowed herself a small smile. 'You're being very masterful, David.'

'Well, someone has to be. Now tell me everything.'

Laura told him everything, except that she had shared a bed with Francis. She did not disclose that particular detail for fear of hurting David's feelings, she told herself. In reality she was deeply ashamed and wanted to blot out the memory of it.

When she had finished, David sipped his wine thoughtfully for a moment or two. 'From what I recall,' he said, 'the papers were quite specific about the fact that Fram was an heir to a considerable fortune. Not only was he to have become

Lord Campling of Campling Hall but he had already inherited the major share of your father's money – am I right?' Laura nodded.

'Did Fram have a will?'

'No – he was only a child, we . . .' She hesitated, looked close to tears, and then rallied. 'I understand from Anthony that in the circumstances, without a will, Fram's inheritance goes to his parents.'

'Precisely,' said David.

'Meaning?' Laura knew what he meant but she wanted him to spell it out.

'Meaning, I think Francis is operating true to form. I think he's probably short of money – he could well be in serious financial trouble in Crete, and he's over here to try and get his share of Fram's money. He's a rotten sod, but he's not stupid – he'll have worked out the inheritance position.'

'That's appalling,' said Laura, 'if it's true.'

'I'm afraid it's almost certainly true,' said David, 'and what's more, you know it – I can see it in your face.'

'I don't know it,' Laura protested. 'He said he came to comfort me when he learnt of Fram's death. It must have come as quite a shock to him, David, to find he had a son.'

'Do you really believe he would have risked arrest purely to comfort you? He walked out of your life without any thought as to how it would affect you – there isn't an ounce of decency in the man, Laura – he has to have an ulterior motive.'

Laura felt compelled to defend him. 'I think you're being a little harsh, David.'

'Am I? I've known him a long time, Laura. We were at school together – remember. He's weak, greedy, lazy and he can't tell fact from fiction.'

'You are speaking of my son's father,' Laura said, her voice trembling.

David studied her in silence for a moment. She was stretched to breaking point emotionally, he could see that. Still in the early days of coping with her son's death, the reappearance of Francis could very well push her over the precipice. 'Have you agreed to see him again?' David asked.

'No. He wanted to come round and talk tonight but I said I

wasn't sure I could manage it. You see, I'm very anxious that Holly shouldn't meet him. She's bound to spot the similarity to Fram and I don't think she could handle it at the moment. She knows Max was not Fram's father, if she thinks about it, but I don't think she ever does. She loved Fram very much, he was her brother and now he's dead. To suddenly be presented with his father would be too much.'

'Laura, can you stall him in the country for a couple of days – preferably without the need of seeing him?'

'When you say "a couple of days", how long do you actually mean?' Laura asked.

'Well, say the whole of tomorrow, which is – where are we – Thursday, and all of Friday up until Friday evening. You could fend him off by telling him you can see him Friday evening. If you can do that, you can leave everything else to me.'

'What is "everything else"?' Laura said.

'I need three telephone numbers,' said David, 'Anthony's number in Australia, your family solicitor's and Katrine's in Athens.'

'Why my mother's?'

'We need to find out what Joseph Clarke is up to in Crete. If I took a flight out to Athens tonight, scooped up your mother and went on to Crete, we could get to the bottom of his situation out there in a few hours, with your mother's command of the language.'

'Is that wise?' said Laura.

'We'll be discreet.'

'We might be doing him a terrible injustice,' said Laura.

She was still clutching at straws, he realized, desperate that her son's father should not be the villain he appeared. 'Perhaps,' he said, in an effort to comfort.

David took Laura home then, and outside the front door he hesitated. 'Do you think you should perhaps confide in Scotty?'

Laura shook her head. 'No.'

'Is there anybody else then you would like to know about this, so that they can give you some moral support if Francis should cut up rough in any way? I don't like leaving you to cope with him over the next two days, but there's no other way round it.'

'No, it's a risk telling anyone else. Don't fuss, David, I'll be alright, I promise. In a strange way I feel a little better since Francis reappeared – more alert somehow.'

'OK, if you're sure. Now try and relax and leave everything to me.' He kissed her and drove off into the London traffic.

Stalling Francis was far from easy. He rang Laura constantly. 'I don't understand why you won't see me,' he said. 'I've come all the way to London, taking God knows what risks to try and help you in this difficult time, and then you say you're too busy to see me. I love you, Laura, I always have, and I really want to help, but we must meet.'

'Francis, you can't walk out of someone's life and then reappear thirteen years later and expect VIP treatment. I can't see you tonight, or tomorrow night, and I don't have to explain why – I just simply can't.'

'But after last night, I want to be with you, Laura, to touch you and comfort you, and there's so much I still don't know about Fram.'

At the mention of her son's name, Laura nearly weakened. 'Friday evening, Francis, I promise, now please leave me alone, I'm awfully tired.' He rang twice more during the evening, once to ask if she had changed her mind, then lastly simply to say goodnight. Laura felt as though she was under siege, and more than a little panicky. David had been right – coping alone with the situation was not easy. She tossed and turned all night, images of Francis and Fram floating before her. She kept waking, hot and sweaty, and then suddenly shivering with cold. Her head ached, she felt sick and absolutely exhausted. On Thursday morning, Scotty took one look at her, sent her back to bed and took Holly to school by taxi. It was only half-past nine in the morning when Francis started bombarding her with telephone calls again. She felt a rising sense of panic – if only David were here to help her.

Scotty brought her a cup of coffee to the bedroom. 'Who is

this man who keeps phoning you?' she demanded. 'I'll send the laddie packing if he's upsetting you.'

'No, it's alright,' said Laura.

'Why don't you let me answer the phone?'

It was tempting but Laura knew if she didn't keep speaking to Francis, he would come round. 'No, it's alright, Scotty – honestly, I can cope.'

'You look like hell,' said Scotty firmly, and disappeared with a disapproving look on her face.

Somehow Laura staggered through the rest of the day and into Friday but there was still no word from David. Not knowing when to expect news, she convinced Francis that she could not see him until ten in the evening. He was almost abusive at the delay and Laura was at her wits' end, when around four o'clock in the afternoon, there was a phone call from David. 'Where are you?' she asked.

'At Heathrow, with your mother, we're on our way to you now. Are you alright, Laura?'

'Sort of,' said Laura, her voice very wobbly.

'You don't sound it, just hang in there – we should be with you within the hour.'

True to their word, they were. In a moment of inspiration, Laura arranged for Holly to stay the night with a friend, and with Scotty safely ensconced in her little basement flat, they were free to talk uninterrupted.

Katrine swept Laura into an embrace. 'My poor darling, this is too much, just too much for you.'

The relief of seeing her mother was enormous. In the dark days immediately after the funeral, she had shunned the company of both David and her mother. Next to Holly they were the people she loved most, and because she believed she destroyed everyone she loved, she had decided to avoid them. Now suddenly, they both seemed very dear and a very necessary part of her life.

'Have you been to Crete?' she asked, looking from one to the other. David nodded. 'Good grief, you must be exhausted – let me get you some tea or a drink.'

'No, we're fine,' said Katrine, 'sit down and we'll tell you all about it – but first, how has Francis been behaving?'

'He's been awful,' said Laura, 'he rings me up all the time. Honestly I don't think I can bear much more – it's such a relief you're here. Oh, and he's coming round here at ten o'clock tonight.'

'Good,' said David. 'In a nutshell, Laura, Joseph Clarke is in considerable debt in Crete. It's true he does own three tavernas but he's over-extended himself. Basically, they're far too grand for Crete and they're not making enough money. The staff haven't been paid for weeks and he's used up all his credit with suppliers. In other words, as we suspected, he's in big trouble.'

Laura sat in silence, listening to the details of David's news. As in the past with Francis, she felt a sense of disappointment. She always wanted to believe the things he told her, she always had. The idea that he might really risk imprisonment to come and comfort her when their son had died, was just what she wanted to hear. Of course she had known his motives were suspect, but to be confronted with the cold evidence was just too much. Above all, it was insulting to Fram and his memory. She burst into tears.

Katrine came and sat beside her and took her in her arms. 'There, there, darling, don't worry, David and Anthony have sorted it all out.'

Laura made a stupendous effort to pull herself together. 'How do you mean, sorted it all out?' she asked David.

'He needs paying off, it's as simple as that,' said David. His mouth was set in a firm line and he looked very different from the normally mild David. 'In reality, of course,' he said, 'there is no question of him receiving any money from Fram's inheritance, because the only way he can claim it is to admit who he is. If he does that then he will be arrested. However, it is not simply the legal position that's at stake here – Francis has got at you emotionally, at the most vulnerable moment in your life. Anthony recognizes that, too, and I must say, he has no illusions about his brother. Anthony's view, and I agree with him, is that you should pay off Francis with a lump sum and then provide some sort of trust to stabilize his lifestyle and provide him with income, but no capital. What Anthony has proposed is an immediate cash payment of £250,000, and

I have the cheque here in my pocket waiting only for your signature. Once Francis is back in Crete, Anthony will set up a trust fund based in Switzerland, which will pay him an income of approximately £30,000 a year. He can live like a king in Crete on that, but there is a condition.'

'What's the condition?' Laura asked.

'That he never contacts you or any member of his family again and he accepts that Francis Melhuish is dead.'

'What if he *doesn't* accept the deal?' Laura said.

'Then Anthony has instructed me to telephone Scotland Yard and have him arrested.'

'Oh David – no!'

'Don't worry,' said David, 'he'll take it, it's a very generous offer, far more than he deserves, but as Anthony says, it's money well spent, to get him out of your life. The man is unspeakable – to do this to you in the circumstances, I just can't bear . . .'

'There, there, David, don't upset yourself,' said Katrine. 'You must be calm and unemotional. Just explain the facts, man-to-man. You must avoid telling him of your personal views on the subject when you see him.'

'When *David* sees him!' Laura said. 'It's me who will be seeing him.'

'No,' said Katrine, 'David and I discussed it on the plane, it's quite wrong for you to ever see him again – you just can't take it, darling. David will give him the money and explain the terms. We picked up a ticket for Francis at the airport. He's leaving the country at 9.15 tomorrow morning, although he doesn't know it yet.'

Laura extracted herself from her mother's arms and stood up. 'Look, don't think I'm not grateful to both of you for what you've done, I just couldn't have coped without you, but I must see him myself, I really must.'

'No, Laura,' said David, 'it's madness, he'll upset you too much. Please let me handle this, it's what Anthony wants, too.'

'Anthony's in Australia, and with all due respect, my relationship with my ex-husband is my affair. I agree completely with the proposal you are offering Francis. It *is* generous and if money is his reason for coming to England, then obviously he will take it. However, I do have to see him and tell him about it myself.'

'Why?' David raged. 'Are you still in love with him?'

'No,' said Laura, 'it is simply because he is Fram's father.'

There was nothing either David or Katrine could say to that. By half-past nine they had left, having both booked themselves into rooms at the nearby Portman Hotel, in case Laura needed them. 'Will you ring us when he's gone?' David said. 'Please, Laura.'

'Alright,' said Laura, 'I will, I promise. Now please go otherwise you'll meet him on the doorstep.'

Francis arrived promptly at ten. He looked considerably less ebullient than the last time they had met. He was very pale and seemed strained and nervous. He accepted a whisky from Laura, made a half-hearted attempt to kiss her, and when she rejected him, he seemed almost relieved and sat nervously on the edge of the sofa.

She did not waste any time coming to the point. 'Is that what you really came for, Francis?' She handed him the cheque. He looked at it in silence for a moment, colour suddenly flooding into his cheeks. 'This is incredibly generous of you, Laura.'

'It is generous, Francis, but it's not from me, it's from Fram. Arrangements are also being made for a trust fund to be set up in Switzerland for you. It will give you an annual income of £30,000 a year.'

'Good heavens, what on earth have I done to deserve that?'

His confidence was back, Laura marvelled – in a trice he was his old, arrogant self. 'Absolutely nothing,' she said, coldly. 'I should add that there is a condition to all this.'

'What condition?' Francis's eyes narrowed slightly.

'That Francis Melhuish is sent back to his watery grave. If you accept this cheque and the income from the trust fund, you may never contact me or any member of the family again. If you break the agreement, we will hand you over to the police.'

Francis looked genuinely hurt. 'But I thought you and I . . . well, after the other night.'

'That you and I, what?' said Laura, 'might get back together gain, is that what you thought – surely not?'

'Well, I don't know,' said Francis, 'but you have always een the only one who really mattered, Laura, I'm sure you now that.'

'How could I possibly know that?' said Laura. 'I do know ou took horrendous advantage of me the other night when I vas so shocked and emotionally unstable, I did not know what was doing. It didn't endear you to me, Francis, in fact quite ne reverse. I don't trust you, don't respect you, I don't even ke you. I hardly think that's any basis for reinstating our elationship, do you?'

'You always were very hard, Laura,' Francis said.

'Perhaps you made me that way,' Laura said. 'And, inci-entally, here is the final part of the deal,' she handed him the irline ticket. 'The flight for Crete leaves tomorrow morning, ıst after nine – you have to be on it. It's booked in the name f Joseph Clarke, of course.'

There was a lengthy silence. It seemed as though Francis ıight still be considering the deal except that the cheque was lready in his pocket. At last he spoke. 'I accept the terms,' he ıid, quietly.

'It's what you came for, Francis, isn't it?'

'I came to comfort you, I told you that.'

'Couldn't you be honest just for once, just to me?'

'I am being honest, Laura. I am a little stuck for cash at resent, I'll admit, but that's not why I came.'

It was hopeless, as it had always been. Francis and the truth id not travel the same road. It was not just that he deluded ther people, she realized suddenly, he deluded himself as 'ell.

'So,' said Francis, 'you seem to have sorted out the rest of ıy life – what happens to the rest of yours?'

Laura shrugged, the fight had gone out of her. Francis had ın true to form, there was no point in being angry or isappointed. 'I don't know, concentrate on bringing up Holly) be a well-balanced, happy soul is the extent of my ambi-ons. Since . . . since Fram died, I don't seem to be able to oncentrate on very much.'

Francis hesitated. 'There is one thing I would like to as you – could I have a photograph of him, to take back to Cre with me?'

They stared at one another in silence, suddenly emotio between them running high.

'Yes, yes of course.' She looked across at the photograp standing on the bookshelf. 'That's the last one, the most u to-date.'

'I'd like that, if you can get yourself a copy.'

'Oh yes,' said Laura. She walked to the bookshelf and lift down the frame. She was crying now, but she kept her ba towards Francis so he could not see. 'I'm glad you asked f this,' said Laura, thickly.

'Are you?' He was on his feet and close behind her.

'Oh Francis, I just can't bear life without him.'

She turned and Francis took her in his arms, pressing t photograph between them. 'It'll get better, Laura. I know i a hackneyed phrase but time does heal,' he said gently, stroki her hair.

'Everyone says that. What they don't understand is that don't want time to heal – I don't want to stop feeling as I d

'You must,' said Francis. 'I never knew him but I'm su he would not have wanted you to have this degree of su fering.' He led her back to the sofa and they sat down. F smiled. 'Tell me, how do you think you came to get pregna – when was he conceived? You certainly weren't in the fran of mind to start a family at the time.'

'That last time on the boat, the afternoon before you di appeared, that's when it happened,' said Laura.

'Did it? How do you know?'

'I don't know, I just feel it instinctively. It was your parti gift as it turned out – the best present anyone has ever, or w ever, give me.'

'I'm glad you feel like that,' said Francis, simply.

Silence fell between them again, and they both knew it w time for Francis to go. He stood up, picking up both t photograph and the ticket. 'So,' he said, 'it's goodbye, n only to you but finally to Francis Melhuish, too. I shall thi of you often, Laura, and wish you well.'

'And I shall think of you,' said Laura, realizing how true 1e words were.

They walked together to the front door. Francis opened it, :tting in a blast of cold air. 'Oh, for the Cretan sun, he said, 'ith false gaiety. 'Goodbye Laura, my darling.' He studied er face for a moment. 'I know I'm not a very good man, but f all the people that have drifted in and out of my life, it is ou I've come nearest to truly loving – you and the child we reated. Extraordinary isn't it, to love someone I never met.'

Tears flowed down Laura's cheeks again, for instantly she ecognized in Francis something she had never seen before – bsolute sincerity. Just for that fleeting moment, she had seen im for what he was – a sad, lonely exile, with no home, no amily, no roots and no real identity. He bent forward and issed her, a long, deep kiss full of passion but not of a sexual ind. Then he drew away and stepped out into the cold night air.

'Goodbye, Francis.' Laura's voice was little more than a 'hisper.

'Goodbye, my darling,' he said, with a sad little smile. 'The ame's Joseph, remember.'

He turned and walked away, and as his shadowy figure isappeared into the night, Laura felt as though her guts were eing wrenched from her. It was the symbolic final severing f the umbilical cord – the last true link with Fram gone prever. She shut the front door and went into the sitting oom. There was still the indentation on the sofa where 'rancis had sat, his empty whisky glass stood on the table. he walked to her desk, lifted the telephone and dialled)avid's hotel.

'Are you alright?' David said, anxiously.

'Yes, I'm alright.'

'He's gone?'

'Yes. You were quite right, he accepted the money without ny fuss – it was what he came for, without a doubt.'

'The bastard,' said David.

'I'm very tired, David, thank you for all you've done. Give 1ummy my love. I'll go now, if that's OK.'

'Will you ring me in the next few days?'

'Yes,' Laura promised. She replaced the receiver and went

upstairs, but made no attempt to go to her room. Instead she went to Fram's and lying down on his bed, she clutched his teddy bear to her. It was sodden with tears before she finally slept.

THE END:
Oxfordshire, Christmas 1985

CHAPTER THIRTY-FOUR

(love Christmas at David's, don't you?' said Holly. 'I just ouldn't bear to stay in London, Christmases are supposed to e in the country, in fact *everything* should be in the country. Aummy, why can't we live at Meadows Reach and then I could ave a pony and cats and dogs and goats, and . . .'

'Stop, stop,' said Laura, laughing. They were driving down ne M4 in Laura's smart new Range Rover, complete with Latrine, Scotty and Dougal, the cairn.

'I still think it's too much for a bachelor, having to cope ith all of us women, and he won't even let us do the cooking,' Latrine said.

'Oh Granny, he does it every year, we've told you.'

'Yes, but he doesn't normally have Scotty and I as well.'

'I agree,' said Scotty. 'The poor wee lad will be worn to a azzle.'

'No, he won't,' said Laura. 'David's never worn to a frazzle, 's not his style.' She spoke warmly and affectionately and Latrine, in the passenger seat, glanced at her daughter to try nd read the expression on her face. She had lost count of the mes she had prayed that David and Laura would marry and ttle down. It seemed such an extraordinary relationship – ney were like brother and sister now. They stayed in each ther's houses, they took Holly on holiday together, spent ng weekends in the country, yet Laura assured her they ways had separate bedrooms. 'It's just not that sort of relaonship, Mummy.'

'But it was,' Katrine had said wistfully.

'A very, very long time ago,' Laura reminded her, yet surely nere had been a note of regret in her voice, Katrine fancied.

In the years since Fram's death, mother and daughter had rown close again. Katrine came over from Athens frequently nd spent long periods in the house in Harley Street. All the old animosity between her and Laura had gone. Laura needed her mother's moral support these days and didn't mind admitting it. Katrine had grown close to Holly, too, who was very much the effervescent child that Laura had been, both in looks and temperament. Please God, do not let the same things happen to Holly as have happened to Laura, Katrine thought again and again. For the light had gone out of Laura's life. She was kind and caring to her child, she had written a couple of books, so she was not idle, she entertained a little, she was always impeccably dressed, the house tidy, warm and welcoming. But Katrine knew that Laura was simply existing eking out the rest of her days until she could be with Fram or so it seemed. And Fram, himself, was a taboo subject except between Holly and Laura. That, too, upset Katrine Fram had been part of the family and he should be a part of the family still – much discussed, often referred to, but Laura could not take it, and therefore he was never normally mentioned in her presence.

They came off the motorway and drove over Henley bridge and through the town. David's little cottage, which he had once shared with Serena, was on Turville Heath, high up in the Chilterns above Henley. They drove up the Oxford Road and turned off on to country lanes. It was a cold day but with bright sunshine and the hedges sparkling with frost.

'Oh I love it, I love it, I can't wait to get there,' said Holly 'Why don't we live with David if we can't live in your old home, Mummy. You know you hate London as much as I do.'

'Stop, Holly,' said Laura, 'it's Christmas Eve. I don't deserve all this nagging on Christmas Eve, now do I?'

''Spose not.'

'Particularly bearing in mind that tomorrow is both Christmas Day and your birthday, and I still have hold of all your presents. I might decide to give them to Dr Barnados, if you don't behave.'

'You wouldn't!' said Holly, confidently.

'I might.'

They turned into an almost concealed driveway, and there was David's cottage, with its thatched roof and white walls. It was almost too good to be true, like a cottage in a picture book

Beyond it stretched fields, and a stream bubbled its way through the garden.

At the sound of the car wheels on gravel, David came to the door, smiling broadly. He limped across to the car and opened the door for Katrine. 'Katrine, how lovely to see you. Welcome to England! You look wonderful, as always.' Katrine embraced him warmly and regarded him thoughtfully. He had turned into a very good-looking, middle-aged man. The confidence he had lacked as a boy, presumably due to his disability, was now very much in evidence – he always seemed calm and master of every situation. His dark hair was almost grey now but was as curly as ever, and he still looked very trim and fit.

'David, David!' Holly threw herself into his arms, nearly knocking him over.

'Good God, look at the size of you,' he said, 'you're nearly as tall as me.'

'That's not difficult, Shorty.'

'Holly, don't be so rude,' said Katrine, horrified.

'Go play with your doll, Brat-face,' David said. They stuck their tongues out at one another and Katrine, not for the first time, was aware of the rapport between them. It was all so sad.

David greeted Scotty and then turned at last to Laura. 'Hello, old thing,' he said, 'you look tired.'

'I am a little, though why I should be, I don't know, since I had absolutely nothing to do to prepare for Christmas – you do spoil us, David.'

He ushered them all into the cottage. A fire blazed in the huge inglenook fireplace in the sitting room. The house was beautifully decorated with holly and mistletoe and there was a tree round which a great pile of presents was already heaped. 'I'm keeping you on short rations until tomorrow, because I want you to enjoy the turkey,' said David. 'So . . . all you have for lunch today is smoked salmon and champagne. Do you think you can cope?'

'Just,' said Laura, laughing. 'You *are* naughty, what a treat! I'd better unload the car.'

'Later. Have some champagne and relax.'

Lunch was a happy affair and afterwards, whilst Scotty and Katrine washed up, David drove Holly over to some friends of his, whose children had ponies and where it had been arranged that she should spend the afternoon. When he returned to the house, the two elderly women were fast asleep in chairs in front of the fire and Laura was wandering around the cottage restlessly, having unloaded the car and clearly having nothing else to do.

'What do you fancy,' said David, 'a walk, a drive, a collapse on your bed?'

'You're going to think this strange, David, but how would you feel about us taking a look at Meadows Reach?'

'Of course, why not? Shall we wake your mother and see if she wants to come, too?'

Laura shook her head. 'No, I think I'd rather just go with you.'

They left a note to say where they were going, shut the front door quietly and drove the short distance to Marlow. 'What's prompted this, after all these years?' David asked.

'Holly, I suppose,' said Laura. 'She goes on and on about our living in the country and she's right, of course. I cling to the house in London because of Fram, but every time Holly and I have some leisure together, we find ways of spending it anywhere but in London. It's mad.'

'Yes, it is,' David agreed.

'Anyway, enough of me, how are *you*? I haven't seen you for ages.' It was true. Normally Laura and David met every two or three weeks, sometimes just for dinner, sometimes for a weekend, but they spoke, on the phone, very regularly. However, during the last three months, David had kept a very low profile. He had not been to London once, he had telephoned infrequently, and there had been no invitations to Turville Heath, except this one for Christmas. Laura was grateful to him for asking her mother and Scotty as well, but a little surprised, too. She would have preferred it with just the three of them.

'Yes, I'm sorry I've not been around much, I've been busy at work.'

'Are you expanding again?' Laura asked.

'No, not really, just involving myself a little more in the business.'

'I'd decided it was a woman,' said Laura. 'It is about time you let someone make an honest man of you.' She spoke the words lightly and with apparent sincerity. In reality, the thought of David in a serious relationship with someone else appalled her. Since the day after her father's funeral – so long ago now, before Holly, before even her marriage to Max – the relationship had been entirely platonic. It was easy, restful and comforting, but in recent months Laura had also found it unaccountably disturbing. When he casually touched her, she found she did not want him to let go. When she heard his familiar voice on the phone, her heart always leapt, as it did at the sound of his very individual footsteps on the stairs. She did not want any more from the relationship, she told herself, and yet the thought of him with someone else was something she could not bear to even contemplate. I must not be so selfish, she told herself, whenever she thought about it – which of late had been frequently.

'Don't be silly,' David was saying. 'I haven't time for another woman in my life – worrying about you and Holly is a full-time job.' Somehow Laura did not find his words reassuring.

Laura had not been back to Meadows Reach since the day she had handed it over to the custody of Mrs Jenkins, in the aftermath of Katrine's decision to live in Greece. She received regular reports from Mrs Jenkins and over the years had authorized maintenance work, but that was it. At Mrs Jenkins's cottage, she asked David to stop the car. 'Oh, Miss Beecham, how lovely to see you, Happy Christmas!' Laura had never been anything else but "Miss Beecham" so far as Mrs Jenkins was concerned. 'I hope you'll find the house in order, Miss. You should have warned me you were coming and I'd have lit a fire. It will be cold as charity in there.'

'Don't worry, it'll only be a fleeting visit. I just thought I'd look in, as I was in the area.'

'We do miss you,' Mrs Jenkins said wistfully. She gave Laura a key, and stood waving to them until they were out of sight round the bend in the drive.

As they drew to a halt by the front door, Laura thought of the many Christmases she had spent at Meadows Reach, but more especially of the last one, the one when she had been reconciled with her father and Fram had been no more than a baby. At the memory, she felt tears pressing at the corner of her eyes.

'Are you sure you want to go ahead with this?' David's voice was gentle beside her.

'Yes, please.'

'Do you want to go alone?'

'Oh no, no, with you.'

They wandered from room to room. 'It's beautiful,' said David, 'I'd forgotten.'

'Yes, it is,' said Laura, 'and peaceful, too.'

'You continue your exploring. I'll go and see if I can find some wood and light a fire in the drawing room. It's perishing.'

He disappeared and Laura was suddenly grateful to be alone. She explored every room in the house and then wandered out into the garden, down to the river. She thought of all the places she had lived and realized they all counted for nothing compared with Meadows Reach. This was home.

When she came back up to the house, David was standing in front of a roaring fire which shot sparks up the chimney and sent dancing shadows round the walls of the drawing room. They took off a dust sheet from one of the sofas and pulled it up to the fire. 'All we need now is a bottle of wine and we'd be complete,' said David.

'Not such a stupid idea,' said Laura, 'there's bound to be some in the cellar still.'

'No sooner said than done,' said David, 'lead me to the cellar, old thing, and you can fetch some glasses, while I select a wine suitable for the occasion.'

Laura showed David to the top of the cellar steps underneath the main staircase and then went through to the kitchen. She felt happier, she suddenly realized, than she had in a long time. The tranquillity of the house relaxed her in a way she could not remember feeling since Fram's death. She found two glasses and was on her way back to the drawing room when suddenly from the cellar steps, there was a cry followed by a clatter and a thud. 'No, no, David.' Laura almost threw the glasses on the ground and ran to the top of the stairs. Not this, she thought, not this on top of everything else that's happened. 'David, David!' She flew down the cellar stairs. They were damp and greasy underfoot and she almost fell herself. 'David!'

'It's OK, I'm here. Stupid bloody fool, I've broken the bottle, too.' He was sitting at the bottom of the cellar stairs, surrounded by broken glass and rubbing an elbow.

'Oh David, are you alright? Are you hurt?' Laura fell on her knees beside him, tears wet on her cheeks.

'Hey, what's all this, of course I'm alright. What a bloody clumsy idiot, I am – sodding leg. Help me up, there's a good girl.'

She helped him up. She was trembling all over and without any conscious thought she slipped her arms round him and pressed herself against his chest. 'I thought I'd lost you.'

He tried to make light of it. 'It would take more than a few old cellar steps to finish me off. Come on, you're cold. Let's get you back up by that fire and put some wine down you.' He moved out of the circle of her embrace, leaving her feeling bereft and awkward.

They found another bottle, helped each other up the steps, Laura collected the glasses and after a search for a corkscrew, they opened the wine. It was a 1969 Burgundy. 'The year Fram was born,' Laura said.

David raised his glass. 'Then to Fram,' he said.

'To Fram,' Laura replied. She was sitting on the hearth, the light from the fire highlighting her dark curls and bringing colour back to her cheeks. Her eyes were sparkling, still wet from the tears. She had never looked more lovely. David caught his breath and turned away for a moment. 'David, what is it?'

'Nothing, nothing,' he said. 'I'm sorry I frightened you just now.'

'I'm sorry I over-reacted,' said Laura. 'Since Fram I always assume the worst when there's an accident.'

There was silence between them and for the first time Laura could ever remember, there was an awkwardness, too. Oh God, there is someone else in his life and he just doesn't know how to tell me, she thought. She looked at him carefully. His face was in profile as he sat staring into the flames, a faraway look in his eyes. His hair curled into the nape of his neck as it had always done – touchingly, like a small child's. She remembered how she used to love kissing him there. His hand rested on his knee. With frightening clarity she remembered his caresses – how they had maddened her, taken her to dizzy heights she had never known with anyone else. Her heart was banging in her chest, she felt herself blushing at the vividness of her memories. She shifted position, agitated and uncomfortable on the hearth.

David looked up sharply. 'Are you alright down there?'

Laura nodded, not trusting herself to speak. He smiled at her and then returned to his fire-gazing. What's wrong with me, Laura thought, wretchedly, but she already knew the answer – she had fallen in love with David Lawson all over again, just at a time when he seemed to have little need of her.

Restlessly, she stood up, stretching her cramped limbs, and walked over to the bay window. She remembered as a teenager coming into the room with her mother to find David being grilled by her father, sitting just where she now stood. It was that same night they had made love for the first time – the memory of it now made her feel dizzy.

'Penny for them, old thing.' Laura turned at David's words and stared at him. In all her relationships with men, Laura had been the pursued not the pursuer. She had never known the terror of possible rejection, never felt that her whole future happiness depended on what she said next . . . not, until now. Her heart was beating so loudly that she could hardly hear her own voice, yet now was the moment, the point of no return. 'I was thinking about the first time we made love and wishing . . . wishing you would make love to me now.'

The colour drained from his face. 'What?'

'You heard,' said Laura. 'It may not be what you want to hear, but you heard alright.'

David set down his wine glass but made no attempt to move. 'I don't think that would be a very good idea, Laura.'

She was on the point of giving up, retiring hurt and

humiliated, but something in his face stopped her. What did it matter if she made a fool of herself – wasn't he worth fighting for. 'If it's because there's someone else, then, of course, I understand, but if it is because of the past, can't we put it behind us and start again?'

David stood up and straightened his leg iron. He walked to the opposite side of the room as though to put as much distance between them as possible. 'No, of course there isn't anyone else – I just don't want to change our relationship – we're fine as we are.'

'You mean you don't love me?' Laura said.

David dropped his gaze, concentrating on scuffing the edge of the carpet with his foot. 'Of course I love you, but not like that. I want us to be friends always, loving friends.'

'But not lovers.'

'Not lovers,' David confirmed.

'I see.' Laura crossed the room to the fire again, her face set, her heart like lead. 'I suppose we'd better be getting back, they'll be wondering what's happened to us. I'm sorry if I embarrassed you.' She began clearing up, replacing the dust sheet, putting the cork in the bottle.

'Laura.'

She looked up, and the expression of misery on her face shocked him. 'Yes?'

He struggled with the words. 'It's not that I don't find you attractive, in fact you're the . . .'

'Please, David, don't humiliate me further by trying to explain. I understand, truly.' She picked up the empty glasses and disappeared through to the kitchen.

Her mind was numb as she washed and dried the glasses. To get back to Turville Heath as quickly as possible was the top priority now. Surrounded by other people, she could pretend nothing had happened, and then on Boxing Day she would think up an excuse for them to have to return early to London. After that . . . her life stretched ahead of her like a desert without David Lawson a part of it.

She could not bear to go into the drawing room again. Instead she stood in the doorway and called out to him. 'Come on David, let's get going.'

He was standing by the bay window now, his back towards her. She started to move towards the front door, and then stopped. His shoulders were hunched and shaking. He was crying.

She ran to him and put her hand on his arm. At her touch he turned and drew her into an embrace so tight she could scarcely breathe. His tears brought tears to her own eyes. 'What is it, what's wrong, David?'

For a moment he did not speak. 'I'm sorry, it's just that I'm frightened, so frightened.'

'Frightened – of what?'

'Of you.'

'Me?' Laura managed to draw away from him a little so that she could see his face. 'Oh David, why, why?'

'It's difficult to explain, it's best left, Laura. The past is past. Let's try and get over this afternoon and concentrate on salvaging our friendship.'

'No,' said Laura, 'we must talk about this.' Holding tight to his hand she led him back to the fire. He sat down, Laura threw on some more logs, and settled at his feet. 'Tell me, David,' she said.

He took a deep breath, wiping his eyes as he did so. 'I suppose I've always had a bit of a chip on my shoulder about my disability. There are a lot of things I can't do which other people take for granted. Everything is more of a hurdle – taking a woman to bed for the first time, not knowing how she will react, for example.'

'I understand all that,' said Laura.

'Yes I know you do, and I'm only mentioning it because I suppose it explains why when the old ego takes a knock, I find it so difficult to recover.' He hesitated. 'I've loved you all my adult life, Laura, passionately, completely and right now more than ever before.'

Laura gasped. 'Then why . . .?'

'Listen, please. You've rejected me twice, Laura. I understand why, I think, I'm even sympathetic, but on each occasion, it has taken me years to rebuild my life. You're like a drug to me – I can't leave you alone, even now – but in our current relationship, I feel . . . well, relatively safe, I suppose. It's the best way to describe it.'

'You make me sound awful – some kind of monster.'

'No – it's my love for you which is the monster, not you yourself. Please try and understand – you're wonderful but you're volatile, so unexpected. I never know what will happen next. I can't risk another rejection – you probably think I'm behaving like a complete wally but honestly, to go through all that again would have me in the nuthouse for good.'

How do I break through his shell, Laura thought, how do I reach him to explain?

'I've changed, David – since Fram's death particularly. I'm a boring, middle-aged housewife these days – not the exciting person you fear will walk off with your heart again. I love you, I want to show you how much, to make up for the bad times.'

'Are you saying you'll marry me?' David asked quietly.

Laura shook her head. 'I won't ever marry again, David, not after two mistakes, but I'll live with you, and work night and day to make you happy.'

'Always something held back – never a complete commitment. I can't live like that, Laura.'

'No room for compromise?'

'None.'

Suddenly anger came from nowhere and welled up, almost seeming to choke her. 'Well, sod you, David. Sit in your safe little cocoon, if that's what you want, too frightened to take a risk with life. You'll grow old and wither away all alone, but true, no one will have hurt you. So what, one of your legs doesn't function properly, does that give you a passport out of living? You're so free with your advice – you're always telling me what to do, what to think, what to feel even. How about looking at yourself, or has the great mass of self-pity obscured the view?'

'How dare you!'

'I dare David, because just like you know me so well, I know you. Only real friends can tell each other the truth – do you remember saying that to me?'

'Yes, when Fram died,' David said.

'That's right, David, when Fram died. You talk of the tragedy of a broken love affair. Believe me, you don't know what tragedy is when compared with the death of a child.' She stood up, eyes blazing. 'Let's get out of here, take me back to your cottage, there's no point in talking any more.' She started towards the door.

'Come here,' said David.

'No, I want to go.'

'Come here,' David shouted, getting to his feet.

Mesmerized by his anger, she walked back to him. He seized her by the shoulders. 'I could shake you until your teeth rattle, I could beat the hell out of you until you were black and blue, but I'm not going to.' His hands were hurting her.

'Let go, David!' She was almost frightened at the violence in him.

'I'm not going to, but I am going to do this.' His mouth closed over hers savagely, bending her backwards until she thought her back would break. She tried to cry out but she couldn't. His hands began tearing at her clothes. 'Stop it, David!' she managed at last.

'Not on your life.'

Somehow she was on the sofa again, as he pulled and tore the clothes from her body. His lips were everywhere and suddenly his full weight was upon her. There had not been time to take off his own clothes. He forced her legs apart roughly and in the moment before he plunged into her, their eyes met. Somewhere deep within her, with that one look, he lit the fuse. She let out a long, low cry and raised her body to meet his, moaning, sobbing out his name and begging him never, never to stop.

When they woke it was quite dark. The fire had almost gone out and they were freezing cold.

'What will everyone think has happened to us?'

'First things first, darling, I must get you warm again. Where can I find some blankets?'

'Blankets are in the bathroom, in the airing cupboard, second floor on the right.'

He returned in a moment and covered Laura with the blankets. 'Now I'll build up the fire, don't move.' In a few minutes he had the fire blazing. 'Wine, what happened to the wine.' He grinned. 'We needn't have washed those glasses after all.'

He found the wine and poured them both a glass. Laura half sat up on the sofa, swaddled in the blankets. 'I feel wonderful,' she said.

'You look wonderful, you are wonderful.' They kissed and David groaned. 'Hang the responsibilities, what I actually want to do is get under that blanket and ravage you again, and again.'

'We'd better get dressed.'

'No, lie there,' said David. 'Will the phone be connected?'

'I shouldn't think so,' said Laura.

'I'll whip down to Mrs Jenkins's cottage then and ring Katrine to say we've been delayed.'

'What on earth will you tell her, David?'

'I'll think of something. I'll ask her to ring the Davidsons and get them to deliver Holly back home. I know they won't mind. You stay exactly where you are and don't you dare get dressed – I have plans for you.'

'In that case, I won't move an inch.'

Mrs Jenkins looked a little surprised to see David but ushered him into their front room and pointed out the telephone. 'Katrine?'

'David, where are you? I've been so worried.' Katrine always sounded very Greek on the telephone.

'I'm so sorry – Laura and I got delayed – we're still at Meadows Reach, I'm afraid.'

'What does it look like?'

'Wonderful. Mrs Jenkins has done a first class job,' he said loudly, for Mrs Jenkins's benefit, who he felt sure was listening at the door. 'Katrine, we may be a little while yet. Would it be possible to ring the Davidsons – their number's in my address book – and ask them to deliver Holly back to you?'

Something in his voice must have betrayed him for Katrine was suddenly laughing aloud. 'David, my darling, I'll stuff the turkey and make up Holly's stocking, I'll keep the home fires burning, I'll do anything . . . anything, but please, please don't hurry back.'

'How did you know?' said David, incredulously.

'When your very dearest wish in all the world comes true, a person always knows,' said Katrine.

'She won't marry me, I think I ought to warn you that,' said David.

'Won't!'

'No, but she will live with me. It's a start, isn't it?'

'Oh David, I'm so happy. I shall cry a little and then I think Scotty and I will get drunk.'

'Then don't wait for us,' said David laughing, 'we may be some time.'

CHAPTER THIRTY-FIVE

David Lawson had never been happier, as he drove down the drive of Meadows Reach, one balmy May evening, five months later. He, Laura, Holly and Scotty had been living together at Meadows Reach for three months and it was now hard for any one of them to imagine having ever lived anywhere else. Holly was happily settled at a local school, David's business was going well and Laura was writing another book. Holly adored David, and he and Laura were so in love they could hardly bear to be out of each other's sight.

Laura's move from London had been full of emotional complications, but Katrine had found the key. Fram had spent much of his babyhood at Meadows Reach, she reminded Laura, so by moving there, she was not abandoning him. It was still a delicate subject – Laura's happiness was fragile, and subject to sudden and prolonged fits of depression, but as each day passed, her peace of mind grew and broadened.

Holly came hurtling down the drive on her bike towards David, did an impressive wheely, and chased him to the front door. As he stepped out of the car, she gave him a quick hug. 'Hello, gorgeous, how are you?'

'Yuk,' said Holly.

'Yuk – why? It's a wonderful evening, it's Friday night, no more school until Monday.'

'It's Mummy, she's in a foul temper. You should be warned, David. Nobody, but nobody can do anything right. She's even shouted at Scotty.'

'That is serious,' said David, smiling, 'no one shouts at Scotty if they want to live. I'll go and sort her out – where is she?'

'I don't know. I slammed the door and walked out, I'm not going back into the house until she's in a nicer mood.'

'Tell you what,' said David, 'bicycle ten times up and down

the drive and by the time you've done that, I promise I'll have sweet-talked her for you.'

'You're nicer than she deserves,' said Holly, severely, and peddled off with a face like thunder.

David laughed. Mother and daughter were so alike in all ways, but when they argued, they were identical. 'Laura!' he called as he came through the front door.

Scotty appeared in the hall, and the expression on her face was hardly encouraging. 'She's upstairs in her room,' she said sullenly. Scotty adored David and the lack of ecstatic greeting was truly worrying.

David climbed the stairs as fast as his leg would allow. 'Laura?' She was sitting at her dressing table staring at herself in the mirror. A quick look at her reflection told him she had been crying, though now she seemed dry-eyed.

'Oh, it's you,' she said, listlessly.

'That's not much of a greeting for the hunter returning triumphant to the homestead. Rumour has it you're in a bad mood. What's up, darling?' He came over to her and kissed her.

'Do you really want to know?' Laura swung round, her face was stricken – with grief, anger – it was hard to tell.

'Well, yes, I do – I wouldn't ask otherwise.'

'Don't joke David, I'm not in the mood.'

He shrugged his shoulders and sat down on the bed. 'OK, I'm listening – what's up, darling?'

'I'm pregnant.'

A smile practically cut David's face in two. 'You're what! You're pregnant? Oh, darling, how wonderful.' He went to take her in his arms.

'Wonderful!' said Laura, recoiling from him. 'I can't have a baby, I can't.'

'Why ever not?' Then he stopped short and sat down on the bed again. 'This is something to do with Fram, isn't it? The real reason you didn't want us to marry was because that would naturally lead us into having children – is that right?' Laura nodded, her head bowed. 'Let me get this straight,' said David, 'you feel that if you have another child you're being disloyal to Fram, in some way?'

'Especially if it's a boy – I just couldn't bear it.'

'If it were a boy,' said David, 'it wouldn't be Fram, but it would be someone who needed your love just as much as he did.'

'I can't, David, I can't go through with it, I'll have to have an abortion.'

'Abort our child!' David was appalled. He stood up and began pacing the room. 'I'll never forgive you if you do that, Laura, never.'

'Oh, so that's all I am to you, when the chips are down – just a vehicle for procreation!'

'Don't be silly,' said David. 'I've known what a sensitive subject this is which is why I've never raised it, but it's not my fault you got pregnant.'

'Oh charming, so whose fault is it?'

'Come on,' said David, 'you know exactly what I mean – you're the one who must have forgotten to take the pill, but I can't help saying that now it's happened, I'm really pleased – it's all my wildest dreams rolled into one.'

'I'm sorry to disappoint you,' said Laura, 'but on this issue, you are not going to have your own way. I simply can't go through with it.'

'David, David.' There was a knocking on the door.

'What is it, Holly?'

'I've gone up and down the drive ten times. Is Mummy in a better mood?'

David glanced at Laura. 'She's not feeling very well, darling. Go down to the playroom and I'll be with you in a minute.'

'OK.'

'We'd better talk about this later,' said David.

The battle raged for three days. For David, it was an agony – the woman he loved was planning to destroy the life they had created. At first he just could not believe she was serious, and when he realized that she was, it filled him with a despair he had never known before. Finally, it reached a point where he could take no more. 'I'm going away for a while,' he said to Laura at breakfast on Tuesday morning, when Holly had left for school.

'To punish me?'

'No, I just don't want to be around when you do this thing.'

'Where will you go?'

'I don't know, but when I've worked it out, I'll leave a message at the office, so you can always get hold of me in an emergency.'

'Will you be coming back?' Laura's voice trembled.

David met her eye. 'I . . . don't know,' he said. 'The way I feel at the moment, probably not, there's only so much pain one can take.'

'There you go, talking about *your* pain again,' said Laura, bitterly. 'You're upset at the idea of losing a child you've never known and loved. Imagine how you'd feel if you'd known this child . . .' she touched her stomach, '. . . for twelve years, and then he was taken from you.'

'You told me once,' said David, 'that you seriously considered having an abortion when you were expecting Fram.'

'Yes,' said Laura, 'yes, that is true.'

'Can you honestly say, even though you know what you know now – that he had only a short life to live and that his death would cause so much sorrow – that you would rather he had never been born?'

'Of course not,' Laura shouted at him, 'how could you say such a thing.'

'In the circumstances I think it's a perfectly valid question. You're about to kill our child, so it occurred to me you might have regretted not terminating Fram's life before it began, too. All ways round, it would have caused less trouble in the end.' The remark was intended to deeply hurt and it did.

'Get out of here, get out!' Laura stood up clenching her fists, tears of anger and sorrow streaming down her face.

'Don't worry, I'm going,' said David.

In the end he went to Norfolk, to Blakeney. The flat marshes with their ever-changing colours calmed him. He walked a great deal, too much in fact so that his leg was painful each night and kept him from sleeping. He borrowed an old ketch and went sailing once or twice but mostly he just sat on the edge of the quay staring out across the marshes, wondering where he had gone wrong and what he could have done differently. That he loved Laura with a passion he had felt for no other woman, was without question. If he could not have Laura, he wanted no one. However, if she was intent on destroying the life of their unborn child, he could not imagine his love for her surviving intact. What would be left, would not be enough on which to build a future together. Yet again, there was Holly to consider. To walk out of Laura's life was bad enough. To walk out on Holly's was another matter – the child had experienced more than her fair share of misery in so short a life, and she had come to depend on him.

He had intended to stay just a few days but when the hotel told him that his room was needed, he did not feel ready to go back and face Laura, so he rented a cottage at Salthouse, just a few miles up the road. It was right on the edge of the marshes, facing due west, so that the skies at sunset were incredible. The weather was warm and surprisingly balmy for north Norfolk and for the first time in his life David did absolutely nothing but sit and think.

He had been at the cottage for ten days when one afternoon, as he was sitting in the porch in the last of the sun, a bottle-green Range Rover drew up outside the gate. His heart soared and then plummeted – it had to be Laura and for a moment he felt like running away. He didn't want to hear what she had to tell him. He was emotionally exhausted to the point where he felt he could take no more. She walked up the path towards him. She was looking very pretty in jeans and a cool shirt. 'David?'

'Hello, Laura,' he said. He got up wearily, 'So you've come to seek me out. How's Holly?'

'She's fine, very well in fact. Her team won a rounders match last night and she scored the most runs.'

'Good old Holly.' They didn't touch, they stood facing each other. 'Would you like a drink or cup of tea?' David asked, awkwardly.

'Not particularly,' said Laura.

'It must have been a long drive.'

'Not too bad, let's sit in the sun.' They sat down on the little seats either side of the porch. 'It's a beautiful spot here,' said Laura.

'Yes, it is. I've always loved this part of the world.'

'Boats again,' she smiled.

'Yes.'

'David, I haven't had an abortion.'

The joy that suffused his face shocked her. 'You haven't?'

'No, and I have some more news for you. It appears we've rather overdone it.'

'H-how do you mean?'

'Perhaps we ought to have a drink after all – a brandy?'

He shook his head. 'Stop messing about, Laura, what do you mean?'

She smiled and took his hand. 'How does the word "twins" grab you?'

They married a month later in Hambledon church, with Holly as their bridesmaid and all their friends and relatives around them. To everyone it seemed like the happy end to a story that had been fraught with drama and sadness, but for Laura the nightmare lingered on. Twins – because of the position of the babies, the gynaecologist was unable to tell her their sex – baby daughters she could cope with, a baby son . . . her mind recoiled from it. She knew termination of the pregnancy would have meant losing David, but the price she was paying to keep him often seemed too painful to bear.

The pregnancy was easy, though she was so large she could do little more than waddle. It was a great source of amusement for everyone, especially Holly.

Laura and David celebrated New Year's Eve quietly at home that year. 'Almost forty,' Laura said, 'I can't believe it.'

'It's alright for you, youngsters – what about me?' said David. They smiled at one another and held hands. They had grown closer during the pregnancy, their relationship had never been stronger, but would it stand the rejection of a son?

In the second week of January, still two weeks before the babies were due, Laura's gynaecologist decided to take her into the hospital, bearing in mind her age, and after a couple of days, he decided to induce the babies. By now, Laura was in a state of abject terror – not at the prospect of the pain but of its outcome.

David, too, was frightened. He was aware he had forced her into this pregnancy and was equally aware of the danger of twins at her age. He sat beside her, holding the hand into which the drip was now going, and prayed that this woman, who had come on such a long journey to find happiness, would not once again be crossed by fate.

It was a difficult birth. The pain was more acute and prolonged than Laura could remember before but at least this time she had her husband with her, right beside her, holding her hand and mopping her brow, and it made everything very different. Finally, at twenty minutes past one, on January the 27th, the first baby was born. David's daughter, with his pointed chin and beginnings of his curls. David was ecstatic, Laura too – a little girl – it was just what she wanted for him.

The pains began again almost immediately. The first baby was taken away and the drama mounted. The baby's heartbeat was intermittent, suggesting stress. 'Listen to me, Laura.' Through the blur of pain, she could just hear the doctor's voice. 'We're going to have to get this one out fast – it's the only chance it has, push old girl, push with all your might.'

'I can't,' Laura gasped.

'You can, come on.' He glanced at David, 'I'm sorry, I'm going to have to ask you to leave. I'll need to use forceps.'

'I can't leave,' said David in anguish.

'You must, just for a moment, we're fighting for your baby's life, Mr Lawson.'

Strangely enough, without David, Laura's struggle with her body was easier to cope with. She had needed him there until this moment, but now the concentration required was too acute – she was fighting the pain, fighting the hysteria and fighting to understand what the doctor was saying. 'Wait, now push. OK, stop, wait, I said. Right, push again, harder. Come on, come on, Laura, harder.' The pain ripped through her. She had not wanted these babies, but now faced with the battle for life, she was not going to let her child die. 'Come on, harder, that's it!' There was a triumphant shout. 'Hey, here it is, here we have it, one last push, Laura, come on. There we go . . . a little boy, you have a son, Laura. Hold him, just for a second, he needs warming up, hold him close, now.'

Laura opened her eyes and stared into the face of her son. The baby had a dimple on one cheek and a tiny cleft chin extraordinarily like Bernard's. His hair was very dark, not curly as his sister's, but dead straight. This was no Fram substitute – this was someone else entirely.

David was suddenly beside her. 'Darling, you're so clever. Are you alright?'

'Yes, yes, I'm fine.' She said, not even looking up from her absorption with the baby.

David's voice was thick with emotion, but he tried desperately to sound casual. 'What do you think of this little lad, then?'

'He's lovely,' Laura said. 'Katy for the girl as we agreed, and I thought we might call this one Justin, after your godfather. See his dimple, David and look at his chin . . .'

'Can we take the baby now, Mrs Lawson? Just to wash him and check him over.'

'Can I have them back soon? They are alright, aren't they?' Her obvious anxiety was of overwhelming relief to David.

'Yes, they're fine, Mrs Lawson, and we'll have them back with you in just a few minutes.'

Left alone for a moment, David bent over the bed. 'Thank you,' he whispered. 'Don't ever imagine I don't know what this has cost you.'

'Don't thank me,' she said. 'I owe everything to you. God knows, David, it's taken us a long time, but we got there in the end, didn't we?'

'We certainly did,' said David. He hesitated. 'Is everything really alright?' The question was heavily veiled but they both knew what he meant.

'Yes,' said Laura, 'everything's wonderful.'

CAMPLING HALL

19th March 1987

When the National Trust acquired Campling Hall, it was considered to be of sufficient architectural, historical and national importance to justify inviting the Queen to officially open it to the public. The date chosen for the opening had been a happy accident – had he lived, it would have been Fram's eighteenth birthday.

After the official opening ceremony, members of the Royal Family, the Camplings, the Lawsons, their friends, and a spattering of dignitaries from the various institutions involved, gathered in the newly nominated Francis Melhuish Chapel, for a service of dedication.

Anthony, David and Laura had thought long and hard about how Fram's inheritance should best be used. In the end they had formed a trust fund specifically to help children with heart disease, for of all the people in Fram's life, Holly had been closest, and she owed her life to modern surgery. The idea of naming the family chapel after Fram had been Anthony's. They had linked it to the trust by means of a plaque at the entrance to the chapel, giving details of the fund which bore Fram's name and asking for public donations. The large collecting box had already been emptied twice, even before the chapel was opened. The regular troop of builders, masons, architects and designers, who had helped prepare Campling Hall for its grand opening, had been deeply moved already by the story of Fram's brief life and had given generously. It was a story with an appeal, which as theatrical jargon had it, would run and run. Around the walls of the chapel were the family portraits of the former Lord Camplings, going back to the fourteenth century, and joining these now was a portrait of Fram – the Lord Campling who never was – painted by Brian Organ from a series of photographs Laura had given him.

The service was brief and moving, the high spot being

when Holly lit a candle and placed it beneath her brother's portrait. All Laura's greatest friends were there – Eleanor and Chris, with Thomas and Eddie, now two grown-up young men; Diana and Giles with their brood; Bridget and Buck, flown over specially from Canada, looking strong and brown and more like one person than two. Harry Sutherland was given a special place with the family, Gerald Seaton was there and Holly's doctor, Simon Nettleton, who had given them immense technical help at the time of setting up the trust. Fram's best friend, Oliver, was there with his parents – so tall, almost a man, it was hard to believe that Fram would have been of an age. Katrine, of course, had a place of honour. She looked as vigorous as ever, yet she was nearly seventy. Scotty, keeping an eagle eye on the twins, was as much in control as ever.

After the service was over and the Royal party had left, Laura sat down quietly in a pew, David beside her. 'Happy or sad?' he asked.

'Both.' She smiled at him, lovingly. 'Fram would have been amazed at all this fuss – he was a very simple person, really.'

'He'd have been proud of his mother,' David said.

Laura smiled. 'I hope so.'

'I know so.' Then, always attuned to her moods, he said, 'Would you like me to leave you here for a while?'

She smiled gratefully at him. 'Yes, please.'

The whole event had been much documented already in photographs and editorial comment in the press, but all day Laura had carried a camera around with her. Now, left alone in the chapel, she took two or three photographs of the improvements and embellishments that had been made, and finally a photograph of the Organ portrait, with Holly's single candle burning in front of it. The photographs were developed a few days later. She selected the best and added them to the carefully prepared scrapbook, which included the press write-ups of the day's events and details of the trust fund. Fram's press was very different from how it had been at the time of his death.

When the scrapbook was completed, Laura placed it in a thick brown envelope, with no letter or accompanying comment of any sort, and mailed it to Joseph Clarke, Ayios Nikolaos, Crete.